T0363217

About Darry Fraser

Darry Fraser's first novel, *Daughter of the Murray*, is set on her beloved River Murray where she spent part of her childhood. *Where the Murray River Runs*, her second novel, is set in Bendigo in the 1890s, and her third novel, *The Widow of Ballarat*, takes place on the Ballarat goldfields in the 1850s. *The Good Woman of Renmark* is set on the mighty Murray in the 1890s once again. Her latest book is *The Last Truehart*. Darry currently lives, works and writes on Kangaroo Island, an awe-inspiring place off the coast of South Australia.

Also by Darry Fraser

Daughter of the Murray
Where the Murray River Runs
The Widow of Ballarat
The Good Woman of Renmark
The Last Truehart

Elsa Goody
Bushranger

DARRY FRASER

mira

First Published 2020
Second Australian Paperback Edition 2021
ISBN 9781867208075

Elsa Goody, Bushranger
© 2020 by Darry Fraser
Australian Copyright 2020
New Zealand Copyright 2020

Except for use in any review, the reproduction or utilisation of this work in whole or in part in any form by any electronic, mechanical or other means, now known or hereafter invented, including xerography, photocopying and recording, or in any information storage or retrieval system, is forbidden without the permission of the publisher.

This book is sold subject to the condition that it shall not, by way of trade or otherwise, be lent, resold, hired out or otherwise circulated without the prior consent of the publisher in any form of binding or cover other than that in which it is published and without a similar condition including this condition being imposed on the subsequent purchaser.

All rights reserved including the right of reproduction in whole or in part in any form.

This is a work of fiction. Names, characters, places, and incidents are either the product of the author's imagination or are used fictitiously, and any resemblance to actual persons, living or dead, business establishments, events, or locales is entirely coincidental.

Published by
Mira
An imprint of Harlequin Enterprises (Australia) Pty Limited (ABN 47 001 180 918), a subsidiary of
HarperCollins Publishers Australia Pty Limited (ABN 36 009 913 517)
Level 13, 201 Elizabeth St
SYDNEY NSW 2000
AUSTRALIA

® and TM (apart from those relating to FSC®) are trademarks of Harlequin Enterprises (Australia) Pty Limited or its corporate affiliates. Trademarks indicated with ® are registered in Australia, New Zealand and in other countries.

A catalogue record for this book is available from the National Library of Australia
www.librariesaustralia.nla.gov.au

Printed and bound in Australia by McPherson's Printing Group

MIX
Paper from
responsible sources
FSC® C001695
FSC
www.fsc.org

Dad

One

My brother is dead.

The bold, confident script swam before her eyes and Elsa Goody dropped the page onto her lap. She took in deep silent breaths until the taut pain eased in her chest. Finally lifting the letter again, its words weighty, she angled it towards the candle and read to her dying father. Her voice shook as if unused to speech.

'To Mr Goody, Goody Farm near Robe, In the Colony of South Australia.

'Dear Mr Goody, it is with regret I write to tell you that I have, today, buried your son, George. He has died this morning.'

These words from a stranger—this Mr Ezekiel Jones—carefully scribed, were impossible to absorb, to comprehend. How could her brother be dead? And—*where*? In Casterton. The place was fully three days' ride from here, in another colony.

George. Her eyes closed a moment and the picture of him was clear. Wild, wavy hair, the colour of stringy-bark honey, framed a pale face under dark amber eyebrows—like their mother once had, like Elsa's own. His small nose and luminous green eyes were

1

also just like hers. How alike they'd been when they were young children, especially when he'd lopped off her long tresses—with the shears—which then resembled his own much shorter mess. She should've been more wary of her twelve-year-old brother when he'd come back from the shed, hands behind his back and a peculiar look on his face. His strike had been swift and wickedly gleeful, and suddenly there lay ten years' growth, the tight bundle of thick curls lifeless on the ground. She'd belted after him, not able to run him down as he charged across the home paddock laughing himself silly. The little devil had nearly got away with it too, telling Pa that she'd done it herself.

Their other three siblings, two dead and only Rosie left, had not looked like their mother at all. Now that beloved George was dead, there was no one around to remind her of her mother, Kitty, who'd died long … Where was the locket with her mother's likeness in it? Tucked safely inside Elsa's cherished keepsake was a curl of her ma's soft deep golden-brown hair. *Oh, now's not the time to wonder where it is.*

She stared at the letter, her vision blurred, until she blinked and took a breath. It had been so kindly written by Mr Jones, and from so far away that she should give it her full attention. It had come from a farm outside Casterton, in the Western Districts of Victoria. *Gracious me, George had got all the way there on his adventure.* The date on the letter told her that he'd died almost two weeks ago. *What was I doing around here on that day? Why didn't I feel something strange or telling?* She couldn't remember. She'd have been doing her usual chores—trying to coax the vegetables to grow, or re-aligning that fallen fence-post, and digging it deeper into unforgiving earth. Maybe she'd been chopping wood. Nothing unusual.

Tears hadn't come when she'd first read the letter. Collecting it from the post office in town earlier today, she'd opened it as she walked the couple of miles back to the house; the faraway postmark had been a mystery she couldn't resist. After that, it had been a walk home from hell.

Still no tears, even now, after reading it to her father. Anyway, this was not the time for her tears. There was much to do about this, but for the life of her, she couldn't think of what right now.

She folded the page in her lap and looked at her pa. Propped up in his bed with all of their meagre pillows stuffed in behind him, Curtis Goody remained silent. His drawn features were shut beneath his lank white hair, the dark blond of his youth completely gone. Where had he vanished to, her father? So few years ago he was vital, strong and alive. Perhaps all the deaths, his wife, his sons, had left a gaping wound that finally sapped his life.

He stared across the dim room that was the sum of their house. 'Read the line again where he talks of regret,' he said, and shifted under the blanket draped around his bony shoulders. Perhaps he could feel the night-time chill beginning to settle in but she had nothing else to keep him warm.

Holding the candle closer and unfolding the letter, she cleared her throat. '... *it is with regret I write to tell you that I have, today, buried your son, George.*'

Nothing but the chirrup of birds calling before they took to their nests for the night filled the silence. The little flame flickered and, worried her gulping breath would blow it out, she dropped the letter again. Cupping the wick with her hand to guard it, the flame steadied on the tiny piece of wax. There were only a couple of candles remaining in the house, so she'd have to hurry to make some more—although with what, she didn't know.

A murmur came from her father yet she heard the words, the deeply borne grief, as loudly as if they'd been shouted in her ears. 'My son, my last son. My fault. I let him go wanderin'.'

Alarmed, she said, 'I'm sure not, Pa.'

'Oh yes, oh yes,' he cried softly—his breath troubled by illness and bereavement. 'Too easy on him.'

The letter remained on her knees as she carefully set the candle down on a sturdy little stool that served as a bedside table. When they still had their cow, it had been their milking stool. Now the cow was gone, there was no milk to churn for butter. No butter, no money. Their whole farming enterprise, sheep mainly and a few cows, had whittled down to that last old girl once her father became too ill to manage.

Strangely, she thought about that cow now, about when it had delivered its first calf. The baby bull was born dead. Its mother had stood over it for hours, cleaning it and trying to encourage it to life. Only when she finally plodded away, lowing mournfully, accepting her baby was dead, did Elsa find George and have him help take the small body away. George buried their dead animals; he said it respected them. She'd understood, or thought she had, but her siblings had thought it senseless. Their father had indulged him.

When the cow had been ready to calve the next time, Elsa was more prepared. Old Mr Conroy, a bullocky, had told her about lathering soap over a person's hands and arms, which helped to ease them inside the birth canal to grab the calf. Despite the massive contractions, and the calf slurping back in, Elsa had managed to pull the infant heifer into the world. She'd stayed with the baby, and watched as the cow hovered, waiting anxiously until the poddy could stand on wobbly little legs to take her first drink.

Elsa missed that cow. Missed the calf who'd been sold when it was old enough for market. How many times had she nursed both mother and baby—clearing feeding problems, massaging teats to milk, cleaning their makeshift stall, keeping watch for wild dogs, stitching cuts to the mother and calf when they'd stampeded over a rotting fence.

She'd done a lot of stitching, of her brothers' wounds, too, as well as tending to animal births and helping to build fences, and clear the well, and keep the cartwheels oiled, and the leather goods pliable, and—

Oh, goodness. Stop. She couldn't help wanting to escape the reality of George's death. She so missed her brothers … how big and boisterous the family would become when they all got together. Rosie was never much fun, and she seldom even visited. She was always glum and snappy, so when the older boys had died, Elsa had clung to George until he'd left home. Now he was dead too. No more big family, no more siblings to laugh with, to wrestle, to belong …

A breeze crept in between the timbers of the walls, its crisp, sly tendrils mocking her. She'd have to mix some pug—clay and straw—find the gaps and fill them. *Another chore.* After her mother had died, her father never finished the stone house he and the boys were building, so the timber hut with its clay fillers was all they had. Kitty was missed, such a force in their lives. Cheery, Elsa remembered, and fun, and her lean arms would hug hard and make the breath whoosh out of you. And she loved Pa. Her hands would cup his face and she'd plant a kiss on his mouth—*right in front of us.* He loved it; he loved her. No wonder the life started to leave Pa when Ma went.

Elsa grasped her father's hand, its large and nobbly-knuckled fingers cool and dry. She leaned in. 'There's more in the letter, Pa.' She edged closer to the candle and held the paper near the flickering light.

Concentrating on the letter, she found the script looked as if done by a firm hand, assured of its task. Elsa imagined the hand had hesitated, but once decided, the words had flowed, and the page had been filled with elegant prose for their loss.

Glancing at the flourish of Ezekiel Jones's signature, she wondered about his name. Not often heard these days, biblical and—

'Go on,' her father rasped.

She collected herself and continued reading aloud. *'He has died this morning. He lies by a great eucalypt on my land, a place of peace and comfort, and he faces the colony of his birth. He was brought to me for help after injuries inflicted by bushrangers in the district, but alas, his wounds were too great, and he succumbed to merciful death.'*

Bushrangers, Elsa thought. *Good Lord, in this day and age.* She kept her head bowed, felt a distance as if all this was happening to someone else. The letter was a thoughtful missive to strangers—compassionate, sincere, and the writer must have known the family would suffer immeasurable loss upon reading it. It seemed to her that he was reaching out to say he shared their sorrow. The lump in her throat grew. His words warmed her, as if his gentle hand had settled on her shoulder, sharing some of the burden of hurt.

Curtis Goody took in a long noisy breath. 'He was impetuous, that boy, and he thought nothing could stop him.' He withdrew his hand from hers. 'First our John by snakebite, then our Ned by fever. And now our George …' He tapped her hand and she looked up. 'We didn't find the snake that killed our John, we couldn't fight the fever that killed our Ned, but—' He beat a fist weakly on his chest, his mouth a grimace. 'If I were a well man and not dyin' myself, I'd go after those bushrangers for killin' our George.' A lone tear rolled down his cheek.

Elsa took his veiny hand and laid it down. 'Rest a bit, Pa.'

'My sons. All gone. And I don't have the fight left in me.'

Her pa would hate anyone to see that tear, but as she was only his daughter, it wouldn't matter. *Only his daughter, not one of his sons.* She cut off that thought. Elsa reached over and with the edge of her pinny dabbed at his face to wipe the tear, ignoring that he'd alluded to his own impending death. On one of the few visits from the doctor the family could afford, they were told that his illness was most probably in the organ called the pancreas and not curable. Dr Wilson had left sleeping draughts, no doubt powerful tinctures against deep and burrowing pain. Elsa glanced at the little glass bottle by the bed. It wouldn't be the right thing to administer another dose now, so close to the last one, even to help ease her father's heartache—grief would only bide its time anyway, so it might as well be faced now. Besides, she knew she had to be careful with the doses. The doctor did say that at this stage in her father's illness she could use too much. Her hand hovered over the bottle. She withdrew sharply.

Breathing deeply, she said, 'I should write back to Mr Jones to thank him.'

'Aye. Would be the right thing. Perhaps our George left some possessions.'

Elsa nodded, although thought that would have been odd of her brother, and Mr Jones hadn't mentioned anything. George had only the clothes on his back. She said, 'Tomorrow, I'll go into the town and tell our Rosie.'

'Your sister will be terrible afflicted by this news.'

'She will,' Elsa agreed. *As I am terrible afflicted.* But her sister would soon forget her grief with the promise of the farm coming to her and her husband now. Rosie was older and had married at sixteen, in the year Elsa was born. When the fortunes of the town were growing, Rosie and her husband had done well as bakers. Now Robe was in decline, and folk had left in droves, leaving only a small population trying to eke out a living in the South Australian coastal town. Once a thriving port but now in competition with stronger rivals, it was a shell of its former self—a beautiful shell, with many grand and stately, but empty, buildings.

The port was one thing; the farms struggled too. Not that her father owned much land, but with the boys gone—the last of her brothers, that scallywag George, had refused to work the farm—Elsa's future now looked bleak. She didn't believe for one minute that she would feature in her sister's plans.

Elsa could almost hear what her father was thinking. His eyes were closed, his jaw was set, and his breathing was now measured. He pulled the blanket a little tighter around himself.

'You must bring Rosie home, here,' he said, an urgency in his tone. 'I must speak with her first. Frank is the only man in the family now, but I don't want Frank to ...' His voice drifted off. He frowned, his eyes averted from Elsa's.

Frank, Rosie's husband. A puffed-up lardy ball if ever there was one, in body—Elsa was sure he ate much of their bakery's profits—and in soul. She couldn't understand her sister ever having taken to a man who strutted about the town hardly doing a thing, while his wife worked down to her bones, sweltering in front of the wood-fired ovens for the best part of every morning, after kneading and shaping loaves and buns in the hours prior. Rosie had lamented over the years that she hadn't had any babies and wondered if she'd worked too hard for her body to bear children. It'd been a while since Elsa had heard her sister's laments.

And that husband of hers is so lazy, it's a wonder Rosie thought she could possibly become— Again, Elsa stopped those thoughts. Not her business why they hadn't had children. Rosie was getting on in years now. She'd be over forty this year—she could easily have been Elsa's mother although she didn't look like their mother. She had their father's features. A narrow face (that could turn too sharp once she put on that determined, bossy pose), a long nose and a strong chin. Her hair was a paler shade than Elsa's, much subdued compared to Elsa's rich and wild mane, and not likely to attract attention. Rosie's brown eyes appeared, to others, to warm towards folk. Elsa had found that bemusing when she heard talk of it. Rosie—warm? But whatever her thoughts of her sister and brother-in-law, one was insistent and clear: Frank did not inspire her confidence.

She leaned towards her father to whisper, 'I'll bring her. But Frank doesn't have to do anything for you, Pa. I can administer if you name me in a legal paper. You know the laws have changed.'

By the look on his face, if he could have harrumphed, he would have. Mr Curtis Goody had been unimpressed by laws regarding property changing in favour of married women, and allowing women to have the vote in South Australia. 'Slip of a thing like you,' he grumbled but not unkindly. 'You're the youngest, my farm girl. Better that you marry Pete Southie and not get Frank offside any longer.'

'Pa, I'm not a slip of a thing. And you know why I would never marry Mr Southie. He's an awful creature.'

'Now, I'm sure he's not as bad as you say,' her father wheezed. 'I'm sure the man didn't mean to bump into you like that.' His hand, with its thin and dry skin, rested on top of hers and patted absently.

Her father's memory was still sharp. Pete Southie had been making a pest of himself when Elsa had refused to acknowledge him. One day not long ago, he'd stalked right into the house, pressed his suit for her, offered marriage and then he'd *pressed* himself on her. When she complained loudly and with a crack of her dustpan on his head, Southie had claimed that his enthusiastic attention was an accident.

Enthusiastic? Accident? Did the man think her a fool? She had in no uncertain terms told him what she'd thought of his enthusiasm. While he'd controlled his zeal from then on, it was the leery grin he'd give her whenever she'd seen him since that set her teeth grinding. She should've crowned him more than once with the dustpan.

'Besides, Elsa, he is a friend of Frank's. It might benefit if you marry.' Her father was nearly out of breath. 'To keep this land, you girls have to …' His voice drifted off again and in the silence that followed, she soon heard a soft snore.

Bah, Frank. Elsa knew she had no chance to change her father's mind. Never did have, really. As long as there were men in the family, her father was convinced that she'd be looked after. She wasn't about to be allowed to administer anything, much less something as important as The Property. Of course, with three older brothers, what were the chances she'd ever have been considered anyway? She shrugged. There was no use fighting for it, not within her family anyway, *what was left of it*—her voice would still not be heard. Well, she'd always made it heard but would be ignored.

There was a light shining though, despite the grief. She would have a voice in the upcoming elections this year. Very soon, in April, women in South Australia would have a vote. The colony was the first place in the country where women were legally about to vote—including Aboriginal women. It will be wonderful. *Such excitement.* And that same day the country would have its first referendum as well: should laws change to allow the introduction of religious education into state schools?

Oh, it would be a grand thing. Elsa was glad the polling booths would be in Robe township at the council offices, not the old and draughty Courthouse; previous polls had been conducted there and complaints were loud. The candle's flame flickered as another, more erratic, breeze blew through. *Be careful, Elsa.* She cupped the flame to steady it.

The voting business was all very well—and of course she felt invested—but there was much else to consider right now. With her last brother gone, how could she possibly work the farm on her own? *Oh, George.*

Would things be better if she'd married and had lots of children and made her own big boisterous family? Apart from Pete

Southie, only one other man had offered. She'd sent both roundly on their way. Oh, there was young Henry Benson who had her heart a-flutter at odd times like when he'd smile at her as she walked past his father's forge, or when he'd stand too close if they were ever in the bakery at the same time, waiting for yesterday's items that had been reduced. He was too young, only nineteen, and it always made her feel foolish, that reaction of hers to him. Was it time to review? After all, she was getting on now too. At twenty-four, she knew she risked being overlooked in the marriage stakes.

What if marriage was indeed the only way she could keep the land?

Disgusted with herself that the thought had even entered her mind—it'd be like selling her soul—she looked down at the letter again. The candlelight wavered and threatened to extinguish. The signature leapt up as if dancing under the sputtering flame. *Ezekiel Jones*. To have buried her brother, her dear George, in a place of peace and comfort, he must be such a kind and loving man.

Unexplained warmth settled in her.

Two

Zeke Jones watched his eldest, Gifford, walk the horse down the track. It was maybe five miles from his sheep and wheat farm to the little school in Casterton. While at nine years of age, Giff was capable of the walk, his younger siblings, Gracie at eight, and Jonty at six, would struggle. So they were both atop the bareback Milo, a gentle tan-coloured gelding. The horse would wait patiently at the school with the few other horses that would have delivered children who lived far away. Later in the afternoon he would plod home over the flat paddocks then take the rise over the low hill and down to Zeke's gate, returning with his charges.

Three dogs, all black-and-tan male kelpies—Itch, Scratch and Zeke's brother Jude's dog, Bizzy—danced around their feet, barking and yipping their excitement. Zeke allowed the dogs out of their pen to see the kids off for school. The only other times they roamed free were when they worked the sheep, or when Giff had to give them a run. His kids loved them, but Zeke was not giving the dogs a soft life. Casterton had been producing fine litters of this new breed, small in stature and big on personality. They were bred as working dogs, and their reputation was growing.

The kids would be home again at last light or so. It was now about seven in the morning, Zeke reckoned. There was much to do, and a few remaining sheep to sell off; the day would go fast. He'd long been hearing of the bonuses the government offered for butter and cheese factories in the colony, so that meant dairy cows were in demand. New infrastructure and the money to pay for it would be needed if he sold out of sheep altogether. Hoping he might've somehow missed tallying by a hundred pounds or so, he'd check his sums. He'd stocktake his milled timber again but he knew he only had enough to fence another small yard. When his older brother Jude came back, he'd discuss combining their holdings once more. Zeke could use his input, financial and physical ... if only Jude were willing and able.

As he waited for the kids to get to the gate, he checked the sky. Light scudding clouds skimmed a high breeze. A darker billow above them hinted at rain. *Season's changing, the mornings are cooler. Time to get on with it.*

The kids yelled goodbye, waved at him, and Milo plodded away with them. The three dogs turned for home and suddenly alert, they tore into a gallop back towards the house, charging past him. Following, his mind on his ledger, he stopped short. '*Jesus*, Nebo. Do you have to sneak up on a man?' The dogs had crowded around his brother who lounged on the verandah post.

Nebo bent to rough-house the dogs. 'You said to wait until after your brood had gone off to get their education for the day, so here I am.' He pushed off the post, ignored the dogs barking. 'A herd of roarin' bulls could've crept up on you the way you were daydreamin' into the sunshine after your kids.'

Zeke flicked a wrist. 'Boys, away,' he snapped, and in silence the dogs trotted off, ears sharp, tails wagging. He'd tie them up as soon as he got rid of his brother.

At forty-one, Nebo Jones was older by three years. Lean and rangy like Zeke, close enough in height, dark haired and dark eyed, they'd often been mistaken for one another—in their chequered past, that had been a problem for Zeke. He was a little sturdier around the chest than Nebo but not by much. Nebo had more angular features, and when vexed he could be gaunt. Haunted was the word Zeke mostly used to describe his troubled brother. Today, he looked more relaxed.

'Did you bring it?' he asked Nebo and pushed past him into the house.

'Could do with tea and a plate of eggs,' Nebo said, following through the house and outside to the kitchen. Once inside, he slapped a packet wrapped in newspaper onto the table.

Zeke turned to stoke the oven. 'We'll eat quick. I have work to do.' He shook the kettle, checking for enough water, and put it on the cooker. Glancing behind at the packet, he said, 'Is that all it is?'

'He was a lone boy, Ezie,' Nebo said, a smirk lighting his face. He knew it irked Zeke to be called by his childhood nickname. 'Didn't have much on him but a locket with a snip of hair, a handkerchief and three spare buttons.' He pointed at the parcel. 'All there, as requested.'

'Surprised it is all there, knowing you,' Zeke said.

Nebo pulled a chair away from the table and sat, legs stretched out, crossed at the ankles. Any closer to Zeke and he'd be in the way, which was probably his intention. 'Nothing of value in it, nothin' to interest me. The boys reckoned I shoulda chucked it away.' The 'boys' were Nebo's no-hoper mates who lived with their women in the bush. Small-time thieves, some said. 'When you told me you'd written to his family, seemed only proper to bring it in.'

Zeke pulled a small basket from the mantel and took out eight eggs. He cracked them, dropped the contents into a bowl and tossed the shells into a bucket. Jonty's hens had performed well. At least something was still working in the right direction on his place. 'Proper? Good of you. A bushranger, out of time and place, brings in a dead boy's only trinkets. Must have a heart after all.'

Nebo rubbed his face with one hand. Zeke could hear the rough scratch of it, thought of his own unshaven face. He never could come at the great beards some of his friends had grown; too many times had he seen their dinner stuck in their whiskers. Or worse, yesterday's dinner.

Maybe Nebo should grow the beard since he called himself a bushranger—that way no one would mistake him, the clean-shaven brother, Zeke, for being a petty thief.

'At least I'm not a reformed bushranger,' Nebo said. 'Nothin' sorrier in my opinion.'

Zeke snorted but didn't take the bait. He'd never been a thief, just known to stick up for his wayward brother. And that had got him into plenty of trouble because whenever it happened, it never happened softly.

Nebo frowned. 'I don't care to be shooting lads, you oughta know that. I told you it wasn't me, or mine. I got a feelin' that lazy slob Billy Watson mighta known something, but even when I gave him a roughin' up, he still never said. I just sent him on his way.'

'Billy Watson?'

'That no-hoper tub of useless thinks he's Billy the Kid.'

'You think he had something to do with this boy's shooting?'

Nebo shrugged. 'Damned if I know. But the poor kid was in a sorry state when I found him, and I just wanted to get him help. God knows, none of us want anyone dyin' on Jude's place again.'

Zeke glanced at him. Not like Nebo to show he cared much about anything except himself.

'If it was Watson,' Nebo said, 'I didn't want him comin' back for another go but it's got me stumped why he'd be on Jude's, anyway. He knows there's nothin' there.' He let out a long breath. 'The boy's dead, and I made sure he got a decent burial here.'

'You could have buried him out in the scrub,' Zeke said, then thought of the boy's family. He wondered if his letter had got to them. George had said he had a father and two sisters. He grabbed a heavy iron pan and sat it on the stovetop. He spooned lard into it, watched it melt and sizzle, then poured in the eggs.

''Cept he wasn't dead then, was he?' Nebo said. 'And I wasn't gonna wait for him to die out there, either. I knew you'd honour the lad, Ezie, is why I brought him here.' There was no smirk on his face, nor in his voice. Nebo had carried George onto Zeke's verandah, yelling for help. He waited with George still in his arms (who was sobbing a sister's name, Nebo told him later) while Zeke and his daughter Gracie hurriedly made a bed inside for the near-dead lad. 'And you buried him close by Maisie and your other little fella so I knew that's exactly what you did.'

Zeke let that go. He wasn't about to get into that old conversation—argument—with his brother about anything to do with Maisie, Zeke's dead wife. Any mention of their last child who'd survived birth by only days still tugged at his heart. He had to let that go, too.

He pushed the eggs around with a large wooden spoon. Reaching up to the mantel again he drew down a cloth-wrapped bundle and threw it on the table in front of his brother. 'Here, cut some bread.'

'You're a real homebody, bakin' bread and all. Bet you got those kids of yours doing all the chores, the laundry and such. If you get them runnin' this place, you can come to work with me. Better pay.' When Zeke gave him a look, Nebo said, 'All right, if not that, Mrs Hartman next door would take them. She's been on her own a while now, an' getting' on. She's everyone's granny.'

Mrs Hartman was only a few years older than they were, maybe their older brother Jude's age. What would that make her—around forty-five or forty-six? Zeke didn't bother responding.

Nebo tore off chunks of bread, still warm from the cooker this morning. 'What'll you do with that?' he asked, pointing at the newspaper-wrapped packet.

'Might wait a while, see if I hear anything from the family.'

'You could just send it on to that same address, anyhow, couldn't you? Pity I never got it to you before you mailed the letter.'

Zeke stopped stirring eggs and stared at his brother. 'Yeah, pity you never got it to me when you landed a near-dead boy on my doorstep.'

'I found it *after*, by accident, when I went back to Jude's place, just to check. I swear.'

Jude's place was all but abandoned. Judah Jones had lost Anne, his wife, and two daughters to diphtheria nearly five years ago and he'd been roaming around the colony since. He'd come back every so often; Zeke imagined that it was to see if he could bear to stay again, but he never did. Nebo and Zeke looked in on the place from time to time, and the last time Nebo had been there, he found the badly injured lad and had brought him here.

'Check for what?' Zeke asked.

'For who'd done this to him, left him for dead. Might've been some clue. Maybe Billy-bloody-Watson left something behind— if it was him. The kid mighta thrown away other possessions, trying to hide them when he maybe seen someone comin'.'

There was a moment's silence when Zeke stared at his brother, searching for answers. 'Well, wouldn't have been Jude who shot him.'

'It wouldn't have. Unless he's really out of his head now.'

'So, that locket must've meant something to the boy. You don't carry a locket with a picture of a lady in it, and a lock of hair, unless it means something to you. As for mailing it, I trust a letter in the post. I don't trust a packet of jewellery in the post.' He continued with the eggs as they crackled and spat in the pan.

'Jewellery.' Nebo barked a laugh. 'If it was valuable, you wouldn't have it, I'd have sold it. It's nothing more than cheap stuff, sentimental at best.' He tapped his fingers on the table.

'Aye. That's right. You checked it over first,' Zeke said, a curl on his lip. 'Then old *sentimental* you gave it back to him. After he died.'

'*Bah*. I'm glad not to be stuck with it. You forget I'm not a soft-heart like you.'

Zeke grunted. 'Like I believe that,' he said. 'You bring me the boy, then his treasures instead of throwing them away, even though they're worthless. If that's not soft-heart, what is?' He threw a pinch of salt into the pot and stirred. 'Poor kid was just too far gone for me to save him.'

Nebo looked a little uncomfortable. 'It was late when I found him.' He sat up, cleared his throat. 'Anyway, looks like Billy Watson has gone to the troopers.'

'About the boy?' Zeke scooped some eggs onto a plate and slid it across to his brother. He scraped the rest out for himself and then landed the empty pan with a clatter onto a bench—a thick piece of sawn timber. The hot pan seared it, and wisps of smoke arose. He sat down to eat.

'That and other things.' Nebo loaded bread with eggs and took a bite.

Zeke's own chunk of laden bread hung in the air as he looked up. 'You can get right back on that horse of yours—wherever you've left him—and get the hell off my place. The last time there was "that and other things" the troopers came and threatened me and the kids if I didn't give you up.'

'They were just tryin' to rattle you. You didn't tell 'em where I was.'

'Trust me, only because I didn't know.'

'You wouldna done it.' Nebo stood and took the boiling kettle off the stove. He poured water into a teapot, threw in a handful of tea leaves from a tin he found on the mantel. 'But I'm surprised they haven't got you watched again already.'

Zeke squinted at his brother. 'You'd know. I bet you've been watching this place for days.'

'True. No troopers around.' Nebo set the teapot down on the table.

'What've you done this time—"that and other things"?'

'I had to do him over a bit.' He held up his hands before Zeke could yell. 'Not the kid you buried. Watson. He's not so smart. Just gave him a roughin' up like I said before, just a tickle, but I heard he ran straight to the troopers so we had to move camp to be careful. The police are gettin' more interested—'

'You're outlawed then?' Zeke frowned at him.

'Nup, no warrants against me. And until I'm so named, no man can legally shoot to kill me. Not the police or any other bastard. I'm just a pest but I'm not outside the law.'

The *Felons Apprehension Act 1878* made it possible for anyone to shoot and kill declared outlaws—no need to arrest them, no need for a trial. Zeke figured Nebo knew how close to the wire he could run.

'But they can still shoot you.'

'Not to kill me. I'm safe.'

'Jesus, you're a fool. Shot is shot. Dead is dead. They'll name you an outlaw, anyway, in due course.'

Nebo waved him away. 'I'm not that important. Been no real bushrangers since Ned Kelly, poor bastard. Too many settlers around; too many police now. I just steal a sheep here and there, just for a feed. Get a laugh out of taking the wind out of some blow-hard's sails … But then, I'll tell you this, one of my boys took Scotty's missus off his hands, and that caused a ruckus.' He shrugged as if to say *what could I do?*

'*What?* He kidnapped a woman?'

'No, Ezie, he didn't kidnap anyone. What in God's name d'ye take us for, pirates? If I find any nasty arsehole takin' a woman by force, I'll put him away without a backwards glance.'

Their mother, *and* their father, God rest their souls, had instilled a respect in all their boys for any women in their lives. Zeke knew that Nebo had spoken the truth, but anything else was fair game. Still, he mocked his brother. 'You—the big, bad bushranger.'

'I steal sheep, I said, a cow maybe. But I don't steal women. Who-ever heard of that this day an' age?' He shifted in his seat, looked a bit uncomfortable. 'Any of mine goes there and I'll kill 'em.'

'You couldn't kill anybody.'

Nebo shrugged. 'You never know.'

'I do know.'

'Just let me tell the story, will yer? It wasn't kidnap at all. It seems the young lady herself, Mrs Tillie Scott, took a shine to my boy Glen Barton—'

'Barton? He did kill someone, though, didn't he?'

'*Jesus*, Ezie. Yeah, Barton. And it was self-defence, witnesses and all.'

'Ah, and that's why he hides out in the scrub, then.'

'Fer crissakes, leave off. So, while Scotty himself was away hid-ing his end in someone else, Tillie asked Barton to come get her, and he did. So Scotty gets all funny on it, prob'ly more because Tillie took her horse Salty with her. You know the one? Bloody brilliant little gelding won at the races last year.'

Zeke was busy eating now and didn't look up. He knew the horse.

'That was the thing that made us move again. We'll keep our heads down for a while. Troopers will forget all about the other stuff.' Nebo went on, 'We got quite the society happening in our bush camp, hidin' in the scrub. All the boys each have a little woman.'

Zeke nodded. 'Impressive. A real Robin Hood and his merry men. Haven't come across a Maid Marion for yourself yet?' When there was no quickfire response from Nebo, he could've kicked himself: he'd just done what he'd tried to avoid—opened a conversation he was sick of having.

Nebo's frown appeared, furrowing an already lined forehead. 'You had the only Maid Marion for me.'

'Don't start.' Zeke pushed his plate away. 'You're forgetting about poor Henrietta Porter. Henny was a real loyal one, and you barely gave her the time of day.'

'She wasn't Maisie. *I* saw Maisie before she latched eyes on you.'

Zeke slammed an open palm on the table. 'Maisie wasn't for you. Don't goad me, Nebo. Henny hung around waiting for you to stop chasing *my wife*.'

'Well, she didn't wait too long,' Nebo said, ignoring the vehemence in his brother.

'I reckon six years was long enough. And by then Maisie was already dead and still you—'

'Now, you stop,' Nebo yelled and bounced a fist off the timber table as he shoved out of his chair. He paced to the door and back, pointing a finger. 'You dunno anything about anything.'

'I know plenty.' Zeke had had enough. 'Tell me what it is you want and then get the hell out. I got work to do. Not wasting any more of the day, going over ancient history. Again.'

Nebo rubbed his nose, scratched his chin: all signs that he was trying to hold onto his temper. 'Don't want anything. Just came for a visit, brought that packet. But now you're asking, I do have something to tell you. It'll mean you're in it whether you like it or not. Cobb & Co's coach is coming right by here next week, travelling from Mt Gambier to Casterton. Still gotta make good some details, like where and when to stop it, but it's said there's rich folk on board.'

'I'm not bailing up Cobb & Co, or anything else. Besides, coaches are giving way to railways. Rich folk travel by rail.'

Nebo cocked his head, agreeing, but said, 'Rail don't go everywhere yet. The spoils would help you out, too.'

'I don't need that kind of help.'

'You used to enjoy yourself.'

'Getting you out of trouble? I don't think so.' Zeke eyed his brother. 'You'll end up killed, doing a hold-up. Get a job like the rest of us.'

'A job. You call this a job, what—this farm? There isn't enough land to do anything with and you know it. How many sheep can you run?'

'If your boys hadn't been stealing them—'

'My boys weren't stealin' from you. I'm sure of it, I'm tellin' you.'

Zeke shook his head. 'I don't want anything to do with any hold-up. I don't want to know about it. I don't want to see you back here talking about it. You're a risk to my kids.'

Nebo nodded, all too agreeable now. 'Ah yes, your kids. How are they? How is the little tacker, Jonty? Always had a soft spot for him.'

Zeke should've known that was coming. His brother had been angling for something the whole time, as was his way. He felt the pressure build, deep in his gut. His blood had seemed to heat faster in days gone by, a rapid boiling that threatened to spill, sometimes had. And it was fierce when it did. He'd always been the fiery one of the three brothers, always the one whom people kept on the good side, whom they knew to steer clear of. By now, he'd learned to beat down the flare of blind rage.

Nebo lifted his chin, still goading. 'He has the strong look of both his parents, boyo.' He threw the contents of his tea out onto the dirt outside. 'So we'll never know, will we? Can never tell what some of the ladies get up to.' He tossed the empty pannikin at his brother—the smirk on his face souring—ducked into the doorway and left.

Zeke let the cup clatter past him as Nebo disappeared from his sight. He heard the dogs barking and Nebo's snarl at them to shut up.

Jonty was Maisie and Zeke's child. But the boy had a strong resemblance to his uncle Nebo, more than Zeke's other two children did. Nebo always made it sound as if Maisie had at some later stage hankered after him, that maybe she'd let him dabble there. From time to time when it suited, Nebo would needle Zeke about it. It mostly always worked, like today, but Zeke never let it take him over. With Maisie life had been rocky before the last babe, and worse after he'd died. Nebo never niggled Zeke about the dead child, and he was never aware of what caused their marital troubles. He just knew there was a chink in Zeke's armour and that's all he needed.

Even as Zeke heard Nebo's horse galloping away, he stood, planted by the familiar rage, so white-hot he could see stars.

He knew Maisie and Nebo had never, ever gone there. He knew it in his heart, no matter what trouble there was between him and his wife. Nebo always pushed it, always tried to ignite an explosion in his younger brother, giving Zeke a pain in his gut. He bent to sweep up the cup and set it on the bench with a soft tap. Grabbing his hat, he stalked off to catch the dogs and tie them, then he'd go to the place where he had buried his infant son and not many months after buried his wife.

He knew he never would but some days he wondered if he could kill his brother.

Three

'Elsa,' her sister said, surprised as she opened the bakery's front door. 'This is very early. The store's not even open. And my goodness, look at your hair. It's all over the place. You know to plait it tight and not loose.'

Elsa had trudged into town, her heart heavy, her head empty. Even as hot and bothered as she was, she'd known not to go around the back door because Frank didn't like that. She pushed inside, not bothering to fuss with her hair. 'It's not about Pa, in case you're wondering,' she said pointedly.

'Then what?' Rosie snapped, impatient. 'I'm very busy getting ready to open.'

The aromas inside the bakery were irresistible. Elsa's stomach growled, and she could feel her mouth water, the saliva pooling over her tongue. Hot baked bread was cooling on the vast benches. Buns with fruit dotted through them sat alongside, and rows of jam tarts, their edges neatly pinched and perfectly formed were behind them. She feared she would dribble as she told her sister the awful news. Just to be on the safe side, she wiped a hand over her mouth.

'It's George,' she blurted. 'He's been killed in Victoria.'

'Oh!' Rosie's hand clapped over her throat. 'Oh no, not George. Not our George. How? Who—'

'I came for some stores and the post yesterday and there was a letter to Pa. A kind gentleman from Western Districts in Victoria had sent it to inform us.' When she'd had to come to town, Elsa hardly bothered any longer to visit her sister in the bakery. She'd usually been ignored so there was no point. She would do what she had to do, turn around and go home.

'Victoria?' Rosie looked bleak. 'George travelled far on his adventure.'

Frank came lumbering into the storefront. 'I heard a cry, what is it?' Flour-dust handprints were on his apron and a dollop of custard was stuck high up on it, as if he'd taken a bite of something and missed his mouth.

Rosie was groping for the bench to hold herself up. 'It's George. Elsa has just said he's been killed.' She leaned back heavily on the bench, with a hand on her throat. Her brow furrowed as she waved Elsa away.

Elsa blanched at that. She just needed someone to—

'Lord love us, that's awful,' Frank cried, and pressed a fist to his chest. 'Where? When?'

'Casterton,' Elsa said dully, resigned to standing in the store without an embrace from her sister.

'Good Lord. That's days from here.' He was now by Rosie's side and patting her shoulder. He didn't seem to notice she edged away. 'And Curtis?' he asked. 'He's not taken a downturn, I hope.'

Elsa knew Frank was genuine for news of his father-in-law; however, later in the day, it would all be about the business of family and succession. She swallowed that down. 'He is distraught, of course.'

'Frank,' Rosie said, dashing tears and pinching her nose. 'We must close the store today.' She groped inside her pinafore pocket to pull out a handkerchief.

All three looked at the produce on the benches. Elsa itched to grab bread and buns, but dared not. Not yet.

'Rosie, dearest,' Frank began, his eyes wide in his florid face. 'We need to remain calm. You must go to your father, and I will stay in the store for the morning. You know how busy it gets.' Now his gaze darted around the store. 'And after midday, I will close up and then we will decide on a course of action.'

That was sensible, Elsa decided. But how would she cope with Rosie in their house—or hut as Rosie called it—with her father? Still, it had to be that way.

Rosie tucked loose hair back under her cap. She dabbed at tears and daintily wiped her nose. She looked all blotchy, crying for her lost brother.

Elsa felt the lump in her throat again, yet still, tears would not come. It was as if grief was holding them back and not letting go.

'Off you go then, dearest, go with your sister. But be back soon.'

Rosie looked up. 'I'll take the cart, Frank. I'm not walking miles there and then miles back.' Not expecting resistance, that was clear, she pulled open the ties on her pinafore. 'Wait out the front, Elsa. I won't be a minute. Frank already had the horse hitched up for his delivery rounds earlier this morning.'

Frank was retreating to the kitchen and Rosie was about to follow him out the back. 'Might I pack some of this delicious produce to take home for Pa?' Elsa asked guilelessly. Today she expected no resistance—Frank did turn and gave Rosie a small nod. They'd never been generous, and Elsa had found on some occasions that if she encountered Frank in the store and not Rosie, she'd had to hand over her pennies. Rosie had never taken money from her but never offered much either.

Her sister pointed at the bread, loaves that looked crusty and still had steam floating above them. 'A loaf and a fruit bun,' Rosie said loudly. 'You haven't brought a basket so take mine. It has a

cloth in it. Both of which need to come back when I come back.'
Her sister stepped behind the curtain.

'Yes, Rosie,' Elsa said to thin air. Words were exchanged
between husband and wife and then the back door opened and
closed.

Rosie reappeared from behind the curtain, moving fast, her voice
low. 'Take four loaves and four big buns, and I'll put in a couple
of tarts. The meat pies we'll pack under all of that and cover with
the cloth. Hurry,' she said, as they heard the horse and cart being
driven around to the front.

Surprised, but as bid, Elsa packed the items into the basket and
covered them quickly. Ushered outside by a flap of her sister's
hands, she waited until Frank had pulled up the cart. He stepped
down and Rosie climbed up unaided. 'Come along,' she said to
Elsa, while taking the reins.

Elsa put the basket into the cart and climbed up to sit by her
sister. A quick wave of hands between Rosie and her husband,
and then Rosie snapped the reins. The horse and cart pulled away.

As they drove, Elsa knew she'd be interrogated over the news,
but it didn't happen right away. Except for an occasional snivel,
and a hiccup—Rosie was letting out her grief—there was no
other sound from her sister. Glancing sideways, Elsa could see
Rosie really was struggling, yet when she ventured a reassuring
hand on Rosie's arm, her sister had shaken it off, irascibly.

On the way out of town, Elsa studied the horse, Peppin, pulling the cart. He wasn't always harnessed. She knew Frank sometimes saddled him up and rode the poor thing around if there'd
only been a few deliveries. And these days with a reduced population in the town, that seemed to be the case. She wondered why
he'd been harnessed today. Perhaps Frank was feeling the weather
again and hadn't wanted to ride or walk. He was always so florid
in the face lately.

A fresh breeze whipped up her hair. She found a length of worn calico ribbon in her pinafore and tied it back. As the light gusts brought the scent of the sea, in the morning light she could see white-tipped waves in the distance. She breathed deeply, closing her eyes for just a moment to capture that hint of salt and seaweed. The strong bouquet of the coastal daisy, its new shoots piney and sweet, was a reminder of a familiar part of home. All the scents of home never failed to make her feel as if there was some reason for her existence, but she couldn't ever capture what that reason might be. It just felt like hope, a fresh start every time she smelled it, and like—

'Now with George gone,' Rosie said, all matter-of-fact. The cart had gone past the last of the buildings and pedestrians in the town and was headed out along Main Road. Lake Charra came into view, and the women crinkled their noses as its sulphuric odour drifted by. They passed the handsome Lakeside House at a steady pace. 'And Pa too ill and not likely to recover, you will have to think about where you'll live.'

Elsa was taken aback. 'Will I just?' she said, trying to keep down a sudden burst of anger. 'Pa is not yet dead, if you don't mind, and I will stay there until he has departed. As for George, can we not give him at least a little of our thoughts before you bundle me up and get rid of me?'

Rosie scoffed and a breath puffed out. 'Not what I meant.' Her nose was swollen and red, but the tears had stopped. 'Do you know when George died? Did this letter writer tell us?' She seemed very insistent, even angry perhaps.

Not the reaction Elsa expected from Rosie on this occasion. Perplexed, she said, 'It seems about two or three weeks ago, by the date on the letter.'

'Took a long time to arrive, then, didn't it?' Rosie was snappy. 'Could've walked faster.'

Elsa shrugged. 'Anything could have happened to delay the mail.'

'Well, *come along then*. Did the man say how he died?'

'Bushrangers killed him.'

'Bushrangers?' Rosie erupted. 'There's no such thing anymore.' She looked at Elsa before sharply turning back to concentrate on the road. 'Where?'

'I told you. Casterton. It's in the Western Districts.'

'Elsa, that is a huge area. Where exactly? What else do you know? Was he robbed?'

'I—would presume as much, and that is such a horrible thought. I have no other details but what was in the letter. You'll see it when we get home.' Elsa felt a round of painful thuds strike from within as her pulse raced. Her poor brother. He would have had nothing to hand over to bushrangers—*is that why he got himself killed?* 'There are so many questions, Rosie, we may never have the answers.'

A mile along, Lake Fellmongery, named for the now declining business of removing wool from sheepskin, appeared on their right. Fresh air—not long to go now before their turn-off. Rosie flicked the reins. 'Come on, Peppin,' she yelled ahead. 'Get a move on.'

Peppin trotted his way to the hitching rail out the front of their father's house and waited patiently to be tied. Elsa alighted, put down the basket and patted his muzzle, whispering her thanks. She knotted the reins loosely over the rail.

Rosie braked the cart and jumped to the ground. She glanced down the yard beyond to the clearing where the unfinished house stood. Its first row of packed stones was covered in long strands of dead weeds that seemed to have no end, and sturdy thistles reached high on its walls, bereft of a roof. 'Waste of money and effort,' she muttered. 'Bring the basket, Elsa,' she ordered, pushing open the door to the hut.

With the basket already in hand, Elsa decided she'd resisted the baked goods long enough. Hanging back just a little, she snuck a hand under the cloth, pinched off a small piece of fruit bun and popped it into her mouth, chewing delightedly, swallowing hurriedly before she reached the door to the hut.

But a lump of chewed bun stuck in her throat when she heard her sister wail.

Four

Even though Curtis Goody was not the heavy, densely muscled man he had been before being stricken, the sisters had a hard time trying to take their father's body from his bed to place him into the back of the cart.

Rosie had wailed afresh, and who could blame her? If only Elsa could wail out her grief too, but nothing came. The blow of George's death had numbed her, but this—her father now dead—so soon after. She couldn't take it in. Couldn't work her mind around it.

She'd slumped by the bed watching Rosie, who'd been frantic, trying to wake their father. Of course nothing had worked. Of course not. Death was final, a hollow silence, an eerie space, which before had been filled with noisy life. Elsa had only been away from home perhaps three hours and in that time, life had left him, quick as that. Gone.

Had he minded dying on his own? Or had he waited until Elsa left so he could slip away by himself, resting his weary heart without disappointing those clinging to him and keeping him in this life? That was it—that was probably it. It was his time, and he'd just decided to go. *But oh, that silence, that space.*

The last weeks of his life had left him feebly coloured and now that life was gone, he was even a paler shade than before, tight-skinned and waxy. He was still warm to the touch—perhaps Rosie was right: he would soon wake. *He looks like he needs a shave.* Elsa would do that for him. *Perhaps Elsa is going mad, thinks Elsa.* Her mind was whirling in strange loops.

Now, with their father's body covered in the cart and under the shade of a gum tree, they'd returned to the hut. In her own grief, she hadn't taken any notice of her sister who seemed to be babbling. '… few minutes, only a few minutes, a few minutes more …' and the repetition was beginning to sink in. Then Rosie was rushing from corner to corner of the hut, muttering, 'Where would he put it?' She pulled Elsa's cot from the wall, upended the milking stool. Fiddled about in the disused butter churn. Swiped along the top of the rough homemade bricks of the mantel. Tipped up her father's cot and peered under, sweeping a hand over the floorboards underneath. She flipped through the raggedy story books and old copies of *The Bulletin* from which Elsa had always read to her father (before he got bored with the same old stuff. They'd been too poor lately to buy more).

Rosie stood up and paced, scanning the rough walls and the scrappy ceiling. Elsa clutched her arm, stopped her for a moment. 'Where would he put what? What are you looking for?' She gazed around at the mess: there was an awful lot of straightening up she would have to do— Oh, what did that matter, now?

Rosie flung herself onto a small bench seat, one of a pair her father had fashioned so the family could perch and eat from a trestle table. Her hair was mussed, her cheeks had bright pink spots where colour bloomed and her nose was pinched.

'Rosie?' Elsa was still waiting.

'Pa had buried a tin of money. It was full of sovereigns.'

Elsa stared, open-mouthed. 'Full of sovereigns?'

'At least thirty of them, he said.' Rosie glanced at Elsa, it seemed without seeing her.

'That's a fortune,' Elsa breathed.

'Yes, it is,' Rosie cried. 'He was supposed to tell me where it was hidden when George took off on his adventure. George had to have known where it was, because he would have inherited after Pa's death. But now both of them have gone—' Rosie burst into fresh tears.

Shocked by the news, Elsa shot to her feet. 'Where did he get such money?' Her father might have told her about it. Should have told her. It would certainly have helped them.

'He said he'd found it when he first bought the property. Whose ever it was, they'd been long since gone by that time.'

'That's astounding. No one missed thirty sovereigns?'

Bleary-eyed and waspish, Rosie said, 'Clearly not, Elsa.'

'I—have no knowledge of such a tin.'

'Of course you wouldn't,' Rosie snapped. 'Besides, what would you have done with it if you did know?' She stood up again, rubbing her chafed hands together.

Elsa spun around, anger flaring. 'But what would you do with it, sister? Give it to that lump of a husband of yours?'

Rosie turned on her. 'No. I was going to leave him with his bakery. Let him do the work for a change.'

Elsa's mouth dropped open again. 'Leave Frank?'

'I was going to get the tin and run from here. Go far away and start my life again, venture out of this dying place to find somewhere exciting. Somewhere I could breathe again and live my life.' Flattening her hands on the table, she leaned on it and seemed out of breath.

'And so—leave me?' Elsa was incredulous. 'Leave me penniless?'

'Oh no,' Rosie cried, gaping in horror. 'Do you suppose George took it with him and it's now in the hands of the bushrangers?'

Obviously, Rosie's issue had nothing to do with Elsa's indignation. But this was her big sister talking. This was a woman she'd always looked up to—not necessarily had liked all the time but had certainly looked up to. 'I'd say so. George was the sort to have spent it, not kept it or kept it hidden.'

Rosie held her head and grimaced. 'That's true, the silly boy.' They all thought of George as a boy, no matter that he was older than Elsa by two years. 'Perhaps that's why he was murdered. He might have flashed the coin around—that would undoubtedly attract attention.' She exhaled. 'I'll leave. You don't have to come. I don't need you.' Her tone was sharp.

At forty, Rosie was part of a world Elsa had not yet begun to explore. The baby of the family, Elsa had been protected by three older brothers and the firstborn Rosie, and never dreamed she would be left behind—by all of them as it was turning out.

'What—you'd really do that? Abandon me? Had you found the tin of coins earlier, where would you have put me, or sent me?' Elsa heard her voice become shrill. 'And now, with our father dead, where am I to go? You still have Frank if you stay—'

'Oh, I don't know what I mean,' Rosie shrilled. 'Damn and blast Frank.' She waved her arm around the room: 'Are there any other hiding places here? We have to be sure.'

Elsa spread her hands, confounded by all of this. It was all wrong. George was dead, her father was dead—his body going cold in the cart—her sister had gone mad and now there was nowhere left for her to go. She would be told to move on if Frank really did take over administration of the property—which of course he was legally able to do.

Springing out of her stupor, Elsa checked under her bed for any loose boards. Squeezing her arm behind the old cooker she felt for anything wedged in behind it. She dragged out the pine box that had been their pantry cupboard and looked behind that.

Nothing. Hands on hips, she checked around. There was no place to hide a tin. The rafters were open to the poor roof, so there were no hidey-holes there. Besides, why would he leave it here if he was going off on his adventure? 'He's taken it with him, I'm sure of it.'

'You haven't looked very far,' Rosie said.

'You haven't looked at all.'

'It could be anywhere,' Rosie muttered. 'But I think you're right. He would've taken it with him.' She frowned. 'What about the broken-down horse stall?'

Elsa gritted her teeth and marched outside to the stall, Rosie on her heels. 'In you go,' her sister said.

Careful no rotting roof timbers there fell on her head, Elsa scrambled around in the dirt, and came up with nothing. Brushing aside thick cobweb, she said, 'Short of digging up the whole yard, what else do you suggest?' She heard her voice rise to shrill. *No, no, no.* What was *she* doing? She pushed past Rosie and headed back towards the hut.

Inside, she dusted off, annoyed with herself. What were *they* doing? Good Lord. Their father was dead. There was something far more pressing to do. 'Rosie, wait.' She held up her hand. 'Wait,' she said more calmly. 'We have to plan, yes, but first we have to get Pa to a coffin maker, get him buried properly without folk accusing us of a terrible thing.' Elsa knew the ramifications of all this was still a jumble.

'What terrible thing?' Rosie asked, looking frightened.

'Rosie, what if people say we had done something to Pa for this tin of coins? Does anyone know? Does Frank know?'

'I don't know, I don't know.' Rosie clamped her hands together. 'No, Frank doesn't know, I'm sure of it and don't be ridiculous. We wouldn't kill our own father for it.' And then understanding dawned. 'Oh, my God.'

'You see, don't you? We must be very quiet about this tin. We must ask Frank for the money to bury our poor pa—'

Rosie wailed yet again.

'—and then plan …' Elsa rubbed her face hard with both hands and swiped them into her hair, dislodging more from its loose plait. Impatient, she swiped at the thick, unruly locks. 'We must find that tin and hide it anew. If Frank does know of it, we must claim ignorance. He must not find it.' Elsa's mind was working fast. She knew their land was so small that it wouldn't bring much if they were to put it up for sale. And Frank would still have the right to administer their affairs if their father had named him. 'We could just sell up.' Her heart sunk at the thought.

Rosie shook her head. 'The whole district would go for a song these days, why would this patch of worthless scrub be any different? You know the Robe port is all but dead. People are abandoning their farms, their homes and their businesses.'

'Frank wouldn't abandon your business.'

'He might if he knew about the gold coins.' Rosie seemed annoyed when Elsa shook her head in disbelief. She went on, 'If he closed the bakery, he would expect me to go with him wherever he went.' She held her head as if it pained her. 'But I don't want to be married to him any longer. I don't want to be his wife.' It was another wail, one probably borne out of years of thought.

'How can you not want it? There's no solution to that, is there?'

'I could divorce. All the more reason for me to find the tin.'

'Oh, Rosie. What grounds for divorce do you have? He has to be proven guilty of cruelty, or desertion or adultery. And we know he has provided for you—even if you're the one doing all the work. No magistrate would release you.'

Elsa had read enough newspapers; she knew of the terrible scandals divorce created. All the same, she couldn't see that there was much going for marriage. Just look at her sister: so unhappy that she would plan such a desperate move as to run away from everything she knew and risk her life by being alone in the world. A fallen woman is how she would be labelled. Hers would not be a happy or a safe life and yet Rosie was prepared to forgo all of it. What sort of turmoil drove that? Divorce was terribly frowned upon, and a woman who instigated it would be almost untouchable afterwards. She despaired for Rosie.

It irked Elsa though, that Rosie would choose to abandon her, too. She would have to look after herself. If her only sister could forsake her for a tin of coins, who on earth could Elsa trust now but herself?

Five

In the bakery, Elsa watched with growing concern as she realised Rosie was losing the battle with Frank. Even though he had offered what appeared to be sincere condolences to them, he hadn't softened one iota. Not that Elsa had expected it, but she'd been sure Frank had respected their father. Perhaps not.

It was time for her to step in. 'I apologise for interrupting, Mr Putney—Frank,' she started. Frank hated being interrupted, especially when they were standing inside the store. (Mind you, he didn't mind interrupting others when he felt like it.) He also hated being called by his first name in public. Someone might come in and hear, and it could be misconstrued that he was letting his sister-in-law be impertinent. That was the least of her worries; right now her father's casket was being measured up at the blacksmith's—who was also the coffin maker. 'But might I not work for you too, in order to repay you for the purchase of our pa's coffin? We certainly don't want him going to his grave with only his clothes on.'

Rosie had frowned at her sister, but Frank hadn't seen that. He turned to look at her. 'It would need quite a lot of work to repay that sort of money.'

A few pounds was all, not a lifetime's worth of work, Elsa was sure. She forced a wheedle into her voice. 'And you well know I'm a hard worker. Why else would we still be able to live on the farm?' As she spread her hands, she realised just how dirty they were, the creases stained with the colour of the earth and her nails scuffed and dark.

Frank chortled. 'The farm. Good-for-nothing piece of dirt right now. Still, might be worth something in the future. We'll bury him there. That way I won't have to pay for a hole to be dug in the town cemetery.'

Elsa swallowed down the affront and didn't dare look at her sister. 'Yes. We can do that, he'll rest beside Ma, that's preferable,' she said agreeably, her eyes smarting. 'I can dig a hole if necessary.'

Frank went back to his till but didn't open it, just stood there, lord of the manor. 'In that case, as soon as the smithy has finished the coffin, you'd better start digging. There's no time to waste—it's already early afternoon and this warm weather will finish off a body quick enough.' He checked over his shoulder and addressed Rosie. 'You may take today for your sister and the sad duty. If the reverend can perform a ceremony, we'll have it the day after tomorrow. That's enough time.' He turned away; they'd been dismissed.

For the first time in a long time, Elsa saw the Rosie she thought she'd known for years. Her sister's face reddened and her mouth flattened to a thin line, but she said quite calmly, 'Thank you, Frank.' However, when Rosie glanced her way, Elsa noticed the lightning flash in her eyes. She then tilted her head, indicating they should leave.

Rosie swept ahead of Elsa and left by the back door, snatching off her pinafore and grabbing her hat. They'd only been back in the town with their father's body an hour, yet Elsa knew Rosie had been expected to don her work apron as if nothing was amiss.

Upon their return, Rosie had disappeared into the house attached at the back of the bakery. Elsa was left standing on her own quite embarrassed as customers filed in to be served by Frank. For whatever reason, Rosie had taken her time, then returned wearing a clean pinafore over her day dress.

Now, trailing her sister, who marched to the smithy's, Elsa felt quite outside herself. Having to ask for a coffin to be built was one thing; being unsure that funds would be made available to pay for it was another. Unsettling and wrong. Frank had the money to do it. A person had a right to be buried with decency. It was their father, after all.

'Miz Putney,' the smithy yelled at Rosie when they entered the forge area. He always yelled, whether he was in his forge or not. He yelled over the roar of his fire and the clanging of his tools on the huge anvil, even, it seemed, over thin air. Perhaps it was easier for him to do so all the time. He tipped his cap. 'Miss Goody,' he blasted at Elsa. 'Got yer pa's box all ready. Had one half done, just had to saw off a bit on account of he's short.' He pointed to a coffin standing on its end on the far wall. Then he wiped his forehead with his forearm, smearing more soot and sawdust over himself. With singes on his eyebrows and one sideburn almost completely gone, he must have got too close to his fire at some point.

Rosie crossed the shed to check the coffin.

'Thank you, Mr Benson,' Elsa said. She didn't have to yell. 'We'll need help to get Pa into it and then into the back of the cart.'

He nodded, made a sad face, then whistled through his teeth. Young Henry, his son, appeared, just as blackened from soot as his father. His teeth gleamed against his dirty face. 'Hello, Miss Goody.'

Henry was only about twenty and had a confidence that was a bit disconcerting. Still, she wouldn't take any notice of someone so cheeky and full of himself, even if he did have that heady I'm-interested-in-you stare that on other occasions had made her insides tingle. If he'd been older, Elsa *might* have taken a shine to him. So forthright was his stare today that she couldn't help the patter inside her chest—on the day of her father's death, if you please. She turned away, dismayed with herself.

'Lad,' Mr Benson yelled. 'We have to help the ladies load up their pa.'

'Right you are.' Henry sidled past Elsa, his eyes now kind with sympathy (so he'd just redeemed himself), and when he got to Rosie, scuttled around her to hoist the coffin over his shoulder.

Elsa followed as he took it out to their cart. Their horse, Peppin, still harnessed, was fully under shade, and so poor Pa would have been relatively cool. When Henry and Mr Benson got in the back of the cart, and the coffin followed, poor Pa was unceremoniously hefted inside it.

As the lid was slid over the top, Rosie started to say something but stopped. There was no reason to stop them closing the coffin. Mr Benson pulled out a hammer from the bag slung about his thick waist. With three or four nails clamped between his teeth, and more in his hands, he whacked them into the lid, securing it. Elsa ears had begun to ring.

'Guessin' you done spoke to the doc and got yer pa a death certificate,' he shouted while concentrating. He flicked a quick look at Rosie who nodded curtly.

Elsa let the lie slip by. She hadn't thought of that, but nobody would dispute their father had been dying, and was now dead. They would register it soon. *But first, please God, let's bury my poor pa.*

Finally, Mr Benson was done. 'That oughta keep him tight,' he yelled and jumped down from the cart. He snatched off his hat and Henry followed suit. 'Right sorry, Miz Putney, Miss Goody.'

They nodded at both of them. 'I'll send me bill to Mr Putney, directly,' Mr Benson said.

Rosie stopped him then. 'No need. Here. Five pounds, isn't it?' She clutched the notes and held them up for him to see.

Elsa gaped.

Mr Benson shook his head. 'Two pounds too much, Miz Putney.'

'If we can have Henry for this afternoon at our farm to dig a hole, would that make it about right?'

'Miz Putney, it's still—'

'For God's sake, man. We're trying to bury our father,' Rosie said, glaring. She thrust the notes at him. Elsa closed her mouth.

Mr Benson pocketed the money. 'Whenever you're ready, Miz Putney.'

'We're ready now.'

At Mr Benson's lift of his chin, Henry leapt into the driver's seat. Rosie and Elsa climbed up beside him.

'Thank you, Mr Benson,' Elsa said as Henry released the brake and the cart lurched forward.

As she helped Henry dig a decent enough hole for her father, right alongside her mother's grave, there was no time for Elsa to speak to Rosie on her own. Digging had been easier than she'd imagined. The earth around had already been loosened—of course at the time of her mother's interment a while ago. Also because George had always intended to plant shrubs there and had begun to work the soil, never imagining that their father would lay there so soon. *Dear funny, sentimental George.* Elsa wondered if she and Rosie should try and bring George back home for burial here. But she decided against putting it to Rosie. It would be a terrible task, grief aside. They'd have to dig up George from wherever he was. Elsa wasn't so sure she could do it.

Henry did most of the harder work as they steadily dug into the solid earth. The only talk was when someone needed a drink. Sweat dried on Elsa's face and neck. She had dirt all over her— face, neck, dress, boots. Didn't matter, the job had to be finished, and Elsa was used to being dirty; it was part of working the land, and it was honest work. She'd get to bathe when she could.

Once a decent depth was reached, Henry slaked his thirst by slurping from the ladle inside the water barrel nearby. Then he dunked his head in the horse's water trough. He slung his hat in it too and wrung it out. 'I'll be off then,' he said, as he placed it back on his head.

'No, Henry.' Rosie stopped him. 'You need to help us get the coffin down into the hole and then fill it in. A shilling, just for you,' she said. 'Come along. We need to get it done quickly.'

It was a juggle getting the coffin off the back of the wagon. Once they'd manhandled it to the ground, they only had to carry it a short distance to the hole. Then Henry jumped into the pit and directed Elsa and Rosie to push it towards him so that one end of the coffin could hang over the edge.

Elsa stepped back. *Gracious me.* They'd hardly have managed as well without Henry.

He worked the casket down until the narrow end rested on the cool ground. He ducked underneath it and crept it all the way until he was ready to fully lay it down.

'Best not to look at this bit, ladies,' he called up, his hands holding the broad part of the small coffin.

Rosie turned away and grabbed Elsa's arm, forcing her to do the same. Elsa, bewildered, heard a loud thump and a curse then Henry saying, 'He's in.'

Both Elsa and Rosie turned back for a moment to see him step on the coffin to climb out of the hole. They stood side by side now. Rosie took a deep breath as she gazed down on it; Elsa could see tears again trailing on her sister's cheeks.

'I'm so sorry, Pa,' Rosie whispered. She swiped her face, smearing dust over the sheen of perspiration. Rosie looked as dirty as Elsa felt.

Henry took up a shovel to lean on. He'd already knocked off his hat, ready for paying his respects.

Elsa and Rosie gripped hands. It was strange. *The whole thing is strange. I feel very strange.* The lump in her throat was growing again. Here they were, filthy, their father just dead these last few hours and George three weeks gone …

Now he is in his grave and there is a blacksmith's son standing by with a shovel and the day has suddenly become very hot and I really feel quite peculiar as I'm saying a few mumbled words with my sister for our father and now clods of earth are being shovelled back into the hole and—

She took a breath. It was done. Their father was beside their mother. Henry was whacking the back of the shovel on the low mound of earth covering the hole. Then he dunked his hat in the water trough again and helped himself to another drink. 'If there's nothin' else you want doin', Miz Putney?' With a shake of Rosie's head, he pocketed the shilling offered, slapped on his hat and looked at Elsa. 'I'm better'n that mad Pete Southie that's comin' after you. Remember that, Elsa Goody.' He waved and began walking back to the town.

Rosie regarded her sister. 'You will tell me about that later.'

Elsa looked away. 'Nothing to tell.'

She stood by the graves. Her mother's had a cross on it, which was leaning a little in the loose soil. The roughly carved letters read: KITTY GOODY. DIED 1889. LOVED WIFE AND MOTHER.

George had made it, and had, just weeks before he'd left, painted the letters he'd previously meticulously carved. Elsa reached down and straightened the cross. Who would they get to make one for their father? Her throat squeezed.

'We must get a stone marker for them,' she rasped. 'One so that the words don't disappear.' At her sister's silence, she looked across.

Rosie was on her knees, doubled over and weeping silently. This time when Elsa put her hand on Rosie's shoulder, she wasn't brushed away. Still her own tears wouldn't come. There should have been tears for the loss of her father, and for her mother and her three brothers. Elsa would have to let Rosie cry tears for her as well.

Elsa had directed her sister out of the afternoon sun and into the hut. A bowl of now dirty water and a freshly filled pitcher stood on the narrow table inside. They had each divested their dresses and washed. They'd sat, still in their boots and their chemises with pinafores tied over, and sponged off the dirtiest bits on the dresses. Once they'd been brushed down, the garments were left to dry over the hitching rail outside. No one would see them. No one was expected. No one would come. News of their father's death would eventually reach the few folk still left in town, and maybe tomorrow people might visit to offer condolences.

Elsa had given the last of the bought feed to Peppin. Then she'd rubbed him down and he seemed content enough. Now back inside, she used the washcloth again and felt refreshed. She retied her apron, feeling better having it over her chemise.

Rosie had done the same and was patting her face dry. 'I've wanted to talk to you about something all day, something I've thought carefully about.' She discarded the towel, placing her palms flat on the table. 'It came to me this morning when I left you in the shop,' she said as she twisted her wedding ring off and put it back on again.

'What is it?' Elsa had let out her hair and was trying to drag her mother's brush through it, the only thing of Kitty's she now had. Setting the brush aside, Elsa piled her hair up into a twist and pinned it as best she could. 'Tell me,' she prompted.

'You are a grown woman, now, well and truly, as I am,' Rosie said and hesitated.

Elsa frowned. *This does not bode well.*

'And we know that there is a tin of money somewhere,' Rosie began again.

'We know there *was* a tin of money,' Elsa replied.

Rosie let that go. 'And as there are now no brothers of ours anymore ...'

Elsa was listening. Her sister had a plan but, right now, she couldn't presume what it might be. 'Yes?'

'We need to look after ourselves.' Rosie was looking at her and for the first time Elsa felt as if it was as an equal, not a merely tolerated baby sister.

Elsa's eyes were scratchy and dry. Her throat hurt from the lump in it that still hadn't subsided, and she had begun to feel overwhelmingly tired. She sighed. 'Of course we do, but you are ready to leave Frank and to leave me here to fend for myself, so I can't see how *we* could do that.' She was tapping her fingers on the table. 'However, if I stay here, and you still have money in your pocket, I'd like to have a cow again and that way I can—'

'We should both leave here, now,' Rosie said, and closed a fist against her chest. 'Or at least first thing in the morning. We have the cart, and Peppin. Frank is not expecting me back tonight.' She patted her side. 'And I do have some money in a purse here.'

Elsa thought for a moment, her mouth set. 'Is that why we had to bury Pa so quick?'

'No. That was plain necessity.'

'It was too quick.'

'Have it your own way, but the weather was against us. It is done.' Rosie sighed. 'If you don't want to come with me, I'm still going, and I will take Peppin and the cart.' She stood up. 'Yes, no point waiting, is there? I'll go now so that you can sit here on your righteous backside and be the spoiled brat of the family you always were. Good luck finding something to eat while you're at it.' They both glanced at the basket of bread and buns and pies left abandoned this morning. 'We should truly eat those pies soon,' she said a bit more softly, 'but after that, *good luck* finding food.'

Elsa could not believe what she'd just heard. 'I was not spoiled. I worked as hard as my brothers when they were here—' *Oh, that sounded so odd.* 'But I have my own mind, and I will always speak it.'

'And get away with it.'

'Not so. On his dying bed—' *That was only this morning.* 'Pa said that he wouldn't consider that I administer—'

'All those grand ideas about the rights of us women.' Rosie shook her head.

'Yes,' Elsa declared. 'The laws allow it now. And you well know there's to be an election in April and I intend to be the first woman to cast a vote.'

Rosie scoffed. 'Where? In Adelaide?'

'No, here,' Elsa cried. 'There is to be a polling booth here, in Robe. We are in the Albert electorate.'

'And so next you'll be our new governor, I expect.'

Elsa scowled. 'I will be exercising my right to vote,' she said between her teeth.

'And that's a nice word-for-word quote you've read at some point,' Rosie said, a dismissive wave of her hand following. 'If I'd known that by saving all those newspapers for you, we'd have a raging suffragette—'

'Suffragist,' Elsa corrected. 'And for your information,' she erupted, 'the governor is appointed by the queen, not by the general public.'

'You'll stand for parliament, then,' Rosie goaded.

'No women have decided to stand. If *you'd* read all the papers you saved for me, you'd know that.'

'God, listen to you—no wonder people laugh.'

Elsa bristled. She certainly didn't mind being vocal about her views. Perhaps other women were smarter than she was—keeping their views to themselves. But what good would that do? 'I don't care if they do laugh. I'll stand up for what I believe in, otherwise how will things ever change?'

'Yes, yes. And as impoverished as you are, no doubt it will serve you well. All this reading, and standing up for what you believe in, and changing everything by having one single vote.' Rosie dusted herself down. 'Well, I can't waste time squawking about that. I've made up my mind and I'm not turning back. I'll take a few things from here and be on my way, so that I can stand up for what *I* believe in.'

'Oh? And that's to leave your husband and be destitute, is it?'

'Don't be churlish. You know nothing of marriage.'

'And I don't want to know.'

'Spoken like a true brat—you don't want to know. In that case, make no comment.' Rosie looked around. She picked up her father's bedclothes and sniffed, then tossed them back.

Elsa thrust off her seat. 'Then tell me what it's been like so I can understand why you want to leave.'

Rosie set her mouth and ignored her. She went to Elsa's cot and picked up the sheet there, decided it was good enough to take with her and began to strip the bed. Elsa snatched the bedclothes out of her hands. Rosie countered, 'I'll be sleeping in the cart, Elsa, so I need to take some bedding. At least you'll have time to wash Pa's bedclothes tomorrow before you need them here.'

'*Rosie.*' Elsa dropped her bedsheets back on the cot.

Rosie stamped her foot and shouted, 'Well, you're just standing there like some nincompoop, not doing anything. It's time to go.'

Elsa's thoughts were spinning again. 'I—haven't had time to check things over here.'

'Check what things—all the gold and silver?'

Elsa glanced around the hut that now looked so foreign. 'I—wanted to look for Ma's locket, and I need to consider what to take, if I'm to leave. How can we leave with nothing? We'll both be impoverished—'

'My mind is made up. Hurry up and pack some clothes. And I can tell you, you won't find Ma's locket. George took it with him. Good old sentimental George.' Rosie cast about, looking for something. A small trunk caught her eye and she went to it, opened it and pulled out its ragged horse rugs until she found an old canvas satchel. 'This will do for your smalls.'

Elsa stared at Rosie. 'George took it? Oh no.' Then she felt real tears beginning to smart. 'Ma's locket was the only thing with a picture of her.'

Rosie flipped the satchel to the floor. 'I know,' she said with empathy. 'And now there's nothing of Pa left either.'

'Yes, but he was going to live forever.' Tears filled Elsa's eyes, but she dashed them away before they fell, and blinked and blinked to make sure they'd disappear. She set her jaw. 'I hadn't given a thought to how I'd fare here in the hut with no one and no money. And now, suddenly, that doesn't even matter.' Hearing her own words, she looked with surprise at Rosie. Then she wiped her nose and went to the little milking stool that had been upended in Rosie's first manic rush around the hut. Underneath it was Mr Jones's letter. She picked it up and smoothed it against her chemise then held it to the light. 'If George is buried on this man's property, we must go there.'

Rosie threw her hands in the air. 'Into Victoria? There are wild men there, and bushrangers again, the letter said.'

'It was just a description, I'm sure,' Elsa said. 'There haven't been real bushrangers anywhere since—'

'Anything George had with him in Victoria would've been stolen by whoever killed him. Call them bushrangers or not, I don't care, I won't go there,' her sister cried.

Exasperated, Elsa threw her hands in the air. 'So where did you think you'd go, Rosie?' The expression on her sister's face answered that. She'd not thought that far. Taking a breath, Elsa changed her tone. 'I hear the Western Districts is quite a beautiful area. Besides, this man, this—' she consulted the letter, 'Ezekiel Jones was kind enough to bury our brother.' Her heart gave a little thud as she mentioned the man's name. *How odd*. She folded it, put it back in its envelope and tucked it into her bodice. 'Perhaps he would be kind enough to offer us more information. George might have told him things.' She paused. 'Like where the tin might be. It would be better to get that information face to face, don't you think?'

Rosie shook her head, frowning. Elsa knew she was thinking. 'We could write a letter instead,' she said, not quite ready to give over to Elsa's idea.

'And how would we receive an answer if we run away?'

Rosie paced the room, flicking items up from where they'd been cast, checking in case she'd missed something. When she spun back to Elsa, she grabbed up the satchel. 'All right, we go to Victoria. But pack this with what you need, and let's go now, so we don't get caught by some unexpected sympathiser for our dear pa's death.' She tossed the bag onto their father's bed then flung open the hut's flimsy door, and marched smack bang into a leering Pete Southie. She propelled backwards in shock as he hovered in the doorway.

Elsa sucked in a breath, her chest tight.

'Ladies,' he said and whipped off his hat as he stepped inside. He was a broad-shouldered, stocky man with bushy eyebrows and black and grey whiskers shaved haphazardly. The sour tang of fresh sweat, the earthy odour of rangy horse and the stench of stale tobacco smoke pervaded the hut. 'Where are ye going if you're packin'?' He glanced at Elsa.

Elsa wasn't fooled by that smile. It wasn't kindly, it was a leer, for sure. His gaze roved over her, then flicked to Rosie. She pulled her pinafore strings tighter. They were both only wearing pinafores over their chemises. *Think quick, girl.* She glanced around at the disarray, at the fireplace, at the old kettle waiting to be packed, at her father's bed with the linens crumpled on it. At the little bottle of sleeping draught left by the doctor. 'We're closing up the house to decide what's to be done, and we're going back to the bakery, aren't we, Rosie?' she said as Rosie came to lean against her. She gripped her sister's shaking hand.

'A good thing I arrived then, to see ye're all right. I can escort ye back.'

'We're all right,' Elsa said, squeezing Rosie's fingers before she let go. 'I suppose you'll be wanting tea after the ride out.'

Southie's eyes lit up. 'I would. Ye're being generous today, Miss Elsa.'

Elsa glanced at Rosie who was frowning, her gaze still on Pete Southie. 'Him just buried, our pa would have wanted us to offer hospitality.' She noted her sister was saying nothing. Rosie's mouth was firmly closed.

'He was a good man, Curtis Goody was,' he said and helped himself to a chair, swinging it in front of the door. He sat, elbows on his knees, staring intently at them.

Blocking escape.

Feeling Rosie stiffen, Elsa said, 'I think there are still hot coals in the cooker, so tea shouldn't take long.' She pushed at her sister. 'The tea, if you please, and there's a third cup somewhere.' *Think.* As Rosie crossed to the mantel, Elsa turned to her father's bed linens. *Aha.* 'We have to take all this to town to wash because the well here is nearly dry again, isn't it, Rosie?' As she gathered the old sheets, she swept the little bottle from the bedside table into her pinny pocket. Turning, her arms full, she faced Southie.

He shot to his feet. 'I'll put them in the cart for ye, duly,' he said and reached over to grab them from her arms.

Elsa flinched as his hard fingers, gathering the bundle, scraped both her breasts. She gritted her teeth and kept her features stony as he sat back down again. He scrunched the bundle flat, shoved it under his feet and folded his arms, watching one woman then the other. A sting of pinpricks rushed across the backs of Elsa's hands. *Fear?* No, not that. *Danger.*

Rosie poked an iron rod into the cooker, stirring the coals. Elsa wondered about the poker, but watching Rosie, she knew her sister wouldn't take any action with it. *She's too jittery.* She watched her sister drop the tamp with a clang and thump the kettle onto the hotplate. Water splashed and spat. Rosie shoved three pannikins across the stovetop and threw a hard glance at Elsa.

Elsa ignored it, steadied the cups and asked him, 'Sugar?' She drew the tin from above the cooker and hovered it over a rusty pannikin.

'You know I do, Miss Elsa. Four spoons.'

She waited imperiously. Dared him with a glare.

'If ye please,' he added, and shuffled in the seat.

Four spoons, indeed. Such extravagance, you great gormless hog. Go wallow in a swamp somewhere. Elsa took a spoon from the hutch drawer and cranked open the sugar tin. She fiddled, and with her back turned, palmed the little bottle in her pocket, flicked the tiny cork from its neck and dropped tincture generously into the cup. Belatedly, she wondered if it was too much. *Too late.* A scent of cinnamon and cloves wafted up. She capped the bottle and dropped it back in her pocket. Rosie saw, and chewed down on her lip.

Elsa spooned sugar into a cup. *Why does boiling water take so long?* She jiggled the kitchen utensils. She reached for the ancient teapot on the mantel, lumped a handful of tea leaves into it from the little box on the same shelf, and set it on the stovetop. Rosie snatched up the switch broom and swept madly along the hearth.

'Sad day,' Southie said, no doubt warming to this picture of domesticity. 'You ladies thinkin' straight, though, getting ready to go to Frank's bakery an' bein' under his wing an' all.'

Rosie bristled.

Elsa, rolling her eyes, turned her attention to the tardy kettle. Then—at last—the damn thing was boiling. She snatched it up, poured hot water into the teapot and immediately filled their cups, careful to keep her eye on which one was meant for Southie.

'Ye've not steeped the tea,' he said, pointing an accusing finger.

Terse, Elsa kept pouring. 'We like it like that.'

'In my house—'

'We're not in your house,' she snapped, and glared again. Making a big thing of stirring his sugar, she finally handed it to him. 'You know we don't have milk.'

'Perhaps I can fix that for ye one day, Miss Elsa.'

Miss Elsa wanted to fix him with a clunk on the head. One of Pa's iron boot lasts, which sat by the edge of the hearth, would do nicely but it was too hard to get to.

'When you consent to—'

'Our father has just died, Mr Southie,' Rosie announced, flinging the broom to the floor. 'And we've just learned of George's death, too. There'll be no talk today of consenting to anything,' she hissed.

Southie blew into his tea, slurped, grimaced at it, but said nothing.

He's lucky he got it in a cup and not dumped in his lap. What would boiling water have done there? Elsa didn't think long on that.

Rosie was busying about doing silly, useless things with maddening efficiency, straightening discarded utensils, brushing down cleaned benches, grabbing the dishrag and flapping it at anything within reach.

Waiting, and watching her sister at work, long minutes passed. Elsa felt the sweat slip down under her chemise. She rubbed the spot, then when Southie's gaze followed, she dropped her hand and turned to Rosie. 'We have all we need of Pa's things to take to Frank now, Rosie,' she said quietly yet loud enough for Southie, behind her, to hear. She nodded encouragement to her sister.

Thankfully, Rosie responded in kind. She seemed to be quite collected now. 'Yes, you're right, Elsa. Frank will know what to do. Perhaps we should go soon.'

'Yes, we should.' Elsa turned back to Southie. 'What say you, Mr Southie?' she asked, and as she looked at him, he slumped, glassy-eyed, and fell over backwards off the chair. His tea spilled, and the empty pannikin rolled over his chest.

Both women froze. Then Elsa grabbed his cup and poured her tea into it. She swished it quickly with a finger then tossed the contents onto the floor, emptying it of any laudanum residue. Its smell was distinctive and she didn't want it to linger. Rosie flung out her tea then used the dishrag to grab the kettle and pour hot water onto the coals in the stove.

'And on the floor here,' Elsa directed with a finger pointing over the puddle of tea staining the floorboards. She stared at Southie as steam misted the room. 'He's well and truly sleeping, but I don't want to risk staying any longer than we must.'

Rosie stared at her, agape. 'You're a scheming witch, Elsa,' she said, a light in her eyes. 'I never knew you to be so—'

'Practical, inventive,' Elsa finished for her, and stepped around the fallen man. 'All this talk of bushrangers has made me quite daring.'

'Elsa, the bushranger,' Rosie said in wonder, hands on her hips and her gaze on Southie's prone body.

'Hardly. Bushrangers had guns and such.' Elsa bent to peer at Southie's closed eyes.

'A lady bushranger. Choice of weapon, laudanum.'

'Not a time for funny, Rosie. We have to drag him away from the door. Help me. Let's roll him over there.'

They'd loaded the cart in a frenzy. Elsa had taken most everything she could. Clothes, of course, and her spare pair of boots, the thin, ragged blankets, the flat mattresses, and any pillows still worth keeping. There wasn't much when it came down to it, but the kettle, cups and tea provisions had to come with them. A pot. They'd have to cook from time to time, but she didn't know what. The match book—she ran her hand over the mantel and found it. She grabbed tins of flour and sugar, salt. Preserved fruit that Frank had so kindly 'donated' to her father.

Avoiding Southie's body (he'd be all right, she'd given him only a little more tincture than prescribed for her father), she looked around the hut. Their father's old rifle took her eye. It leaned against the ancient sideboard, a piece of furniture her mother had brought with her from Mt Gambier when they'd married. Elsa thought about the gun, knew that it worked because she'd been the one to clean it on Curtis Goody's say-so. Bushranger she'd be. She grabbed it, rested it against the table and searched the sideboard drawer for bullets already made. Only three, but at least they'd be dry. If she had to, she'd purchase powder and make more ammunition. She stopped a moment. She knew her father's will was also in there. She rummaged around, found the thick envelope and held it up. 'This is coming with us, too, Rosie.'

They dropped the dirty dishrag over Southie's eyes—just in case—stripped off their pinafores and donned their cleaned dresses. Elsa snatched up the pinafores and a blanket for across their knees, for when the sun would drop and the temperature with it.

Impatient to get away, Rosie marched for the cart. She pushed their belongings into it, shoving aside the shovel Henry had used, keeping things packed tight as Elsa handed her everything she'd gathered.

'I'll get newspaper for our nature calls,' Rosie piped, and ran back inside.

Elsa slid the rifle in behind the driver's seat and tucked the bullets and the will into a small wooden toolbox attached nearby to the floor of the cart. In it was a pot of axle grease tightly clamped shut, oily rags, a mallet, leather straps for something-or-other, and a tin of nails. All useful for something.

Rosie returned, threw a small bundle of newspaper into the cart and beckoned with a wave of her hand. 'Come along, the day is getting away. How much longer will he be unconscious?'

'Probably for the night.'

'We should untie his horse and let him run home,' Rosie said.

Elsa looked at the nondescript brown gelding, still saddled, standing quietly under a tree. 'Best not,' she said. 'But there is one more thing we have to do. I'll need you to help me.' She didn't wait for Rosie to get down but headed around towards the water trough. There on a timber stand was a barrel of water.

Rosie called, 'How are we going to manage that?'

'How are we going to manage without it? Come on, two of us can do it. Bring the cart.' Elsa climbed onto the stand and with the heels of her hands, hammered the lid down tight on the barrel.

Rosie gee-upped Peppin. Wrangling the barrel between them, they managed to hoist it onto the cart and slid it all the way along until it sat snug against the driver's bench. Rosie got back into the driver's seat, huffing and puffing, and muttering, 'Hurry up, hurry up.'

Elsa took one last look inside the hut. She stepped over Southie, only a moment fearful he would suddenly wake, and from stout nails on the far wall she grabbed her father's oilskin coat, as well as her own wide-brimmed and battered hat and the hand-me-down blue woollen jacket she'd worn for years. She'd tie one of her brother's long leather belts—much too big for her—around her waist to keep the jacket closed because she'd lost buttons and never bothered to replace them.

Outside she took a moment to stare at the pair of graves, one fresh and one much older. She felt strange. She turned to look at the hut, squat, dilapidated—it appeared as if it was a life that was no longer hers.

Ezekiel Jones's letter was safely tucked into her bodice, and knowing she was on her way to meet him, the man who'd buried her brother, there was that odd flutter in her chest again. Mr Jones might be one hundred and ten years of age, and not able to help at all. *Why on earth do I feel so unsettled about meeting him?*

Rosie's call distracted her. 'Up you get, Elsa. We're off to see that letter writer of yours.' Nothing unsettled about Rosie's thinking, it seemed.

Whether he was ancient or not, they were going to meet Mr Jones.

Six

Zeke knew it wouldn't be his kids when he heard horses approaching; it was too early in the day. When he looked up from the post hole, sweat dripped into his eyes, and he blinked away the salty sting of it. Autumn and still the sun was hot as Hades. He lifted off his hat to wipe a forearm over his face, then replaced it.

A couple of troopers reined in. 'Mr Jones.'

'Afternoon.' Zeke leaned on the post-hole digger, glad for an excuse to stop pounding it into unforgiving ground. A fence line had to go in—it was hard work, but it was his work. He didn't keep many sheep these days and was often hired on other properties to build or repair fences. 'You're out of luck if you think Nebo is around.'

'Not after him.' The constable, a young fella with a wide black moustache that seemed too big and too mature for his face leaned over his saddle. 'We heard that you buried a man not long back.'

'I did. Dr Smith wrote a death certificate and I notified the registrar. Wrote a letter to his folk. I buried him on my place, being a good distance out of town. All legal.' Zeke looked at the other trooper, another young one with tufts of downy fair hair unshaven on his chin. 'What's this about?' he asked the older one.

'Heard that he might have had a run-in with your other brother.'

Jesus. 'Jude hasn't been in this area much since his wife and girls died. Comes back for a while and goes again.'

The fluffy-chinned trooper shifted in his seat, gathered the reins. His horse shied, stamped his feet, and took a moment to settle. The lad said, 'Heard the fella who was killed mighta been hidin' out in Jude's old place.'

A fiery zing shot through Zeke's gut as he thought about that. Jude could very well be back in the district, and it wouldn't be unlike his older brother to slip back and not announce it. The death of Jude's family had taken a toll on his mind. These days, he was dour, reticent, and lived almost like a hermit. He seemed to roam here and there, always returning, and he didn't always let his brothers know he was back. But he wasn't a violent man. Nebo would have said if he'd seen Jude at his place.

'What about Nebo?' the older trooper asked.

'I'm not his keeper.' It was a half-hour's ride from here to Jude's place; no time at all for Nebo to get to, but Zeke would have to walk it because his horse, Milo, had taken the kids to school. Had Nebo been to their brother's abandoned place and found the Goody boy, shot him as a trespasser then brought the dying lad to him? 'You said you weren't here about him.'

The constable on the nervous horse gave a short laugh. 'Not here to get you mad.'

Zeke ignored that. 'I don't know if Jude is back, I haven't seen him. I haven't been up to his run for a while,' he said. 'What makes you think he had anything to do with the boy's death?'

The mustachioed policeman lifted a shoulder. 'Talk.'

'I don't listen to talk.'

'Everyone listens to talk,' the trooper said. 'We got instructions to let you know that we'll be watching out for both your brothers.' He smoothed his thick moustache. 'Why is it you don't run on the wrong side like they do?'

Zeke took up the post-hole digger again. 'Wasn't aware they're on the wrong side. And I don't care to be.' He stove the digger into the ground and rotated it hard by its handles.

'Good day to you,' one of the troopers said.

Zeke flicked them a look and nodded. They wheeled their horses and rode away. He waited until they were out of sight then threw the auger to the ground. He packed up and headed for his house, too late to go to Jude's place now. He'd wait until tomorrow, after the kids had left for school. Then he'd walk over to Jude's property to see what he could find out himself.

Zeke always met his kids at the mail tree by their gate. That way they'd have more time together before they got home and had to do a few chores. Gifford was on foot as usual, Gracie was walking by his side and Jonty swayed on Milo's back. Seemed like the little fella was tired. He'd perk up when he had to feed the chooks and collect their eggs.

But the chooks would have to wait. Zeke swooped up dark-haired, sturdy Gracie and swung her around. He hugged the raw-boned Giff, ruffled his dark coppery hair, stiff with dust, and noticed how the boy fell into him. Lately, some days Giff was still a lad, like today; other days he was trying to be a man and didn't want affection from his pa.

Then Zeke lifted Jonty off Milo and carried the sleepy boy down the long track to home. He hugged him close, this third child of his. This boy, his boy whom he loved, who looked so much like his mother. His thick dark mop was in need of a cut.

Skipping alongside, Gracie never seemed to tire. She loved books, loved music, and when Mr Henshaw at school would lend her something to bring home—under dire threat to return it—she treasured it as if it were gold. She was fierce in her convictions and stood a little apart at the tiny school. Sometimes he feared for her wellbeing, but she seemed content in herself. He wondered why she preferred solitude to making friends.

She held her father's hand as they walked the driveway. 'I do wish I didn't have to do sums, Pa. I try hard, but I'm much better with me reading and me letters.'

'Sums are good to learn. Try a little harder.'

'Oh, I will. But I know I'll never be really good at them—'

'Girls aren't good at sums,' Giff said, leading Milo.

'Am if I want to be.'

Giff cut off the argument. 'Pa, Dougie Carter said Uncle Jude was back. His pa saw him riding down Jones Track.'

Ah. So someone had seen his brother on the old property's track. At one stage, the track connected all the properties their father had owned on the one lot, before it was split into three and reallocated.

Zeke swung Gracie's hand in the air and squeezed Jonty with his other hand. The boy had slumped over his shoulder, secure and comfortable there. 'Did he now? I haven't seen Uncle Jude yet. I might have to visit tomorrow.'

'Can I come?' Giff, suddenly wide-eyed and hopeful, had always wanted to be around Jude.

'It's a school day tomorrow.'

'Yeah, but if I take these two then come back—'

'School is just as important for you, too. If Jude is home, he'll be here a while.'

Giff frowned but didn't argue.

Zeke looked over at him. 'You know he takes a day or so to settle in. Let's leave him do that first before we visit.' By the look of it, Giff found that a reasonable request. 'And he wouldn't think too much of you missing school, either.'

Giff's shoulders dropped. 'I just wanna work on the farms, Pa. I could look after Uncle Jude's when he goes roamin'.'

Gracie still skipped along. 'Me too, Pa,' she chimed. She pushed forward. 'And before you put your tuppeny's worth in, Gifford Jones, girls do work on farms.'

Zeke hid a smile. Hitching Jonty before he slipped any further, he said to Giff, 'School first. And I'll decide when you leave school. I'll be talking to Mr Henshaw about your marks and until they're good enough—'

'Mine are good now, Pa,' Gracie said and poked out her tongue at Giff.

'Mine too,' he answered, poking out his tongue at her.

'Until they're good enough on my say-so, no one leaves school.'

At the house, Zeke set Jonty on his feet. The lad grumbled for a bit but there were chores to be done. Today was Giff's turn to rub Milo down and feed him then feed the dogs, Gracie's turn to lay the table for dinner, and Jonty was to collect eggs as usual, and fill the bowl for wash-ups. There would be fights, yells, and a push here and there, but all in all his children got along well. He was careful to watch Giff for any of the brooding his two brothers displayed, but it hadn't showed itself, and it might never. He would be a happy man if Giff remained free of it, and free of Zeke's own temper.

As the children went about their tasks, Gracie hummed a tune, Giff talked to Milo in low and measured tones, and Jonty crept inside with the eggs, storing them on the bench in a basket. Then he filled the water bowl, concentrating on not spilling a drop. Zeke felt his chest expand. He and Maisie had made these kids in those early days with love, in the days before she changed, in the days before his heart had gone to sleep. Filled only with his kids now, there was no room in his heart for anyone else, even if he had noticed someone. It was shut off to another woman, and its sleep was deep.

He looked at his good kids. He would see to it that they turned out to be good adults. A niggling thought wormed in. How much longer could he do it by himself? The older they got, the more the farm would be required to support them. He'd need a strong lad to help with that. But Giff was still a couple of years off eleven, the age at which Zeke had decided he could finish school. And Gracie. Well, she'd need a woman's help—Zeke knew he'd be well over his head in that department, and he only had five, maybe six years if he was lucky. He looked at Jonty whose tongue was on his top lip as he tried to prevent the wash-up bowl from slopping water over the rim. Jonty was already missing a mother. Gracie had told her father that Jonty sometimes called other mothers Ma and would hold onto their skirts. Zeke figured he'd grow out of it but it pained him, all the same.

The older two had a few hazy memories of Maisie, but Jonty was too young when she'd died. An aneurysm of the brain, the doctor had told a bewildered Zeke. It had happened so fast, with no warning. Maisie had died at twenty-eight, four years ago. Mother at the time of a five-year-old, a four-year-old and a two-year-old. It hadn't been long after their fourth child was born. Perhaps the heartbreak of his death had brought on the deadly aneurysm. He didn't know.

His thoughts turned to his brother. Jude had been spared the infection, even after tending to his wife Anne and both daughters, Clementine and Bess, until their deaths. In the early days afterwards, Jude said he'd rather have gone, too. Zeke wondered if Jude's roaming was due to guilt that he hadn't saved his family, that he'd survived.

Jude had been there for Zeke, only a year later when Maisie died.

Then there was Nebo, not touched by loss, but lost nonetheless.

Next morning when Zeke waved his children off to school, the barking kelpies at his heels, Giff had given a forlorn look as he led Milo down the track. The moment they turned onto the road, Zeke called back the dogs and tied them up under a shady old gum. He filled a water flask, slung a bag over his shoulder and set off for Jude's place.

Rolling grassland hills and hints of green cheered him. No rain yet, but early dew might have teased new shoots to the surface in the last few days. He'd given up on growing wheat; the market had dropped away. Dairy cows were the word among those who gathered in the town, and maybe cattle for meat; the postmaster had said he'd heard a fair bit of talk about that. Zeke would have to do something soon to bring about a change in his fortunes. And not the same way Nebo was trying to change his fortunes— by robbing others of theirs. He laughed to himself. It wasn't a great place for a bushranger's headquarters. Country was so wide open there was nowhere to hide. But he had to give it to Nebo; Zeke had no idea where he kept his band of merry men.

If Zeke found Jude was at the property, he'd speak to him again about a joint venture. Jude had long stated that his heart wasn't in the land since Anne and the girls had gone, since life had been sucked out of him. Zeke felt that couldn't last forever but at the same time, he just didn't have the money to do anything about it and buy his brother out. He needed him to agree to form a partnership. The more he thought about it, the more he liked it. No point planning; first, he had to see what state Jude was in.

He strode on—the house was only a few hundred yards away over a low rise. The hut stood close to an unfinished stone dwelling. It had been an exciting time watching the house form, and Anne could barely contain herself that perhaps, within that year, she, her husband and two girls would live in such a grand, though small, house. It wasn't to be, and the shell of her dreams had stood unfinished for years. The hut would be patched up and re-patched when absolutely necessary. No sooner would Jude finish mending some part of the hut, he'd up and leave.

Movement caught Zeke's eye.

'G'day, Zeke.'

Jude looked the same as ever as he stepped out through the doorless entry of the stone house. His battered hat was pulled low, sleeves were rolled and his waistcoat opened over a seen-better-days loose shirt. His moleskins were well worn; he was a working man of the land, as Zeke was. Zeke just didn't know where he'd been working, if at all.

'You're back, brother,' Zeke said.

Jude spread his hands out. 'Here I am.'

At forty-two, Jude was still lean. He had a frown, always, so his features looked dark and brooding—he'd always been a thinker. Zeke reckoned Jude's trouble now was that he was trying not to think at all. He had dark hair just like his brothers, but with a distinctive wave that swept back from his face and fell behind his ears. Shot with grey these days, it matched the beard stubble glinting with silver. There were even patches of snowy white in the whiskers.

'Back for long this time?' Zeke knew not to step forward for an embrace of any sort. Since Anne had died, Jude kept his distance from everything but his horse. Even Giff stood back. Poor Gracie wasn't aware; he could barely pat her shoulder before retreating from her hug as quickly as he could. Perhaps she reminded him too much of his daughters. Gracie hadn't seemed to mind. She still hugged him whenever she saw him.

'Who knows?' Jude looked around as if seeing the place for the first time. 'I reckon someone's been here, maybe camped.'

Zeke dipped into his bag and pulled out the flask of water. He took a long swig. 'A young fella came by, we think someone found him here, or maybe he was hiding here after he got into trouble. Nebo came around—just checking on the place, he said—and found the boy shot up bad, brought him over home.'

'Nebo didn't shoot him?'

'Don't reckon he did. So he brings the kid to me, and we got the doc who did what he could, but the kid dies. Took his time, poor bugger. Raved on about his home and family. Just looking for adventure, I think, and came off second best.' Zeke scanned the area too. 'You find anything I should know about?'

'Like what?' Jude asked.

'Maybe he left something, more than what Nebo brought me.'

'Found nothin' so far but you're welcome to look.'

'The troopers might have been by here. Seen them?'

Jude shook his head. 'No.'

'They reckon they're watching this place.'

Jude grunted as he walked past him. 'I'm ready for another drink of tea. You want one?'

Zeke followed his brother as he headed into the hut. Inside, the place looked like it had done when Anne and the girls still lived here, except that Jude had burned all their clothes and bedding. Two cots sat end to end on one wall, stripped of everything but the rawhide straps to hold the mattresses. On the bigger bed, Jude's, his swag was still rolled up. He would throw that on the ground outside, or if the weather was bad, take shelter in a rough humpy out the back.

On his way through the hut, Jude grabbed a pannikin from a simple hutch where other kitchen utensils were stored. He left through the back door to where a small cooking fire had burned down to smoking coals. He threw on a handful of leaves, tossed down a few sturdy twigs and flames soon licked beneath the billy.

His own pannikin rested on one of the rocks that circled the firepit.

Jude's horse was tied to a rail under the shade of a eucalypt. The saddle had been slung over a fallen branch.

'You been here a coupla days?' Zeke asked.

'Aye. Your kids good?' He took a seat on a sawn-off log. 'Dogs good? Bizzy?'

Zeke did the same. 'Kids and dogs, they're all good. Giff grumbles about going to school. Gracie loves it. Jonty's just Jonty.'

'Will be grand to see them.'

Interested to hear that, Zeke only nodded. Coming from Jude, who these days would run as fast and as often as he could from home and family, it sounded like a change for the better.

Jude dipped his cup into the billy and indicated to Zeke he should do the same.

'Matter of fact,' Zeke said, dunking his pannikin, 'Giff reckons he's ready to look after this place while you're gone.'

Jude nodded. 'Don't reckon you'd let him out of school.'

'Not yet.'

'And Nebo? He still pretending he's a bushranger and hiding in the scrub somewhere?'

'He is. He came by yesterday to bring me the dead boy's possessions. Nothing of value that I could see, except sentimental. A woman's locket for one thing.'

'Sentimental,' Jude agreed. He pushed his hat back, scrubbed a hand through his hair and re-settled his hat. 'I was checking things over while I was in the stone house just before,' he said, staring into his tea. 'I might start work on it again. Might need a hand, time to time.'

Zeke hadn't been prepared for that. He nodded as if considering. 'Good idea.'

'Been listening to a few things about the place. About what might work now.' Jude hadn't looked up. 'Beef cattle, maybe.'

'Need good fences for beef cattle.'

'Need a lot of things. Need to *do* a lot of things … I haven't even gone back to my girls' graves.' He looked away. 'Can't bring myself to just yet. Maybe tomorrow. I should, I know. I've let that go a bit. I've let the whole place go, I reckon. Time to get on.'

Zeke nodded, liking what he was hearing. He knew not to make a fuss. 'Nothing that won't come good when you put your back to it.' He tugged at his hat, rolled his shoulders. It felt good that maybe his older brother had found his way and come home. For a time, anyway.

Jude held his pannikin with both hands, hunched forward. 'Been thinking that we might be able to join up, somehow. Depends what you're doing.'

Keeping the relief out of his voice, Zeke said, 'Fencing's been keeping the money coming in, but the blocks are small, money's tight. I'm not putting in crops again, not buying more sheep. Was thinking dairy.' He watched for Jude's reaction.

'Might work, too.'

The talk moved and shifted, ideas were tossed around. While their voices remained low, controlled, Zeke could have sworn his brother seemed lighter in himself. He sensed Jude must have considered returning for a while and for whatever the reason, he was glad of it.

The sun had climbed higher in the sky. While he wanted to sit and talk, wanted to be close to his brother, he knew he had to get on, get his chores done. They had more things to discuss, but the chores needed doing now, today.

Zeke got to his feet. 'It's good that you're back, Jude. If it was later in the day, I'd say we have a rum.'

'Time of day never stopped us before.' His brother dropped his pannikin, stood, his attention focused over Zeke's shoulder.

Zeke turned. 'Know him?'

A lone man on a horse was coming up the track. Didn't seem in a hurry.

Jude shook his head. 'No, looks like he's come a long way. Horse is loaded up.'

There was a swag over the saddle behind the rider, and stuffed saddlebags. A rifle. Zeke said, 'He's out of the way here. Must want something particular from you.'

The man pulled his horse up at a respectful distance. He tipped his hat with a forefinger. 'Greetings,' he called, and dismounted. He wasn't a tall man, was solid but not portly. He had thick forearms, and big hands that looked used to hard work. He had brown hair that tufted out from under his hat, was unshaven but not bearded. Maybe he was as old as Jude, it was hard to tell.

Zeke's gaze flicked to the rifle on the other side of the man's saddle.

Jude nodded. 'Morning. What can I do for you?'

The man stood with the reins loose in his hands. He nodded at Jude then at Zeke. 'Name's Curtis Goody. I believe one of you fellas buried my son.'

Seven

Elsa decided enough was enough for the day. The sun was low, and soon it would be too dark to see where they were going, even if they thought they knew. 'Rosie, we have to find a place to stop now.'

'Yes, yes.'

Rosie was squinting to focus on the road ahead, her hands tight on the reins. She'd wept silently for the first hour and there'd seemed to be nothing Elsa could say to help. Now Elsa wondered how much she could see out of her eyes—her own eyes would have been swollen shut by now, had she been crying as much.

'Then stop,' Elsa said and reached over to put her hand over Rosie's. 'Let's see if we can pull off the road hereabouts.'

Sighing a long breath, as if she had to be finally convinced, Rosie pulled on the reins and Peppin slowed to a stop. She stood up and looked around. 'Perhaps a little further where there's a clearing on the left. Looks as if others have done so before us.'

Taking up the reins again, she directed the horse, and the cart eased off the road. After braking, the sisters alighted, and both went for the cover of bushes.

'Oh my goodness,' Rosie said, mildly. 'It's not called relieving oneself for nothing.'

Elsa laughed a little. 'I was too scared to pull off the road earlier in case we were being followed.'

'Too bad now.'

As they returned to the cart, Elsa said, 'I don't presume to know where we are but as long as we stay on this same road, we should find ourselves in Penola in about two more days' time.'

Rosie looked at Elsa, who was pulling out a blanket and a pillow from under a pile of clothes. 'And how would you know that?' she asked.

Elsa handed her the blanket. 'You remember Mrs Jessup? Her grandfather, old Mr Conroy, would talk about it. I visited him with Pa when we'd go there selling our milk. He had a map he used to carry, printed on skin of some sort. He showed me, and we would pore over it while he told his stories. He was a bullocky who used to take the Chinamen to the goldfields along this road after they got off the ships at Robe.'

'Yes, yes, I know, but he did that fifty years ago,' Rosie snipped.

'It's still the same road,' Elsa said evenly. 'He lives with Mrs Jessup now that he's got so old. I used to love to sit and listen to him. He said he got very rich by escorting the Chinamen.'

'Oh, and he looks very rich now,' Rosie derided, her arms full of the blankets and pillows Elsa had been handing her.

'He said he remembers one woman walking down the main street jiggling her many sovereigns, showing off that her husband had become so rich.'

'A nice thought, all those sovereigns. All *our* sovereigns, if we can find them.'

In the dim light, Elsa looked about. 'We need a place to unhitch the cart. Peppin must rest properly.' She lifted a shoulder to ease an ache and heard the crinkle of Mr Jones's letter in her bodice. If she could trust putting it somewhere else, she would, but for now it was safe. For some reason she liked having it close to her.

'Well, what have I got the blankets for then, if we're to work a while longer?'

'So we don't have to get back into an unstable cart when it's not hitched up.'

Rosie almost smiled. 'My dear little sister, when did you ever get so practical?'

From very early on, Elsa thought but kept it to herself. 'Come on, while it's light, let's set ourselves up. I don't think we'll want to build a fire tonight.' She headed for the edge of the clearing.

'Why not?'

Looking at her sister, Elsa said, 'Frank just might come looking.'

Rosie's face threatened to crumple again.

'And we should eat those pies before we need to cook anything. They won't be any good tomorrow,' Elsa said. Oh no, it looks like Rosie's going to be in tears again. 'You're not changing your mind about leaving, are you?' she asked as her sister held on to the snivels.

'Not at all,' Rosie said sharply, and followed her. 'It's just that, suddenly, all this is reality. George has died. Then Pa dying. I've left Frank. You're with me. I'm worried about what I've done.'

'Perhaps it's regret.'

Rosie hesitated. 'No. It's fear.'

They found a big enough space to unhitch the horse from the cart. While Rosie held Peppin, Elsa undid the over girth, removed the breeching straps and pulled the rails from the tugs. It took some effort, but Peppin was patient. Then she pushed the cart back a little way and set the rails down. Puffing, she scrambled for a rock to wedge under one of its front wheels. A short, thick piece of fallen tree branch sufficed for the other wheel. Dusting off, she took Peppin from Rosie and led him to a tree.

'I'm impressed,' Rosie stated.

'We should roll our bedding out over there,' Elsa said, pointing to the other side of the cart. 'If it rains, we can get under the cart.'

They settled in, ate a couple of the pies and took a drink from the water barrel. Elsa filled a small pail for the horse and he drank, seemed satisfied and comfortable.

Before the sun set completely, they'd removed their hats and brushed out their hair.

'I don't think I should ever take my hair out,' Elsa said as the mass of her wild mane resisted the brush. It crackled and bounced down her back as she pulled and tugged at it before she became impatient and retied it for bed.

Now that it was dark, a silence descended on the world that to Elsa seemed peaceful after the day they'd had. Stars were bright, there was a half moon and the sky was mostly cloudless. After bunching her pillow to give it a bit of plump, Elsa lay back on it. Rosie had also plumped her pillow and side by side, they stared into the night sky.

After a moment, Rosie said, 'You haven't shed one tear yet.'

'I know.'

'You must be sad, though.'

'Of course I'm sad,' Elsa said. 'I don't know why I haven't cried. I feel like I have a great lump in my chest where my heart is, but that's all.' She rested a hand over where the letter was safe in her clothing and took in a deep breath to stay calm.

As they continued gazing at the sky, Elsa tried to get around a little rock that poked the thin mattress under her backside. It had been a long time since she'd slept on the ground. Her little cot at her father's hut had been better than this, she thought.

Rosie started to sniff again.

'It'll be all right.' Elsa squeezed her sister's hand but Rosie didn't squeeze back. 'We'll find Mr Jones, we'll find the tin and then we'll be all right.'

'And then what?'

'I don't know,' Elsa said. She had thought Rosie might have had some plan but clearly not.

'We can't go back to Robe,' her sister said.

There was no Pa to come back to, and no George. Frank would take over the farm. Elsa frowned. She'd have to try and find a lawyer to advise whether Frank would automatically administer the property, if Rosie declared she had left him. And would it mean they no longer had any rights to the farm? Perhaps daughters could inherit. Maybe there was hope, slim as it may be; they couldn't possibly afford to engage a lawyer right now to find out. *Perhaps* they could do anything if they found this tin of sovereigns.

She wondered what would happen if they did return to the farm. No good could come, for sure. Rosie was a runaway wife; although Frank wouldn't realise it until tomorrow, it was true. How could Rosie possibly go back after that—even if she wanted to?

What if they didn't go back? What if they stayed in Victoria? What if they found Casterton appealing? She felt a heat bloom in her cheeks. Why on earth would she think of that? Her hand went to the letter tucked under her chemise, against her skin. How strange that it seemed to warm.

Oh, that's silly. They had to go back—*to come back home.* Or at least she did. There was her one fervent wish—to be the first woman at the voting booth in Robe on the twenty-fifth of April this year. That was still many weeks away. She had to be back in South Australia by then, and if not able to be in Robe, then in another town where there would be a polling place. That might be a better plan; she'd avoid Frank that way, and Pete Southie. She tried to remember what other towns in the area had been reported as a place to vote. Nothing came to her. She would investigate how to vote as an absentee; all she needed to find was a post office and be able to prove she was a resident of the colony. *Gracious me. Another obstacle.*

She was tired. Her throat hurt from the strain of holding back emotion, not that she was doing it on purpose. Perhaps it was just a good sleep she needed—

'Elsa, I said we can't go back to Robe.'

'We'll think of something.' She patted Rosie's hand, and after a while turned on her side to face her. 'Do you happen to remember if in the newspaper there was another polling booth mentioned, one closer to the border perhaps?' She waited a few seconds before realising her sister wasn't thinking but had dropped off to sleep.

Elsa sighed and rolled onto her back again. Stars twinkled. A breeze rustled the leaves. Peppin sneezed. She closed her eyes.

Elsa woke to Rosie coming back from her morning ablution, shovel in hand. It was barely light, but a good time to get going, so she set Rosie to packing up the bedding. 'Give it all a good shaking,' she said while she found a tree to step behind and do what she had to do.

'Yes, madam,' Rosie replied, throwing the mattresses on board before flapping the blankets hard.

After trying to retie her hair into some order, Elsa walked towards the cart. The night's sleep had been welcome, but she wasn't sure yet if she felt refreshed. No point complaining, they might have to sleep rough for a while before their fortunes changed.

Fortunes.

Stretching her back, Elsa limbered a little before starting to hitch up the cart again. She directed Rosie to hold Peppin at the bridle as she tied the straps in place. Checking the over girth again, satisfied the horse and cart were ready, she took up the driver's seat. Rosie had loaded the blankets and pillows, had handed Elsa her hat and tied on her own, and had dug around in the basket for two of the fruit buns.

'They're a bit dry,' she said, looking at hers and holding one for Elsa. 'Would be lovely with some tea.'

Elsa took a bun as they pulled back onto the road. 'Maybe tomorrow we can light a fire.'

'Tomorrow?'

'If we're lucky—and we treat Peppin well—we'll be more than halfway to Penola.'

Rosie shuffled on the seat to get comfortable. 'And then how far to this Casterton place?'

Elsa flicked the reins and Peppin moved forward into a comfortable trot. 'That I don't know but there are bound to be signs, and I'm sure some of the good folk of Penola will be able to direct us.'

Rosie brushed loose hair from her face and tucked it back under her hat. 'You sound cheerful today,' she said, as if disdaining.

Elsa looked sideways. 'Perhaps if I sound it, I'll begin to feel it. But I think the good things we are doing will help.'

'What good things? I'm leaving my husband. I'll never be able to return to Robe for all the gossip that will abound—'

'That we're going to find George,' Elsa cut in quickly. 'That we're going to find Ma's locket, and perhaps the tin. Not to mention that we will be giving our heartfelt thanks to Mr Jones for his kindness.' She gee-upped Peppin as a flutter slid across her chest. *For goodness sake.* If she just kept her thoughts on the task ahead, she'd be all right. No need to snap at her sister, though sometimes Rosie could be so thick-headed. And selfish. Now she could feel her gaze. 'What is it?'

'I'm looking at you anew, little sister. Sometime in the last few years you've grown up.'

'Inevitable,' Elsa said, annoyed. The prick of bristles replaced the flutter.

'I wasn't condescending. You have taken to our situation with great calm.'

'What else to do?' Elsa cried, and the burst surprised her as well as Rosie. She flicked the reins again then reminded herself that Peppin needed to take them a long distance. A little speed for a while wouldn't hurt. As he picked up, she felt the breeze on her, and the rush of heat inside dissipated. 'I have to worry about my future, too, and how I'll manage from now on. If I stay in Robe, what on earth would I do? I've done nothing but think of my options.'

Rosie retied her hat and brushed down her skirt. 'You could marry.'

Elsa scoffed. 'Marry who? And how quickly do you expect I might be able to manage that?' Now the bristles shot up her back. 'Besides, I didn't think you thought so highly of marriage.' Her glance at Rosie was rewarding: she spied a bloom of colour on her sister's face.

After a little time, Rosie said, 'That Henry Benson has his eye on you. I remember what he said to you. I saw him looking at you and flirting with you.'

'And what timing,' Elsa said, and raised her eyebrows. 'I'd just heard of my brother's death, and Henry was there helping us dig a hole for my father's grave. Besides, he's a boy.'

'Oh, and don't for one minute think I didn't notice how you reacted.'

Elsa felt the bloom on her own face now. 'I don't know what it means. I just ignore it.'

'It means you're well ready for marriage. And well past the age, too. You're practically a middle-aged woman.'

Elsa was incensed. 'At twenty-four?'

'Ancient. You should've been married by now.' Rosie straightened in her seat, clasping her hands in her lap, as if it gave her more authority on the matter.

'Rubbish. Other women my age are unmarried.' Although she couldn't name too many right now. She shook that off. 'Besides, if I choose to, I would marry a man, *not* a boy,' Elsa insisted.

'Why not accept Henry Benson? Most of the single men have left the town, gone off looking for work.'

'Because he's only a *boy*.' Elsa shook her head. 'And I haven't thought further than that,' she said quickly.

'You have.'

Elsa huffed. 'All right then. I've had a good look around and found nobody worthwhile.'

'Is that so?' Rosie wasn't giving it up. 'Hmm. True, I suppose. Pete Southie's not much of a candidate, is he?'

'It was never him. I don't want to talk about that awful man.'

'I've heard he's been on the lookout for a wife and is very determined. Talk was recently that he'd found someone but she'd spurned him—' Rosie looked at her, incredulous. 'Oh. Was that you?' she asked, teasing.

Elsa's lip curled. 'I only have to look at him and my skin crawls.'

Rosie sighed. 'Agreed. Then Henry Benson. You could train him to be a good husband.'

Elsa rounded on her. 'You're making fun of me. I don't want a boy and I don't want anything like that lecherous Peter Southie. I want a real man. Like our big brothers were men. Like John and Ned. They were kind men.' Her chin puckered. *Why are tears starting to prickle now?*

Rosie was quick to squeeze her hand. 'They were real men, you're right, and kind. They've been gone long years.'

Elsa felt the gulp coming up from her stomach. Felt the hiccup happen as she tried to speak. 'So, you see, there is a high bar for any man who might come into my life.' Her face then screwed up and the tears broke.

Rosie seemed at a loss. 'Tears? Surely not for some unknown man?'

Elsa shook her head, sobbing. 'No. For all *our* men, for all our boys. They're gone and there'll be no one to replace them. Even George,' she said. 'George, the adventurer, the gadabout. He would have made a fine man once he grew up a bit. And now, now—'

'Oh dear.' Rosie slipped her hands over her sister's. 'Give me the reins and get your handkerchief.' She watched as Elsa complied. 'You know, our big brother John never liked Frank,' she said as Elsa cried into her hanky. 'He always said he was a lazy sod. But did I take any notice? No. At sixteen I was ready for the world. I could take on anything.' Rosie gave Peppin a light flick. 'Ned, well, he was a bit younger and not so vocal. He just kept away from Frank.' She looked at Elsa who nodded as she blotted her eyes. 'But Pa thought Frank was wonderful. A baker and all that. He—*we* had a good business when the port was doing well. What business wouldn't thrive in a place where the only rival in the colony was the port of Adelaide?'

Elsa felt the pressure in her chest ease. A last sob escaped and the hiccups dwindled off. She couldn't speak yet.

Peppin trotted along at a good pace in Rosie's hands. 'Do you know, Elsa, that there were a couple of men vying for my attention even after I married Frank?'

Elsa was surprised by that. 'How does that happen?' Her voice was hoarse. 'Once you're married, that's it, isn't it?'

'Well, it's supposed to be. But I wasn't dead, I was just married. I suppose people take your eye here and there over the years, and it's up to you to ignore it. When things got bad with Frank—'

'Bad?' Elsa looked at Rosie through eyes that felt squishy. 'What do you mean?'

'Not physical danger. Frank wasn't like that. Not like that Mr Greenaway—terrible man, bashing poor Mrs Greenaway and thinking nobody knew it.'

'Nobody does anything for her,' Elsa said, sniffing.

'No one can.' Rosie squared her shoulders. 'But it wasn't that way for us. Bad as in I admitted to myself that I'd made my bed and had to lie in it. I learned early on that I didn't love Frank. Never would. But what do you do?' She bit her lip and shrugged.

'What did you do?' This was all news to Elsa. She'd never thought for one minute that her big sister had a life that wasn't happy and successful, and that she might have had thoughts that strayed ... *Were they only thoughts that strayed?* She sucked in a breath.

'Nothing. What could I have done? Back then I was too young and scared to do anything. I just wondered what things might have been like if I'd taken heed of John's words. I even felt a little ...' She cast a glance at Elsa. 'A little jealous of you, that you would grow up and perhaps choose better. I used to listen to you talk about the newspaper articles on the suffragists, or those written by some of their number.' Rosie gave a laugh. 'And then I'd see Frank's disapproving look—'

'Oh yes. He'd make his mouth go like this.' Elsa made the face, puffing out her cheeks and pouting.

Rosie blurted a laugh. 'That's the one. And then once you'd left the house, I'd get into such trouble about the newspapers. If I was reading them, too, he'd say he was worried I would become—' She dropped her voice to boom her last few words, 'Independent in my thinking.'

'And you have.'

'Not really. I don't care to have the vote.'

'But having a vote means we can change the way things are, change the way the world sees us because we now have a voice.'

'Oh, Elsa. How long do you think it would take for that sort of change? And would it stop what happens to Mrs Greenaway? We women would still be helpless in the face of a bunched fist coming at us. Change would take too long for what I want. But then, some would say I got what I wanted, at sixteen.' Rosie gave a short laugh. 'I just didn't understand. And I did try to be a good wife. Back then.'

Startled, Elsa asked, 'Back then? Does that mean—'

'No. I never strayed. But as soon as I learned Pa had died, especially after hearing about George too, I knew I couldn't stay with Frank. All our brothers gone, our parents both gone, only you left—and I wasn't worried about what you thought.' She took a deep breath, looking embarrassed. 'The only thing now is knowing that those gold sovereigns are somewhere out there and that they are my chance.'

Elsa swiped the handkerchief over her nose and tucked it away to wash later. Shaken, she said, 'Was I really not in your—'

'I meant to say, the sovereigns are *our* chance, Elsa. If we find them, if we stay together, we will be all right.'

Elsa felt the gulps coming on again. She had always been the little sister and long treated as if her opinions were not worth anything. Elsa knew how capable she herself was, and yet how often she'd been overlooked. And now Rosie had practically spelled it out for her. She *had* been overlooked and had nearly been once again. That's why life at the farm with her father had suited her well. She went about her business—learning from her father of course—but had no one telling her how to live. Not until the subject of marriage had come up. Her father had tried but he hadn't won that one. If she was going to marry someone, it would be her decision … and she'd want a good marriage, not one like Rosie's.

'From now on,' Rosie said, casting a sidelong glance at her, 'I'll never do anything I don't want to do. If we don't find these sovereigns, I'll find work somewhere to keep us.'

And there it was again. 'I'll find work, too. I'll keep myself.'

'Of course,' Rosie said too fast.

A new determined Rosie seemed to have emerged quickly, but the old Rosie was still there. Elsa would remain wary.

They didn't speak for a while. Peppin kept up a comfortable pace, and the flies weren't too annoying. There wasn't much of a breeze, so the dust flying around was minimal. It would only be about eight or so in the morning, the temperature still cool.

Rosie eventually broke the silence. 'I wonder when Frank will think to come looking for me.'

'Will he go without you cooking his lunch?'

'Yes. But not his dinner.'

Elsa tried to calculate how far they'd travelled and how far ahead of Frank they would be. 'We'll drive as far as we can,' she said. 'Even a little bit into the night if the moonlight is good. But I've still got my eye on Peppin. He'll be as important to us as food and water.'

The cart racketed along the hard packed earth of the road as it stretched ahead. Hardly a bend or a turn so the sweep of the landscape could barely be seen through the dense scrub. After a little time, Rosie said, 'I wonder if Southie has woken yet.'

'I don't care.'

'Would he come after us?'

Elsa gave a little shiver. 'I don't think so. He'll go straight back to Frank.'

Saying nothing, Rosie nodded. She flicked the reins gently again and Peppin picked up a little speed.

Elsa rubbed her hands together and wiped them on her dress. Keen to change the subject, she said, 'I don't know how far we've come, but old Kangaroo Inn is about thirty miles from home. If we get there in daylight, I say we push on a bit further.'

'Wish the inn was still in its heyday. We could've taken some refreshment there.'

'And come across all sorts of travellers and stragglers, and people drunk and rowdy. There was even a murder there, you know, and it's still unsolved.' Elsa was trying to remember what she'd heard people mention when they spoke of travelling the Robe to Penola road. 'Besides, it'd be the first place someone would look, checking to see if we were camped the night. I believe there's still shelter there.' She should have listened more carefully but how was she to know she'd need that information?

Rosie raised her eyebrows. 'I doubt a murderer would still be lurking, although perhaps there'll be those old-fashioned bushrangers around,' she said, all wide-eyed.

Not offended, Elsa said, 'I know you're making fun of me again, but you were the one scared of bushrangers and wild men. We don't know who or what we'll come across. Two lone women—'

'And a rifle, don't forget.'

'Only three bullets.' Then Elsa looked at her sister. She shrugged and smiled. 'Formidable, then,' she said, nudging Rosie.

Rosie nudged back. 'Indeed.'

Eight

Lily Hartman stood waiting for Mr Carrick to serve the customer in front of her. She'd come three miles from her farm for groceries in Casterton and thought she would treat herself to a fragrant cake of soap before returning home with all her stores.

Though what on earth she was doing, buying as much as she had, was beyond her. She looked down at the basket over her arm. Stan had been gone nearly seven years—why had adjusting to her widowhood proved difficult from time to time? Mostly she only bought for herself but every so often, she'd buy for two, and cook for two. Perhaps wishful thinking. She did miss a man in her life.

Lily was careful not to eat for two, and of course her finances would not stretch to that extravagance and neither should her waistline. When she overcooked, she had to eat the same thing for days before cooking again.

She felt like she'd aged decades since he'd died—and felt silly now, waiting in line for a cake of soap. As if that would make her feel more youthful or restore her scatty memory. She could make some soap if she put her mind to it. She should leave. While trying to decide to stay in the line or go, she put a hand to her hair. Just for something to do, really. She always kept the fine blonde waves—threaded with silvery sparkles she liked to tell herself—neat and tidy in a simple knot at the back of her head. Jiggling her basket, she decided to stay in the store. Besides, it would look odd if she just vacated the line after having waited so long.

They'd say, 'There goes that poor old woman, can't make up her mind whether to be here or there.'

She wasn't *that* old. Forty-five wasn't old. She was just a bit worn out, that was all. She smoothed her cheeks. Her skin was still firm, and she was careful to stay out of the sun. So far, her old-fashioned large brimmed hat, hanging on the hook behind the door at home, did the trick to shade her while she tended the vegetable garden.

Waiting patiently in line, she studied her free hand, palm up then palm down. Only a little dirt was ingrained, just from the reins of the cart, she was sure. And there were crepey wrinkles on the back of her hand, but so what? Her fingers were still strong with no sign of arthritis, and her nails were neat, clean and short.

Oh, there's a delicious aroma coming from the back of the store. Mrs Carrick must be cooking Mr Carrick's lunch in their kitchen behind the curtain. *Hmm.* She did miss baking a good meal, and having it appreciated by a hungry man. The scents of fresh bread and roasted mutton wafted across the store. Lily's mouth watered, and she thought perhaps she should avail herself of a meat pie from across the road at Casterton's finest bakery—the only one—for the ride home.

More extravagance, Lily Hartman. Unnecessary.

Aggie Flagstaff was in front of her talking to Mr Carrick. 'You might have heard, Mr Carrick, that one of those Jones brothers has turned up at his house again.'

That grabbed Lily's attention. *One of those Jones brothers.* She knew which brother that would be. She hadn't heard it herself before now but was glad to know.

'Would that be Judah Jones?' Mr Carrick asked, placing packets of tea and sugar into Mrs Flagstaff's already loaded basket. 'I'd heard he was back.'

'Yes, and it will be a good thing if he pulls himself together this time and goes back to working that place of his.'

Mr Carrick glanced behind her and inadvertently caught Lily's eye. He cleared his throat. 'Mrs Hartman, I won't be long.'

It didn't stop Aggie Flagstaff, who turned around. 'Hello, Mrs Hartman. You were friendly with Mr Jones's wife, weren't you? Poor woman, and her two daughters. Such a tragedy.' Mrs Flagstaff's cheeks wobbled at the same time her hair wobbled when she shook her head. 'But no point in the man wallowing in his sorrows, wasting time any longer. The good Lord gave us lives to live and Mr Jones should be well over his mourning by now.'

Lily only glanced at Mr Carrick who had the good sense to keep his mouth closed. 'I was good friends with Anne Jones, Mrs Flagstaff,' she said, her voice low. 'And a finer woman, and indeed a finer family, I have yet to meet.' She had the pleasure of seeing Aggie Flagstaff take a moment to digest that. 'It's no wonder Mr Jones has taken some time to adjust to his terrible loss. Unless experienced, no one can understand a bereavement such as he has suffered.'

Mr Carrick nodded to Lily. 'As you, yourself, have experienced, Mrs Hartman.'

'Oh, Mr Carrick, that's kind,' Lily said. 'Dear Stan had been ill for a long time, as you know, and I'm blessed all three of our children are still alive and healthy. But Mr Jones was not so blessed.'

Mrs Flagstaff appeared flustered. 'Well, whatever it is, now he's back, he should gather himself together. Do something about that disgraceful brother of his.'

'Mr Ezekiel Jones?' Lily asked innocently.

'No, no. Not him, though he's been bad enough in the past. Got a temper on him, he has. It's the other one with that horrible biblical name.'

'All the brothers have biblical names. Mr Nebo Jones, then?'

'Unchristian. I'm sure they're pagan names.'

'But they are in the bible, Mrs Flagstaff,' Mr Carrick said and kept a straight face when she gave him a look.

'In any case,' she retorted, her cheeks on the wobble again. 'He purports to be a bushranger, of all things. Next, he'll be calling himself and his cronies the Kelly gang. I'm surprised the constables let him carry on as such.'

Mr Carrick spoke in a conspiratorial whisper. 'They have to catch him at it first.'

'That Nebo creature clearly thinks it's all a lark. Mr Judah Jones should take task over the way his brother terrifies good people.'

Lily glanced at Mr Carrick, who'd kept his face deadpan, before she said, 'They're grown men. I don't see that it's any of Mr Judah's business to control his brother.'

'Until his brother bails *him* up somewhere.'

Mr Carrick's eyes widened. 'Have you been bailed up, Mrs Flagstaff?'

'I most certainly have not,' she said. 'There'd be such trouble if I had been, I can tell you that.'

'Something to look forward to then,' Mr Carrick said, and smiled his shopkeeper's smile. 'That'll be one pound two, thank you, Mrs Flagstaff.' Distracted, bemused, the woman dipped into her drawstring purse and handed over two one-pound coins. He pressed change firmly into her hand. 'Good day to you.'

Mrs Flagstaff turned and spoke to Lily. 'Well, I only meant—'

'Yes, good day, Mrs Flagstaff. Mr Carrick, if I could purchase one of those lovely bars of Pears soap?' Lily thought no more of Aggie Flagstaff as the woman swept by her on her way out.

'Certainly, Mrs Hartman.'

Lily paid for her soap. With her heavy basket of goods over her arm, she nodded her goodbyes to others lined up behind her and left the shop. She headed for her horse and cart tied to the hitching rail in front of the merchant store across the street.

The bakery was close by, but she wouldn't need that pie now. It was just as well she had a few extra things in her basket, and in her pantry at home. Perhaps she'd begin baking again. Her neighbour, that very kind man Mr Judah Jones, had returned to the district. He would most probably need a good meal every so often.

Nine

It came as a surprise to Frank when Pete Southie, standing outside the shop's back door holding his head, said, 'I'm tellin' you, Frank, there's no sign of either of them. Grave's fresh dug, but no one's around, and no horse and cart.'

Frank firmly expected Rosie to be back any time now—he'd already closed the shop for the afternoon. One night away from home to tend to family matters was enough and now she should be back to tend to him and his bakery. He undid his apron, hung it on a hook inside and took in the state of the place—*abominable*. Rosie would have her work cut out, so she'd better show herself soon.

Annoyed, he stepped outside and pulled the door shut. 'Perhaps they're visiting someone,' he said, though he couldn't think who.

'Don't think so. The beds are stripped.'

Frank frowned. 'Maybe the women thought to make a new start, burning the bed linens or something.'

'Mate, even the mattresses are gone. Oilskins gone, food, the billy, all gone.'

Folding his arms and now uneasy, Frank eyed Southie. 'What were you doing out there?' This bloke—a man Rosie always said had a shady gleam in his eyes—smelled of the day's sweat, and cow shit. Frank rarely let him inside the shop.

'Payin' my respects. What else?'

'So you went inside the house?'

'I yelled out, walked around the place. Thought I'd check in there when I, uh, heard nothin'.'

Simple enough explanation from Southie but where *was* Rosie, and his sister-in-law, Elsa? 'Well, I can't do much about it, now. Rosie's got our Peppin and the cart, so I've got no transport. 'Sides, I reckon they'll be back directly. Hard to hear that you've lost your only remaining brother and then you have to bury your father. I expect they've gone visiting some lady friends for tea and tears.' But inside, Frank knew.

Southie rubbed his ear. 'Well, if you say so, Frank. But if they're not back tonight, I'm happy to go look for them for you. I'm fair taken with Miss Elsa, as you know.'

Frank wasn't thinking of Southie's matrimonial quest. He was trying to think if there'd been anything Rosie had said that he might have missed. All he remembered was that she was going to purchase a coffin. Sometimes the smithy delivered them. 'The coffin maker. Let's go see if Mr Benson is still in his shop.'

Outside, Frank tugged at his collar. He shouldn't have needed to. The autumn air of the late afternoon had cooled. The crisp breeze brought in the whiff of seaweed and salt as gulls squawked overhead.

As they neared the forge, Frank could hear Mr Benson banging the hammer, shaping a tool on the anvil. The smithy looked up, nodded and waved. He dropped the hammer onto a bench nearby. 'Afternoon to you,' he yelled.

Frank lifted a hand in greeting. 'Afternoon. Did you deliver a coffin out to my father-in-law's place yesterday?' His chest felt peculiar in the dense air of the forge.

'Your missus and her sister took it in the cart. My boy went with them and helped dig the hole.' Mr Benson's yell brought Henry out from behind a doorway. 'There he is.'

'Hello, Mr Putney.' Henry ignored Pete Southie.

'Lad, you buried my father-in-law yesterday?'

Henry glanced from Frank to his father. 'Miz Putney said it were to be done quick.'

Frank blew air into his cheeks and held it there a moment. 'I see. Yes, of course.'

Mr Benson yelled, 'Somethin' amiss, Mr Putney?'

Frank shook his head. 'I don't—'

'Did they say they were going somewhere, young Benson?' Pete Southie cut in.

Frank felt his chest grip. The heat was overwhelming, even at this time of day, worse than the heat from the ovens in the bakery. *Too hot.* He ran a finger along his collar and loosened off the top button.

Henry Benson stared at Southie then scratched his forehead. 'Don't recall that. Looked to me as if they were gonna settle in. No mention of returning to town here, otherwise I'da got a lift. I walked back in.'

Frank felt sweat on his scalp. *I need to get out of here.*

Southie stepped forward, a menace in his tone. 'How long were you out there for, boy?'

Henry lifted his chin. 'Long as it took.'

Mr Benson yelled, 'Here, Mr Southie. My lad was back well by sundown. What's your issue?' A frown creased his brow.

'Pete,' Frank grabbed Southie by the arm. 'I have to get out of here.'

Southie shook him off. 'What did you get up to out there, boy?'

Frank felt a pain shoot across his chest. *Too hot in here. Have to get out.* All he could think of was that Rosie had left him. It all added up. The overnight stay, the horse and cart gone, bedding and other items gone. *She's run off.*

'I got up to digging a deep hole to put Mr Goody into and then—'

Frank turned, reeled towards the doorway, banging against benches and walls as he stumbled. Once outside, he slumped to the ground and took deep breaths. The pain in his chest had gone, and now cold shudders racked him as the sweat cooled all over his body.

Pete Southie strode out. 'Frank. What the hell happened?' He squatted, dropped a hand on Frank's shoulder.

'Get me back to the bakery,' Frank wheezed.

'Jesus, you've gone all white in the face. Is it a heart attack? I'll get some help—'

'Not a heart attack. Just get me back to the shop. Had one of these before, it'll pass. It'll pass.'

Southie hauled Frank up and dropped a shoulder under his arm. 'What is it then?' he grunted, trying to get Frank fully on his feet. 'Shit, yer a heavy bastard.'

Back at the shop, Frank lurched in the back door and waved Southie away. 'I'll be right. It passes, and I have medicine I must take.'

Southie stood in the doorway. 'Anything else you need, Frank?'

'I need a horse. I need to get to the Goody hut,' Frank said, his chest easing. 'If my wife has gone somewhere, I need to know her father's will is safe.'

Ten

Nebo poked at the campfire with a long stick. 'Do y'reckon Billy Watson told the troopers where we were?' He looked across at Glen Barton who had sat on the ground holding a pannikin of rum.

'Not if he knows what's good for him.' Barton swallowed from the cup. His blond hair, dirty and flattened, looked as if he'd sat a bowl on his head rather than a hat. He picked up a glass bottle, yanked out the stopper and poured another generous shot. 'Reckon you scared him well enough.' He held the bottle out to Nebo.

'Roughed him up a bit, is all. Don't want any loudmouthed gun-happy fool shooting at anything that walks and bringing it all down on our heads. Don't want murder on my plate.'

'Gentlemen bushrangers, that's us.'

Nebo snorted. 'That's us. But it's a good thing we moved camp. The troopers won't find anything if they do come looking.'

Barton studied his cup. 'Zeke gonna ride with us?'

Nebo shook his head as he poured from the bottle. 'I give up on him. He won't do us over, but he won't do a job with us.' He mulled over what he'd just said. 'He's got his kids. Be no good for them if he got caught.'

'You know they got troopers on some of the coaches now.'

'And we won't know which ones until we get there.' Nebo stared into the rum. 'Just need one big haul. Then we can all go our separate ways and not have to do it again.'

Barton barked a laugh. 'You sound like a loser at cards, mate. Just one more round and me luck'll change.' He lowered his voice. 'You got family, Nebo, your brothers. Go work the land with Zeke or Jude. Why live this life? A sheep here and there, a few pound notes for grog money, gettin' the law all hot and bothered when they've got nothin' else to do.'

'Could ask the same question of you.'

'I got no family to worry about.' Barton glanced over at Tillie who was dunking washing in a tub on the edge of the clearing. 'And Tillie, well, she doesn't have much either, now.'

'Zeke and Jude, they should put their places together, make a bigger place. Maybe then there'd be work for me.' Nebo tossed the rum dregs to the dirt. 'I told them that but they don't listen.' He wiped a hand across his mouth. 'What about Wally and Fred?'

'They're in,' Barton said. 'These are desperate times. Wally's not keen for any more after this one. Will ye look at him? He's right at home bein' a family man, and he wants somethin' better than hidin' from the troopers all his life.'

They both looked across at Wally and Fred who were sitting at their own campfires with their two women. It seemed a homely affair, serene. Humpies with canvas laid over the top made crude huts. Wally, a stripling black-haired lad in his mid-twenties and his girl, Sal, blonde and buxom and big with child, had begun to make mud bricks, which had the others laughing, but short of stealing building supplies there was nothing else with which to construct any shelter. And winter was coming. It was always cold in these parts.

Fred and Alice had two layers of canvas over a sturdy tent stacked with brush. They worked mostly on small pieces of furniture, storage boxes on legs to keep off the damp ground when it rained, a meat safe or two, cots for themselves and for the others.

'And Fred,' Barton continued, 'he has more talent in his hands than for just bein' a bushie. He could make his mark if he had a chance. Alice is good, too. They'll be all right. Just one more job.'

Fred, his dark brown hair flopping into his eyes, bent over something Alice had in her hands. She looked up at him, brushing her long fair hair out of the way before she reached up and tucked Fred's behind his ears.

They all had skills; they could all survive in the bush. But what good was that when because there was no work—only another bloody depression—there was no future? Couldn't live out a good life scratching around on Crown land, keeping one step ahead of the law just to survive. Nebo turned that thought over. Barton was right: Nebo could—*should*—work with his brothers. He knew it was pride that got in his way. His own pride.

Jude had once exploded that his youngest brother was a no-hoper, a lazy bastard out for a good time and nothing else. And Zeke had only given Nebo the eye when Nebo had played up to Maisie—who mostly ignored him. He admitted Zeke could've clobbered him, beaten the daylights out of him, yet he didn't. Nebo got him back for not paying him attention; he kept Zeke wondering about just which of them fathered Jonty.

Nasty, that was. He knew it. He wasn't proud of it, just couldn't seem to stop himself. He knew it was jealousy, plain and simple.

One last job. That's all it would take. A good haul, and then everyone goes their own way.

Tillie Scott, a slim woman with glossy pale red locks, came up behind Barton. 'You're goin' to need to set them rabbit traps, darlin',' she said and ruffled his bowl-shaped head of hair.

'You could do it, lass,' he said. 'I got business here.'

'I could, but I won't,' she quipped and slapped his shoulder. 'I told you, I'm no slave.' She smiled a bright smile. 'And if I'm to stay, someone needs to till me some soil for spuds and other vegetables,' she said, and tapped Barton's nose before she wandered off.

He watched her go, bemused. 'I'd send her back if I wasn't so taken by her,' he said, and swigged his rum.

'You poor, poor bugger. Better get yourself a patch of dirt quick, so you can dig in those spuds and get all homey. Don't knock your luck.'

Barton's attention was momentarily on Tillie's retreating figure. 'Speakin' of luck,' he said and took the bottle back from Nebo. 'I reckon I know where we could jump that coach up from Mt Gambier. What about at the ten-mile out of Casterton? That's not far from here. Plenty of scrub.'

'Sounds all right but it'll be broad daylight by the time it gets there.'

'Yep, but far enough out of town, and day after tomorrow it's due. No one will know what hit 'em. No one expects bushrangers anymore. All them hopefully rich ladies with golden garters.'

Nebo grunted. 'Not harmin' any ladies. I just want gold coins, notes, a bit of jewellery.' He tossed back the last of his rum while watching the other two couples.

Barton stood up to head to his own tent, and to his delectable Tillie as he'd put it. Nebo heard low murmurs and companionable laughter. He turned his head to regard his own camp, his meagre possessions. A swag and his saddle lay under a low stretch of canvas held up by short stout poles. Fred had nicked it for him on a visit to Casterton. Nebo's horse was nearby, tethered with the other horses.

He looked around. A nice patch of dense scrub, it was in off the road a way, and that suited his purposes. A creek was close, the water low but flowing. He'd be all right if this one job went off to plan.

Looking back to his camp and then to the others in his band, he laughed at himself. *Quite the society*, he'd said to Zeke. Sal had her hands in the bucket packing mud with leaf debris, concentrating, leaning forward over her rounded belly. Alice's quick and strong fingers were using a knife to turn a piece of hewn timber into a sturdy table leg. She handed it up to Fred to examine. She took it back and continued. Tillie had emerged from under her canvas, tied an apron over her dress and was now tending to a fragrant pot over their cook fire.

He was missing that one thing, the thing he'd been hankering for ever since Zeke had married Maisie, and it wasn't just slipping his cock inside a warm tight body. A wife remained elusive.

Eleven

Elsa slowed Peppin as soon as she could see the Kangaroo Inn on the rise. Worn out and hungry, all she wanted to do was stop, alight and try to ease the burning bruises on her backside. Being in the driver's seat all day on these roads did her rump no good at all.

'Are you sure you want to drive right past?' Rosie said, adjusting her hat in the late afternoon sun. 'This looks to be quite an imposing place, so if there's no one else here, why not stop?'

Elsa kept hold of the reins while wiping a forearm over her face. She flexed her fingers. They smelled of leather and dust, were greasy with sweat—she should have thought to bring gloves. She was desperate for a bath, or at least a deep bowl of clean water. 'We'll see. I think I'd rather be off the road. If others are travelling—'

'You've mentioned that already. But I'm tired.' Rosie cleared her throat. 'You must be tired, too, all the driving.' She balanced on one side of her backside and rubbed the other. 'I feel like I should get off and walk the next hundred yards.'

As they pulled up to the stone buildings, despite plentiful daylight the sisters were confronted with an eerie silence. Once a grand staging place for Cobb & Co, the inn had provided a haven for coach drivers, horses and travellers alike needing a reprieve. Now abandoned and crumbling, the place was unnerving.

Rosie alighted. 'I just want to stretch a bit.' When Elsa protested, pointing out the dangers, she said, 'Come on, we won't be long.'

Having climbed down from the seat and tied the reins to a sturdy branch on a shrub, Elsa went to the water barrel and poured a drink for the horse. She told him how good a boy he was and that it wouldn't be long before they could stop for the night. Peppin seemed satisfied, nodding that he agreed. Hands on her back and stretching, Elsa looked around. Rosie had wandered a little way closer to the abandoned inn.

'I read that it was built ages ago, before the gold rush, and now it belongs to a Mr Donald, on Gillap Station,' Elsa called, still stretching.

'You'd think he'd upkeep it. It could still be useful if he did.' Rosie wandered even further. 'I'm finding a privy spot.'

'Hurry up,' Elsa answered, and went in the other direction to find her own.

When she returned to the cart, Rosie was already on board. 'If we have to leave here, let's go. Your stories earlier today of murderers and drunken travellers have begun to send shivers up my spine,' she said. 'There's something sad about all of it here.'

They pulled up again, Elsa estimated, about three miles further. A cleared patch of scrub allowed them easy access to a spot off the road. As she directed Peppin, she decided they'd gone into it far enough when, looking back, she couldn't see the road; she reasoned nobody travelling would be able to see them now.

Rosie clambered into the back of the cart and threw the mattresses and blankets to the ground. Elsa unharnessed Peppin, chocked the cart after loosening the girth and the straps, and used the rag from the wooden box to give him a short rub down.

They needed to find running water soon, Elsa thought. *Oh, to have a bath.* As her sister shook the mattresses she was huffing and puffing and dust flew everywhere. Then there was the matter of their dirty clothes. Peppin was also grimy with sweat and dirt, and the barrel of water (just for drinking, Elsa had declared earlier) wouldn't last forever.

'I'm glad we're almost to Penola,' she said as they settled on their beds, their cups of water carefully set on the ground. 'We can find a well, but better to pay for a bath somewhere. And we're nearly at the end of these,' she said, handing a bun to her sister. 'They feel more like rocks than buns.'

'It's something in our stomachs.' Rosie broke off a bit and popped it in her mouth. 'I'm sure the good township of Penola has a decent bakery,' she said around the chewing.

Elsa shifted, wriggled on the mattress and then sat still, a long sigh escaping. 'It feels good to be off that cursed cart.' She took a bite of stale bun. 'I'm not sure my backside will ever recover.'

'Wriggle a bit more,' Rosie said, still chewing.

Elsa reached over and sipped from her cup. Oh, for some tea. Her father immediately popped into her head. She remembered the way they would sit around the fireplace in the hut and sip a strong cup of tea while they waited for the rabbit stew, or mutton if they were lucky, to heat for dinner.

'What is it?' Rosie asked. 'You just gave a loud sigh.'

'Did I?' Elsa took another bite, chewed and swallowed. 'I miss Pa. And George. Suddenly the future is a yawning chasm.'

'It's been a yawning chasm for a while for me.'

Rosie was so matter-of-fact. Elsa propped on her elbow. 'I didn't know you were unhappy; you've never indicated. I just assumed that married life must have made some people a bit grumpy because they had more responsibilities or something. It seems to me lots of married people are grumpy.'

'Some married people,' Rosie said and glanced at her. 'For a long time, I've been wondering if there was ever to be anything else to life. I haven't been able to bear a child. I live with a man who's mean with money and mean-spirited, who thinks I'm there to work myself to death for his bakery. It should be *our* bakery, but he always refers to it as his. I dressed how he wanted me to dress. My interests were frowned upon, being with my family was frowned upon. And all for what? To be rewarded with a love-less marriage, and now my youth gone. I didn't want that to be all there was for the rest of my life.' She gave a big sigh. 'When you came to tell me about George, I thought that it would be my chance to stand up to Frank and tell him I would be looking after Pa. That he could work the bakery himself.'

Daylight was fading but Elsa could see her sister's chin firm up. She thought that Rosie might have been holding on to some other emotion, but Elsa couldn't think what it would be.

'I know you were looking after Pa,' Rosie said. 'I just wanted to be closer after all these years. I think Pa knew what was between me and Frank, but he wouldn't say anything about it. A woman's place, and all that.' A little laugh escaped. 'When I got home to the farm with you, after worrying all the way there that Frank would be angry, I wondered if I'd gone mad wanting to leave. I began thinking I should scurry back home, and there was Pa, dead. And something inside just—clicked.'

Elsa lay down. In the silence now, she tried to understand what she'd just been told. Rosie had been sixteen when she married Frank. There were many years Elsa remembered an aloof Rosie, an older sister out of reach. When Elsa would become bewildered by her sister's disinterest in her, their mother would pat her hand and say, 'Don't bother your sister, dear. She's a married lady, with grown-ups' worries.' Their father would simply turn away. Sometimes Elsa wondered if he was pained by something Rosie had done, but he never said. Learning just now that her sister had changed because someone had asked it of her seemed foreign, but then again Rosie had been with Frank all of Elsa's life—that person was the only Rosie she'd ever known. Her leaving now seemed very brave, or very reckless.

At the first stars appearing, Elsa asked, 'So, are you afraid of the future?'

Rosie waited a beat. 'I am, but not fearfully afraid, if you know what I mean—not enough to go back. I'm on a path now that I don't want to get off. The freedom ... I feel almost euphoric and I really can't think straight. Perhaps that's the running away. Perhaps it's grief as well.' She finished the last of her bun and took a drink. 'I know things will be very tough if I can't find work, but I am determined to do better.'

'You always laugh at my interest in women's suffrage, and now you sound just like us.'

'Oh, and you identify with the suffragists, now, do you?' Rosie, the taciturn sister she knew, looked over at her.

'Don't be mocking again. It's not just about the vote, you know, and I do intend to vote—absolutely. It's one step towards being independent in this world and allowing our voices on political matters to be heard.'

'Political matters? It's hard enough having our voices heard in our own homes before we go shouting about something else. You still sound like you're reciting from a page.'

'Rosie, I know there are lots of women who feel the same way.'

'How do you know? I don't see too many in Robe.'

'There are a few, of those who are still in Robe, that is. But I read the newspapers. Many women feel the same. Only a few years ago, for instance, thousands signed a huge petition—'

'Don't get on a soapbox, Elsa, I've heard you before. That stuff is not for me. I do want my independence. Or more importantly,

I do not want to be tied down again like I have been. And that's that.'

Elsa thought a little before replying. It sounded as if Rosie was trying to shut down the conversation, and she was used to that. This time, though, things with Rosie had to be different. Elsa had read a report from parliament citing one minister who had declared it would be dangerous for women to vote: that the very heart of a man's home and family life was at risk if it were to happen.

'How can we be independent when we're not allowed to be?' she asked Rosie. 'How will it ever come about, when even some of us women don't want to be? Some people imagine we couldn't cope, or that their worlds would come crashing down if we got an education or kept and managed the money we earned ourselves.' They were all the things that Rosie had just taken a stand against. Didn't she fully realise that she was already thinking independently of the man in her life? Elsa wanted to grab her sister's hand but refrained. *Not yet, not yet.* 'That's what our vote is for, to ensure we have that basic right to be what we want to be, and I'm going to add mine at the election.'

There was another long silence. Night was coming quickly. Soon they'd share a blanket over them to keep the insects away and then sleep would come. But for the moment, Elsa could almost feel the air hum between them as Rosie's thoughts churned.

'Well, in that case, we must ensure that we are back in our colony and find a place to vote, for I believe Victoria has not allowed women to go to the polls,' Rosie said, surprising Elsa. 'I have a feeling we will have to be very busy in order to do that.' Then her sister turned away on her side.

'It's the only thing I want to do. And I will do it. I will come back and vote.'

'Of course you will,' Rosie murmured. 'Now, do stop going on about it, it'll give me nightmares. Go to sleep.'

There were things Elsa would like to have asked her sister, but they'd have to wait. She twisted the blanket they needed out from under her and tossed it over them. Rosie grabbed an edge, pulling it over her head. It didn't matter that she'd turned away; at least she was mulling it over.

The last thing Elsa remembered thinking was how her own life might look in the future. She had no family left except her runaway sister, no home and perhaps no fortune if they didn't find George's tin. *Poor George. Poor Pa.* Her heart thudded. Destitute was the word that came to mind. Her future? She couldn't see anything. Suddenly she wanted a good cry to take her over.

Elsa popped awake. *What was that?* She stopped breathing. *There, not far. On the road,* coming from Robe. A light bobbed in the pitch dark, a voice snarled. A whip cracked and thunderous hooves and the rattle of a vehicle hammered the road not twenty yards from where they camped.

Her heart banged against her ribs. Peppin let out a soft nicker, but that didn't worry her—he wouldn't be heard over the din of the vehicle on the rutted road. But the shock of knowing they would have been found had they stayed at the Kangaroo Inn ruin made her feel sick.

Sucking in shallow breaths, she snuck her hand across to find Rosie's strong, warm fingers had already reached for hers. The traveller's noise faded in the distance, but Elsa stayed frozen, rigid on the flat mattress until no other sound could be heard. No following rider or coach. No wandering men carousing after a night on the rum.

'They couldn't have been after us,' Rosie whispered, letting go of her hand. She turned onto her side and went back to sleep.

For Elsa, the night was long as she watched the stars, hour after hour, edge their way towards the new day.

They were away at first light. The hard ground under her thin mattress hadn't helped Elsa doze at all after last night's fright. She could feel the insistent niggle of a fatigue headache as she packed the cart.

They'd made steady pace with little conversation, and Elsa assumed Rosie felt the same, even though she'd slept. Now, with a rider approaching from Penola way, their tempers were tetchy.

'Get us off the road, quick.'

Elsa straightened up. 'There's no easy place to pull off, Rosie. There's that great drain all the way along on one side in this section and no way through the scrub on the other.'

Rosie was hanging on to her seat as the cart bounced behind Peppin who was into a slow trot. 'We'll just have to hope it's no one we know.'

'Even if it is,' Elsa said as she tried to steady Peppin's speed, 'we have a perfect right to be here. Besides, they're coming from the other way. Just keep calm.'

'I am calm,' Rosie snapped.

'Right.'

The rider held up a hand, indicating he wanted to stop. Elsa's thoughts spun. If she just waved in return and pressed on, it would be rude and likely gain notice—two women flying past in a cart, not stopping for a friendly chat. Then again, if they did stop—

'Oh God,' Rosie said through her teeth, her voice jumping with the corrugations in the road. 'It looks like Mr Milton, all that white hair and that long beard.'

Elsa groaned. Mr Milton, a retired solicitor in Robe, had known them all their lives and would easily recognise them. He'd wonder why they didn't stop. It would be the first thing he'd report to Frank back home—the detail of whether they stopped or not.

'We have to pull up,' Elsa said and dragged in the reins. Peppin slowed.

'Why? Let's just go straight past him—'

'Ahoy, young Goody girls,' Mr Milton shouted and raised his hat high in the air, waving it before he shoved it back on. Hauling his horse to a stop, he waited until their cart was alongside. 'Or I should say Miss Goody and Mrs Putney—I'm getting so old, I still remember you both as little children. And always a pleasure to see you.' His smile revealed big teeth, a gap between his two front ones. His long white beard was dotted with insects.

Elsa and Rosie spoke in unison. 'Good day, Mr Milton.'

'And you're a long way from home, now,' he said and peered into the back of their transport.

Rosie started. 'Well, we—'

'Our father has died, Mr Milton, just after we learned our George had died. We are going to—' Rosie dug her hard in the ribs with an elbow. 'Penola, to inform relatives. It's so much quicker than sending a letter in the mail, you see.'

Mr Milton looked appalled. He snatched off his hat again. 'Oh Lord, my deepest sympathy. Your George, so young. And your father, too?'

'He was ill, you see,' said Elsa, moving slightly away from Rosie. 'And the news of our George's death was an added shock to his poor health.'

Rosie flapped her pinny, dabbed her eyes with a corner of it then madly waved off the flies that came at her from Peppin's tail.

'Of course, of course. I knew Curtis was ill. I'm so sorry,' Mr Milton said. 'When did all this happen?'

Elsa, ignoring Rosie's glare, said, 'We got word that George had died weeks earlier just three days ago and Pa died the very next day, so as Pa has no kin, we thought to inform our mother's family.'

'In Penola?' The gap-toothed smile was wide, but he looked perplexed. 'I thought Kitty's people were in Naracoorte.'

'In Naracoorte,' Elsa said, agreeing quickly. 'After we've seen other relatives in Penola.'

Mr Milton shook his head. 'Dearie me, young ladies, it's all terrible news. But George—what happened to young George?'

Rosie put her face in her hands and Elsa heard a sob, for George's demise, of course, and just as much for Mr Milton's benefit. He began to look uncomfortable.

'Mr Milton, a terrible thing.' Elsa's voice hiccupped. 'He was shot, they said, by bushrangers.'

'Oh, my Lord,' Mr Milton said, shock creasing his face. 'This day and age? That's truly terrible, Miss Goody. Not in these districts, I hope.'

'Oh no,' Elsa said. 'Somewhere far into Victoria.' Rosie's elbow wasn't able to reach her this time.

He frowned. 'Well, it isn't safe for you to be driving around without a man to escort you.' His horse, dancing beneath him, bumped Peppin, who barely turned his head. Clouds of black dots took flight, flies rising off the backsides of both animals before settling again. 'Two young women, alone. I should think perhaps that's asking for trouble,' he scolded.

Elsa gave him a dark frown. 'We're not alarmed to do it, Mr Milton. So far, we are very well as you can see, and we'll be extremely careful. But it is a timely thing for us that we've met you on the road,' Elsa said, ignoring the eye Rosie gave her. 'We passed Kangaroo Inn some hours before dusk last night, and we've travelled a good distance today. Surely we can't be far out of Penola.'

Rosie spun back towards Mr Milton.

He sighed as if in relief. 'That's true, Miss Goody. I reckon two, three hours at the most.' Looking Peppin over, he said, 'He looks to be in good nick. He should do it easy. But if you're to get there before sundown today, I shouldn't keep you any longer. Will you be staying there a while?'

'We'll be on our way—to Naracoorte—as soon as we can be,' Elsa said.

He looked at Rosie. 'I hope you're feelin' better, soon, Mrs Putney. I'll be sure to tell Frank that I saw you, so close to Penola and safety.'

At the well-meant offer Rosie swallowed down a wail. She finally managed a tearful, 'Thank you, Mr Milton.'

He batted at flies before he held up a finger. 'But I must make mention, ladies. When you come back, it'll be time for you to address your father's will. I still look after a few old clients, and your father was one of them.'

Elsa was surprised. 'We have his will with us, Mr Milton,' she said.

Mr Milton gave her a look, stroked his beard and picked out a bug or two. 'That so? A formal will?'

'It looks to be.' Elsa fumbled for the toolbox in the back.

'Should Mr Putney not have it for safekeeping?' he asked Rosie, pointedly.

'He is far too busy at the bakery,' Rosie said, sniffing. 'Too busy to even visit the farm to ensure its security, so we brought it with us.'

Elsa was impressed by that. She reached into the box, pulled out the will envelope and held it up for him to see.

He leaned over and squinted. 'Can't read it from here but it does look like my seal.'

Elsa wasn't about to give it to him; she could barely trust herself with it much less anyone else. 'It is your seal, dated two years ago,' she said, tucking it away again.

'Wait a moment.' He dipped his head, thinking, and his saddle squeaked as he shifted his backside. 'I have Curtis's will in my safe at home, I'm sure of it. Oh, Lord, my memory. When you return be sure to check with me before you open that,' he said and stabbed a finger at the packet. 'One of them will precede the other. And right now,' he grumbled, 'I can't remember what will was done when.'

'We will, Mr Milton.'

Mr Milton put on his hat, still frowning. 'Good day to you both,' he said, and with a wave galloped off.

Elsa snapped the reins and Peppin got going.

'Why did you tell him Penola?' Rosie burst, any semblance of tears gone.

Elsa shot her a look. 'Where else could we have been going on this road?'

'He'll no sooner get back to Robe and everyone will know where we've gone, not just Frank.'

'For heaven's sake,' Elsa cried, glaring at her sister. 'Everyone will know already. And besides, I said we were going on to Naracoorte.'

Rosie threw her hands in the air then thought better of it as the cart rattled along. 'Then you've got us going all over the countryside,' she said, exasperated. 'All I want to do is get to this Mr Jones and find out if George left—'

'Yes, and by saying we're going to Naracoorte, it will put people off following us through Penola. They'll go in that direction, and not into Victoria.' Elsa, annoyed, glared across at her sister. 'Keep up, Rosie.'

'Oh.' Rosie chewed her lip. 'Yes. I see.'

'And when we get through Penola, I have another idea, just to be on the safe side.'

Her sister groaned. 'Oh no, what now?'

Elsa flicked the reins and Peppin sped into an even trot. 'When we leave Penola, we don't stay on the main road to Casterton. We find tracks and cut through to the road up from Mt Gambier. If anyone comes after us from Robe, we won't be on the same road.'

Shaking her head, Rosie said, 'Not only taking us all over the colony, but now intent on getting us lost as well.' Her mouth pinched. 'We've eaten everything. We could die out here.'

Elsa was glad her sister hadn't wailed, but exhaustion was giving rise to doom and gloom. 'There'll be places to buy food in Penola, Rosie. I noticed the other day you had a handful of money, so we won't starve.'

'It won't last forever. We'll have to find that tin of sovereigns, or some work somehow, somewhere.' Rosie shuffled on the seat. 'I have no mind to starve.'

'Exactly my sentiments, sister,' Elsa said. She hoped the sinking feeling in her stomach wasn't despair.

By the time Penola came into view, Elsa's stomach was cramping with hunger. Rosie had fallen silent over the last, long miles of dusty road and low, wooded plains. From time to time the only communication between the two was a glance, or an encouraging smile.

The sun had dropped, so it was late afternoon by the time they turned into what looked like the main street and pulled up at a hitching rail and a horse trough. Peppin wasted no time.

'Over there on that corner,' Rosie said. 'A hotel. Perhaps they'll have lodgings. It looks big enough.' She took off her pinny, using it to slap dust and dirt from her clothes.

Elsa began to worry that this was a plan that could go very wrong. She slumped in the driver's seat and considered the unwelcoming building, a single-storeyed ugly thing, squat and sturdy. A pub. A few men hovered around the front door. She hoped, if nothing else, there was a restaurant inside and that the menu would be hearty—she could eat the side of a bullock. She climbed to the ground after Rosie.

Her sister marched across the road to the arched doorway of the building. 'Good afternoon. Is there a meal and lodgings at this establishment?' she asked one of the men.

The four men standing there tipped their hats. A man with a dark straggly beard and a pipe between his teeth took off his hat. 'There is, missus. But ye and yer daughter might be better off askin' the Josephite sisters for rooms.'

Elsa bit her lip as Rosie stiffened. Her sister adjusted her collar. 'Thank you. So long as this place has a good meal and a good room it will suffice.'

Sucking her cheeks to stop a burst of laughter, Elsa was glad Rosie hadn't corrected the man. Being seen to be mother and daughter would help, but clearly her older sister had been taken aback. Still, bless her heart, Rosie squared her shoulders and spoke to her.

'Come along, Myrtle. We shall go inside and speak to the publican.' Rosie swept by the men who stood aside in deferential, though short-lived, silence.

Myrtle.

When they entered the hotel, the smell of beer—yeasty and sweet—fell over them like a mist. Raucous laughter came from one of the rooms they passed, and tobacco smoke drifted out, along with the strong odour of hard-working men. Rosie strode by. Another room was closed, and further along there was a larger saloon. She stopped in the doorway, aware she wasn't allowed into the bar, and called out over the rumble and hum of boozy conversation.

'Would there be someone in charge to rent us lodgings?'

As the notes of a female voice rang out over the confabulating, the immediate hush, taciturn and sullen, delivered a room full of belligerent stares towards them. Elsa glanced at Rosie, who had her own imperious stare directed their way.

Finally, an aproned gentleman approached the doorway. The hair on his head was slick with oil, parted on one side, the over-comb not quite covering a gleaming bald patch. A pencil nestled over one ear. His moustache, prolific in its growth, was thick and black.

'I'm the publican, I can do that for you. If you'd come this way?' He indicated with his hand that she should step back and let him pass. 'Excuse me, missus,' he said to her. His glance then fell on Elsa. 'Excuse me, miss. This way. This way.'

With the threat of female trespass now removed from sacred space, the important palaver in the bar continued, at first as if recovering from shock.

Elsa had to admire her sister.

They followed the gentleman to a reception counter, its window covered with a curtain drawn across it. 'Wait here a moment.' He took out a large key, opened a door to the side and disappeared only to reappear as he swished aside the short drape. 'Now then,' he said, taking the pencil from behind his ear as he opened a ledger book and peered at it. 'One room is available with four beds.'

'We don't need four beds,' Rosie said. 'There is only my—daughter and I.'

'If you don't want to share the room with other female guests, you have to pay for the four beds.' He waited a moment before raising his brows as if annoyed. He replaced the pencil behind an ear that had more hair on it than he had on his head and closed the ledger.

As if there'd be other guests. 'Do you have a room with one double bed? My mother and I don't mind sharing,' Elsa said sadly. 'We have travelled very far to inform dear relatives of two deaths in the family, and we are so very exhausted, we could sleep on the floor.'

Rosie blinked but her high-and-mighty gaze stayed on the publican.

He looked from Elsa to Rosie and sighed. 'Well, it's a slow time, and not many travellers. I could let you have the room and only charge for the two beds.'

Elsa brightened. 'Oh, sir, you are kind. My mother and I do thank you.' She noticed Rosie's mouth set in a line. 'We also need to stable our horse and secure our cart, if you would let us know …?'

'For a shilling more I can get a lad to do that for you. Now then, how many nights will you need?'

'Just the one, thank you,' Rosie said.

'Sign and put your names here.' He turned the ledger towards her, pushed over an ink pot and nib pen and waited until she'd signed—an illegible flourish—and printed Mrs Conroy and Miss Conroy on the page. Taking back the ledger, he peered at it then handed her a door key dangling from a wooden tag, the number three carved into it. 'Just down there and it's on the right, Mrs Conroy. You'll be able to get water for the pitcher at the well out the back, and you'll find the outhouse further along the path.'

'And where might we purchase a meal, sir?' Elsa asked.

'Across the hall,' he said, pointing to a closed door. 'It opens at six-thirty. The fare is simple. I think tonight it's mutton stew with boiled potatoes, green beans and gravy.'

Elsa's mouth watered. She glanced at the clock on the wall behind him. Only an hour to wait, thank goodness. She sighed. By the time they found the room, found where Peppin and the cart would be stabled for the night, had a wash and a tidy up, the hour would fly by.

'Come along, Myrtle,' Rosie said, and swished along to the room.

'Yes, Mama,' Elsa answered, holding in a laugh as Rosie marched ahead of her.

The room was stuffy, and the four beds were barely far enough apart to step between. But when Elsa sat on one, the relief was welcome. 'It feels wonderful.'

Rosie put her nose to the covers. 'Except for a little dust, it smells clean enough.'

'I'm sure it'll be all very fine, Mama,' Elsa said.

'Don't push it, Elsa.'

Retrieving what little they wanted from the cart to bring inside for the night, they washed their faces and dusted themselves down as best they could. *Oh, how delightful to get rid of the dust.* Now to present for the evening meal. They were the only diners, but the dinner was hearty, and Elsa ate fit to bursting.

Rosie asked to purchase a bag of bread and fruit, some fresh local cheese and some ham, 'So that we can be on our way early in the morning to, um, Naracoorte,' she told the waitress.

That organised, they made their way to their room, slipped out of their dresses and shoes, washed again, this time a more lengthy affair after Elsa had found another bowl to cart water from the well. Even with only cold water, Elsa scrubbed gleefully. They climbed into their beds. Daylight was fading fast, but it would have only been about eight in the evening.

As she settled under the covers, Elsa felt the weight of grief crawl through her; thoughts of their pa, and George, crowded her head and her heart. She clamped it down, wanted to soothe it away but it was a hard, tangible thing that gnawed at her, plumbed depths that she'd forgotten she knew. Too deep for even tears to rise to the surface now, she just took a couple of swallows.

Rosie sighed loudly. 'Oh, I imagine this is what heaven feels like,' she said, her voice muffled as she turned onto her side. 'A lovely bed, and all to myself.'

Distracted, relieved, Elsa mulled over what Rosie could mean. Perhaps now was a good time to appease her curiosity, to slip into conversation with her older sister who would be a font of knowledge and experience. 'So, if being alone in bed feels like heaven, what's it like to share a bed?' At first, she thought Rosie hadn't heard her. 'I mean—'

'I know what you mean.' Rosie still faced away. 'I think.'

Still there was nothing, so Elsa pressed on and said, 'To—sleep by the side of a man.'

More silence, then, 'The sleeping part is the easy part, if you can get to sleep over the snoring, and the farting loud enough to rival Peppin's.'

Elsa cracked a laugh. 'Rosie!'

Her sister turned onto her back. 'I think what you're asking me is what our ma would have told you once you were old enough, but she didn't live long enough to do it. Is it really up to me, now? I suppose it is. You're old enough to know, well over marrying age. Nearly an old maid, I should think.'

'Not true,' Elsa retorted knowing it was a tease but felt the creep of a blush on her face all the same. 'It's not that I don't know what happens.'

'Really? Have you—'

'No,' Elsa was quick to say. 'But I've had enough experience on the farm watching the animals. I got the—general idea. It never looks a pleasant experience for the female.'

There was a silence again. Then Rosie said, 'The mechanics are the same, so to speak, but the delivery is not always violent. I've heard it whispered that it can be pleasurable, but I can't imagine it. Sometimes it's not even noticeable.'

That relieved Elsa, but also confused her.

'I didn't know what to think when I first married Frank. I do wish our ma had said more than "close your eyes and it won't feel so bad".'

Elsa felt the blush burn.

Rosie went on, her voice flat. 'She didn't say anything more than it was to be endured, and that it is a duty. And believe me, that's all it is. I wouldn't have done it if I didn't have to.' Then she gave a short laugh. 'And now I don't have to.'

Elsa chewed her lip. 'Does it hurt?'

A hesitation. 'Sometimes.'

'Why do we have to do it?'

'Don't be thick, Elsa. That's how babies come.'

'Clearly not always,' Elsa shot back and then regretted it. 'I mean, we are told to be so strict before we marry because we might become fallen women, yet once married, it doesn't always follow that doing ... *it*, means we get children.'

'Ma had five.' There was the silence again. 'And have you been strict, Elsa?'

'Of course.' Elsa didn't say that no one had approached her. Well, not seriously. Henry made her squirm a bit, made her want to press her knees together when he looked at her *that way*, but it didn't make her feel unpleasant, in fact the opposite—*but* he was too young. Mr Southie made her feel unpleasant, and her mouth twisted at his image. Shying away from that, and emboldened, Elsa asked, 'So what exactly does happen, Rosie?'

Rosie drew in a loud breath. 'Oh Lord, why me?' she muttered and exhaled just as loudly. 'You're in your bed, the one you share with your husband. On your back. He climbs on top of you, pushes a sweaty hand under your chemise and he feels about between your legs—I presume so he knows where to put his man-thing.'

Elsa cringed. *Man-thing.*

'Then, he lifts his own nightshirt and his man-thing springs against you. Hard, sometimes. Not always. Sometimes not for long, either, before he gets to you, and then it won't work.'

What does that mean?

'If it's hard enough, he opens your legs and pushes it into you.'

Elsa's legs tightened.

'Then he thrusts a bit with his hips, makes a loud groaning noise, spills himself either inside you or on your leg, then falls off you.'

Spills himself.

'Then he goes to sleep. Snoring, and … et cetera.'

'What does he spill?'

'I thought you said you watched the animals. Spills the stuff that makes the babies.'

'Oh.'

'Then you have to clean yourself up, otherwise you'd have to sleep in it.' Rosie waited a beat. 'Are you suitably disgusted? That, sister, is duty, and we must endure it in order to have children. I can think of no other reason why we are ever talked into it, or worse, forced into doing it. It is not pleasant.'

Elsa's lip curled. 'After what you've just told me I don't think I'll ever do it.'

Rosie gave a little laugh. 'When you know you can't get out of it, you'll do it.'

'Perhaps I won't marry,' Elsa said. 'And you, never having had children—does that mean you did your duty all for nothing?'

Rosie sniffed and cleared her throat. 'Most likely. But I had thought at one time to find other means to—' She stopped abruptly.

'What?'

'Nothing.' She blew out a breath. 'Besides, I must have been getting too old because lately Frank has hardly seemed interested enough to bother me. Which is a good thing because clearly since I'm not able to have children, I don't miss all of his huffing and grunting on me. Oh, it was just awful. Thankfully, the last time was well over a year ago.' She stopped again and sighed. 'And now that I've painted you that charming picture, if it's not enough to give you a sleepless night, I don't know what is.' Rosie turned away on her side.

Elsa propped on her elbow. 'You were going to say something about other means. Other means to do what?'

'Oh, never mind that.'

'Other means to do *what*?' Elsa insisted.

'It's late,' Rosie railed.

'It's not. Are you going to tell me what you were about to say?' Her eyes had adjusted to the dim light in the room. Rosie began to turn back and then stopped.

'No, I'm not. Another time, perhaps. Now, if you don't mind, I'm going to go to sleep and have another glorious night without wondering if someone is going to fumble in my britches. Goodnight, Elsa,' she said, her tone clipped as she settled on her side, still facing away.

Elsa lay down again. She couldn't imagine what would make her want to endure what Rosie had just described. She thought of those men in the bar and shook herself away from that. Thought of Henry and the look he'd given her at times, and things tingled deep between her thighs. Then she thought of Rosie doing her duty with Frank, but the picture was so awful, so very intrusive—*and* distasteful of her to even be thinking of it—that the tingles immediately dissipated and she put it out of her head.

No wonder some women didn't marry. No wonder there were nuns. Not that she felt called to God at all, but they could certainly escape such male desires because nuns were forbidden to lie with men. But Elsa didn't like the idea of becoming a nun, either.

But 'what other means'?

She sighed and yawned widely. Rosie's even breathing signalled that her sister was asleep, so Elsa turned on her side. Lots of young women she knew hankered to be married. It couldn't only be the way Rosie described. Surely there was a decent man, someone quite different to Frank.

A kind man ...

After a restless hour wondering if life really could be better than this, she spent a dreamless night.

In the morning, Elsa set off at the reins. Peppin had been harnessed by the lad who'd stabled him, and Rosie climbed on board after her.

Rosie leaned over. 'How do we know which way to go?' she asked, close to Elsa's ear. They hadn't asked for directions to be sure that if anyone did follow, no one would be able to say where they'd headed.

'Casterton is to the south east, so if we take the main road this way, I'm sure it'll be right. There's bound to be a sign, and then we'll veer off. I remember from Mr Conroy that there were a few tracks the teams used to cut across to the Mt Gambier road when they needed to.'

The sun's early rays had swathed a golden glow over the road. Elsa was squinting into it, but Peppin, refreshed, trotted confidently.

'It makes my nerves twitter, Elsa.'

Elsa took a deep breath. 'Mine, too,' she said and glanced at her sister. 'Besides, it's not a great distance, and if we feel too nervous, we can always return the same way.'

Settling herself, Rosie shook her head. 'There's that adventurous spirit again, dear girl. Thought you'd have grown out of it by now.'

Elsa shrugged and clicked the reins again. 'I always knew there was another world outside my own. But by the time I grew up, our mother was gone, and our older brothers were gone, suddenly there was the farm to look after, and then Pa. George was still dreaming all day long about how he'd go adventuring. And he would go off, here and there, and leave me to it.' She looked at Rosie with a rueful smile. 'Then there was only me. And now you, too.' She let Rosie squeeze her hand and then she shook away morose thoughts. 'So I'm taking up the adventure. If Frank is to make the farm work, there'll be nothing in Robe for me.'

Rosie looked at her sharply. 'What makes you think Frank will make the farm work? He might sell it.'

Elsa made a face. 'I don't know what he'll do, but he is the only man in the family now.'

'Did Pa say something to you about it?' Rosie burst.

'Don't be upset. Pa wanted me to marry. He didn't want me administering, and so when he mentioned Frank on that last day, I just assumed he meant that Frank would take over and—'

'What did he say about Frank?'

Elsa thought hard. Her mind had been woolly on that day—so much had happened. 'We were talking about how badly you'd miss George.' She frowned, remembering. 'Then he said that I was to bring you home, so he could talk to you first. He said "first". And that Frank was the only man in the family.' There was something else in the conversation with her father that Elsa couldn't quite put her finger on. 'I got the feeling he wanted to tell you something, or have you do something, but he didn't say.'

Rosie stared off into the distance, shading her eyes once or twice, then ducked her chin to gaze at her hands. She finally said, 'Let's find one of those tracks and get off this road.'

'I thought we'd give it two to three hours, and then try to turn off.' Elsa looked at her sister. 'Had Pa spoken to you earlier about something to do with the farm?'

Rosie looked at her and nodded. 'I had forgotten. Nothing ever seemed likely. George was headstrong but I always thought he was invincible, too. Pa had said a long time ago, after Ned died, that if something happened to George, he would name me administrator for his affairs.'

Elsa's mouth dropped open then closed again as flies tickled her face. 'Did he write anything down?'

'It would be in his will.'

'I have that.'

Rosie glared at her. 'I know but it won't be worth a thing if it is opened,' she rebuked sharply.

'It's sealed,' Elsa cried. 'I know a lawyer has to see it.'

Rosie sat up straight. 'I don't know if he wrote anything down. Truly, I didn't take a lot of notice because at the time, it hardly mattered. Even when George went off on his adventures, I never gave it a thought. Why would I? Being married to Frank I would have to hand it all to him, anyhow, even if my name was on a will.'

'No, you wouldn't. The law changed years ago. You know that.'

'And I know Frank,' Rosie said, a wry twist on her lips.

Ahead, a ragged, scrawny clutch of four children appeared at the side of the road. Three boys and a girl. Dead rabbits were slung over their backs and shoulders, certainly a good meal or two there, and no doubt some coin would be exchanged for the pelts. The dirt-smudged faces stared up solemnly in the early light and one of the taller lads raised a hand holding up a furry body.

'Tucker for a few pennies, missus.'

Rosie shook her head.

Elsa waved back, well remembering those days of her own past. 'Thank you, no.' She clicked the reins again and as they drove by, he called, 'Hoo-ray, miss.'

Shifting again, the memories rankling, Elsa said, 'If you thought we were being adventurous by leaving, now we have to make sure we find that tin of George's to pay for a lawyer. That'll be our real challenge. There might be more to our future in that tin than we think, if indeed, it's still to be found.'

'All those sovereigns,' Rosie said. 'What a mess.'

Elsa squared her shoulders. 'None of that. We are strong women, and we will find our way out of this.' She raised her chin higher. 'We are the Goody sisters. Better, we are intrepid Mrs Conroy and her clever daughter, Miss Myrtle.' Looking over at Rosie she saw a glimmer of a smile.

Twelve

Nebo shot to his feet as Glen Barton galloped in. 'What is it?'

Glen threw himself off his horse. 'That Billy Watson, the great fat redheaded git who's got it in for you. Seems he's told tales after all. We gotta get out of here, quick. He's put the finger on you for bashing him and says we're cattle and sheep duffin'.' He ran across to Tillie when she appeared out of their tent. 'I'm packin' up,' he called back. 'Movin' further in. We can all go there.'

Christ. Nebo threw his pannikin to the ground. Well, he knew it wouldn't have lasted for long, especially after he'd had a go at Watson. But going further in—and by that Glen meant into swampy country between the Mt Gambier road and the Penola road—they'd be that much further away from the ambush site they'd chosen to bail up the coach.

But we'd also be that much further out of sight. Retrieving the pannikin, he looked up. Clouds had gathered around the sun, and more were on the western horizon. Might mean rain tonight. *Shit.* He wished he'd have been able to buy that tent he needed.

He laughed to himself. He needed a house to live in, not a tent.

One more job. Then he'd go on the straight and narrow. Patch things up with Jude—Ezie was another matter—maybe work Jude's farm for him while he went off roaming the countryside.

Wally was flicking mud from his hands and as he pushed hair off his face, it smeared on his cheek. 'Nebo, we're movin', as well.'

Nebo watched Sal straighten tiredly, a hand on her back and her belly protruding as she listened. 'I don't know how long we got till the troopers ride in,' he said. 'You're right. Best to pack up now, and quick.'

Wally hesitated, glanced at Sal who nodded. 'I gotta go somewhere safe. Sal hasn't got long to go, she reckons a month. I can't be draggin' her all over the place.'

Nebo knew one thing for sure—he didn't want a baby birthin' right when he needed all the boys for this job. ''Course not, 'course not. We need to find a place, bit of higher ground somewhere.'

'Yeah. Me and Fred found a spot,' Wally said. 'Needs work, some drains dug, but it's a good site. Good water in a couple of places nearby. We'd be hid from the other road, and it's not far in. Good access.'

'Closer to the Penola road?'

'It cuts in between real neat, right in a patch between the two roads. We can still get to the coach easy enough.'

Nebo stared. So the boys had already scouted for another place. What did that mean? Wally didn't look away, didn't look defiant, either, just matter-of-fact. *No use gettin' all nervous about it.* Wally had done the right thing—was lookin' after Sal, and the new little one to come.

'Let's go, then,' he said.

'Yeah,' Wally said. 'But Nebo ...'

Fred began to pack away a few remaining tools into a large bag. Alice was stuffing bedding into a couple of sacks. Glen and Tillie worked on dismantling their humpy. They'd all been way ahead of him on this. 'What?' Nebo said, short, annoyed.

'After this last one, this last job, I'm heading maybe to Portland. Heard there's a bit o' work there.'

'And Sal?' Nebo didn't know what else to say.

'We'll be all right.' Wally turned and walked away. Sal turned with him, picked up the last of her still-damp bricks and hurled them into the scrub.

Fred had begun strapping his bags to his horse. 'It's a good camp, Nebo, where we're goin' now. But like Wally, I'm off after this. Me an' Alice can make a living on good farmin' land further south. Or maybe if there's a timber mill somewhere, we can set up business.'

Nebo bowed his head and stood, hands on hips. They'd talked about it. All of them? He looked up at Glen and Tillie. Glen shrugged at him. 'I'm not botherin' about a place here anymore. I got family in New South Wales, on land south of Sydney. Nobody knows Tillie there. This last job will maybe buy me a cart and we can head off.'

Nebo looked around. Wally had nearly packed everything they owned. Sal was shrugging on a bag. She'd walk miles like that, even heavy as she was with child. She had to; they couldn't get her on Wally's horse, and no one had a cart.

Fred was tying Alice's tools onto a spread of oiled canvas, then he rolled it up and tied it to his horse. Alice threw him her bag and he strapped it on.

Glen and Tillie were sorting seed into little paper packets. Glen folded them into squares and folded again before tying them off with twine. He shoved them into his saddlebags and said, 'We reckon you'll find your way, Nebo, find what it is you want. We gotta get along as best we can, too. So, one last job.'

One last job. Nebo couldn't even get mad. They were right. *One last job.*

Thirteen

Zeke stood back from the man who said he was Curtis Goody. He'd brought him from Jude's place to the boy's gravesite. The day started out cooler, but now late in the afternoon, heat had built under a thick layer of cloud, and the wind had dropped to almost nothing. Storms ahead, maybe. Hopefully rain.

The man dragged in a deep, pained breath as he knelt to place a hand on the hot earth of the mound over the boy's body. Sorrow welled in Zeke's chest; he too remembered the pain of losing a loved one.

Jude had stayed behind at his place. Before Zeke left to walk back with Mr Goody, his brother had called him aside. They'd left the man studying the area inside Jude's unfinished house where Nebo said he'd found the injured boy.

'Tell 'im nothin', Zeke,' Jude had whispered, hurried and low. 'He hasn't told you anything about the boy. And who told him where to come? Yeah, I'm suspicious. Tell 'im nothin'.'

Now, even though he was in the shade of the huge gum tree, sweat trickled down Zeke's back. The older man got to his feet. Funny, he'd forgotten to take his hat off as he'd said a prayer. Or that's what Zeke presumed he'd done—he'd heard him murmuring while he was on his knee.

'Mind if I camp here the night?' Goody asked, his frown dark over an unsmiling face.

'Don't mind. But might be weather comin' in.' Zeke pointed to the sky.

'Been in worse.' Goody turned back and stared at the grave again. 'Boy didn't leave any possessions behind?'

'Had none when he came to me,' Zeke answered. He kept his head down, as if in respect.

The man grunted. 'Tell me again how he came to you?'

'My brother found him.'

Jude had been tight-lipped when the man had begun asking his questions, and Zeke had followed suit. He'd never been abrupt like his older brother, but he took Jude's lead this time and didn't offer too much. As if by a silent agreement, neither Zeke nor Jude brought their middle brother into it.

'He couldn't look after him there. You've seen how he lives.'

'And the boy died where?'

The boy, not *my son*. 'At my house.'

The man glared then grunted again. Changed his stance a little. 'I thank ye.'

Maybe a man in pain, Zeke thought. 'You're welcome to a meal here with us. I've got hungry kids comin' back from school, but we could stretch a rabbit stew to one more mouth.'

The glare came again, and then a shake of his head. 'Grateful, but no. How did he get here? Cart? On a horse? Walkin'?'

'On a horse. He couldn't walk.' It was Nebo's horse, but Zeke wouldn't offer that.

'A horse? Could he have gone somewhere else before your brother found him?'

Jude's right; this is strange. 'Doubt it. Reckon whoever shot him left him for dead. Or thought he was already dead. I sent you a letter, first he died.'

The glare darkened. 'A letter?'

'Sent to your farm. You didn't get it?'

A short shake of the man's head again. 'I—uh, followed soon after the boy left home, wanted to track him down, bring him back before he got into too much trouble. Missed the letter.'

'Well, his sisters would have it now,' Zeke said. 'Sad for them. No pa there to help them with the news.'

The man thought a moment. 'Aye, the womenfolk,' he said, as if just remembering he had daughters. 'I should get back to them,' the man said and stared off into the distance. Then he looked at Zeke. 'He—uh, talk a bit, did he, before he died?'

'Not really talk. Whispers about this and that, about his mother, that he had two sisters. How he was the last boy, his brothers gone too.' Young George had called out more than once about a sister on the farm: Ellie—Alice? He hadn't been too coherent by then.

The man nodded. 'I'll stay up here a while, if you don't mind. Won't be disturbing you?'

Zeke hesitated but said, 'Stay as long as you like.'

The man nodded, looked away again, as if in thought, but he said nothing more.

Zeke's kids would be just about at the mail-tree now. He needed to see them, hug them tight. He strode off, not sure if the man had watched him or not.

Giff pushed his plate away. 'When we gonna see Uncle Jude?'

His three kids stared at him. Jonty had his fork laden with potato and gravy halfway to his open mouth. Gracie set her knife and fork on her plate.

Zeke took another couple of mouthfuls, chewed and swallowed. Nearly time for another batch of stew the way these kids were eating. There'd have to be an extra loaf of bread a day, too. 'Tomorrow's not a school day, so how about we do our chores early and get over there?'

Satisfied with that, it seemed, Jonty angled his fork into his mouth and chewed.

'Good,' Giff said. He stood up and took his plate to the pot on the stove. Scraping out his last ladleful, he turned and looked at Zeke, offering the spoon. 'Pa?'

Zeke shook his head. He could easily have eaten another plateful, but Giff needed it more than he did. Jonty was a slow eater, but he'd soon finish his. Gracie never asked for seconds.

Giff helped himself to the remaining mashed spud and the last drop of gravy. Back at the table, he said, 'I reckon he could use some help fixin' up the roof again.'

Zeke agreed. 'You'd be right. Don't know that he'll be expecting us, though.'

'He will.' Giff concentrated on the last mouthfuls. 'He always knows we'll come as soon as he's home.' He dragged the last of his bread through the cold streaks of gravy on his plate.

Thank God for my kids. If there was going to be a way back to his brother Jude, it would be through these kids. They'd never given up on him, as gruff as he'd appeared, as often as he'd pushed them away. They just let him be Jude. Where had they got that from?

'Can I leave the table, Pa?' Giff asked, and without waiting for the nod, he stood and the others followed, Jonty's cutlery clanging. 'We need to take some food for tomorrow.'

Having stood too, Zeke and the other children took their utensils to the washing-up bowl that sat on a bench under the window.

Giff left Gracie at the bowl—it was her turn—and he took to rummaging in the only vermin-proof cupboard they had. He pulled out a sack with a drawstring. 'Gracie can go to the orchard. I'll go check the traps after I feed the dogs.'

Zeke peered outside. There was still enough light for Giff to find his way around. Plenty of rabbits to trap, plenty of stew to cook. And the pelts were fetching good prices.

'Trappers are gettin' up to eight pounds a week if they're smart,' Giff had told his father. Zeke knew it to be true. Knew how much that sort of money would mean to his family; he just wanted his eldest son to be a boy for a while longer—he was nine—and not have to work for his living yet.

He wasn't winning.

Zeke watched Giff hand the sack to Gracie who'd finished the washing up. She headed out behind her brother to pick the last of the apples before the birds and the insects got to the lot. Jude had said years ago that he'd build a cold store. Zeke might have to remind him of that.

He called after Giff. 'And not out too late. Jude will want a fair day's work out of you, not a sleepy-head.'

Giff lifted a hand in acknowledgement. Coming up ten, the boy was young, too young, but other families had their children working on the farms, hoping to survive without paying an adult wages. Times were tough so education had to play second fiddle to family survival for many. At least he had his kids close by, not like some who'd been sent away, or some whose fathers had abandoned them.

Never. That would never happen. His kids were everything to him. The boy could trap all the rabbits he liked as long as he stayed close to home. He watched, his chest expanding. The dogs, tied up, barked madly as Giff took his determined strides across the paddocks around the base of the hill.

Fourteen

Elsa's backside, no longer numb, hurt with every bounce of the cart. Her bones—*her teeth*—rattled as Peppin doggedly followed orders and took them off the main road. It had only appeared to be a slight grading through an opening of low scrub but was proving hard work.

'Goodness gracious,' Rosie yelled, one hand hanging onto the vehicle, the other onto her hat.

'It's all right,' Elsa yelled back. 'Nearly done.'

'We should've got off and walked him into the scrub.'

'Done now,' Elsa replied and sure enough, Peppin's stride was evening out. 'Check the water barrel.'

Rosie craned her neck to see into the back of the cart. 'Looks like the lid's held together.' She turned back again. 'And I'm glad the cart held together. Are you sure that was the right thing to do?'

'No. But the wheels seem all right, so we just have to be careful from now on.' She pointed ahead. 'Do you see those faint wheel tracks there? I think this will be one of the places where others have cut through to the Mt Gambier road.'

'Wish I was as sure as you are,' Rosie grumbled. 'How long will it take before we get to the other road?'

Elsa didn't know; couldn't rightly remember if she'd ever known. But thinking back to Mr Conroy's maps, and his tales of bullocky adventures, she didn't think there was much in it. 'I'd say a day's drive at most.'

More grumbling from Rosie as she hung on. 'Looks like there might be rain coming.'

Elsa believed so too. Rain would make things less than pleasant—if the trip so far could be called pleasant—and not just for their getting wet. She knew this country held water, and drainage was poor. If there was a lot of rain, they risked getting bogged, risked Peppin, so they'd have to be vigilant. She looked skywards briefly. Great rolling clouds breezed overhead. The temperature was still a little too warm, but the threat of rain was there.

She would have to carefully wrap their father's will to try and waterproof it. And the letter from Mr Jones. Any moisture could run the ink—even her own perspiration. As soon as she could, she would check the letter she'd tucked in her bodice. Better still, she'd remove it to the satchel. 'Pass me the satchel, Rosie.'

While Rosie took the reins after grabbing up the canvas bag, Elsa wrapped the letter from Mr Jones into her smalls. Then she took her father's will from the toolbox and did the same with it. That done and the satchel once again secured over the back, she said, 'We'll push on, try to find a decent place before nightfall.'

'I hope we meet that other road by then. Otherwise, I'd rather go back and stay on the Penola road.'

Elsa heard the catch in Rosie's voice. 'We have water on board, we have a gun and we're not far from either road. If we stay with these old tracks, we should be all right. And if we haven't found the other road by first thing tomorrow, we'll retrace our steps. Don't be frightened. Nothing will go wrong.'

'I'm not frightened.'

Elsa knew that was a fib. She glanced at her sister. Sure enough, Rosie looked worried, her face drawn, and her mouth was set in a line. But Elsa was sure this track was one that would lead them to the Mt Gambier road. 'Tell you what,' she said. 'If it gets too hard on Peppin, we'll get off and walk him. All right?'

Elsa thought Rosie nodded, but with the cart bobbing on the rough track it was hard to tell. Funny, she thought Rosie had more gumption in her. They were on the road to finding poor George's resting place, and hopefully their mother's locket and the tin of gold sovereigns. Rosie was escaping from her loveless marriage to Frank, and that also meant that Elsa would not have to deal with that awful Pete Southie anymore. And—Elsa was on the way to find Mr Jones, the kind letter writer.

Nothing would go wrong.

Fifteen

Lily had finished tidying her cookhouse after baking up a storm of meat pies and fruit pies. Well, not that many—she'd really had to rein herself in. But six mutton and potato pies in just the right amount of gravy, and six apricot and apple pies, all in her famous pastry (that is, famous in her own kitchen) and baked to perfection, stood cooling on a timber bench under an open window.

Just the thing to tempt a hard-working man.

Goodness. I hadn't realised how much I'd been looking forward to Judah Jones returning.

She stood for a moment and examined that thought as she dusted the flour from her apron. *Rubbish, Lily.* Stan had been gone a long while now, and lately, thoughts of Jude had often crept into her daily grind when she least expected them. She knew what that meant—she was ready for another man in her life and on the face of it, Jude suited her well. He'd always taken her eye—even though she'd been a good and faithful wife—and she knew him to have been a kind and honourable man.

Over the last months he'd been away this time, she'd taken it upon herself to hitch up her horse and cart and drive to Jude's place, taking flowers from her garden. The first time it was to lay them on the graves of Judah's wife and daughters, which she had done, and found that the graves hadn't been looked after as lovingly as she'd expected. Well, he had been away travelling somewhere, and clearly his two brothers hadn't thought to do it.

She remembered Anne, Jude's wife, and his daughters Clementine and Bess very well. They had been a much-loved family, and although theirs weren't the only deaths to diphtheria in the district, it had hit the town particularly hard.

So Lily had set about weeding and tending to the graves. She'd taken some cuttings from her place and planted some shrubs of wattle around the site. When grown a little, they'd give a homey feel, somewhere to come and reflect in the peace that this place offered. It made her feel better to do it, in any case. She would love that someone might tend her final resting place when the time came.

Oh, she was sure her children would visit her grave when they got tired of their busy lives in the city. Oliver and Edward and Loretta. All in Melbourne. The boys were studying engineering at Melbourne University, thanks to an inheritance for their education from Stan's late uncle, and Loretta had a position as governess for some well-to-do folk in South Yarra.

No one had married yet, but she was hopeful Loretta would accept her beau, young Bertie Drake, a carpenter—oh wait, was his name Drake or Darke? She must check her daughter's letter; she'd received the latest one several weeks ago. Where was it? (Nary one from the boys since just before Christmas though, over three months back.) And that reminded her, she'd already started a reply letter to her daughter. She should finish it off and get it into the post. Loretta would be interested to learn that Mr Judah Jones was back in the district. She might very well have changed her tune about her mother marrying again, especially as she herself hoped to marry. Perhaps her daughter now understood the

need for companionship, although she hadn't been happily effu-
sive when Lily had mentioned Judah in earlier letters. It would be
lovely to talk to all of them in person, but visits from her children
were rare.

Hmm. Lily had indeed spent too much time on her own. If her
children didn't need her, she had to get on with life here, in Casterton. She didn't enjoy Melbourne. Too busy, too impersonal—
and the smell! (Her boys had assured her that once they graduated,
they would be working on the new sewerage system due to begin
operating at Werribee.) She was happy enough in the Western
Districts, so wanted to rebuild a life here, and Jude Jones was in
her sights.

The trouble was, her children hadn't felt she should rebuild
her life with another man. Loretta was her youngest and had
been quite adamant in the past that her mother remain a widow.
In fact, she'd been particularly irritable about it, and Oliver, the
eldest, had become very prickly about the subject, too. Edward,
her middle child, had simply refused to discuss it. Of course, it
was clear all three would have conferred. There was almost no
point once again trying to explain that she would not be replacing
their father with a new man in her life, but rather wanted to find
a companion—

No point. It only made her unhappy to think her children
wished for her to continue to be alone. Even though Lily hadn't
had a mind to heed them, it did unsettle her.

A blowfly buzzed over her pies. She swished at it and found a
tablecloth to cover her baked goods. Would it be the right thing
to pack a few pies, cut a bunch of flowers and just, well, arrive at
Jude's place fully intent on going to the gravesite?

She hesitated. Sighed. She knew she'd do no such thing. Having strong feelings for a man—and one who was mostly absent
in mind *and* body—was one thing, but to go chasing him was

entirely another. Well, what to do? She'd done it again. She'd baked and baked and now had so much food she might as well give it away as let it spoil.

You stupid woman. You should be well over these girlish thoughts. Perhaps Loretta and the boys are right. I'm being foolish.

Everyone knew Judah Jones was made of granite these days. He barely had a glance for anyone, much less his neighbour's widow. What would he want with a middle-aged woman who'd been left on her dead husband's patch of dirt with nary a blade of grass on it?

But how long would she hope to hold out on that patch of dirt? The little stipend Stan had left was only just enough to keep her going. She had her chickens and sold their eggs. She supplied baked goods to the store when she pestered them to take her excess. She hadn't had a new dress in a couple of years. She was frugal. She was careful with her watering and her vegetable patch, her fruit trees.

And she felt like a lonely old lady. Something Loretta could not possibly understand. Not yet, anyway.

Old lady. She rushed out of the kitchen and into the house, down the short hallway to her bedroom and checked her reflection in the small mirror atop her dresser. She pulled a face. Yes, there were fine lines. Yes, there were grey hairs—barely discernible—weaving their way through her fair hair. Yes, she would pluck out that stray chin hair *right now* but all in all, she was presentable. She looked well. Contained. Dignified. And still with an imp in her eye when she felt like it.

Her shoulders slumped. *What is wrong with me?*

Nothing, she decided a moment later and straightened up. *Nothing is wrong with me. I will cut my flowers, take one pie for myself to eat—perhaps two, just in case—go to Mrs Jones's grave, and the graves of her dear daughters, and do what I've always done. God knows, no one else does.*

With that decided, she brushed the flour from her apron again and went back out to the kitchen. She collected her secateurs—sent over from her cousins in England—being only the finest of ladies' gardening tools, to cut the hardy, prickly and blooming *Anaïs Ségalas* roses. Such colour, so lucky to have the mauve-crimson variety, rich and vibrant. And such romance in their name—not the woman they were named for unfortunately. This strange lady was all about sticking up for her rights as a woman—even way back in the late 'forties. Then she seemed to have turned her back on the very same thing. *Hard to keep up with, Lily, so don't try.* But the blooms would make a memorable bouquet for the dear departed mother and daughters.

Now there's a thought—the *Anaïs* is hardy enough to plant nearby. She would try and propagate some cuttings and use them for a garden around the graves. One should be joyful of the lives of loved ones who'd gone, not only lament their passing.

Under a clear sky, Lily pulled the last stubborn weed from around Miss Clementine's resting place and sat back on her heels. She'd worked steadily for over an hour relieving the hard earth of the stalwart and healthy but useless tufts.

Goodness, it's warm today. Everyone says that it's too warm for autumn, but there you are.

She watered the little cuttings she'd planted before the summer, pleased that most had survived and that they looked as sturdy as expected. Yes, the *Anaïs* would do well here. If only there'd been a nice big gum tree for shade. There wasn't one nearby, anyway. The undulating hills and plains were naturally grassy, with only a few patches here and there of tall, wooded areas.

Looking over her shoulder, she could see all the way to Ezekiel Jones's property. The brothers had a good number of acres each, but some family issue had got between them and they'd decided to keep things separate. Most people believed that bigger holdings would better survive, and their separate blocks were not that big. She swung her gaze around to where she knew Judah Jones lived—just beyond the low rise, not very far at all—and wondered if he was at home, wondered if she should chance a visit ... despite good sense.

Sighing at the futility of denying herself, she pushed herself off the dirt, gathered up her gardening tools: the secateurs, the little digging spades, a pitchfork and the shovel. She wrapped the smaller items in their burlap bag and tossed them into the cart then grabbed up the rake, a heavy piece that Stan had made for himself, and slid it into the back. Flexing her back, she twisted left to right, stretched. She patted her horse, Cricket, on the rump and climbed onto the cart.

As Cricket turned his head for home, something caught her eye rounding that low rise. It was a surprise to see a lone man she didn't recognise on a horse approaching at a walk, not fifty yards from her. Had he been to see Jude? Why was he coming up this way? No reason to visit the gravesite unless he was a relative perhaps, and paying his respects.

He lifted a hand in a greeting, and a shiver skittered down Lily's back. All very well that she was trespassing but she had very good reason. *Just who is this man?* No one she knew. She decided she wasn't going to stop to find out. She didn't have a good feeling; that shiver had come from nowhere, and she always trusted that. She gee-upped her horse and drove towards him, having to do so in order to turn the cart left onto the track that would take her home.

For a wild moment she thought he'd directed his horse across her path, but he pulled back. Her heart raced. She barely nodded as he called, 'Good day,' and flashed her a big smile.

Definitely do not like the look of him. A man who looked as shabby as he did and yet had gold in his teeth could not be trusted. She kept going, her heart in her throat, until she could sneak a look behind to make sure he hadn't followed her. What on earth she thought she'd do if he did follow was beyond her. She couldn't even reach the gardening tools to throw at him—

Lily Hartman. How silly. For goodness sake, the man hasn't done anything and you have him already a criminal intent on harm.

Cricket answered the flick of the reins for more speed, and when Lily was certain she wasn't being followed, and was equally certain she couldn't be seen by the man, she steered her horse to the right and onto the barely used back track to Jude Jones's house.

She really began to feel silly at the same time she felt gladdened and relieved to see Jude's makeshift hut appear just around the hill. Smoke from his fire rose idly out of the chimney, and nothing at all looked amiss. What she expected to see she wasn't sure.

Goodness me. Any story she would give the reticent Judah Jones would sound as if she'd made it up, that her reasons for suddenly appearing uninvited would be transparent. *Yes, Judah. I had to come because I saw a man on the track and he smiled at me and his teeth were glinting gold.* Well, she couldn't very well turn the cart about now; she'd be seen by Jude for sure. She pressed on to his house, would just tell the plain truth of it, and hope she wasn't roundly told to get along and stop making a fuss over nothing.

What a fool you can be at times, Lily Hartman.

Sixteen

Pulling on the cart's handbrake, Lily got to the ground and slung Cricket's reins over Jude's hitching rail. She stretched then leaned in the back and lifted out her basket of goodies. She stood a moment longer, practising once more her explanation for why she was just barging in on him without an invitation.

'Well, hello, Mr Jones. Jude. Judah. I thought perhaps you could do with—'

No, no, no.

'Hello, Judah. So glad you're home. I wonder if you'd like some pies I've—'

No, no, no.

'Good afternoon, Mr Jones. I was just passing by after someone told me that—'

Oh, Lily. For goodness sake. Just go up and knock on the door. He must be in, it's wide open.

'Mr Jones,' she called as she approached the door. 'It's Lily Hartman, your neighbour.' No answer. Unsure of her next move, her steps faltered. She called again, her hand on her hat as if holding it against a breeze. There was no breeze; it was just something to do as she stood awkwardly in front of his hut. 'Mr Jones, are

142

you there? It's just that I was at your family's gravesite and I saw a man ...' A noise. She listened. A voice, a groan more like it. *Oh Lord.* She swept forward to the doorway and saw him, blood everywhere, trying to get himself up. 'Oh, my Lord,' she cried. 'Judah.' Rushing inside, her basket flung away, she dropped to her knees, her hands spread, trying to see where the blood was coming from. Her hem was soaking it up.

He recognised her, reached for her to help him sit. 'Lily, you're a sight for me eyes.'

'Judah,' she whispered urgently, her arm around his shoulders. 'Can you crawl? Can you turn over? We must get this blood stopped. I must find where you're bleeding.'

'Leave me, love. Get Zeke.'

'Let me strap it, wherever it is. I can—'

'Get Zeke.' He collapsed over her and then she saw it. A big bladed knife had partially dislodged from his side, and blood flowed freely out of the wound.

She knew not to pull it out—it could cause a rush of blood, worse than what was pouring out already. She had to stop it, but his weight was on her ... She tried to move. Slipped again. She pushed him as gently as she could until he rolled off her lap, his face down on the floor. She turned his head. As long as he still lived, he'd at least be able to breathe.

Bed sheet bed sheet. There wasn't one. *Towel.* Nothing. Curtain. *Curtain!* She scrambled to her feet, away from the creeping pool of blood, and ripped it down from over his makeshift window. A faded gingham check. She shook out the dust. Poor Anne, his dear wife, had probably toiled over the embroidery on it.

She bunched it, packed it into his side. The knife dislodged completely and she cried aloud while jamming the fabric with as much pressure as she dared. With her free hand, she groped under him, undoing the knot of his soft leather belt. She tugged it off him and rolled it over the bandage, fumbling to get it back under his body to tie it off tight.

Get Zeke. She couldn't do any more for Judah here. *Get Zeke.*

There was nothing else to pack the wound. His face was grey, his eyes closed. She lurched to her feet, careful not to slip in the pool of his blood that seemed to follow up her dress then drip from her hem.

Dear God. Ezekiel's place was five miles by road, an hour. If she crossed country, maybe a half-hour drive. Rough, though. Hard with horse *and* cart. But the time she'd waste unharnessing Cricket, and riding bareback …

Run. That would be quicker.

What was she thinking? She'd have a heart attack.

Unharness the horse and ride. Ride for Ezekiel's.

She bent and swiped hair from his face. 'Judah, I'm going to get Ezekiel. You be alive when I get back, you hear me?'

Leave me, love, he'd said.

She flew out the door, flew to the horse and cart. She secured the reins more tightly on the rails to hold a now skittish Cricket. Wrangling with the over girth, she loosened it and slipped the poles out of the brace and moved the worried horse out of the trappings. Cricket would be nervous, able to smell Jude's blood on her clothes, able to feel her fear. She patted him, hoped to soothe him. She talked to him, walked him to Jude's house-fence rails and climbed up, one hand still gripping the reins. She bunched both hands in his mane and hauled herself over his back.

Oh, my Lord, I haven't done this since I was a girl.

When she squeezed her knees, pulling her bloodied skirt out of the way, and dug her heels into Cricket's sides, he leapt into a gallop, and across the yellow grassy fields they raced.

Seventeen

Elsa sniffed and dabbed at her nose with the back of her wrist. A light mist was falling and when she looked up, she could only see a faint patch of blue as the clouds rolled along.

Rosie clambered down from the driver's seat, handing the reins over to her sister. 'Where in God's name are we?'

They'd pulled up at the crest of a short incline and in front of them was a track, wider than normal. 'I think we've just shot out onto the Mt Gambier road.' Elsa looked left and right, and as far as she could see in either direction, the road appeared to be well used. Peppin had marched resolutely towards a clearing from the rough track they'd been on all day and tugged them up onto a narrow but well-used road.

'Oh good. So, which way?' Rosie was brushing herself down.

Elsa wondered about how safe Rosie'd be if she was on her own—she had no sense of direction at all. 'Left. We can go on a little further and then get off the road again for the night.'

Her sister groaned. 'Another night? How much further to Casterton?'

'I've no way of knowing that, and I'm certainly not going to attempt driving in the dark.' Elsa slid across the seat. 'Can't be far. Come on, get back up. We need to go and find a good place. Hurry up.'

Disgruntled, Rosie snorted as she climbed into the passenger's seat. 'Bossy. Perhaps you should be Mrs Conroy and I'll be Miss Myrtle.'

Elsa flicked her a wry glance. 'It'd never work.' She felt Rosie's elbow dig her in the ribs and she laughed. 'Gee-up, Peppin,' she said, and they lurched forward at a trot.

The mist was clearing, the day bright in the afternoon sun. Elsa settled in. This road was a far more comfortable drive, and their journey, at least so far as Casterton, was nearly at an end.

Elsa's stomach rumbled as she slid between the thin mattress on the ground and a light cotton cover. A good drink of water hadn't held the rumbles off for long, and the fruit and cheese from the pub in Penola that they'd shared had only taken off the edge of her hunger. Now that darkness had descended again, Rosie was sighing deeply, almost every second breath, but at last seemed to finally relax beside her.

Then she startled Elsa. 'I'll say this much, and only this much,' Rosie began. 'I've thought long and hard, since the other night, about telling you.' Her voice was low and firm.

Elsa waited, the silence growing. She felt she knew exactly what her sister was about to say. It would be to answer her question—*what other means?*

'When I realised I couldn't have children, it felt very bleak, Elsa.'

There was another silence. Elsa had never thought of not being *able* to have children, just that, even if she did want to, perhaps she was getting too old for someone decent to come along and want to marry her. It must feel bleak, because her sister had experienced it to say so.

Rosie went on. 'I've heard it said—oh, it doesn't matter where—that some women can go quite mad if they don't have a child.'

Good gracious me ... Elsa put a hand to her chest.

'And I certainly didn't want to go mad. Even though I might now appear to be,' she said, a droll note in her voice. 'I had read the newspapers—you'll be surprised to hear of more than just suffragist interests—about some stories from Melbourne and from Sydney. From Adelaide, too, about poor women, or about fallen women who have babies they shouldn't have had, or who'd had them and couldn't afford to keep them. So they sell them.'

Elsa sucked in a breath. 'That's terrible.'

'Is it? To try to save a child's life, or to try to save your own?' Rosie took a breath. 'If they sell an unwanted child, or one they can't afford, they both live for a little longer. Or that's what I thought was the reason for the practice.'

Elsa could barely imagine where this was going.

'At one stage I wanted a child so badly I was staring at just about every newborn in their mother's arms, or in their carriage, in the main street of Robe. And I was feeling very strange. I didn't dare reach out to touch the infants for fear I'd snatch one up and run away with it.'

Elsa groped for her sister's hand, but it wasn't within reach. 'Did you have a madness of some sort, after all?'

'Perhaps. The idea of it was certainly driving me mad.' She sniffed. 'I told Frank as much, and all he said to me was that there was naught to be done if my body would not take up his—seed, and that I was clearly defective. That if I couldn't be trusted in public with the children who belonged to others then I should stay behind closed doors.'

'Oh, dear God, Rosie,' Elsa cried. 'That awful man.'

Rosie took in a deep breath. 'So I showed Frank the newspaper articles, said to him that I should like to buy one of these poor babies. They get sold off to baby farmers, you see, terrible people who, if you're the unfortunate woman, take your money on the promise of looking after the infant until you can buy it back and be able to support it. When it becomes clear their real mother is either no longer fit or can't be found, they sell the babies on. Or worse.'

'Or worse what?'

'Do you remember that terrible case reported in Sydney a few years back? The man's name was Makin. His wife was Sarah. He was hanged for murdering the babies.'

Elsa turned on her side to face her sister. 'Rosie, that's a horrible story.'

'It's true, and baby farming still goes on.' Rosie sucked in a deep breath. 'I had it in mind to try to buy one of these babies. Maybe from Adelaide, or somewhere close by.' She paused. 'Of course Frank wouldn't have it. Of course not.'

Elsa heard Rosie's voice drift above them into the night sky. Why had she not known this about her sister? And Frank. 'Surely if he knew you couldn't have your own—'

'He said that it would bring shame on him to suddenly have his wife appear with a baby that was clearly not his.' Then she huffed. 'Never mind about me,' she said as an aside. 'He said that the child would most likely be diseased and tainted with its slatternly birth-mother's blood.'

So shocked, Elsa had nothing to say. There was no need to condemn Frank to Rosie; he'd already done that himself. She tried again to find her sister's hand and felt Rosie's fingers close over hers.

'So I felt like I could either descend into my madness, or try to make it so that I no longer cared.' Rosie squeezed Elsa's fingers and then let them go. 'I don't know how well I succeeded in not going mad, because here I am running away with nary a penny to my name. But I know I no longer care for Frank.'

'You're not mad,' Elsa said quietly. Subdued, she asked, 'Are there many babies, do you think, unwanted?'

'Oh yes. Many. And it makes me very sad.'

It made Elsa sad, too, and the threat of tears felt like a huge wave rolling through her, but Rosie had endured it. Poor Rosie would not want her pity. Well, it wasn't pity—it was empathy; still, it wouldn't help to cry. Those poor children; those poor women.

'Are there baby farmers everywhere?' Elsa asked.

'Probably. There are, I've heard, some ladies who look after unfortunate women, to try and help them keep their babies if they can. They house them, find them meaningful work but they too are frowned upon. They have to take their work underground, so to speak.'

Elsa suddenly wondered why on earth she had decided to leave the sanctuary of the farm and go in search of her dead brother's belongings. The outside world seemed a dark place. Either that or she had been well sheltered from some of its horrors.

'You know a lot about it, Rosie.'

'I do; I made it my business, but Frank refused to budge,' she said. 'He would not have it, would not abide any more talk about it. A child of his own, or none at all, and I was to accept his position on that and think of his standing in society. That was, for me, the last straw.'

Lardy-ball, Elsa seethed.

Rosie caught her breath. 'But now I must try and forget all of that and get a good night's sleep. I feel quite out of sorts, dear Elsa.' Abruptly, she turned away, and stifled a sob.

Poor Rosie—

But what had she said? *Dear Elsa.* Not even dear little sister. Rosie had called her dear Elsa.

The next morning, Rosie was still out of sorts, but in a different way. 'I thought you said it can't be far,' she said, sounding annoyed. She shuffled on the seat alongside Elsa, one hand holding the outside rail. There was no mention of last night's revelations.

Elsa looked across. 'It can't be far,' she reiterated, then thought she heard the rumble of thunder and looked up. Strange, not a cloud in the sky. She craned her neck to look over her shoulder and saw only a distant line of cloud, too far away for a storm to be heard. They'd rounded a sweeping bend and were travelling steadily.

Rosie was still talking. 'Well, hurry it up. The sooner we're in civilisation the better. Can't he go any faster?'

Elsa kept her voice even. 'Peppin's done a good job so far, no point pushing him now. He's got a nice steady pace on him.'

'Give me the reins.'

'No. We need him to be rested. You know it as well as I do.'

Rosie folded her arms. That proved not a good idea, and she dropped them to hang on to the cart. 'You were always much better with animals than me.'

Elsa's brows rose at the concession. That was a first, she decided. She didn't dare comment; knowing how tired they both were, niggling each other now would make matters worse. 'Not long to go now, I'm sure of it.' She waited a beat. 'Do you hear thunder?'

Rosie stared at her, incredulous. 'No.'

Peppin jerked against the reins. Elsa held on. 'Maybe he does. I thought I did.' Not willing to try and slow down the horse to listen—he was straining against her tug on his reins—Elsa gave Peppin his head. He was insistent.

'Yes, now I hear it,' Rosie cried and looked up. 'But there are no clouds.'

Peppin whinnied, snorted, and pulled ahead. Elsa tried to hold him back but he surged forward. Her heart leapt. He shouldn't be doing this, he should be calm …

The thunder increased, but it wasn't overhead—it was behind them, the rumble of wheels over the main road. Then the crack of a whip sounded and a man's yell urging his team faster.

Oh my Lord—a coach is behind us, no way of knowing we're here …

'Elsa,' Rosie screamed.

Peppin squealed and tried to bolt. Elsa sucked in a breath and held on. Rosie grabbed the reins with her, but the horse had spooked. He was too strong. Elsa had to let him go and just try to hang on.

'Pull him up,' Rosie screeched. 'Pull him up. He'll kill us.'

'I can't—that coach will kill us, plough right into the back of us.' A quick look over her shoulder and the big Cobb & Co coach, pulled by four galloping horses, was truly thundering behind and closing in on them. Men waved their arms madly in her direction from on top of the vehicle.

'Jesus Christ,' Elsa heard a man bellow. *'Jesus Christ!* Brake, man, brake. Hold the horses!'

Wild screams from inside the coach jolted her. 'Peppin, go,' Elsa cried and cracked the reins hard on his rump. Their poor horse answered with all he had, and they shot forward as the coach hurtled in pursuit.

And Rosie screamed, desperately hanging on, bouncing against Elsa and screaming some more. Elsa's ears were ringing so loudly with it she thought her eyes would water. Then, unbelievably, up ahead— *No, no, no …*

Two masked men on horses shot out of the scrub and onto the road. One with bright red hair curling out from under his hat had the butt of a rifle sitting on the bulge of his big stomach. He blasted a shot in the air high overhead.

Peppin wasn't having any of it—not Elsa dragging on his reins, not a gun going off in front of him, not a coach hurtling towards him from behind. He ploughed ahead, blindly, terrified and squealing, heading for the horsemen …

Until he slammed on his own brakes. The horse veered sideways across the narrow road, and still attached to his straps, the cart rocked precariously on an angle.

Elsa shrieked as she pitched forward between the cart and Peppin's stomping hooves. The cart rocked from side to side and the timbers squealed as a crack seared down the middle of one of the brace poles. Elsa's teeth rattled. Her hat flew off her head but stayed secured under her chin. Her hair sprang out of its pins and was whipping her face. The only things that stopped her falling under Peppin were her arms hung over the rigid rails. Then he pig-rooted. A bone cracked in her foot under a hind hoof and she grunted as the pain shot up her leg.

'No, no, Peppin,' Elsa breathed, scrambling out of the way. She hauled herself up, clear of Peppin's kicking, and froze. Her eyes were fixed on the flaring nostrils of badly spooked coach horses—still galloping, so close. Then she was staring into the open mouth of the coach driver, his eyes wide in horror, his teeth bared and white against his dense black beard.

Death approaches swiftly …

Rosie, already hurled backwards on the cart, had scuttled to the ground. As she scampered off the road, skirt clutched, stumbling, she shouted, 'Run, Elsa!'

Run!

Elsa couldn't move. The driver's black beard seemed to move in slow motion, the man's mouth moving soundlessly.

Rosie had darted back but couldn't get under Peppin's hooves. Suddenly the other masked man, sinewy, dark haired, now on foot, reached under the cart and dragged Elsa out by her bodice. When he flung her aside out of harm's way, she landed in a heap and let go a scream of indignation. Ignoring her, he ran back to his horse and with a leap, remounted. Rosie bunched her hands in Elsa's skirt, tugging her off the dirt road.

Then Peppin decided to drag the wounded cart, hopping and bobbing behind him, to the side of the road. The big coach's horses strained, and with them, the vehicle slid along behind, wheels juddering, brake locking—only yards from where Peppin was still blocking the way.

Elsa braced for the terrible impact ...

Peppin then seemed to pop off the road, dragging the banging cart after him.

The driver was roaring, and his co-driver gripped the reins with him and hauled back. They were braced—

The horses, as one, slewed to a halt. Their squeals fell to heaving breaths. All other sounds fell away. The frightened yelps of panicked passengers thrown about, and the bellows from the men atop the coach grimly hanging on ... It all stopped. In the silence, dust floated in a busy cloud over everything, and stones, flung high, fell like hail, the last one thudding in a puff.

No lives lost, man nor beast.

And in the calm, the redhead man, still on his horse, pointed his rifle at the coachmen. 'Throw down your guns.'

His lean friend swung a rifle at the male travellers. A handgun and a rifle were suddenly tossed to the ground.

'Hands in the air,' he barked.

All passengers' hands flew high in the air.

The driver's rage erupted. 'You coulda killed us all, ye madman,' he shouted, his black beard shaking, his bushy brows twisted over flashing eyes.

Elsa watched in disbelief from the dirt. *Perhaps he has forgone good sense. There is, after all, a rifle pointed at him.*

Redhead fired another round. The *boom* set more screams coming from women and children inside. The coach horses jumped and snorted. Terror bulged their eyes as the co-driver wrangled the reins for control. The bushranger flicked a hand at his leaner mate, who kicked his horse close enough so he could reach down and grab the reins of the two front coach horses.

'Now, toss over the mailbags,' Redhead ordered the driver. 'Anyone with cash and jewellery throw it out now, or I make the next round count.'

Elsa picked herself up off the ground, hopping, while Rosie still had hold of her. Clinging together, they watched as jewellery and coins were flung out of the coach, sparkling in the sunshine before they hit the dirt road, sinking into the dust, or lying in old wheel ruts.

The leaner masked man jumped to the ground and grabbed everything he could, stuffing the precious bits into his shirt.

The driver tugged open the compartment under his seat and pulled out a canvas bag and flopped it onto the ground. 'You and your strumpets won't get away with this,' he blared at the redhead. Then he pointed a finger at Elsa. 'I'll remember your look, girlie, that's for sure. Yer'll not be hiding that head of hair. Yer won't get away with this, any of ye.'

Elsa stared at the driver, mouth agape, stumbling a little as she favoured her sore foot. *What?* She pushed at Rosie who grabbed her again before she could lurch forward.

Redhead laughed, his big belly shaking. His fiery beard was visible, straggly, and showing from behind his kerchief. 'Ah yes, *my* strumpets. Thanks for your help, ladies.' He leaned down towards the women. 'It were all in the timin', weren't it?'

Elsa could hear glee behind that mask. She hopped, gripped her sister to steady herself, her breath hissing as pain shot up her leg.

Rosie was rigid beside her. 'Don't say a word, Elsa. Just shut up,' she said, squeezing out her words from behind clenched teeth. 'Shut. Up.'

Then Redhead shouted to the driver over the high-pitched squeals from inside the coach, 'Get on your way before my strumpets here go in to pick and choose what else you've got hidden.' Swinging his gun towards a male passenger at the back of the coach, he snarled, 'Don't try it. No blood's been spilled yet, so get on your way.'

Cries of 'hurry up' and 'get moving' followed by urgent arm-waving hastened the driver into action. 'No one holds up coaches anymore,' he cried, shaking one fist in tangled reins. 'They'll catch ye, ye bastard.'

'Is that right?' Redhead yelled, his horse dancing under him. 'Well, I'll make it easy for 'em. Tell 'em the name's Nebo Jones and don't forget it. Nebo Jones,' he bellowed. 'Now get that coach movin'.'

The driver cracked the whip over the horses' flanks and the coach lurched forward. Fearful cries from within could still be heard.

The younger bushranger clambered back onto his horse. 'You daft bugger,' he shouted at his mate and took off into the scrub.

Wheeling his horse about to face Elsa and Rosie, Redhead tipped his hat, which was tied firmly under his chin. 'Delighted to make yer acquaintance, strumpets. Yer done good.' Then he too bolted into the scrub.

Rosie stared after him, ducking the dust and flicking stones as coach and riders departed. 'Strumpets? I'll give him *strumpets* if I ever lay eyes on him again. Lucky we weren't killed,' she shrieked, eyes wide, and panic had her voice shaking. She still had an iron grip on her sister.

Elsa too stared after the redheaded thug, outrage fading as a strange thought hit her. *What was the point of being masked if he was going to yell out his name?*

'Two rifle shots,' Nebo whispered in a growl, his stare flicking from Glen to Fred. They'd thrown themselves off their horses and were laying low behind the rise on the other side of the road. He idly flexed gloved fingers, one hand after the other.

'Yeah. Bloody dangerous git,' Fred said, and spat. He swiped away a flop of hair from his forehead.

The sky had clouded over again. It was still glary, and they all squinted towards where they knew the coach had been, listening as it departed, sounds fading in the distance.

'Coach'll be in Casterton in only a coupla hours,' Glen said. He reached over, grabbed his hat and plonked it on hair already moulded by where it had sat before. 'We best get going if we're gonna sort this out.'

Nebo shook his head in disbelief. 'But you heard it, too, didn't ye? You heard some mad bastard yell that it was *me* who just held up that coach?'

Eighteen

Lily, riding hard as she crossed Ezekiel's home paddock, could see the happy children and the horse as they came down the track from the gate, home from school. She could see Ezekiel marching towards them, and she wondered if he always did that—met them on the track.

Her thighs hurting brought her back to the moment. It had been a long time since she'd ridden bareback, even as long ago as in her childhood. Gripping Cricket's sides had come naturally, but she'd forgotten how difficult it was to sustain; she was so out of practice.

'Ezekiel.' She tried to call, but her voice only croaked. She tried again and this time it was a scream. She waved, crying, calling his name.

It was his eldest son who saw her. He was walking ahead of the horse, leading with the reins. He waved back, then hesitated.

Ezekiel turned towards her and waved, too, before he realised something was terribly wrong. He waved his son over, then ran towards her.

Cricket slowed on her command, and as they got closer to Ezekiel, she could see the shock on his face. *Oh God, Judah's blood is all over my clothes.*

'Mrs Hartman, what—'

'Come quickly, Ezekiel. It's Judah. He's been attacked.' She leaned down and gripped his outstretched hand, but she didn't dismount. 'Can your boy go for the doctor?'

She was about to wheel Cricket around when Ezekiel grabbed his reins. 'Wait. You don't look too good either.'

'It's not my blood, Ezekiel.' She felt her panic rising. 'Please, let me go back.'

Ezekiel wasn't letting go. 'Giff,' he shouted, and the boy started at a run, the horse trotting behind with the two younger children bobbing on its back. 'Gracie, Jonty, hop off Milo, quickly now.'

'Please, Ezekiel, let go of—'

'Mrs Hartman, give me your horse. Giff can go for the doctor,' Ezekiel said and spoke to his son. 'Tell him to hurry and get to Uncle Jude's.'

Giff swung onto Milo's back, turned the horse and took off.

The younger children stared at her.

'Down you get, Mrs Hartman,' Ezekiel said quietly. 'Gracie will get you a cup of tea, help you clean up a bit.' He still had hold of the reins and lifted his free hand towards her, urging her to dismount. His face was creased with worry, and she could hear the urgency in his voice.

Suddenly tired, she slipped off poor Cricket and caught Ezekiel's horrified look at the state of her dress. Alarmed, she glanced at the children. The young lad was wide-eyed and silent.

The girl, perhaps seven or eight if she remembered correctly, was solemn, and curious. She went to Lily and held out her hand. 'We'll get you a bit washed up, Mrs Hartman,' she said, in her steady, soft little voice. 'I think you've swiped something over your face.'

Oh dear. Lily took Gracie's outstretched hand as Ezekiel clambered onto Cricket's back.

He looked down at her and said, 'Wait here for me. Look after my kids.' Turning the horse, he kicked him into a gallop.

Look after his kids. Lily took a glance down at her dress. Judah's blood had dried on it and where it had darkened, the fabric was stiff. She looked at Gracie who firmly had her hand and was leading her to Ezekiel's house. Dogs barked and yipped frantically somewhere in the background. She glanced back at Jonty who, after staring at his brother then his father, jogged along beside to catch up to her.

'You're all dirty, missus,' he said, pointing at her skirt. 'Dirtier 'n' me.'

Lily laughed a little, cried a little; the sound of it was pathetic in her ears.

'No one's dirtier than you, Jonty Jones,' Gracie said, matter-of-fact.

He considered that for a moment, tilting his head. 'That's true,' he said with a lisp.

Jonty sneaked his hand into Lily's, and she sobbed some more, squeezing the two children's hands in hers. Then as she walked on wobbly legs towards their house, a few tears flowed for Judah.

Nineteen

Frank Putney knew he should have insisted on going out to Curtis Goody's farm with Pete Southie, but he hadn't liked the idea of riding out there—especially the way he'd felt.

Bad enough now having to close the bakery door early—again—because of it. Closing the shop went against his every fibre, even though he knew he needed to do it. The pain in his chest had radiated earlier, and his arm had had a pain in it too, for a while. Another thing he should have done was get himself over to see the doctor.

Damn that—he knew what he'd be told. *Stop eating so much of your good cooking, Frank.* He leaned back against the long counter in the shop. *Now, admit it, Francis.* It might be more than that angina thing he'd been diagnosed with. It'd be a heart attack. Well, may as well face it, nothing would save him from that if it was going to happen. He rubbed his chest, wanting to believe that the pain was easing. Certainly he was breathing better. He took a deep breath to see how it felt. Yes, it was easier. So, perhaps not a heart attack. Don't think of it as that. Was he trying to bring one on? And who would look after him now if he did become ill?

'Rosie, Rosie, Rosie, what a time to have a fit of crotchets,' he said aloud, brushing a cloud of flour from the timber benchtop.

'You should be in the bakery where you belong, selfish woman, not running off when I need to catch my breath.' He looked around at the empty bread racks, at the boxes that held bags of flour. 'How much money have I lost these last days?' He shook his head, still rubbing his chest. 'You could have said you were ill again—I had no idea. God knows I can usually tell when you go off the rails. I thought you'd been well, lately.' He pushed off the bench and stood with hands on his hips. 'Oh yes, you said you had niggles—couldn't have been too important—I don't even remember what they were. And the shame you've brought on us—you won't be able to hold your head up. I won't forgive this, you know. When you come back, you'll have to work so hard at—' He stopped. He couldn't hear Rosie's voice in his head, arguing with him. How could that be? He couldn't remember the voice of the woman he'd lived with all these years. He scoffed. Well, why would he? All she did was nag.

Pain bloomed across his chest, deep and unreachable. This couldn't be good. He shuffled to the door, careful not to make his heart race, but he couldn't lift his arm to pull the blind over the window. Instead, he leaned back against it, waiting. Again, the pain receded. He took another deep breath. Fear would only make it worse.

Distract yourself.

Pete. Pete had gone out to that dump of a farm.

Come to think of it, Pete had looked a bit green around the gills too. Said he was woozy, bit of a headache. Still, he'd insisted he was fine. He'd said it looked like the place had been cleared out of all the house things. *House things, bah.* Rags and hand-me-downs.

Damn it—I should have gone with him. He won't know what's important and what's not. But what if I'm wrong about Rosie and she and that farmy sister of hers have only gone to visit relatives, after all.

He might be acting too soon. No, no. Rosie would have told him. Then he would have talked her out of it. Dirt-poor the lot of them, especially these days, and likely to want to visit the bereaved and sponge off his bakery, all his hard work—he wasn't having any of it.

Bad enough he had to support old Curtis and Elsa after the boys had gone. And those boys—lazy sods, those three brothers. Never got any work out of them, all too busy with that good-for-nothing farm.

Well, with Curtis gone, and the last of the boys gone—good ol' George—maybe that farm was going to have some worth after all. Now that only the girls remained in the Goody family, the farm would come to him. Curtis had said—

Wait. I haven't seen the will yet. Curtis had said to Frank that he'd look after him—he wasn't fooled by that. The old boy had got Pete to witness the will probably because he couldn't read, therefore couldn't blab, so there'd been no point pressing Pete about it. But what else would Curtis do with the farm *but* hand it to his son-in-law? Rosie wouldn't want it—she had her job in the bakery.

Correction, Frank: Rosie has left her job—and you—and gone. But she'd be back, of course she would. And Elsa; he'd have to put her to work somewhere. He couldn't leave her on the place; she'd never manage it, the little thing, farmy or not. A woman farmer for God's sake. Besides, her ideas were too highfalutin.

There wasn't any money there either, and it would take some considerable funds to restock it and make it work. So as it would come to him—Rosie's husband, the only man left in the family— he needed a plan. Can't be that hard running a few sheep and cows. Once Rosie came back, tail between her legs, he'd show her what was what. That he would.

He nodded. He liked that decisiveness. He liked being in control. He liked—

Sightless, his head flung back and his mouth dropped wide open, rigid around a silent scream. A colossal explosion, deep, so deep in his chest, hurled him into the darkness and far beyond pain.

Pete Southie stood inside Curtis Goody's hut. *The hell?* That he'd come back out here to confirm for Frank what Pete already knew and had told him as much—that the Goody women had taken off. It wasn't just for that, he knew—him being on Frank's orders and all—Frank needed to know what Frank needed to know. It was always the same with that fella, always wantin' things done his way. Right or wrong.

The women had taken off—after they'd put whatever it was in his tea, that much was clear. Last thing he remembered was the woozies. *Enough to knock over a bloody horse.* He still felt a bit beside himself, as if his brains were on the loose. But his arthritis didn't pain him quite so much as before—had to be a good thing. He was all right. Could still ride. Walk. The ache in his head was a bitch, but it'd go; he'd had worse after a night on his homemade rum.

Mischief women. Or just one woman, he reckoned, and laughed. *That Elsa.* She seemed the quiet one, but she'd be a handful. Had a bit of fight in her, that one.

It was still hot in the late afternoon, and the dingy hut was stuffy. He pulled off his hat and rubbed his head. Dirt and sweat tangled his hair. He eyed the room. It hardly looked any different to when he'd last seen it. A cupboard drawer had been opened, the chair he'd sat in had been uprighted, the milking stool moved. *They musta had something to hide to dose me up like they had.* And something to hide from Frank, too.

Pete snatched a piece of brown paper out of his pocket. Frank had scratched the word 'Will' on it for him. Pete could read, not real well, hardly at all if the truth be known, but he could sign his name all right—he'd signed his name on the will as witness for ol' boy Goody a while back. He should be able to find it even without Frank's paper. He just couldn't read all that other curly, flowing, fancy writing.

And when Frank got the farm, then maybe when Pete married young Miss Elsa, he too would have his future secured, him being family then. After all, Pete had saved Frank, for sure, from that heart attack he was having in the smithy's shop.

Now, where to start looking for the ol' boy's will? The girls would've been looking too, and chances were they'd already found it. Still, perhaps they missed other things that might have some value …

He laughed at that too. Nothing else of value here. It wouldn't take him long to peer inside the sad furniture, or to check over the rotting horse stall not far from where old Curtis had been laid to rest. Not too many places to look—the hut was no better than a fancy humpy. So maybe the young Miss Elsa would be pleased to marry him now. *Would be a step up in the world for her after this place.*

He checked the light outside. Even if he found something, he'd have to wait for tomorrow before he reported it to Frank. He knew the baker went to bed early and would get up in the wee hours before dawn to set the ovens firing.

Better get on with it. Better get back to town for a good kip overnight and an early rise, because Frank would want to know quick, first thing tomorrow. Wouldn't do no harm to get in good with his future brother-in-law.

Twenty

Elsa was on her backside in the dirt, on the roadside, staring at her left foot. She could feel the pressure building in her boot and knew it'd have to come off. If the bone was broken, somehow she'd have to bandage it. Somehow, she'd have to manage.

Peppin seemed content dragging the injured cart with him a few feet here and there as he found another clump of grass to chew.

Rosie was on her knees, her hand on Elsa's shoulder. 'That was terrifying,' she said, her voice breaking. 'The coach, our horse dragging the cart. Those men, gunshots.'

Elsa nodded, out of breath as she caught up with herself. *Dear God. That coach could've killed us, not to mention the armed men—*

'Elsa!' Rosie screamed and, in fright, scrambled back, plucking at her sister's sleeve.

Three men on horseback had sauntered out of the scrub onto the road.

Elsa shrugged her off and stared. *Oh no, more trouble—all wearing loose bandanas around their throats.* It was another strange thought, like the last she'd had as that fat bushranger galloped off. *What had that been—being masked and—*

'Ladies,' one man greeted and lifted gloved fingers to his hat. 'You both all right?' He looked over his shoulder to the scrub on the other side and back again. His gaze flicked from Elsa to Rosie, who promptly scooted a little further away. His stare remained on Rosie.

Interest flared in his dark eyes. *Oh no.* 'Yes,' Elsa answered curtly.

Another man said, 'Looks like you might need a bit of work on your cart.' Unruly hair flopped across his eyes. He pushed it back and lifted his chin towards Peppin, who had been grazing calmly, not the slightest bit bothered by the presence of the other horses. Now Peppin was glancing back, as if at the split shaft of one of the poles which was still attached, as if acknowledging what the man had said. The man sidled his horse alongside, murmuring low. He leaned over, patted Peppin's rump then dismounted and began to inspect the long poles.

'We can manage,' Elsa croaked, still with her wary eye on the man who'd tipped his hat. A quick glance at her sister and she could see Rosie was just as transfixed with him.

The man, hands clad in scuffed leather, flicked the reins and his horse stepped closer. 'Can you get up?' he asked Elsa. He stopped, and slid to the ground.

Elsa shook her head. 'Our horse stomped on my foot. I think there's a bone broken.' He nodded but his gaze was back on Rosie.

The blond-haired man dismounted and pushed back his hat, revealing dark blond hair that resembled a thatched roof. He stood, hands on his hips, checking the road left and right and peering into the bush on the other side. He brushed flies away and over his shoulder said to Elsa, 'Heard gunshots, and a coach charge off. Trouble?'

He knew very well there'd been trouble. Elsa began tightly, 'There was—'

'We were driving along,' Rosie erupted, 'minding our own business and the blasted coach came roaring up behind us, spooking our horse and—'

'Let me help you up.' The man with the gloves bent to Rosie and offered his hand, his voice kind, his smile friendly.

As soon as his hand encased her sister's, and Rosie was gently tugged to her feet, she was struck dumb. Her eyes were only for the dark-haired man and Rosie, as long as Elsa had known her, had never, *ever* been struck dumb.

The man with Peppin called over. 'I should be able to strap this with something here then fix it proper-like once we get back to camp.' He was pointing at the split pole. 'I reckon I could repair it, or build something new.' He patted the horse again. 'And the horse is unhurt. Should be no problem.'

'Camp?' Elsa was querulous. 'We're not going to some men's camp—'

'Elsa, shush.'

Astounded, Elsa stared across at Rosie who was now on her feet. Her sister, still gazing at the man who had her hand, smiled at him. 'Thank you,' she said. 'I'm—'

'Rosie, help me up,' Elsa snapped, sure her starry-eyed sister was going to tell this stranger who they were. Her foot was throbbing like the blazes.

'—grateful for the help.' And she was still smiling. *Rosie?*

The blond-haired man had been surveying the road. He jogged over to the other side and peered at tracks in the dirt. 'Looks like they headed off this way.'

'Yes, yes,' Rosie said, managing to detach herself from that gloved hand to offer her arm to Elsa. 'As soon as they'd picked up all the things the passengers had thrown out, they rode off in a hurry. And not that long ago, either.' She gave the dark-haired man a tentative smile as Elsa tried to get up. 'At least we know the name of one of them. We can let the troopers know.'

'What did he look like?' the man at the tracks asked. And when Rosie gave him a stare, he said, 'Beg pardon. My name's Glen Barton.'

Elsa was struggling to stand until Rosie's man helped pull her up. Annoyed, she said, 'They both wore masks.' As soon as she'd made the remark, Mr Barton then removed his bandana and wiped his face with it before casually tucking it in his pocket. 'But one was a big man around here,' she said, holding her arms out in front of her, hopping a little to balance. 'With red hair,' she continued and looked at the man by the cart. His bandana was also disappearing down his shirtfront, his hand shoving it inside.

'He said his name was Kneebone Jones,' Rosie said.

Elsa sputtered quietly at her sister. 'It wasn't Kneebone, Rosie.'

Mr Barton let out a bark of laughter. 'Kneebone,' he cried, highly amused. He called across to the man at the cart with Peppin. 'Hey, Fred. Kneebone Jones held up the coach.'

Fred nodded, wide-eyed and looking very concerned. 'He's a terror, for sure, that Kneebone Jones.'

'Aye, all right, lads, very funny,' the dark-haired man said. He turned to Elsa. 'Our womenfolk back at the camp can look at your foot. That way, Fred over there can take his time working out how to get your cart on the road so you can be on your way.'

Rosie let out a breath. 'Oh. Your *womenfolk*?'

Elsa couldn't believe her ears. *Did she sound—was she disappointed?*

He turned those dark eyes of his on Rosie. 'The boys' wives,' he said and nodded at Glen and Fred. 'And there's Wally back there, too, with his wife. Seven of us altogether.' And then he smiled at her again.

Elsa suspected Rosie could add up without asking the obvious. Her sister, satisfied, returned his stare, and then she smiled too, her cheeks blooming with colour.

All this smiling—Rosie, for heaven's sake.

Elsa nudged her. 'Help me to the cart, would you?' And together they shuffled over. Elsa perched on the step and rubbed her ankle, which didn't do anything to ease the throbbing. The boot would have to come off, and soon, and that was that. But until she knew what was happening, she was reluctant to remove her footwear, especially not to reveal her feet to these men. That was simply not done.

Fred was peering into the back of the cart. 'Have you got an old whip I could unravel, or any rawhide? I can tie something around the pole and maybe, if we're careful, we can keep the horse harnessed and just walk him back.'

'Leather straps in that box,' Elsa said, pointing it out. Better the pole was repaired than not. 'How far is your camp?'

'Less than an hour.'

The dark-haired man addressed Elsa. 'And who might you be, miss?'

At first, Elsa thought not to answer. Then, she thought it wouldn't matter if she hung on to some security. 'Miss Elsa Conroy. And this is my m—'

'Sister,' Rosie said quickly. 'I'm her older sister.'

'Miss Conroy,' he addressed Elsa. 'Perhaps if you can climb into the cart, we'll head off for camp.'

'Would you take us into Casterton where we can find a doctor and lodgings?' Elsa asked. A reasonable request, surely.

The three men fell silent. The dark-haired man looked at the other two. Fred shrugged. Glen raised his eyebrows then shook his head.

Rosie took Elsa's arm, steering her to the back of the cart. Elsa pulled her arm away. 'But I think going into Casterton is a very good idea,' she said.

Rosie kept her voice low, 'Elsa, that's a bit ungrateful—'

'Ungrateful? We don't know these people,' Elsa shot back, just as low.

'We don't know *any people* outside of Robe,' Rosie spat.

The dark-haired man, with his eye on Rosie again, said, 'We won't be taking you into Casterton. Not now, that's certain. And when your cart's fixed, we'll just give you directions.'

'Why is that?' Elsa demanded, while easing herself up into the cart, backside first. As soon as she was in, her boot would be coming off.

Glen walked with Fred's horse and his own and fell in alongside the cart. 'Because, Miss Conroy,' he answered Elsa, 'once that coachload of people gets into Casterton, they'll start talking their heads off and it'll be all over the town and the district that Nebo Jones bailed it up.'

'Quite right,' Elsa muttered. 'He'll get his comeuppance.' She tugged at her bootlaces.

Fred walked to his mount and handed the reins to Glen then headed back to Peppin. To Rosie he said, 'You'll have to go on foot, miss,' and began to lead the cart slowly into the scrub. It juggled over the stiff clumps of dried grass on uneven ground.

Rosie leaned over the side to Elsa. 'Have you forgotten that the coach driver also accused us of being part of the hold-up, our being strumpets and all?'

Elsa shut her mouth.

The dark-haired man said, 'Nebo Jones didn't bail up that coach.'

Elsa laughed, her bravado returning. 'Oh, here we go. I heard him bellow as much.'

'That may be,' he said, mounting and nudging his horse to walk behind the cart with Rosie. 'But that's not his name. If it's who I think it is, his name's Billy Watson. I am Nebo Jones.'

That's what Elsa had been thinking when the bushrangers who'd held up the coach galloped off—why would they cover their faces with bandanas, or kerchiefs or whatever they were called, only to have one of them shout out his supposed name for all to hear? It made no sense, so perhaps this Mr Jones *here* was telling the truth.

As the cart trundled along in the midafternoon, Elsa pulled off her hat to fan her face. It kept the flies away, momentarily at least, but loose wisps of her hair became annoying. There was nothing but her hat to keep it in some sort of order now so, aware of the sun beating down, she slapped it back on her head.

Mr Jones. A common enough name. That was also the name on the letter advising of George's death. The letter writer's name, Jones, would really have been his right name—you wouldn't sign a letter like that and not tell the truth of who you were.

Perhaps this Mr Jones, playing up to my sister, has just picked out a common name to disguise his real identity. Best keep your wits about you, Elsa Goody. Someone had to here, and it didn't seem like it would be Rosie. It appeared her sister's wits had evaporated. She was showing signs of being fairly taken by the so-called Nebo Jones— all eyes a-fluttering, *and still* smiling, what's more. How could that be so? She'd only just left her husband of many years. What about the deaths in the family? It was beyond Elsa's power of reasoning. Although … Elsa could see Mr Jones as he conversed with Rosie. Dark, wavy hair, a little unkempt, his face without a shave for possibly a couple of days. He looked like he was a man on the land, or at least someone who spent a good deal of his time outside. His face and neck and his forearms were sun browned, and his eyes crinkled deeply when he laughed. There was a lively look in them, certainly when he gazed at Rosie.

Elsa didn't get the feeling that this was the letter-writing Mr Jones. *Pleasant looking, I suppose, though nothing to set the world on fire.* Not that Rosie could marry again even if she wanted to—not right away, anyway—but what were this man's intentions? What were his prospects?

Intentions. Prospects. For goodness sake. A long stare at each other and I have my sister married off to a stranger.

A stranger with a strange name, Nebo. Then again, you don't hear of Ezekiel too much either, the other Mr Jones's name. Would they be related? Now was not the time to ask; she'd keep things to herself. Hopefully, Rosie would, too.

As the cart bobbed along, Fred was talking to Peppin as if they were old mates. When she sneaked a look, he'd been stroking the horse's mane and patting his neck. He'd whispered sweet somethings into Peppin's flicking ears, and the dear faithful old horse seemed to love it. And Mr Barton and this Nebo Jones person were chatting affably to Rosie. Chatting, as if on an afternoon picnic. They'd moved ahead, so Elsa was now behind them in the back of the cart, watching the receding road.

'Looks like a good horse you have here, miss.' Mr Barton's voice.

'We do. He's wonderful,' Rosie said. 'We've had him since a foal. He's getting on a bit now.'

'Wise and reliable, then. He seems very sensible and looks like he's been well looked after.' Mr Jones's voice. Elsa imagined he had turned to smile at Rosie. 'So, where have you come from today?'

Oh no. The inquisition.

'Today? Well, somewhere between here and Penola.'

At least Rosie seemed to have the good sense to stop there and not to divulge anything—

'Penola?' Mr Jones again. 'You've taken a wrong turn somewhere to end up here on this road.'

'We were heading to Casterton to—'

'To speak to a lawyer on a matter in the Victorian colony's jurisdiction,' Elsa said loudly over her shoulder. She could almost feel Rosie's glare, but at least her sister had shut up.

Chat rolled on about the weather, about the land in the area needing drains, the crop prices falling. Elsa knew about all those things but refrained from joining in. Rosie knew about bakeries and therefore wasn't offering too much, except for 'Imagine' and 'Is that right?'

Elsa was happy to be ignored. While she nestled into the bedding with her ear on Rosie's contributions to the light conversation, she bent her knee and took to her boot again. No one would see if she slipped it off and checked her foot. As she loosened the laces a little more than she had earlier, she realised that once she removed the boot she might not get it back on again. She had nothing to strap her foot and decided to wait until they arrived at camp—where this Wally and the wives were—for help. At least with the boot not tied so tight, her foot felt some relief. She tried to relax. And closed her eyes for only a few moments ...

'Not far now, miss,' Fred called.

Elsa snapped awake. The sun was low, so she'd dozed for a while. The odour of wood-smoke somewhere close curled around her and she sat up, groggy, twisting to see what was ahead.

Mr Barton had ridden off and the horse's hooves sounded hollow on the hard earth.

'D'ye hear that, Nebo?' Fred stopped and stood high in the stirrups. 'That's mad yells from the camp.' He kicked his horse and took off.

Nebo stopped his horse. 'Jesus.' He stared after Fred.

Rosie leaned over the side of the cart to her sister. 'Do you hear it?'

Elsa nodded. The hairs on her forearms were standing up as she stared back at Rosie. Mad yells—yes, they were—rolling over and over, the wails of someone in extreme distress.

Twenty-one

Zeke flung himself off Mrs Hartman's horse, threw the reins off and hurled towards Jude's open door.

'Jesus Christ,' he hissed at the sight of blood on the floor. There was a trail under his feet. Another trail was headed in the opposite direction out the back door. Then he saw the knife. His brother's boning knife, dull under red smears.

Jude? Where—

A cough. *Out the back door.* Then he heard a voice, wheezing, '*Dammit.*'

'Jude, it's me, Zeke,' he called out, sidestepping the drying blood. He edged to the back wall, now not sure it was his brother outside, and not sure if whoever it was had a gun. Just then his boot landed on something soft. He'd squashed a pie of some sort. 'Judah?' Taking a breath, he sidled into the doorway and chanced a look outside.

Slumped with his back against the wall, there was Jude; his face was white but he was alive. He was breathing. There wasn't any more blood streaming from him.

'Took your time.'

'I just knew you'd say that.' Zeke dropped to his knees. 'Where's the cut?'

'On this side, lower back,' Jude said between breaths. 'Hope he didn't nick anything important. Bled like a bastard.'

Zeke eased an arm behind Jude's shoulders and pulled him forward. 'Mrs Hartman strap you up?' He could see the blood had stopped running, and that the patch of cloth, while soaked, had also begun to dry off.

Jude nodded. 'Fine job. Nice pies, too.' He held an uneaten pie on his lap.

'Naught wrong with you if you're thinking of your stomach.' Zeke studied the cloth stuffed against the wound and the belt wrapped around his brother's waist. It should stay there until Giff brought Dr Smith. 'What are you doing outside?' He helped settle his brother as comfortably as he could, then slid down against the wall until he was on his arse beside him.

'Didn't want to stay sat in me own blood. Managed it, bit weak, but I feel all right.'

'Like I'm convinced of that. Giff's gone for the doc.'

'Yeah.'

'You know who did it?' Zeke asked, swiping a forearm under his nose.

'The dead boy's pa.'

'Curtis Goody?'

'That's him,' Jude wheezed. 'Bastard came back, crept up on me sayin' he knows George had money and papers that belonged to the family. He said he was gonna go look for George's belongings, that maybe they'd been hid somewhere. Accused me of stealin'.'

Christ. He's looking for something? Zeke had already taken Goody to where George was buried. On his own property ... Would he want to go there again?

It'd have to wait. Zeke wouldn't leave Judah, not at least until
the doctor had come. Still, he'd left his two younger kids at his
place, on their own with Lily. But if Giff got the doc, it wouldn't
be long before they'd be here. Maybe a half-hour at the most. He
checked the sky. Still plenty of daylight, three or more hours. As
soon as his boy arrived, and the doctor reckoned Jude was all right
for an hour or two, he and Giff would head home.

First thing Zeke'd do was notify the troopers. *Wrong. Second
thing.* The first was making sure his kids were all right. After the
troopers, then he'd go after this bastard himself. *Jesus, what was the
rest of the family like if this was the father?* But he hadn't picked up
anything nasty about them from George: not about his father and
especially not about one of his sisters from the way the lad had
sobbed for her. Zeke wished he'd caught her name properly.

He checked Jude again. He was trying to raise his arm to take
a bite of the pie. Zeke took the pie, broke off a piece and angled it
into his brother's mouth. Jude chewed slowly.

Zeke asked, 'So what happened?' He sat the remainder of the
pie in Jude's lap.

'Don't really know. I told him I knew nothin' about whatever the
lad had with him, that I was still away when my brother found him,
and to get the hell off my land.' Jude stopped to catch his breath.

Jude had just told Curtis Goody that he'd been away when
George was found. At the gravesite Zeke had told Goody that
his brother had found George. Wouldn't take a genius to figure
out there was a third brother, or that possibly someone was lying.
Either way, Zeke would have to find Nebo before this madman
did. George had touched them all.

Jude was staring at the little pie in his lap. 'What was Lily Hartman doing here?'

Zeke glanced at him. 'She tends your girls' graves when you go
off on your little wanderings.'

Jude let out a deep sigh, closed his eyes. 'Was she all right when she got to you?'

'Out of breath. Unhappy. Why?' Zeke jolted upright. 'Was she here when—'

'No, but next thing after I got the knife in me back, he's headed up the track to where the graves are.' Jude looked at Zeke. 'Then I'm waked up by Lily who's standing over me. If she was at the graves, she mighta seen him.'

So, Mrs Hartman, as well, might be in his sights. Zeke tapped his thigh, thought of Gifford. *Come on, lad. Come on. Hurry up.* He leaned over and peered at his brother's side. No fresh blood. But move that swabbing and who knows what'd happen. Sweat broke over his forehead. He took off his hat and sat it on his brother's head. 'Wait there.'

Jude gave an amused grunt. 'Funny.'

Zeke tramped inside, found Jude's hat on the hook behind the door. He stared out the window in the direction he knew Giff would be coming. Dust was rising from the track. That'd be his boy, for sure. Back outside, he replaced Jude's hat for his and clamped on his own. 'You could have picked a shady spot.'

'Could have. Meant to build that lean-to, but never got 'round to it.'

'Never did.' Zeke squatted again. 'We'll get it done the next few months. My kids are keen for it.'

'They're good kids. Those boys are a chip off your block. And that Gracie, mind of her own, that one.' Jude sucked in air, winced. 'Hold 'em close, Zeke. There's nothin' more important. Once they're gone, there's no gettin' them back.'

Zeke's chest expanded and tears sprang. 'I know it, Jude.' He pressed a hand to his brother's shoulder. He swallowed down the pressure in his throat. 'Nothing comes before my kids.' Taking a deep breath to steady himself, he aimed a thumb over his own shoulder. 'And I reckon that's Giff coming up the track not a mile off. Not long to go now, old mate. Then we'll clean up here, get you home to mine.' He stared at his brother whose eyes had closed, and his heart gave a solid thump. 'Jude?'

Twenty-two

Pete Southie was kicking dirt in the front of the bakery. *I had to oversleep, didn't I?* Dammit. Frank would be spittin' brimstone—and at havin' to open the store on his own. Maybe that's why the doors were still closed. He stared at the women hovering around the bakery door, peering inside.

Without Rosie on hand, Frank would be running behind. *That Rosie. She really left poor Frank in a state. He has to do all this work himself, now.*

Pete knew not to go in the front way and began to walk down the alleyway between the bakery and the saddlery. Frank had always made him come around the back. But something about the shoppers huddled before the door made him stop and head back that way.

A grim-faced dumpy lady in her brown and patched day dress stepped aside as he approached. 'We can see his boots,' she said, alarmed. 'He's on the floor.'

Pete marched onto the footpath past the other ladies. Nose to the pane on the door, his breath clouding it a little, he rubbed the glass. As he squinted, he reckoned that he was staring at Frank's lifeless body.

Mr Benson kept banging a molten horseshoe on the anvil with his hammer. 'And I'm tellin' you, Pete Southie,' he yelled. 'I ain't handing over no coffin if I dunno how I'm gonna get paid fer it.'

Pete held up his hands. 'You know the bakery's good fer it.'

'I know the bakery's good fer it, but not you.'

'The constable said it'll just take some time for a magistrate to get to Frank's affairs—'

'Ever'body knows his missus has gone. Took orf, they reckon. Not comin' back. So who's gonna pay for a coffin?' He stopped banging the hammer and jutted his chin towards an assortment of coffins standing by the far wall.

'How much is it?' Southie asked.

'Won't get much change from a fiver.' The hammer clanged and bounced back off the horseshoe taking shape. Soot and glowing sparks leapt into the stifling air.

Young Henry Benson smirked at him. 'Has to be a big coffin,' he said. 'That's why it's a fiver.'

Pete Southie wasn't real sure about the truth of that, but there was nothing he could do about it. He knew right where he could get five pounds, too. He knew how to get into the bakery. He weren't no thief, not really, not when folk would be looking out for Frank and the bakery. But he knew there was money in the till—and if it meant Frank would have a decent burial, then he'd go get it. Frank had been good to him, least he could do. He'd nip into the bakery, dark of night, and lift a fiver. Or two if there was two—to pay for anything extra required, of course.

'You have to measure him up,' Pete said.

'I don't,' Mr Benson yelled. 'That'll fit him.' He thrust the hammer at the tallest, widest pine box. 'When will I get paid? Dunno where his missus has gone.'

A man with a long white beard approached. It was the retired solicitor, Mr Milton. 'Frank Putney's wife, do ye mean? I know where she's gone,' he said and stepped up to the anvil. He looked at Mr Benson. 'I need you to make me six more of the railway spikes for me shed.'

The smithy nodded, threw down his hammer, picked a pencil out of his pocket and made a note on a piece of raw timber. 'Will do,' he yelled.

The man went on. 'I passed those Goody girls on the road to Penola maybe three or four days back.' He looked at Pete. 'Someone will have to tell Mrs Putney she's a widow now. There's a will to be read, and all that.'

Pete Southie had opened his mouth to say something to Mr Milton then shut it abruptly. All manner of things rushed through his head. Rosie would be a rich widow. Elsa was unmarried. There was money in the bakery's till to get Frank buried—and the funeral could happen while he was off looking for the two sisters.

Tonight, he would get into the bakery and get that money for this damned fool smithy. 'I'll get you your money, Mr Benson,' he said, and he couldn't help his lip curling. He turned to Mr Milton. 'They were going to Penola?'

'They were, to relatives there and then on to Naracoorte. Coming back here after that, I thought.'

Pete would get the priest fella, or the vicar or whatever he was called to get the council men to dig a grave in that fancy walled cemetery. Soon as that was done, he'd take off for the farm, then go after the women. No point trying to run the bakery, but he'd be able to look after the farm for Elsa when he brought her back. He'd make himself useful. She'd like that. She'd be grateful.

He wouldn't mind living on their place. Now, there's a thought. A man had to have prospects, after all. He'd have to take opportunities where he found them.

Twenty-three

Elsa couldn't shake her goosebumps—the person's pain was palpable in that wail of theirs.

Nebo Jones leaned down from his horse towards her sister. 'I'm going to check what's going on. Wait here.' He wheeled and followed Fred at a gallop.

Rosie clasped her hands. 'What do you make of those cries? They sound like—I don't like the sound of them.'

The yells were incessant, crowding Elsa's thoughts. 'We can't be far from the camp if we can hear that. I'm sure I could walk—'

'No,' Rosie cried. 'What if those terrible bushrangers have found where these people live and—'

'Oh, stop it.' Elsa shimmied herself down to the end of the cart and worked the latch free on one side. She shuffled over to the other side and edged down, trying not to put any weight on her sore foot. 'If you find me a stout stick I can use it to hobble a little.'

Tut-tutting, Rosie climbed down from the driver's seat and scouted the area for something suitable. Elsa tested her foot but the throbbing was beginning to make her dizzy. That would clear, she told herself, and took a couple of deep breaths, steadying herself on the cart.

The wails were coming every few minutes.

Rosie thrust a sturdy dry limb at her and Elsa grabbed it, testing again. Better. If only she could keep her feet on even ground, she might be able to limp along. She took a couple of tentative steps.

'Where are you going?' Rosie shrilled.

The distressed cries rose in the air around them. 'I'm heading towards that poor person, wherever they are,' Elsa said.

'Nebo told us to stay here.'

'*Nebo* did, did he?'

'What about Peppin? We can't leave him,' Rosie said, her voice rising even higher.

'Peppin will be fine. We'll come back for him. He won't go anywhere if you sling the reins over that tree branch. Then come help me.' Elsa began to shuffle away.

Peppin secured, Rosie ran to Elsa and slipped under her arm. Steadily, they made their way over the dry, sand-like soil, avoiding dips and mounds to keep Elsa on her feet.

Rosie froze as a man on a horse came galloping towards them. It was Nebo Jones, trailing two riderless horses behind him. 'We have to get you into the camp quick. I'll help you up,' he said to Elsa, and slid to the ground. 'Bein' ladies you know all about birthin' babies.'

At the camp, Elsa waited until Rosie, with Nebo Jones, helped her dismount. She took the stick Rosie had brought with her and adjusted her stance until she could move with some confidence. Waving Nebo away, she limped and hopped until she came to a swathe of canvas thrown over some tree branches. It created a tent of sorts that sheltered the woman crying on the other side from view. A man paced at the side of the tent, shaking his hands as if to bring back circulation.

At the sound of a wild yell, the man stared at Elsa. 'That's my missus. That's Sal. Baby's comin' early.' The wails reduced to whimpers until another contraction grasped the woman.

Elsa bit her lip. She'd told Nebo Jones before they left the cart that she only knew about cows and calves, not about human babies. He'd said, 'That's good enough.' Now she glanced back at Rosie who lifted her shoulders, her face pinched. Her sister would know even less. Her gaze shifted to another woman who hovered a distance away, whose strawberry-blonde hair was twisted high on her head.

'I'm Tillie. I dunno much either. Never had my own yet. Poor Sal's been screaming for a long time now, she wouldn't settle, so Alice went in for the doctor, or the midwife. I sat with Sal a bit, but I couldn't do nothin'.'

Dear God. Elsa looked at Nebo Jones, standing well back from where she was. Fred and Glen were standing with him. 'How far away is a doctor?' she called.

'Hour there, hour back,' Nebo said.

'A midwife?'

'Same. If she's sober.'

'Can you do somethin'?' the man by the tent asked Elsa. His big hands clenched and unclenched by his side. Then he looked at Rosie who shook her head. 'Yer women, ain't cha?' he burst, anger flaring from him. 'Ain't cha s'posed to know what to do?'

Tillie shrank away. Rosie sucked in a sharp breath.

Elsa hobbled a little closer to the tent. The roar through the last contraction had faded to puffs and groans. 'Get me something to sit on,' she said to him, no longer hesitant. 'And something I can make a lather with.'

The man bolted for a pile of pots and boxes and yanked up a billy can. He found a water bowl.

'What are you going to do?' Rosie shrilled at her.

'*We* are going to go behind that canvas and hold her hand. Then I might have to pull that baby out.'

Colour drained from Rosie's face. 'I can't. You can't.'

'If the baby can't come out on its own, it'll have to have help.'

Rosie grabbed Elsa by the arm. 'You don't know anything about this,' she hissed.

'No, I don't,' Elsa snapped back. 'But look at those useless clods,' she said and flicked a hand towards the others. 'No one else does, either.'

Rosie didn't turn, she kept staring at Elsa, a hand at her throat.

And when they both heard another wail beginning, the man rushed back and thrust a crude stool Elsa's way. 'Put it in there by her feet,' she said, and pointed at the canvas.

'Not goin' inside. That's women's business.' He stood like a dumb beast, the stool thrust out.

Elsa glared. 'Did you put that baby in there?' she demanded, hopping on one foot and pointing again at the canvas enclosure.

'Elsa,' Rosie breathed, the shock clear in her voice.

Tight-lipped, the man gave a curt nod and Elsa returned his scowl. 'Then you can damned well witness the result of that and do the least bit more and help her. Put that seat in there for me to sit on,' she ordered, 'so that I can try and get your baby out.'

He glanced at the other men, his face flaming, his mouth still closed in a grim line. Then he ducked behind the canvas, stool in tow.

Elsa heard a female voice pant, 'Wally—I told yer, this isn't good. I know—this isn't good.'

A noise emitted from him before he swung back out from behind the tent. 'I'll get that lather,' he said to Elsa, his face no longer red, but white and sweaty.

'Help me get in there, Rosie. Then hurry up that fool with the soapy water. I know he's frightened, but he's not useless.'

'I'm frightened, much less him,' Rosie said, twisting her hands. 'You're still so plain-spoken.'

'Plain-spoken gets the job done and you will not be frightened. We'll be helping this poor girl, and her babe.' She looked around. Everyone else appeared to have abandoned Sal.

Rosie smiled a little. It seemed to light her face. 'A baby.'

Sal let out another yell; Rosie dropped the smile, lifted the canvas and stepped aside for Elsa. 'In you go, then.'

Taking a deep breath and hopping past her sister, Elsa saw Sal, exhausted, was on her hands and knees. Dark red streaks marked the inside of her thighs, and her dress bunched at her waist. Blood pooled in the earth underneath her as if her body had torn as the baby tried to come out. The woman turned her head, stared up bleakly, her chest rising and falling rapidly. Her face was crumpled, sweat bubbled on her brow and her cheeks were ruddy.

Rosie stepped in beside Elsa, still holding up the tarp. 'Oh.'

Elsa angrily shooed the flies that buzzed close by. 'Rosie, get some drinking water, too.'

Rosie drew a ragged breath, her eyes on the labouring woman a moment then she dropped the canvas and disappeared. Elsa eased down to the stool. 'I'm Elsa, Sal. I'll help all I can.'

Sal, her dark blonde hair slipping from a tie made of twine, stared back. 'Pleased to meetcha, just get it out,' she said, sobbing with the effort. 'I think it's dead.'

Elsa looked between the woman's legs. She could see a small crown.

Rosie called out. 'I have the soap and water.'

Another wail started, but stopped as Sal strained, her neck corded in the effort to push as the contraction bore down.

'Quick, Rosie,' Elsa cried. She slipped off the little seat and onto her knees, her sore foot paining sharply as it bent under her.

Rosie burst in, shoving the bowl of water, and a pannikin, at Elsa. She dared a look at Sal. 'Oh God.'

'Get the cup of water to her.' Elsa sat awkwardly on one knee so her broken foot wasn't in as much agony. 'Support her under the arms at her shoulders.'

Rosie bent and helped Sal take a few slurps then shuffled behind her.

Plunging her hands in the bowl of water, Elsa scrubbed furiously with a square of hard soap to make a lather. She shuffled forward to be right at Sal's thighs, and at the next push, she eased her fingers in alongside the crowning head. The head kept coming and she felt deeper for the little shoulders, wrapping her struggling fingers around them.

Amid Sal's next agonised yell the contraction clamped and the baby pushed out into Elsa's hands. Sal collapsed into Rosie's arms and they sank sideways to the ground.

Elsa glanced at her sister. Rosie's gaze was on her, hopeful, expectant.

There was nothing. No yells. No crying. Only silence.

Silence.

Holding the perfectly formed baby in her lap, Elsa knew that the tiny infant girl was long asleep, and peaceful. Her little face was lifeless.

Twenty-four

Elsa watched as Fred walked Peppin and the cart through the scrub to the camp and felt some relief. She was glad to see her horse and to know their possessions were still intact. Fred took the horse to a tree and tied off his reins. Glen Barton helped to unharness him.

There was quiet in the camp, a hush borne out of misery.

Away from the others, Elsa was sitting on a rough bench. Rosie was at her feet, carefully wrapping a bandage around Elsa's bruised and battered left foot, the clear mark of a curved hoof on it. Rosie's face was still blotchy and red, her eyes swollen and squishy-looking after an hour of gulping great silent sobs, out of sight of the others. She sniffed and said in a ragged whisper, 'You're lucky Peppin didn't crush your whole foot. Perhaps it's as you say, only one bone broken—all your toes move bar one.' She grabbed up Elsa's torn stocking and refitted it carefully. 'It's as modest as I can make it, Elsa,' she said and stood up. 'You should keep it out of sight, though.'

'It's a damned broken foot, Rosie,' Elsa said dismissively, tiredly. 'It has no need of being modest.'

'And that's the second time you have resorted to swearing in the last couple of hours,' Rosie said, rubbing her hands over and over. She twisted her wedding ring, stopped. Twisted it again.

'And why not? Oh, for goodness sake.' The dead baby's little face appeared in her mind again and she closed her eyes. They had both just been a part of something sad and terrible. 'What is a glimpse of a female foot to anyone here in the light of such a tragedy?'

'I know, I know, but ...' Rosie glanced at the canvas again.

Distraught, Rosie had been all for removing the baby from its mother and as soon as possible. *Custom says it's best*, she'd whispered urgently. Elsa had almost barked at her to leave Sal and the baby alone. There was no pressing matter once the afterbirth had been delivered. Wally had taken that away and buried it before returning to sit with Sal who cradled their tiny child. Elsa was sure they'd know the right time to let the baby go, and to bury her.

Because the infant was born dead, there was no requirement to register her, even if they'd wanted to. Elsa asked if they'd name her, but Sal had only looked blank.

Rosie's hands kept moving. 'Still, it is not proper to show your bare legs or feet—'

'Things have not been *proper* since before we left home, Rosie,' Elsa said hoarsely. The hurried burial of their father. Rosie insisting she was leaving Frank. The drugging of Pete Southie.

'The poor mother,' Rosie breathed. 'Surely it must deeply pain her to hold that little body. I can't imagine. I can't imagine.' She looked to be close to tears again.

Elsa had no experience of these things but when she thought back to her animals, their sometimes difficult deliveries, and their reactions to a dead baby, it made sense what Sal was doing. 'She'll let her go when she can, I suppose,' she said. 'She must, at some point.' The sight of Sal holding the baby and rocking her, crooning softly, and Wally, sitting with his back turned, would stay with Elsa for a long time.

'I don't think I could bear it,' Rosie said softly, her voice breaking to a sob. She sat beside Elsa and covered her face with her hands. 'Losing a child. All that time inside you, all the hope ...'

Elsa put her arm around Rosie's shoulder. For a few moments, they sat in the quiet of the afternoon. There was barely a rustle of breeze in the trees, and flies buzzed past, ignorant of the heartbreak. 'It is a tragedy,' she said, and thought of their parents, of what they'd had to endure.

Rosie sat up straight, wiping her eyes clean of tears. 'I know I never will go through that and I hope you never suffer what just happened. But so many things are changing, Elsa. There are so many things I feel now, and things I didn't know I could feel—' She stopped then. 'I'll sponge off those spots of blood from your dress, Elsa. I hope the stains come out.'

Elsa's dress hadn't suffered much from the birth of the baby, but Sal would have to have clean clothes. Rosie had seen to rinsing the poor woman's chemise—it would have to do for the time being—and it was drying in the sunshine at the back of Sal and Wally's tent. Elsa had helped Sal remove the soiled undergarment and then assisted clothing her in her day dress as best she could. Sal had not wanted to relinquish her child to do either.

The blanket on which she'd lain to give birth would have to be burned.

Tillie wandered over with two tin cups of tea and once they were in the sisters' hands, she pulled out a flask of something from her pocket.

'Might dull the pain in your foot a bit, miss,' she said to Elsa with a lift of her chin.

Elsa took a sniff only of the contents of the flask and thought that was pain relief enough. Rosie dropped a splash in her tea then nodded at Nebo Jones. He looked as if he'd been waiting to approach.

'I'm grateful to you,' he said to Elsa, and glanced furtively at Rosie, who kept her head down, her chin still puckered. 'So is Wally, although he can't speak it.'

Elsa nodded, her ire rising. She hadn't helped Sal; she'd just sat there and caught a dead infant—what help was that? Here they were in this stranger's camp, with the poorest of people. She crippled by a broken foot at a coach hold-up. Her sister starry-eyed over some scruffy bush man and now deeply distressed by the death of this poor babe. Their brother dead and buried somewhere in this region with a tin of gold sovereigns and their father gone to his own grave, a sad and lonely sick old man.

A woman rider shot into the camp on a sturdy roan. Fred dropped the draught poles of the cart and ran to grab the reins of her horse. As she swung down, hanging onto Fred, she looked about, and stared at Elsa and Rosie. Then she found Nebo. 'I couldn't get the doctor.'

'No matter now, Alice,' Fred said, steadying her. 'The baby was dead before bein' born.'

'Oh no,' she said and shook his arms. Her glance darted to the canvas drape. 'Jesus, poor Sal.' She took a moment then she looked at Nebo. 'I couldn't get the doctor because he'd gone off with your nephew. Your brother's been knifed by a madman.'

Nebo stared at her dumbfounded.

Glen strode over from Elsa's cart. 'Which brother?' he barked.

'Not Ezekiel. The other one. The one what's just come back to his farm.'

'Judah.' Nebo turned and seized the reins of Alice's horse from Fred.

Glen grabbed his arm. 'Nebo, wait. You can't go. The coach hold-up. Billy Watson screamed it was you. Soon as the troopers know Jude's in trouble, they'll be waitin' for you to show up. They'll trap you, for sure.'

Elsa stared. Alice's words—'*not Ezekiel*'—rang in her ears. She snatched the sturdy stick and hauled herself to her feet. Rosie helped her stand. 'You have a brother named Ezekiel?' Elsa asked of Nebo as he shook off Glen's arm.

'Two brothers. Judah's older, Ezekiel's younger.' He seemed to be deciding what to do, his face creased in a frown, his cheeks hollow. Then he looked at her. 'Why?'

'Ezekiel Jones wrote to our father about our brother, George, who died and is buried on his property.'

Nebo made no move towards the horse. 'You said your name was Conroy, not—George's name was Goody.' His gaze flicked over the sisters but his eyes narrowed at Elsa.

'Uh, Nebo,' Rosie said, straightening, and catching his attention.

Elsa briefly closed her eyes. *Oh yes, oldest of friends now.*

'We feared we would've been followed and thought not to let our real names be known,' Rosie went on, her forthright stare fixed on him. 'We *are* Rosie and Elsa. Our family name is Goody.'

Rosie had omitted her married name and had conveniently removed her thin wedding band at some point, too. But that was certainly not Elsa's worry now. 'I have Mr Ezekiel Jones's letter with me. It's in my satchel,' she said.

Nebo tilted his head at Fred who loped to the cart. He retrieved the bag and brought it back to Elsa. She rummaged amongst her underclothes for the envelope and pulled out the letter, holding it out to Nebo.

He didn't reach for it. 'It's his handwriting, I recognise it.' He frowned as if he was about to say something else to her. Instead he turned back to Glen. 'I have to go see Jude.'

Glen shook his head. 'They'll haul you away. The troopers won't believe it wasn't you. Or the rest of us.'

Nebo thumbed at Elsa and Rosie. 'They are witnesses to say it wasn't me.'

Rosie took a deep breath. 'The coach driver thought Elsa and I were the robber's accomplices.' She pointed at Elsa. 'He said that she'd not be able to hide. Her wild head of hair is unmistakable, and Lord knows,' she said, shaking her head, 'there's no taming it, never has been.'

'Her hair?' he barked.

'Well, just look at it.'

All eyes stared at Elsa's head as if she'd grown another one. Trying to tidy her hair, she picked a twig out of it out. There was dust there too, and dirt. A leaf. She flicked it clear.

Rosie threw her hands in the air. 'We were driving along and suddenly the Cobb & Co was coming fast behind us without realising we were ahead. When it rounded the bend, poor Peppin took fright and we ended up halfway across the road.' She slapped one hand on her hip and waved the other. 'It must have looked as if we'd stopped there deliberately once the bushrangers came out and so the coach driver accused us of being—*strumpets*—and that he'd recognise her anywhere because of her hair.'

Fred chortled but with a glare from Alice he stopped. She then said to Nebo, 'Send her, the young one, to find out about Judah. I can fix her hair so it looks different. If she has a letter from Ezekiel, no one will think different than she's had to see him about her brother. Send her on Tillie's horse Salty, he's rested.'

Rosie gaped. 'That means she'll be on her own.'

Elsa was thinking hard as she tucked the letter back into her satchel.

'That's right, alone,' Alice said. 'There's another way to get to Ezekiel's house, away from the main road. Real easy with good directions. People ain't dangerous around here, she'll be all right.'

'How can you say that?' Rosie cried. 'You've just told us there's a madman out there who's attacked someone, and … bushrangers held up that coach.'

Alice blurted a laugh. 'Bushrangers, *bah*. What cods. If it was that Billy Watson, he couldn't hit his own foot, even if he could see it. His big fat belly would get in 'is way.'

Rosie whipped around and stared at Elsa. 'You're not to go. George lost his life here in this lawless country to thugs, to—bushrangers. Remember that.'

Everyone looked away.

Clutching the satchel with one arm, her foot throbbing, Elsa shifted her weight. 'I do. It's why we're here, isn't it? It's about George, Rosie. About his—things,' she finished firmly, hoping to convey a message to her frightened sister.

'Do you mean a locket he carried?' Nebo asked.

Elsa turned to Nebo. 'You know of that?'

'Zeke has it,' he said, his attention lingering on Rosie a moment before returning to Elsa. 'You said things. Was there something else your brother had?'

'How do you know of the locket?' Elsa insisted. 'Did you know George to speak with him? Were you anywhere near where he was attacked?'

Nebo sighed. 'I found him. Bad injured on Jude's place.'

Rosie clapped a hand to her mouth.

'Bad injured how?' Elsa asked as a fierce burn shot through her chest.

Nebo looked as if he was deciding whether to go on. Then he said, 'Shot. I don't know how long he'd been lyin' there. He didn't know either, but he'd been left for dead.'

Elsa felt her tears sting, and a lump bobbed in her throat.

'I picked him up, put him over my horse. Grabbed up what was strewn around him and set off for Zeke's. I knew he'd look after him.' At their silence, he continued. 'Zeke had him maybe three days. Doc said it was only a matter of time, nothin' could be done.' He took in a deep breath. 'He's buried on Zeke's.'

Nodding, Elsa hesitated before saying, 'I know, so I just want to get there, see where George is and then go.' She decided not to ask any more, she couldn't trust her voice. She hoped that wherever the locket was, the tin of coins would not be far away. But the chances of that looked slim. Poor George had probably been murdered for it.

Thankfully, Rosie didn't look as if she'd ask any more either. She still had her hand over her mouth.

Nebo pointed at Elsa. 'You're going to Zeke's, alone, on Salty.' He held his finger higher in the air when Rosie protested. 'And Rosie, you're staying. So when your sister returns with news of Jude, you can then decide to do what you will.' He turned to Fred. 'Get what Elsa might need from the cart for a short ride and an overnight stay.' He didn't wait for Rosie to respond before he turned to Alice. 'Get her hair fixed.'

Elsa had to repeat the directions back to Nebo. When he was satisfied, Rosie elbowed in and took both her hands. 'I'm worried.'

'You're always worried,' Elsa said, glancing at Nebo who'd stepped away, waiting to help her mount Tillie's horse. She whispered to Rosie, 'But you're not staying here against your will, are you? You want to stay. With him.' She saw the flush creep over her sister's cheeks. 'I'm sure I'll find this other Mr Jones, bring back the locket and any other information about George, and about Nebo's older brother. And then we can go.'

'Look, I ... should come with you.'

Elsa looked at her. 'They won't let you. And you don't really want to. I can tell.'

Rosie, flustered, tried to explain. 'Well, because you're much better at this than me—'

'Besides,' Elsa said. 'Your Mr Jones here is right.'

Rosie bent towards her, eyes flashing under a quick frown. 'He's not *my* Mr Jones.'

'No point hissing at me,' Elsa said. 'He *is* right. Two women in a cart especially after the hold-up will just bring attention. One woman—'

'Will definitely attract attention,' Rosie said loudly.

'Not if I'm smart.' Elsa smoothed her hand over the pinned-up plait that Alice had fashioned for her and tried to make it feel more comfortable. It was tight and her scalp hurt but she'd get used to it. She was glad she didn't have bright red hair like the bushranger's, or that pale coppery glow of Tillie's. She put on her hat. 'Don't worry. He says I'm only two hours' ride from Ezekiel Jones and I've memorised the directions.'

'Elsa, it'll be near dark then.'

'So you need to get going,' Nebo cut in. He walked Elsa to the cart and helped her climb aboard. Then he walked Salty over and held the reins as Elsa clambered from the cart into the saddle.

It was awkward using her right foot in the stirrup to mount, but she managed, thanks to the patient horse. She settled her skirt and slipped her left foot gingerly into the stirrup. She looked across to the canvas drape. No sound, no sight. There was nothing anyone could do for Sal and Wally except leave them to their grief.

Fred and Alice watched her from their own tent, while Glen and Tillie sat at the campfire. Tillie raised her hand in a wave. 'You bring my Salty back. He's a good horse,' she called.

Elsa nodded. 'I will.' Then she looked back at Rosie. 'When I come back, then we can go,' she said. *If you want to go*, she thought, when Rosie gave her a tentative nod. Elsa already knew, as she was turning Salty's head, that when she did return, she could well be leaving without her sister.

Twenty-five

Zeke had re-harnessed Mrs Hartman's horse, Cricket. Once the doc had stitched Jude and declared him wrapped up tight enough to endure a careful cart ride, they got him into the back. They packed him in with his own swag and Mrs Hartman's gardening sacks full of weeds and set off. Zeke wasn't leaving Jude to fare alone in his own house tonight; he feared that bastard Goody might return to finish him off.

Gifford rode Milo alongside the cart. Doctor Smith rode with them until the turn-off to the town. He declared he'd go to the police station and report the stabbing then waved goodbye as he headed down the road.

No difference to Zeke that the doc would report to the police. *I'll find the bastard before them, that's for sure.* What exactly Zeke would do with him, he didn't know. Not until the time came, anyhow. He'd had a couple of hours or so to cool off since watching Jude slip into a deep sleep. The doctor had arrived with a red-faced Gifford, who'd been riding hard. Jude did have a deep cut in him, but nothing major had been nicked, the doc said. He'd be sore, and tired after all the blood loss—as soon as he got to Jude's he'd first asked Zeke if the blood had been black and was very satisfied to learn it was not—but if the wound was kept clean and the man well-watered, he should be good as gold in no time. Twenty good stitches and a swab of medicinal alcohol would do the job nicely.

A relief for Zeke, but that didn't mean his rage was any less, just best cold. That way he'd have a clear head when he hunted down 'Curtis Goody'.

And now, early evening, they were only a half-hour or so out. Dark soon, but enough light to be able to get Jude inside and settled. Would have to be in Zeke's bed, but that would be fine. Was nothing to find another cot, or something makeshift, and some blankets for himself.

He wondered how Mrs Hartman had managed. He shied away from thinking that Goody might have gone to his house, and there being only a woman and two young children, defenceless. He couldn't think of that. She might have asked his kids for his rifle. Might have decided to keep it ready. Or would she have taken the two children to her own place?

Not likely. They'd have had to walk. No. It would've been a better plan for her to stay put. He hoped that's what she'd done.

As the sky darkened over the setting sun and the cart crawled over the undulating terrain, he could see lights twinkling in the distance. His place. And if the lanterns were lit, chances were Mrs Hartman was still there.

'I'll go ahead, Pa,' Giff said.

'No,' Zeke ordered sharply. 'Stay with me.' If something had happened, or if something was wrong, he didn't want Giff in danger too.

The lad sucked in a breath and edged Milo closer to the cart. 'Will Uncle Jude be all right, Pa?' he asked quietly.

'I'll be fine, lad,' Jude wheezed. 'Just damned uncomfortable right at the minute.'

'You're awake?' Zeke asked. 'Good. I don't have to lug you inside. You can walk.'

'I like my chances of that,' Jude said, a breath rushing out.

'I'll help,' Giff said. 'We can do it.'

About thirty yards out from the house by Zeke's reckoning, he pulled up the cart. Giff stopped. Cricket stomped and shied, eager to get closer to a feed bucket, no doubt. It was hard to see in the dim light, but what Zeke could see were candles burning in all the windows. He could hear his dogs in the distance, barking in a frenzy. Good sign. If there was no noise from them he'd be more worried. And the place lit up? He reckoned they were both good signs.

Alongside, he could hear Giff breathing fast and Milo whinnied. Jude was snoring, a soft even rumble, so maybe he was comfortable after all, having fallen quickly into sleep.

Nothing was moving at the house—only the flicker of candle-light. He clicked his tongue and flicked the reins lightly. Cricket took it slowly, and Giff nudged Milo forward.

Closer, maybe ten yards from the house, he saw a window swing open. A rifle propped on the sill, and he heard its bolt slide. He froze. The snoring stopped.

'Who's that?' Lily Hartman demanded.

Zeke nearly let out a sob when he saw that Mrs Hartman had tucked his little kids into their beds. Gracie and Jonty had nodded off, both huddled in Jonty's bed, after a bath. He learned that she'd sat inside the main house, with his rifle close by—Gracie had found it for her—until near dark. Then together they'd lit all the lanterns and candles they could find.

'I made it a game,' Mrs Hartman said. 'I'll replace them for you, and the lantern wicks.'

He shook his head. 'Not necessary.'

'I wanted this place lit up like a beacon.'

Poor Jude hadn't walked from the cart too well, leaning on Zeke and Giff. Inside he'd nodded at Lily and given her a weak smile. Once down the short hallway, into Zeke's room and onto the bed, he'd dropped off into a deep sleep again.

In the kitchen, Giff almost slurped down the rabbit stew and potatoes Mrs Hartman had prepared, but Zeke couldn't find his appetite just yet. He kept getting up from his chair at the little table, going back to watch over his younger two, then returning to ruffle the hair of his eldest.

'Mrs Hartman, I can't thank—'

'Stop,' she said to him. 'You've thanked me enough. They were fine, and we told stories as we made our dinner. They even helped me rinse off some of this mess,' she said, holding out an expanse of skirt still stained with remnant blood. 'When I get home, it might have to be burned. All of it.'

Even in the candlelight, Zeke could see his brother's blood in pools and smears all over her clothes. 'We'll replace your clothes. You probably saved his life.'

'Then what's a few clothes?' She glanced at Gifford at the table. He was staring at the cooker, one eye drooping, then the other. 'Young man, your sister and your brother left the bathwater. In you get.'

Giff didn't baulk. He just nodded, stood up and began to strip off. Zeke herded him to the bath at the other end of the room, drew over the curtain he'd rigged up when Maisie was still alive. Giff splashed for a bit, complaining about the cooled water, soaped up, scrubbed his head and climbed out. He dried off and, wrapped in the wet towel, silently headed for the house. Zeke followed him to the room the boy shared with his siblings and Giff fell drowsily onto his cot, folding like a rag doll. Zeke pulled away the towel and draped a blanket over him. The boy was already fast asleep.

Emotion welled up. Breathing deeply, he willed his heart to stop its pounding. He rubbed his stinging eyes. He walked out quietly, went to his room and peered inside. Jude was on his good side, snoring again.

Zeke wondered where his other brother might be. Wondered if he was safe. Too bad. Tonight, Nebo would have to look after himself.

Back in the kitchen room, Mrs Hartman gave him a small smile. She'd settled in a chair by the stove. 'I'd rather not travel home tonight, so if you don't mind, I'll stay here, in the kitchen.'

'Mrs Hartman, use Gracie's bed. My kids won't surface until dawn, and they can take you home on the way to school tomorrow.'

She nodded, relieved. 'That would be very good.'

After she'd gone into the main house, Zeke tamped down the stove and pinched the wicks out. Back inside, he retrieved the rifle, unloaded and reloaded it, and took it to his room.

Earlier, he'd pulled Jude's swag from the cart and had taken it inside. Unrolling it now, he threw it on the floor near Jude and after toeing off his boots, sank onto it. Tonight, he'd do without a pillow.

As he lay back, his thoughts wandered. The horses had been rubbed down, fed, watered and were sheltered in the stalls. He'd checked the dogs, their barks deafening; they were fine, and gradually settled. Mrs Hartman's cart was parked nearby.

He'd latched the back and the front doors to his house. Only his window was open and unlatched. If anyone came in the night, that's the window through which he'd shoot them.

He closed his eyes.

Twenty-six

Elsa was fuming. It was getting dark too quickly. Nebo Jones must have misjudged the miles and the time it would take to get to where she was supposed to go. The sun was down now, and the last of its glow was just a faint band of light on the western horizon.

Salty was keen to get going—anywhere—but she held him steady. She'd found the old track's crossroads and knew that she had to keep going straight ahead, and not turn towards the town. Was it her imagination or could she see the glimmer of house-lights? If that was the case, she wasn't even a mile from Casterton, on the flats, but she'd been told to keep clear of the town. There'd be low hills, and the Glenelg River to avoid.

Nebo Jones had said if she could see the town, she'd only be two miles or so from where she needed to be. Veer right just after another crossroad, and that would be his brother's back track. Surely there'd be enough light for her to at least make that. She nudged Salty and he lurched into a loping gallop. She let him go for about a mile, then slowed him up.

The night was still and light clouds covered the stars. If there was to be a moon of any sort she hoped she'd have a little light from it. *Gracious*. If not, she'd have to sleep out in the open by herself—she wasn't too keen on that—but she wouldn't dare press on in the pitch dark of night. Apart from sending the horse into a rabbit hole and laming him, she could end up so lost that she might never be found, ever.

She pulled Salty to a halt. She wouldn't dismount—she couldn't, she'd never get back on again—so she waited until he settled and then kneed him to a walk. She hunkered down over his neck, whispering to him. His warmth, the solid mass of him, his confident step in the deepening night all made her feel safer somehow. Her face was so very close to the only being she could trust right now. He would stay on the road, wouldn't he? She knew horses could see a little in the dark.

His hooves barely made a sound on the track. Every other sound seemed to heighten as the night descended, but Salty's soft clip-clop in the dust was barely discernible. It was something she was very glad of when she smelled the faint acrid odour of a campfire.

Oh no. The last thing she wanted was to accidentally come across anyone in the dead of night. *What if it was that madman? What if it was those bushrangers?*

She clung to Salty's neck. Her hands, gripping the reins, twisted in his mane. Her foot was throbbing again, but she was sure it was just because of the pressure of the stirrup. She couldn't even ease her foot out for fear the stirrup would drop away and she wouldn't be able to slip back into it. As a horsewoman, she was a really good farm girl, she thought, and almost laughed at that.

The farm. If Rosie was to stay with her bushman Jones—and it wouldn't surprise Elsa, certainly if the way they both looked at the other was anything to go by … How did this thing work between people? Surely if she was to go with this bushman, wouldn't he want the same things that Frank had wanted? So why would Rosie want that? Then again, if Nebo Jones looking at Rosie felt as nice as when Henry Benson had looked at Elsa, why would Rosie not want that?

A mystery to ponder another night, Elsa Goody.

If Rosie did decide to stay away from Robe, what would it mean for Elsa? Could she go back and claim the farm somehow? She bit her lip. And Ma and Pa were buried there, on the farm, beside their other two sons. It was home. It was family. She should go back. She would go back.

The farm was one reason—she didn't know how she'd deal with Frank after Rosie but there was the other reason for needing to be back in South Australia—she was *not* going to miss out on the first vote for women in the country.

Her eyelids drooped and she shook her head. *None of this dozing off business.* It was not poor Salty's responsibility to get her to Ezekiel Jones, the letter writer—who looked after dear George. It was hers, and she needed to be sharp.

Smoke from the campfire still hung lazily in the night air, the teasing wisps of it bothering her. Was it getting stronger, was she getting closer to its source, or had a breeze picked it up and swung the scent towards her?

She kept her cheek against Salty's neck, resting on the coarse scrape of his mane and breathed in the earthy warmth of him. Her hands were still tightly wound in the reins as she patted him with her knuckles.

That campfire smoke was definitely stronger.

She was hoping Salty would remain quiet and continue to wander at his leisurely pace until—*oh no …* She could *see* the faint glow of the campfire itself. *Oh no. Oh no.*

Elsa held her breath, hugged the horse with hands and elbows and knees, hunkered lower on him and prayed he wouldn't nicker into the quiet night.

No moon, no moon.

She whispered to Salty, 'Stay calm, boy. Calm.' But she was ready to kick him to a gallop if necessary. Squeezing her eyes tight, willing the silence, willing stealth, they crept along. After a time, her body aching, tense and cramping, she took a furtive peek. The firelight glow was behind them. Her breath still came in shallow puffs, her grip easing a little on the reins.

Salty swaggered along with a rhythmic gait, still calm, still silent. She kept him walking like that for the longest time—she couldn't tell how long—until she realised that the smoke of the campfire was no longer floating about her. Had they veered off where they were supposed to? She didn't know. Right now, she didn't care. In the morning she could backtrack if she had to. Things always looked better in the morning.

The air was cool, and the night scents and sounds seemed to have altered. Gone was the dry and peppery waft of scrublands and the gentle whisper of the bulokes, the casuarina, in the breeze. The air was fresher now, as if skimming over open land. She looked up, arms sore, her hands still clasped to Salty's mane. She couldn't see anything; no stars lit the sky. Tiny cold sprinkles fell on her face. A light mist was falling.

Was it an hour gone? Was it two? She tried to sit up straight, but every muscle creaked and groaned. Everything gave her a pain. She needed to stretch and ease out the stiffness.

And there out of the dark night, a box-like shadow loomed ahead, a darker pitch against the wide night sky.

A house.

Salty whinnied. Elsa froze.

Twenty-seven

Zeke woke. He didn't know why. First thing, he smelled moisture in the air, the scent of rain on dry earth. From the swag, he glanced up through the window at the night sky. Black as pitch, so maybe cloud had rolled in and falling rain had woken him.

He waited. No rain. No fat drops landing on the roof.

A horse whinnied. Milo? Cricket? *But they were out the back.*

Christ almighty …

He edged off the thin bedding and crawled to the window to peer out. At first, he saw nothing, then a silhouette. A sturdy beast and a rider, motionless.

Why hadn't the dogs barked? Christ, Christ, Christ.

He sunk back to the floor, felt for the rifle, his hand on the butt. Yes, yes, he could shoot out the window if need be, but who was out there?

The front door? No, take the back door and go around the house to the front. On the dirt, not on the verandah. No noise, no noise.

He snatched up the rifle, then thought better of it. What use would it be if he couldn't see a damn thing? Still, he took it with him as he left his room, Jude's deep breathing the only sound. The

207

door to his kids' room was closed over as he passed so he heard nothing from there.

He walked swiftly, lightly in socked feet and slid the bolt on the back door. The latch scraped when he released it, and the sound boomed in his ears. He held his breath.

No hooves, no footfalls. No dogs barking—probably good; he'd take this bastard by surprise.

Dammit—would the door creak as it opened? He couldn't remember if it did. Why couldn't he bloody remember if his own back door creaked when it opened? *Jesus.* He pulled it an inch, two inches. A foot. A little more so he could squeeze through, the rifle snug at his side.

Crouching, he edged towards the back of the house, feeling his way along the wall, its weatherboards familiar under his hand. At the corner, he stood, daring to move only enough to see across the yard where the horse and rider stood.

What was he doing, this trespasser, just standing there?

Zeke's pulse thudded in his neck. If he moved, chances were he'd be seen. He stared, willing the shadow take a form he could—

Horse and rider turned away. They were moving carefully, stealthily towards the other end of house. If Zeke moved now, he'd be behind them. He lay the rifle flat on the ground, took a deep lungful of night air, then silently sprinted towards them.

Twenty-eight

Elsa couldn't work out what to do. Was this the right house, the house of Mr Ezekiel Jones, or had she stumbled across someone else's house? Should she keep going or just bang on the door, and perhaps risk life and limb?

Either way, there looked to be not a soul about. There were no sounds of chatter or laughter. No candles burned in any windows that she could see, and why would there be? Surely any sane folk would be in the land of Nod now. A flutter scampered in her belly and once again her hands tingled. But Salty didn't seem to be worried, certainly not by her indecisiveness.

What fool's errand was this? She should have smartly told that Nebo Jones that she'd make her way here by the light of day, and not gallivant around country—unfamiliar to her—in the dead of night.

The truth of the matter was that her fear had made her tardy, otherwise she'd have been here in daylight. Instructions on how to get to where she needed to be were clear and concise. Even Alice had agreed with that. It was Elsa's own trepidation—oh, and the threat of some likely murderer who was minding his own business at his campfire—that led her to be cowering in the dark.

For all she knew, she could be in Timbuktu (although she never really learned where that was. Maybe she should if she survived the night).

Salty stood patiently.

The house loomed in the dark almost as some sort of sentinel that she could only catch in full if she turned her gaze away a little. It wasn't that big when she could make sense of its shape.

Well, she couldn't stay out here all night, perched on top of her horse and feeling slightly ridiculous. Or increasingly scared. Not to mention the fact that the heavens might open and she'd get a good drenching. Best to let Salty wander further on in his quiet way and together find somewhere safe and undercover. She tugged the reins and the horse moved off to the right. Elsa bent low on him again, feeling more secure closer to his solid neck than sitting bolt upright. He seemed such an obliging horse—

An iron grip wrenched her from her seat and flung her from the saddle. She landed hard, sprawled, her hands skidding on the ground. Her sore foot bounced and her cry erupted. Salty reared half-heartedly. His hooves came down not far from her face, which was pressed into the dirt as hard hands dug into her back. They shook her. The horse sidestepped, huffed, and trotted away.

'What are you doing outside my place in the dead of night?' The man's voice, irate and low, grated out between clenched teeth.

Hands bunched in her dress, hard knuckles jammed between her shoulder blades. He kept up the pressure on her back, forcing her to stay down. The grip on her bodice restricted her breathing and as she panted, she tasted dirt and leaves, and strangely hoped she wouldn't swallow ants or anything. Dogs barked in a frenzy somewhere. Panicked, she tried to wrestle, but he had her pinned tight. And— *Oh dear God*. Was that his knee on her back?

He was roughly patting down her leg. 'I said, what are you doing— *Jesus*. A dress. You're a woman.'

She was let go, a thrust as if he'd suddenly been burned. The knee came off her and he sprang back. She dared not move, not yet.

'Can you get up?' His voice was gruff, but gentler.

'I'm looking for Ezekiel Jones,' she puffed in a rush, into the dirt, and tried not to inhale any. Then she pushed herself onto her backside and dusted off her hands. The scrapes stung. Her foot had burst with pain, but she dared not do anything about that just yet. She panted some more times to catch her breath before she'd lash out with fists and scratch with fingernails and—

'I thought you might've been a man who's been seen in the area.' He squatted beside her, his voice low again but not furious. Just a whisper, an apology of sorts. 'A dangerous man.'

'Clearly, I'm not he. *Are* you Ezekiel Jones?'

Dogs barked incessantly.

'I am. Just a moment.' He turned and yelled, 'Itch, Scratch, Bizzy, quiet.' One last yap, then instant peace.

The rest of the household hadn't stirred.

'Well, good,' Elsa said, tetchy. 'I was looking for you and I would've been here in daylight, except I messed up my timing somehow.' She could hear herself: indignant, uppity, and scared. She'd been scared, she admitted it. This was not the kind man she'd felt he would be. 'I didn't expect to get sat on.'

He stood. 'Why were you looking for me?' His legs were mere inches from her.

She struggled to get up, couldn't manage it from where she was, and longed to grab hold of those legs and haul herself upright.

He must have been able to see a little. 'You're hurt. I'm sorry for that. Let me help you. Take my hand.'

Her eyes were adjusting, too, and she saw his hand in front of her. She was still scared. 'Don't touch me,' she snapped. She turned over onto her hands and knees and pushed up on one leg, hopping perilously but she managed it. A solid rod of iron bumped her and she realised his arm had shot out. She grabbed it and he steadied her.

'Don't let go if you intend to come in for the night. You'll break your neck in this dark.'

'I need something from the horse.'

'First I'm going to take you to the verandah and sit you down. Then I'll get you inside. I'll get your horse. What's his name?'

'Salty.'

'Salty?' He clamped his arm to his side, pulling her to him. 'You've come from Nebo's camp. That's Tillie's horse.'

'Yes, yes,' she said impatiently, and even to her own ears, it sounded as if she'd whimpered as well. 'It's a long story, but my sister and I were set upon by bushrangers at a hold-up—'

'Bloody Nebo.' It was barely audible.

'—and she's still at your brother's camp. Tillie was there and loaned me her horse to find you.' She limped along, his forearm hard and warm under her hand.

The silence from him felt tight in the night air and only a few shuffles later, he stopped as she heard a soft thump, perhaps his shin on something.

A grunted expletive, then a hissed intake of breath. 'I've found the verandah,' he muttered, his tone wry. He helped her turn. 'Now, there's much more to this story, so you'll tell me all about it.'

She groped her way down and sat heavily. Out of the corner of her eye she saw a flicker, then the glow of candlelight appeared in the window.

'Zeke?' a male voice called softly. A tired face appeared, strangely familiar.

'Aye, Jude, it's me.'

As Ezekiel padded up to his brother, Jude handed a lantern out the window for him to take. As the light swung, Ezekiel's face was also familiar—quite the strong resemblance between the three brothers. Nebo Jones was nothing to write home to Mama about, so to speak, and the older brother looked very much older, handsome in a craggy sort of way. But this brother, this Ezekiel, *Zeke* ... Elsa felt her mouth dry. His face was—

'Seems we have a late night visitor,' Ezekiel told him. 'Go back to bed.'

The face still peered out, eyes squinting. 'You all right?'

'Aye, I'm all right.'

There was a silence and Elsa glanced up. Ezekiel Jones's intense gaze was on her and her breath caught. *'I think'* she thought he said, and his dark eyes were gleaming in the lantern light.

It was awkward. She'd had to lean on him and try to shuffle, hop quietly alongside the verandah, as they made their way to the back door. Inside, she was directed to what might once have been a parlour room of some sort. Barely used, she noted once he'd set down the lantern. He lit another and the room appeared to be used as a store. But in it was a narrow cot by the far wall, and he bid her sit on it. Then he left.

She could hear him murmur to someone down the passage, and when he returned he brought a pitcher of water and a bowl. He set them down on a small table after swiping a stack of old newspapers from it. Turning to look for something, he found it in the corner and pulled a sheet off a piece of furniture. It revealed a commode chair, its chamber pot underneath. Satisfied, he dragged it closer to the cot and left it there.

With a foot he pushed a latched timber trunk into the middle of the room and sat on it, facing her. His feet were clad only in socks, no surprise they were filthy from the bid to run her down. His trousers were tied with a leather belt around his waist and his plain shirt was crumpled. Tufts of dark hair sprouted through the unbuttoned neck. Elsa was sure she had her mouth open. Certainly, her breath was coming a little faster—she couldn't seem to get enough air. But his face—there was the kindness which she believed was in him. His eyes were dark, and a slight frown was a constant over them. His nose had a bump in it, perhaps it had been broken. The set of his mouth was easy, as if he was comfortable, his upper lip under a shadow of stubble, his lower lip over a glint of what might have been two-day-old silver whiskers. There wasn't a hint of a smile, but he wasn't angry, either.

He eyed her. 'Though the hour is not conducive, a little chit-chat might not be amiss. You already know who I am. You must introduce yourself.' He rested his forearms on his thighs, lacing his large and gnarled fingers. Farmer's hands. Well used to tightening leather, straining wire on fence posts, hammering horseshoes. There'd been broken bones. One finger had healed bent. The shape of his hands was familiar to her by way of their work.

'Oh, yes,' she said and nodded, distracted as she'd been by other things. 'I'm Elsa Goody, my sister is Rosie. You wrote to our father, Curtis Goody, about the death of our brother George. You've buried George on your property.'

His brows furrowed, and this time he didn't appear comfortable. 'You're Curtis Goody's daughter?'

She really did not like the sudden dark look that crossed his face. *He doesn't believe me.* 'Yes. And when you're able to get Salty and find my satchel, the letter you sent us is in there. It'll prove who I am.'

He thrust off the trunk and stood over her so suddenly Elsa reared back on the cot. Her feet scuffed the floorboards as she tried to keep some distance. She winced as her sore foot protested.

He thrust a thumb over his shoulder. 'I've met a man who calls himself Curtis Goody, and George's father,' he said, his teeth clenched. 'He attacked Jude, my brother, a day ago. Stabbed him, left him in a pool of blood. What are you up to?'

Baffled, shocked, Elsa cried, 'My pa is dead, Mr Jones. Dead a day after we received your letter about George, barely a week ago. What are you talking about?' Pressing herself against the wall, wary, and her pulse thudding in her throat, she stared as Ezekiel Jones blinked back his fury. *Which one of us is mad?* 'My satchel. Get my satchel, it's got your letter.'

'When I find that man again,' Mr Jones muttered to her, 'he'll wish he was dead.' He spun around, grabbed a lantern and stormed out of the room. Next, she heard his footfalls on the verandah, and a long throaty whistle followed.

A horse whinnied, and she heard more of Ezekiel's murmurs. The dogs had begun to bark again, but another whistle, sharp this time, silenced them. She thought she'd heard children cry out, and then a woman's soothing voice calming them.

She waited, straining to hear something more. It seemed like ages had passed before hurried footfalls sounded on the verandah. Then he was back in the room, her satchel in his hands. He set down the lantern then held out the bag for her.

She grabbed it, frowning and indignant. Just to set him straight, she said, 'I don't know who you think you've met, but it is most definitely not my father.' This time it was her jaw that clenched. She was so angry—she couldn't stop the tears forming, trembling. She dashed them as they fell and they stopped. Her father *was dead*. How could Ezekiel Jones possibly think that he'd seen her father here, in this district? She rummaged in the satchel and snatched out his letter. Threw it at him.

He caught it, checked it. Pulled the single-page letter from the envelope and bent closer to the lantern. Elsa could easily see that he recognised what it was. She watched his features crease, shaken, bewildered.

When he looked up, his eyes were fiery under twisted brows. 'I took him to your brother's grave,' he said, apologetic, perhaps horrified that he'd made such an error of judgement.

He lies by a great eucalypt on my land, a place of peace and comfort, and he faces the colony of his birth.

His written words now played across Elsa's mind in the compassionate tone she could hear in him. The letter, and his voice just now, was not that of a cold-hearted man. They were of someone who had known sorrow, and grief, who'd known the importance of comfort in dark times. She'd felt it when she first read his letter, when she first realised how deeply his prose had touched her. How kind, she'd thought at the time. She remembered it clearly.

Then he looked to the ceiling and spoke, relief in his voice. 'I did not give him your brother's belongings.'

'I'm grateful for that,' she said softly. She held out her hand for the letter. 'Will you take me to my brother's grave in the morning?'

'I will.' He tucked the page into the envelope and handed it back to her. 'I have the packet containing the locket. If you'll allow, I'll bring it to you now.'

Elsa nodded. She thought it strange that he still had it with him, after meeting a person he'd believed to be George's father. He must have had his suspicions. But she was happy and relieved that it would be returned to her and Rosie. As she huddled on the cot, his look at her lingered a moment before he left the room. She laced her shaking fingers and she waited.

Lantern light barely flickered in the still night as she listened to the stirrings of the house. A snore from somewhere, a cry that sounded as if it came from a child's dream, soft footfalls on the boards. She breathed in its scents. Furniture polish—perhaps a lemon fragrance. Musty paper. Dust. It wasn't a new house, but was sturdily built, she could tell. The timber floors were older and shot-edged—the planks butted together—but the walls were more recent tongue-and-groove, as if the place had been refurbished. The planks were most definitely milled, and pine probably. *How lovely—a proper house.* She'd seen others like it at home in Robe. She wondered if he worked at a sawmill, or was this a farmhouse and he ran sheep, perhaps he grew crops. She couldn't tell in the dark of the night, but as lanolin and urea odours were very faint, she guessed that he was more a crop farmer.

Ezekiel appeared at the door, his face blank, a packet wrapped in newspaper in his big hands. 'This is what my brother gave me of George's.'

It looked very small, but recognising it, she knew that inside was a memory that could never be replaced, that was more precious than anything else she had ever held in her hands.

He placed the parcel gently in her outstretched hand. Unwrapping it, she nodded; it was all she could do in response as she drew it to her chest. Her throat closed with emotion so strong she couldn't speak, and a sob almost tore from her. She held on, her stomach tight, fearful she would crack and not recover.

Composing herself, she glanced up through unshed tears. He'd been watching her, and now looked around, as if undecided what to do next. He bent to the trunk, unlatched it and drew out a beautiful quilt, faintly fragrant with herbs and some sort of spice. He dropped it onto the cot. 'I have no spare pillow,' he said. He looked fierce about that.

'No matter,' she said, and it wasn't.

'I'll put Salty in the stable with the other horses.' Then he said, 'Remember, there's a madman out there and this is the safest place for you to be. So don't think about leaving in the night.'

Elsa blinked. Sniffed. She straightened up, the envelope still held tight. 'I'd hardly get very far, would I? I have a broken bone in my foot.' Her foot throbbed as if agreeing with her.

His features softened. 'Someone will help you with your foot in the morning. And ... again,' he indicated his letter. 'My condolences about your father. Goodnight, Miss Goody.' And with that, he turned, his feet whispering over the floorboards as he left the room.

'Goodnight,' she called to his back. 'And thank you, Mr Jones.' He might not have heard her.

She let out a long breath, and still clutching the packet, gathered the quilt around her as best she could and tucked in her feet. She lay down and opened the newspaper parcel, angling it towards the light.

In it was a stiff envelope, folded and clasped with a piece of twine hooked loosely over a dob of cracked sealing wax; it had been opened. She unwound the twine and shook out three buttons, nondescript little wooden ones that George might've made himself, and clearly something he thought he might have needed. Perhaps Pa had it drilled into him, to keep up appearances should his shirt be missing buttons. She couldn't really imagine that, though. She turned one of them over. Something was scratched in it, the letter 'R'. She turned over another and it had the letter 'G' on it. The third had 'E' on it. They were his and his sisters' initials.

George. A sentimental wanderer. Her heart filled, and a sob escaped this time. Next, she withdrew the handkerchief that was wrapped around the locket. As far as she could tell it was clean— *thank you, George.* Perhaps he'd kept it so for securing his mother's likeness. She felt for the tiny clasp and opened the piece. Inside was the sealed but unmistakable lock of her hair, and the picture of her mother Kitty, unsmiling, gazing serenely in profile.

A peace descended on Elsa. No tears. No lump in her throat. She gazed at her mother's likeness and let long-forgotten memories race and tumble over her. She touched the tiny glass under which was the curl of shiny dark brown hair, then carefully closed the locket. She kissed it and, clutching it to her cheek, remained still for long moments. Sighing, she tucked the locket back into the packet. She lay awake, the reminiscences receding, then she leaned over, blew out the lantern light and snuggled down.

Drowsy, she wondered who'd made the quilt, and who'd stored it so lovingly with rosemary and lavender and another spicy scent she couldn't identify. Restless throughout the night, whenever she rolled over, the scent of it brought the picture of Ezekiel Jones's face—when he'd stared at her under the lantern light by his brother's window.

Zeke lay down on the swag again, reached over, lifted the lantern glass and blew out the wick. Darkness engulfed him. He'd had to leave the spare room quickly. He was feeling things that had been long gone, that were now unfamiliar. It made him uncertain.

Elsa Goody smelled of horse, musky, grassy, of leather and dust, and beneath that, her own scent, an ambrosia sweet on her skin, and elusive. He took a deep breath, trying to capture the memory. She'd felt all woman when his hands had slid down her legs seeking a hidden weapon. There was no gun—the weapon had been the surprise of her.

He bet her smile would be as wide as sunshine—if he ever saw her smile. And those eyes of hers, staring at him, at first fearful—he couldn't blame her for that—then angry, and wide, challenging everything he said.

Being the boy's sister, she'd have to learn everything they could relate to her. He'd given her the packet of his belongings. He'd take her to his grave as soon as he could. She'd have to meet Jude.

Damn. There was Mrs Hartman to look after. The kids would help. Maybe he should keep them away from school because of this imposter Curtis Goody on the loose. Who knew what the man would try?

He turned on his side, away from Jude's soft rumbles. His brother seemed comfortable, and out of danger from the knife wound.

But his thoughts wouldn't let him sleep. There was a woman on his mind, a woman with a forthright stare, a proud stance despite a broken foot, and a clear and bright confidence in her speech. A capable woman.

A woman with a supple, strong body. Younger than he, but not immature. A woman to whom he'd responded—on a deeper level than just the obvious (to him, at least), and one who looked as if she'd felt it, too.

Oh sure, his cock was responding, and thank Christ it was—meant he wasn't dead to the pleasures of the world, but he was too tired, and that could wait. He rolled on his back again, closed his eyes and slept.

Twenty-nine

Elsa could feel the flutter on her lashes. What was that? She was asleep, wasn't she? And yet, it was a breath ... It was someone, or something was breathing, steady and low. Close to her face.

No light had crept under her eyelids. No sounds had pricked her ears. Frozen in place, not daring to move, she tried desperately to remember where she was. *Rosemary. Lavender.* Oh yes. Ezekiel Jones's house.

She made a noise. If it was some animal, a dog perhaps, staring down at her, maybe it would scurry away.

'Oh good,' a child's voice said. 'Pa said not to wake you, but I brung you some tea.' It was a lispy whisper. 'I didn't wake you, did I? I'll get in trouble 'cos I'm not allowed to be in here.'

A child's voice. Elsa cranked open one eye and found she was face-to-face with a young boy whose big brown eyes were studying her. He had a tin cup in one hand, steam was rising from it. 'No, you didn't wake me,' she said, her whisper as quiet as his. The moment her eyes had opened, her foot began to throb.

'Then you better hurry up and drink the tea. I have to go to school.' He stayed close, reached out, and stroked her cheek with his other hand. 'You're real.'

'I am real,' she said and struggled to sit up, tangled as she was in the quilt.

'Will you be here when we come back from school?' he asked, still very close to her face.

There was no mistaking whose child this was. He was Ezekiel Jones's son, that was very clear. The boy was as alike to his father as peas in a pod, right down to the line of his jaw, the colour of his eyes, even the tilt of his head. The resemblance was strong to Nebo Jones, as well, but there was no mistaking whose child he was. But there was another dimension there. Not all Ezekiel. The boy's mother would have made her mark on him, possibly the deep dimple in one cheek.

The boy's mother. The female voice she'd heard murmur last night. No doubt Elsa would meet her soon. *So better be quick to put those stupid thoughts from last night out of your stupid head.* She squeezed her scratchy, dry eyes shut and open again. Barely made any difference.

'Will you be here?' he repeated, insistent.

Elsa couldn't see herself leaving today. 'Today I should be here. Tomorrow I might have to go.'

'What's your name?' He still whispered and thrust the cup at her.

'Elsa,' she said and took the cup before the contents landed in her lap. 'What's yours?'

Nose to her nose, 'Jonty,' he said.

'Pleased to meet you, Jonty.'

An older woman peeked around the open door. 'There you are, Jonty Jones. Did you wake the lady?'

'He didn't wake me,' Elsa said in a rush. *Goodness, Mr Jones's wife looks much older than I expected.* She put down the tea and swung her legs off the cot. The throbbing foot didn't let up.

'Come along, young man,' the woman said. 'We'll get you something to eat before school.'

Jonty scuttled out. 'Bye, Elsa.'

The woman stood in the doorway. Her dress was splotched at the hem, as if she'd stood in a puddle, and there were dark smudges on the bodice. She smiled, and her face creased into soft lines and deep wrinkles at her eyes that suggested to Elsa perhaps this woman might have been Jonty's grandmother, and not his mother.

She glanced down at Elsa's bandaged foot. When Elsa looked at it, she was dismayed to see how dirty it had become. 'Oh gracious. That looks awful.'

'The children are having their breakfast, so I've come to take you to the privy and to help you bathe and dress.'

'Thank you, Mrs Jones,' Elsa said automatically. *May as well get that over and done with.* She felt her face warm despite her best intentions.

'My dear, my name is Lily Hartman. Mrs Hartman. I was also a guest of the Joneses last night. It seems we have a houseful of people, three of whom don't usually reside here.'

Not Jonty's mother.

'And for your information, both Messrs Jones are wid—'

Yells and shouts, erupting in an argument, were coming from another room. They were children's voices. A deep grumble from a man followed and the shouts quietened to indignant protests of who was to blame for what. Another deep grumble and there was silence, followed by the stomping of feet as someone left the house.

For a long moment it had all been music to Elsa's ears.

'Are you feeling quite all right?' Mrs Hartman asked.

'Yes, I am. I was just listening to sounds I haven't heard for a very long time.' She put her good foot on the floor. 'I'm Elsa Goody. I had come looking for Mr Jones but got lost in the night.'

'Well, clearly you found him, and it's certainly all very intriguing. Not to mention nasty, I imagine,' Mrs Hartman said, pointing at Elsa's foot. 'Can you walk at all on that?'

'A bone is broken, I think. I can hop and shuffle, and I had a stick somewhere that helped me.'

'I'll see if someone can fashion a set of crutches for you. Shouldn't be difficult for the strapping farm men around here, or at least the healthy one, that is. Come along, let's get you moving. No sense using that thing if you don't have to.' She tilted her head at the commode chair.

On Mrs Hartman's arm, Elsa managed to hobble out of the room, past two other rooms along a short hallway, and outside to the privy. Afterwards she hopped and limped to the cookhouse and Mrs Hartman sat her in a chair. The children appeared to have gone and the silence was pronounced.

At the stove, slicing a chunk of fresh damper from the fragrant loaf, Mrs Hartman said, 'Mr Jones has taken his children to the gate on their way to school. There'll be time for you to have a quick bath,' she said and pointed to a drawn curtain at the end of the room, 'and to wash some of the dust and dirt off you.' She pushed the plate with damper and jam on it to Elsa. 'Put something in your stomach first, dear.'

'I really must speak to Mr Jones,' Elsa started, tearing off a piece of damper and dabbing it into the jam, a dark fragrant berry of some sort.

'He'll be back shortly.' She smoothed her hands over her already neat hair, tied back into a sensible bun. 'I was to go home myself this morning, escorted by the children, but your arrival last night seems to have changed the plans.'

'What do you mean?' Another bite was halfway to Elsa's mouth.

'Mr Jones—Ezekiel, that is—says it mightn't be safe for me to return home just yet, and now with you here, I am to be a—companion for you, and you for me I suspect. There is another Mr Jones here, recuperating, you see.'

Elsa took the mouthful, chewed and swallowed as Mrs Hartman brought another cup filled with hot tea. 'Mr Judah Jones?'

'That's right.' Mrs Hartman smartly turned away, gathering used dishes to take to the deep washbowl on the bench.

Elsa stared down at the woman's dress. 'Is that blood all over your hem?'

'Judah's blood. I found him early yesterday after that man had attacked him.' She put a hand on the small of her back, stretched, and a breathy groan escaped.

'Oh.' Elsa stared at Mrs Hartman's ramrod straight back. 'That's terrible for you. Are you all right?'

'I'm a bit creaky today. I had a long gallop bareback yesterday coming for Ezekiel's help. Out of practice.' Mrs Hartman turned and smiled at her. 'More terrible for poor Judah but he's well enough, considering. Now, if you're finished that mouthful, let's get you into the bath—there's a towel for you on the chair—and then I must get onto some chores around here if I'm to be useful.'

Elsa slid carefully into the shallow bath, but not before Mrs Hartman had insisted she divest herself of everything, her dress, her chemise and her smalls. At first Elsa protested. Not only because she'd be naked, but she'd have nothing to wear afterwards. She had smalls in the satchel; it's just that her chemise was in a very sad state, patched and stitched together. An embarrassment, but who'd have thought it would ever be seen by anyone else?

'Hmm.' Mrs Hartman held it up. 'I'm not sure this would survive a good washing but we'll have to try. In this weather it'll dry in a jiffy. I'll sponge off your dress, Miss Goody, and that will have to do.'

From behind the curtain, Elsa soaped up quickly in the bath. 'Please don't go to too much trouble, Mrs Hartman. I'll be gone from here as soon as I have the information—' She stopped.

Information for Nebo was one thing, information about George was another.

'Information?'

'About my brother, George,' she finished.

'Well, you'll need decent clothes to gather that information, and I won't be—'

Wild yells erupted once again and barking dogs joined the cacophony as Elsa heard the door open.

'Dogs, get out of it,' a loud male voice commanded. 'And you boys, go tie them up. Calm yourselves, and stop needling Gracie. Mrs Hartman, I had a sudden feeling that I should like my children home today, after all. So here we are, back again, right or wrong. You'll have an army to help you with the chores.'

The groans of protest from his children made Elsa smile.

'Out of the kitchen, children. Out, out, out.' Mrs Hartman made shooing noises. 'And you, too, Mr Jones.' After a moment of silence, she said, 'Miss Goody is taking a bath.'

'Oh. Right,' Mr Jones said.

Elsa heard all the voices fade and the door shut, and she slid deeper into the bath. She pulled at the tough leather ties and the pins that bound the taut plait and released her hair. Oh, the relief. Scrubbing her fingers on her scalp, the tension eased. Her hair had always been a pain, always a bother. She finger-combed it before dunking her head. Washing it with the soap Mrs Hartman had provided and rinsing sudsy water with fresh from a pitcher within reach, she squeezed out excess water. Hauling herself out of the bath to the chair she finished off with the towel. Her hair would take ages to dry; nothing to do about that but wait.

Now, there was only one problem. The satchel carrying her clean smalls was in the room in which she'd slept, and no Mrs Hartman in sight. She'd just have to wait behind the curtain, while wrapped in the light, damp towel.

Thirty

As Lily stood outside the kitchen room, her arms draped with Elsa's clothes, she listened to Ezekiel explain, his hat in his hand. He certainly had a nice way about him and had a twinkle in his eye, unlike serious Judah. The other brother, Nebo, well, he just seemed to have a chip on his shoulder, always seemed a bit surly. Ezekiel's voice was low and calm.

'I got nearly to the gate and then I began to worry that if that fella with the knife was still around, my kids might be in danger. So I turned poor Milo around and came back. Would you stay another day or two longer than I asked? Of course, not to alarm you, but it might be for your own safety as well.'

A little disappointed, Lily resisted looking down at her own dirty clothes. 'I was hoping to get some fresh clothes but if you think it best—'

'I'll accompany you to your place for whatever you might need. Jude can look after things for a couple of hours, and Miss Goody is here too. I'm sure she might stay until at least you can get something to …' He faltered and waved a hand vaguely at her blood-stained clothes.

'Oh yes, a relief to get clean clothes, and something for Miss Goody as well.' She paused and looked at him. 'I have left her in the cookhouse so no one is to go there until I say so.'

He raised his eyebrows but only said, 'Understood.'

'And Mr Jones will need his bandage changed.'

'I can do that.'

Lily nodded. 'I'll need to wash the old one. And now, where is your copper for laundry, Mr Jones?' She held up Elsa's dress.

He ruffled his hair and replaced his hat. 'Nothing so grand here, Mrs Hartman. I just boil water on the stove and it all gets done in the bathtub when I can get to it.' He turned to go. 'I'd prefer to get you to your place and back again as soon as I can.'

Lily looked at the chemise and the dress over her arm. 'In that case, I'll have to tend to this straight away.'

'I'll get Gracie. Direct her for anything you want done. If you're ready now, I'll saddle up our horses.' He shouted for his daughter. 'Gracie, Mrs Hartman needs your help here.'

He's very insistent. Lily walked back to the kitchen. 'Are you decent, dear?' she called to Elsa behind the curtain. 'We need to do this laundry in here, apparently. Goodness knows why the man hasn't built a lean-to for a copper. Three children to deal with, and he washes in the bathtub.'

'I'm wrapped in the towel, Mrs Hartman.'

Oh, so lovely to be looking after a young woman again. I do miss Loretta. Lily drew aside the curtain and took in Elsa's wild mass of drying hair, the swollen and bruised foot, and the thin damp towel. 'If you will, sponge off your dress here, then slip it on for the day. We'll get to your chemise now, once I have the water heated.'

'I have clean smalls in the satchel in the room I slept in if some-one would—'

'Hello, Mrs Hartman.'

At the young voice, Lily turned. 'Ah, Gracie. Would you go to the room Miss Goody slept in and bring her satchel?'

Gracie was staring at Elsa. 'Good morning, Miss Goody,' she said, her dark eyes clear and bright. 'I'm pleased to meet you.'

'Good morning, Gracie. I'm pleased to meet you, too.'

'Go along now,' Mrs Hartman said to the girl. 'And hurry back.' *And a houseful of children to look after. Oh, my poor heart has missed this.*

Gracie turned her gaze to Lily and nodded before leaving, a small smile on her usually solemn face.

Lily found a clean rag from the drawer in the hutch and shook it before dunking it in a bowl of water, squeezing out a little moisture and handing it to Elsa. 'Just the immediate needs, and I'll empty the bath and refill it to wash your chemise.'

'I wish I could help. I'm not used to being an invalid.'

'With that foot, dear,' Mrs Hartman said, pointing at it, 'I don't think you'll be doing too much on it for a couple of days at least. Even with crutches, you'll have to rest it. I'll re-bandage it shortly.'

She heaved a pot, heavy with water, onto the stove, and stoked the oven beneath, deciding that the chemise could be washed here, not in the bathtub. Before she and Ezekiel got on their way to her place, she would ask Gracie to empty the bath.

Such a delight to be useful again, to have a family to—

Thoughts of Judah Jones—and that they'd both been under the very same roof last evening—invaded her mind and crowded other sensible thoughts into a corner. *Now, now, Lily Hartman.* She shook herself. *Just put a stop to that before you* lose *your mind, silly woman.*

She dunked Elsa's thin and patched garment in the lukewarm water and, sudsing with the soap Elsa had used, she tried to start a conversation.

'I have a daughter about your age,' she said.

'I'm twenty-four,' Elsa offered.

That surprised Lily. 'Oh, in that case, my Loretta is younger, and is my youngest, she's nineteen. She's working in Melbourne city for well-to-do folk. She should be married too, soon, I think.'

The young woman nodded, sponging at the armpits of her dress.

So, Miss Elsa is clearly not a talker, Lily decided. *No matter.* She went on. 'And I have two sons. Oliver, he's the eldest and Edward, he's the middle child. They're also working in the city.'

The young woman looked up. 'Your sons don't live here?'

'Gracious, no. They're in Melbourne too,' Lily replied, but felt the little thud in her chest as the emotion of missing them, all three of her children, swept through her. 'They have an education to get.'

'Education,' Elsa repeated softly, her head bent over her dress.

'They're doing well, by all accounts, which I might add, are few and far between. Still, you can't expect sons to keep their mothers informed of what they're doing.' *Or a daughter.*

'I should think it only a kindness,' Elsa said. 'If not a duty.'

Lily felt colour rise in her cheeks. 'They do their best, I'm sure,' she said, and even to her ears it sounded like an excuse.

'They mustn't realise what it's like to lose their parents, and how they'd miss them if ...'

Lily heard the young woman's voice waver. 'They lost their father, some years ago. But none of my children are sentimental in that way,' she said and suddenly believed the truth of it.

'It's not sentimental.' Elsa's voice was very quiet.

Lily rinsed the chemise one last time and wrung it out as best she could. 'I'll be right back.' Stepping outside with the wet chemise and towel over her arm, she saw Gracie returning with the satchel held tight in her skinny little arms. 'Here, my dear. I'll take the bag. Would you hang these out in the sunniest place? And make sure they can't fall into the dirt.'

'Yes, Mrs Hartman.' Gracie handed over the satchel and took the wet laundry.

Ezekiel came out of the house with a handful of bandages. From what Lily could see, they were only lightly soiled on the spot where Judah's wound would have been. He was heading for the cookhouse.

Lily stepped in his path. 'I'll have that, Mr Jones,' she said, taking the pile of cotton gauze from his hands and slapping it on top of Elsa's bag. 'I won't be long and then we can go.'

Ezekiel shook his head. 'Mrs Hartman—'

'Just a little more time.' She turned with her arms full and marched back into the kitchen.

From the satchel, Elsa pulled out a pair of knickers, creased and dusty, and shook them, then reached in and brought forth a camisole in the same condition. 'These will do perfectly well under my day dress, Mrs Hartman,' she said.

'We can re-use your bandage for your foot, but I will have to wash Mr Jones's.' She stood for a moment. 'I wonder if there's more of his things to wash.' She turned to Elsa. 'Are you all right to dress yourself, dear?'

'Yes, there are only a few buttons on my dress. I can manage it.'

'Good. I must go to Mr Jones. Mr Judah, that is.'

Oh, it feels so good to have such purpose. She walked smartly back to the house. *Mr Ezekiel is waiting patiently, the dear man. And once returned from getting fresh clothes for myself, I can set to and bake for the family. Goodness knows, there's hardly anything here for all of us to eat. I can gather eggs from home, and the last of my bake from the other day—*

She found herself at the door of the room which Judah occupied. Her heart leapt. Surely that was a good sign—the warm thrills cascading in her belly. She knocked, heard him invite her in with a curt, 'Yes?' So, in she went, her breath in her throat.

Standing in the open doorway, she said, 'Mr Jones. I'm so glad to see you well.' Though he did look a bit pasty. She clasped her hands in front of her to prevent them fluttering to her hair. He wore no shirt, and a thin spread of dark hair, sprinkled with silver, spread across his chest and trailed down to where it met a thick swathe of bandage, wrapped low and firmly around his hips.

'Well as can be, Mrs Hartman.' Gruff, of course. *Of course, he was.* He was Judah Jones. 'All thanks to you gettin' to my brother in a hurry.' He glanced at her. Then looked away. The stubble on his cheeks and jaw was very much greyer than the hair on his head. And he might need a shave soon. It had been some time since she'd helped a man shave …

He was propped on his side, and pillows and blankets had been pushed around him to keep him off his wound. It looked as if Ezekiel had done a reasonable job of the bandage, and she found herself trying not to look at where it was almost covered by the bed linens. He was lean, this Mr Jones, but not thin, like Stan had been. This was a muscled man, well used to manual labour.

Remembering the reason for being in his room, she said, 'I came to see if you needed anything. Your shirt washed, or—'

'No,' he said sharply, then added, 'thank you.'

'Perhaps you'd like some tea,' she said, hopeful.

'Zeke brought tea,' he answered and nodded towards the pannikin on the bedside table.

'Bread and jam? Or eggs perhaps?' she asked and at his hesitation, at last felt she had made a breakthrough. Food. *Time to take charge, Lily Hartman.* 'I'll bring breakfast.'

'No.' He set his mouth. 'No need to wait on me.'

All right, no breakfast. 'Mr Jones, I'm sure your brother would've told you of another visitor in the night,' she went on. 'Another invalid, as it turns out. Would you know how to make a pair of crutches, perhaps to instruct young Gifford?' she asked firmly, her hands now quite still as they laced in front of her.

He cleared his throat and glanced again. 'I would.'

'Right. I shall send him in.' She swept to the chair beside his bed, stepping over a swag on the floor. She retrieved his discarded, torn shirt, caked with blood. 'Ezekiel and I are going to my home now so that I might change out of these clothes,' she said and gestured at her own blood-stained apparel. *His* blood, she was reminding him.

Judah moved a little uncomfortably under her stare. 'Aye. Very good.'

Aye, very good. He can be uneasy all he likes. 'I presume one of your brother's shirts would fit you,' she went on, 'as I don't believe we will be visiting your house on this particular trip to bring anything of your own.'

It seemed he had nothing to say to that. He nodded. At least this time, his gaze, moody and dark, connected with hers for a few moments before he looked away again.

'Good day, Mr Jones.' She headed for the door.

'Mrs Hartman.'

Lily stopped. His voice was hoarse, but his tone was firm. She feared her dreams of getting to know Mr Judah Jones were about to be dashed. All the same, she tried not to allow any such feeling to show as she turned to face him.

Thirty-one

Elsa had stepped into her crushed but clean knickers and pulled on her rumpled camisole. She'd hardly waited for the damp patches on the fabric to dry before she'd shrugged into her sponged-off day dress. She was comfortable enough, and the dress was not really smelly, but she knew it would have to be washed properly soon. She adjusted the bodice to sit comfortably without her chemise underneath and was reasonably satisfied as she patted herself down.

Oh, to be back in Robe, on the farm, and not bothered about what clothes I'm wearing. And that wasn't a good thought—she still had to learn more about what had happened here to poor George. Trouble was, she and Rosie seemed to have stepped into a mess, and all because of George.

Now she had met the brothers Jones, there seemed a monumental task ahead—glean information about George and find out what else might be left of his possessions; get back to Nebo Jones (and his band of sorry followers in the bush camp) with information about Judah Jones; ensure (somehow) that the man with the knife was no danger to her; keep away from Ezekiel Jones.

She'd have to make sure she could do all of that and get back to South Australia in time to vote, even if it did mean tackling Frank on a number of levels. Rosie, for one. Administering her father's property for another. Having to see that awful Pete Southie person.

In the light of day, the tasks seemed monumental. Not nearly as monumental as some that others might be facing. Sal, for instance, the poor woman. *How would Sal be faring?*

Elsa closed her eyes. She tested the toes on her bad foot. Pain seared through. Damn. How was she to get back, at least to Nebo Jones's camp if her foot was still bad?

She took the dusted-off roll of bandage and began to wind it over her foot, the support of it relieving some of the niggling pain. *A nuisance, all in all.* At least she had her boot on the other foot. How else was she going to be able to—

'Elsa, it's a good thing you're dressed.' Mrs Hartman had thrust open the kitchen door and swept inside. 'Mr Jones—Ezekiel— will escort me to my house in order for me to change. He'll bring me straight back. You're not to worry.' She seemed harried, flustered. Bright spots of colour stained her cheeks.

Elsa stared over her shoulder as Ezekiel Jones filled the doorway. *So no visit to George's resting place any time soon.* 'I'm not worried, Mrs Hartman.' She tucked in the end of the bandage, knowing it wouldn't hold for long. 'If you'd be so kind as to bring me a pin of some sort to fasten this off?' She nodded at Ezekiel, who nodded back. 'If you leave me instructions—'

'My children are very capable, Miss Goody, and will attend to any chores you might see fit. I'll have Gracie bring a pin for you. Now, should you find yourself at all uneasy if someone uninvited were to appear, there is a rifle in my room.'

There's a houseful of children to look after. 'Yes, all right.'

'You know how to use a rifle?' he asked, his dark gaze on her.

A slither of fear crept over Elsa. 'I do.'

'Giff will bring it to you if there's a problem.' He turned to Lily. 'Correct me if I'm wrong, but the man in question is nuggety in his build, nondescript except for his front teeth.'

Mrs Hartman nodded, glancing at Elsa. 'They're capped in gold, quite distinct,' she explained and clasped a hand on Elsa's shoulder. 'We'll return very quickly, well before midafternoon, you can be sure.'

Elsa looked up at Ezekiel Jones. 'When you return, would you then take me to my brother's grave?'

'My dear, your foot needs rest,' Mrs Hartman said.

'It does, but—'

'I'll take you, Miss Goody,' Ezekiel said. 'I'll ask Giff to hitch up the cart to be ready for when we get back.' He tipped his hat, and then held out his hand indicating Mrs Hartman should leave ahead of him. He glanced at Elsa. 'We'll have time before sundown when it's a little cooler,' he said and turned in the doorway before striding away.

When the two were outside, Elsa heard Mrs Hartman say, 'I'm very worried about the other Mr Jones. I should've made him some breakfast.'

Ezekiel Jones's voice drifted back. 'Gracie can do that if he wants any. I don't think you need to be worried and ...' Out of earshot, the rest of his assurance was lost to Elsa.

Not long after she'd heard horses leaving, Gracie appeared in the kitchen room. She had a safety pin, about the size of Elsa's little finger. 'I have this for your bandage, Miss Goody,' she said, her soft voice sounding very grown up. She set about fixing it to the bandage.

Elsa gazed down at the little head as Gracie bent over her task. 'Thank you. It will help make it much easier for me to walk.'

'Oh no, you mustn't walk yet,' Gracie said. 'Uncle Judah is showing Gifford how to make crutches for you. My brother has already found long sturdy sticks, and he's smoothing them off with his hunting knife. Jonty has to plait some rawhide, so they're very busy in Pa's room. That's where Uncle Jude is.'

'I see.'

Gracie patted the bandage gently. 'It's all done.'

'What do you suppose I should do, then?' Elsa asked her. Gracie shrugged. In the silence, Elsa tested some weight on her foot. 'You're right. Not ready to walk on yet.' Nor ready for a boot. At least she had one good foot.

The girl's gaze was openly on her face. 'Does it hurt?'

'A bit.'

'What happened?'

'Well, my horse, Peppin, he took a fright and stomped on my foot. I wasn't able to get away in time.'

Gracie considered that, then, 'Where is Peppin?'

'He's at your uncle Nebo's camp. And that's where my sister is, too.'

Her eyes lit up. 'You have a sister?'

A pang of something hit Elsa deep inside. 'Yes. Rosie is her name.'

A frown. 'And where is your mam?'

'She died.'

'Mine too.' Gracie's hand snuck into Elsa's. 'But we have our pa. Do you have a pa?'

'Not anymore. He died, too, not many days past. He was very worried about my brother, George. So that's why we came.' Elsa felt herself calm. 'Did you meet my brother?'

Gracie nodded. 'He was sick when he was here. He talked a lot, some I could understand, but not all. And he couldn't get off the bed or walk or anything.'

Elsa's breath caught. 'Did you look after him?'

Gracie shook her head. 'Not really. Just to wash his face at times. He was very hot, mostly. Pa looked after him, feeding him, giving him water. When Uncle Nebo brought him over from Uncle Jude's place, he was very bad.' The girl squeezed Elsa's hand. 'Then he died.'

Elsa panted a sob. 'Thank you for looking after him until then.' The little girl squeezed her hand again. 'Do you know if he had anything with him, like a bag?' Elsa asked, waiting half a beat. 'Or a box, a tin box?'

Gracie frowned in thought, then shook her head. 'I didn't see anything.'

Elsa sat back, withdrawing her hand from Gracie's. She'd have to wait for Ezekiel Jones to return and ask him, then thought better of it. *Best to wait a bit longer.* She sighed and dragged her fingers through her hair, well dried and now its usual unruly self.

Gracie's eyes lit up again. 'Can I do your hair, Miss Goody?'

'Oh, well, if you'd like to, I suppose while we wait for the magical crutches. But it is a bit hard to handle, and there's so much of it.'

'We have a big hairbrush and I know how to do a plait. I do my own, you see. Pa taught me.' And she turned her head for Elsa to admire the neat braid.

Before Elsa could comment, Gracie fled.

Elsa thought of Ezekiel Jones's big hands, those hard knuckled, gnarly fingers of his nimbly turning a little girl's tendrils into a neat plait. She couldn't imagine her own father would have done such a thing. And certainly not with her head of hair. With Rosie's, perhaps—her hair was straight and easy to manage, usually tied back, neat and contained. But still, Elsa couldn't see her father attempting to fix a daughter's hair.

Rosie would have had their mother's help. Elsa could recall Kitty, but not all that well. When George was alive, she could see glimpses of her mother in him, but otherwise there was very little to remember her by. Except for the locket. And George had taken the locket when he left the farm but now she—

'Here it is,' Gracie said, rushing back into the kitchen and brandishing a beautiful brush, silver plate with a gold trim.

A very old piece already, Elsa thought. Perhaps it had belonged to Ezekiel's wife, young Gracie's departed mother, or her grandmother.

Standing behind Elsa, Gracie began pulling the brush firmly through the mop of hair. 'It's very strong hair,' she said.

'It is,' Elsa agreed, delighting in the luxury of having someone do her hair. 'Now tell me what else you remember about my brother.'

There hadn't been a lot more to glean from Gracie. Once definitely established that any possessions of George's had not been secreted anywhere, there didn't seem a lot more to ask. Elsa sat back and let Gracie play with her hair.

Jonty wandered in. 'Is there bread and jam?' He brought with him a cloud of little flies.

Gracie pointed to the loaf on the bench. He tore off a chunk and took a bite, then dipped another chunk in a pot of thick jam. 'Giff says they nearly done one stick,' he said, his mouth full.

'Oh, that's good,' Elsa said. She might soon be able to hobble about unaided. She hadn't yet met Giff, but it seemed he was a capable lad.

'Uncle Jude says ye're George's mam,' Jonty said, still chewing. 'He's lucky to have a mam.'

Elsa's heart lurched for him. 'I'm his sister,' she corrected softly. 'Like Gracie is your sister, I am George's sister.'

'George told me he had a mam,' Jonty insisted.

Elsa nodded. 'He did.' The brush dragged a bit more and she felt strong nimble fingers divide hanks of her hair and begin to wind what would become a thick plait.

'He told me stuff. And Giff.'

'Jonty,' Grace chided. She whispered in Elsa's ear, 'No one could make out what George was proper saying, miss.'

Elsa thought that might have been the case. Delirium made a person ramble. She would never truly learn George's last words, if there'd been any.

Jonty was eye to eye with her. 'Me an' Giff know where Pa buried him.'

'Is it far from here?' Elsa asked.

'Up that hill a bit,' he said, tearing off another hunk of bread. 'He's buried near our other mam and our little brother.'

Gracious me, more sorrow. 'Thank you, Jonty.'

'Jonty, go away,' Gracie said, and the plait pulled a little tighter. 'I'll take you there when we get you them sticks from Giff.'

Gracie was having trouble managing Elsa's thick locks. She tugged again. 'You will not, Jonty Jones. Pa will take Miss Goody.'

A lanky boy appeared in the doorway. He had a crutch under his armpit, and he limped inside, as if testing it. 'Uncle Jude wanted to see if this would suit ye, miss,' he said without looking at her. He handed over the crutch.

'Are you Giff?' Elsa asked, taking it from him.

'Gifford.' The serious boy still had not made eye contact with her.

'Gifford, I'm pleased to meet you,' Elsa said. He was also his father's son, but there was a lot more of someone else in this boy.

'Giff's pleased t'meet ye, too, Miss Goody. He don't talk much.'

'Shut up, Jonty,' Gifford muttered, and a bright red flush bloomed on his cheeks.

Elsa spoke to Gracie. 'Let me stand up, now, so I can test out this very handsome stick.'

'But I haven't finished your hair. Half of it's hanging out.'

'I'll only be a moment.' Elsa slid the crutch under her arm and using the hand grip, a tapered piece of timber wedged into a hole neatly bored into the larger stick and bound by leather straps, she took a couple of hops. 'It's very fine, Gifford, thank—'

A rifle shot boomed into the air.

Jonty shrieked and dived for Elsa's legs. She rocked against the stick and managed to keep her balance. Gracie stood stock-still, but Gifford raced out the door. 'It was Uncle Jude,' he yelled.

Picking himself off the floor at Elsa's feet, Jonty stood for a moment, undecided. Elsa grabbed him by his shirt collar before he could think to run after his brother.

'Gracie, take hold of Jonty and don't let him go. Come on, we have to go and see your Uncle Jude.' Elsa handed Jonty over and under Gracie's grip, the boy gave a little whimper of fear. 'It's all right, we'll go see him,' Elsa said, hopping to get comfortable again on the new crutch.

Outside the kitchen room, she couldn't hear any yelling. It was quiet, strangely so. Not even the dogs were barking. Eerie. The rifle would have been fired for good reason and that was enough to have her shake with apprehension. She shuffled forward with the two children close by. Gracie was clutching Jonty.

'Can you be very quiet going inside, Jonty?' Elsa whispered as they got to the back door. He nodded. His eyes were wide, but there were no tears, no cries. 'Gracie?' she asked.

'We can creep along the hall. Pa has another rifle in that parlour room you were in. I can get that,' Gracie whispered, taking Elsa's free hand.

Elsa wasn't sure about that idea. As they stepped into the darkened house, she stopped and listened. Still no noise, only the loud thrum of her own heartbeat. Gracie's hand tightened. She squeezed back. How was she going to manage to walk quietly down the hallway on the crutch? She leaned heavily on it and tested her foot with her weight. Pain shot up her leg. No good.

'Gracie,' Elsa said softly as she bent down. 'We need to crawl to that room. Jonty, you must be very quiet and do exactly as I say.' He nodded. 'Leave my stick here,' she said, handing it to Gracie and then slid down the wall to the floor. On all fours she crawled into the old parlour room, the children behind her. There was murmuring in the next room, but nothing like what she expected to hear.

'I know where the bullets are,' Jonty said, his little voice ragged as he tried to keep it low.

'You're not supposed to know,' Gracie growled at him.

He tugged away from her and scrambled to the trunk where he picked out a box nestled inside. He took out three bullets and solemnly handed them to Elsa. She didn't want to think about a child handling ammunition, nor about having to load a rifle, but she slipped them into her dress pocket. If she had to use it, she would.

'Where's the gun?' she asked Gracie. The girl darted over to where the commode had stood and pulled the rifle from behind. It was wrapped in rawhide and slid easily along the floor to Elsa. Unwrapping it, she felt the dust thick on her fingers. She couldn't use it even if she wanted to; the bolt was missing, perhaps insurance against young master Jonty's bravado. Besides, it was clear it hadn't been cleaned for some time. She rewrapped it and said, 'We'll leave it here for the moment. We won't need it, I'm sure.' Jonty looked crestfallen. 'And these bullets might be just the thing for Uncle Jude's gun.' He gave her a grin. 'Gracie, can you crawl along and see if Uncle Jude and Gifford are alone? You'll have to peek.'

Gracie's breath came in little puffs as she nodded and crept back into the hallway. Elsa followed on her hands and knees. 'Jonty,' she beckoned—then pressed a finger to her mouth to let him know he had to be very quiet. He scurried along beside her.

Jude's door was open but an inch. Gracie put her eye to the crack and then looked back at Elsa. 'No one else is in there,' she said so quietly that Elsa thought she might have lip-read and not actually heard her. Gracie pushed the door a little wider.

Elsa held her breath. There was Jude, the rifle at his shoulder and aimed outside. And Gifford, standing beside him, away from the window.

Then Jude tried to shout, his breath failing him. 'Didn't realise it was you, young constable. Sorry for the warning shot,' he called, his voice scratchy. He let his rifle slide to the floor.

Elsa heard a reply, but couldn't make out the words. 'Gracie,' she whispered. 'Call out to Gifford. Tell him we're coming in.'

When he heard Gracie, Gifford turned. 'Hurry up,' he mouthed, waving his arm.

Gracie pushed open the door and crawled in. Elsa followed closely behind with Jonty on all fours beside her.

'Are you all right, Mr Jones?' Elsa asked quietly.

'Bloody troopers. I couldn't see 'em properly so I fired off a shot. Prob'ly get done for it.' He leaned against the wall, barely glanced her way. 'Damn thing's not loaded now.' He cocked his head at the weapon beside him on the floor.

Elsa said to Gracie, 'The stick, please, and stay low.' The young girl scrambled out of the room. 'Mr Jones, you must get back to bed. Your wound is bleeding.'

Gracie scampered back on her hands and knees, dragging the crutch behind her. Elsa grabbed it and hauled herself to her feet. 'Gifford, please help your uncle.'

'Dammit,' Judah breathed. He'd started crawling, and Gifford was trying awkwardly to help his uncle get to the bed, fearing to put his arms around him.

'You come out here with your hands up, Jones,' a man outside yelled.

Elsa struggled to the window and peered out, careful to keep herself hidden. Certainly, two troopers were there, rifles aimed at the house.

Gifford was still struggling with his uncle, not sure where to grab him, but finally Judah flopped onto the bed and rolled onto his back.

Elsa glanced at Gracie. 'Get some clean towels or something for your uncle, to help stop the bleeding.'

'I'll get 'em,' Jonty yelled and suddenly bobbed up, ready to run from the room.

An explosion shattered the window, covering Elsa with shards of glass and timber. A hole burst in the wall behind them. Gracie shrieked and threw herself on the floor, clutching at Jonty, who'd howled in fright.

'*What are you doing?*' Elsa screamed out the shattered window. 'You just shot at a child.'

'Wassat?' The voice from outside sounded genuinely surprised. 'D'you hear that, Mr Clark? It's a woman.'

Gifford dived across the floor to the rifle. He grabbed a bullet from his pocket and scrambled to his knees, frantically trying to pull back the bolt.

Outside a trooper bellowed, 'Don't care it's a woman. Prob'ly one o' them doxies from the hold-up that Watson reported.' He waited a beat. 'We know Nebo Jones is in there, so come out, hands up.'

Gifford still desperately tried to reload.

Elsa dropped to the floor and, sweeping glass gingerly out of her way, shuffled on her knees to him. She couldn't escape broken glass from pricking her bandaged foot but thankfully there were no shards. Still, little chips stung her toes as they found their mark. She slapped at Gifford's shaking hand as he tried to load the bullet. 'Gifford, stop. Put the gun down.'

Lips clamped, mouth in a firm line, he shook his head and tried to snatch it out of her way.

'They'll shoot you, Gifford, if you aim the rifle at them.' She heard the plea in her voice.

He shook his head again, still fighting her.

'Giff.' Judah Jones was up on one elbow. 'Let it go, lad,' he said tiredly. 'That's not the way. Don't be like your other bloody uncle, the one without a whistle between his ears to call for brains. You know better than that.' Gifford slumped, as if the air had gone out of him and he pushed the rifle away, relinquishing it. 'Good boy. Now, crawl back over here,' Judah wheezed. Swiping broken glass out of his way, Gifford slunk over to the bed and sat with his back against it. Jude let a hand drape over one of his shoulders.

The loud trooper roared, 'Get out here, now, Jones.'

Elsa peered out again and then back across the room. Gracie had Jonty in a stranglehold on the floor. 'You two stay on the floor,' she ordered. They both nodded silently, wide-eyed. She shouted, 'Nebo Jones is not here. It's just Judah Jones and Ezekiel Jones's children and me.'

'We know bloody Nebo's in there.'

Elsa almost rolled her eyes. 'You're wrong,' she yelled. 'Judah Jones is in here injured after an attack on him, and he is with Ezekiel's children.'

'He fired at us.'

'He was defending children, defending himself.'

'Not bloody likely.'

'You are damned fools,' she shouted again, angry and frustrated by their stupidity. 'And you'll be more than the laughing stock of the town when this gets out—grown men shooting at children, at innocents.' Peering out again, Elsa saw a cloud of dust behind the troopers, in the distance but certainly on the home track. Perhaps it was Ezekiel riding back. Oh, that thought filled her with hope and with dread at the same time. *Ezekiel Jones.*

'Ain't takin' no woman's nonsense. Nebo Jones, get out here.'

From her vantage point, Elsa now saw two riders were bearing down the track. One whose clothes were billowing—that would be Mrs Hartman. Dear God, would they be killed if the troopers panicked?

'I'm going to come out,' Elsa called. 'By the front door.'

'Yair, so Jones can get out the back way.'

Elsa could see the rifle in one man's hand begin to lower. The other was aimed at the broken window. 'So, go around the back, you fool, as I come out the front,' she retorted.

'You got cheek, woman.'

I'll give you cheek when I get to you face to face. Elsa shuffled back. 'Mr Jones, you'll stay low, stay on your bed?'

'I'll stay here.'

Gifford cried out, his voice breaking, 'They'll kill him if they come in.'

'They won't.'

Jonty whimpered. Gracie dragged him over to Gifford at Jude's bed and pressed the little lad against his brother.

'Your father is coming,' Elsa said, a whisper so low she wasn't sure they could hear. 'I can see him. The troopers haven't heard him yet.'

'They'll shoot him.' Giff's eyes were wide.

'Not while I'm standing out the front.' Elsa turned back to the window. 'I'm coming out now,' she shouted. 'If you shoot me, you'll have to shoot every one of us, every witness, and shooting children is not an act of self-defence, is it?' She dropped to the floor again and slid under the shattered window, dragging the crutch with her. Pricks of pain smarted once again where glass nicked her toes.

They heard a trooper say, 'I ain't shootin' no kids, Mr Kilby.'

'No one's shootin' kids, fool,' the loudmouth growled. 'You, girlie,' he yelled. 'No weapons now.'

Edging up the wall, she could clearly see it was Ezekiel galloping towards the house, Mrs Hartman now left well behind. His reins flicked wildly from one side of his horse to the other, his hat long gone and the locks of his hair streaming behind him. In that glimpse Elsa had never seen anything more wonderful—or terrifying—in her life. He was charging towards the troopers.

'Gracie, you stay with the boys to help your uncle,' Elsa whispered. 'The troopers won't hurt us. Go on, now.' The girl stared at her, wide-eyed and silent.

Elsa needed to keep the troopers' attention from Ezekiel. She slowly pulled open the door, leaned on the crutch and squinted into the bright daylight. Her foot hurt, her toes stung. She squeezed her eyes shut a moment and waited for that split-second click of a barrel.

Nothing.

She opened her eyes. Ezekiel was still too far away. Shuffling onto the verandah in full view of the troopers, she called out, 'It's just me. There are three children inside and an invalid man.'

A push behind her, and a small hand gripped her skirt. 'I'm here, too. Jonty and Giff have got Uncle Jude, so I'm helping you.'

Shock thundered in Elsa's chest. She half turned. 'No, Gracie, go back—'

'Drop it *now*. I can see what you're doin',' the trooper roared, and the rifle came up to his eye again.

Elsa's breath caught. Desperate to keep Gracie out of sight, she froze. Ezekiel was only a few hundred yards from them, but still so very far away, even if he was coming fast. Just a bit more time—

A shot rang out, booming loud in her ears. Behind her Gracie screamed and dropped. Dust flew up from the boards as Elsa crumpled on the verandah.

Thirty-two

Damn and blast that trooper. Sure an' all there was worse cursin' he could yell into the afternoon air, but naught to be done for it—he'd only end up swallerin' flies as he rode along. He wasn't gonna directly cross the law, so no amount of yellin' about it would make any difference.

He kicked his horse into a gallop. Pete Southie knew he was close to Penola and as soon as he got there, he'd get to the first pub. He hoped he'd make it before that cloud burst overhead. Still, he had good daylight and although hungry, he'd slake his thirst with a rum and then fix his rumbling stomach.

Bugger it. Over three days since leavin' the Goody farm and he still got his back up knowing that the trooper had accused him of thievery.

There he was, mindin' his own business—he'd been shovellin' horseshit from the broken-down stable then he'd gone to tidy up the hut (well, to check again for that will or for other things of value. Shoulda known better, there was nuthin'), and the trooper had bust in.

'What do you think you're doing, Southie?'

He musta snuck up on foot, I dint hear no horse. An' there I was checkin' the back of that hutch thing in the hut.

Pete had spun around, guilty as buggery, and stared into the face of a sergeant who'd visit the town from time to time. The man's handlebar moustache looked too big for him, his youthful looks belying bright, keen squinty eyes that burned and seemed to nail Pete to the floor.

'I'm caretakin'—'

'Bollocks. You're looking for something to pinch, that's clear.'

Pete shook his head. 'Frank said he left a will, and he said—'

'The smithy said you might be out here snooping around.'

Bet it wasn't the old boy smithy, bet it was that shit of a kid of his.

The great moustache moved as more of the thunderous voice came out from under it. 'Mr Putney just buried, and you just had to race out here and rummage around where you got no right to be. Yeah, and by the look on your face, the smithy was right.' The trooper thumbed over his shoulder. 'Get out.'

'Look, Miz Putney doesn't know Frank's gone to God. I was lookin' for somethin' that might give me an idea where to go look for her, maybe find her and tell her—'

'You know as well as I do, Mrs Putney was seen by Mr Milton on the Penola road.' The frown was deep, and the moustache had stopped moving.

Pete looked about him. 'Tidyin' up, I was, case she came back. Them sisters will need a decent place to live and it ain't decent now. Look at it.'

'Don't give me that.'

'Is true. And Miss Goody—that's Miss Elsa—I asked her to marry me. I'm lookin' after her interests.'

'Well, I don't know Miss Goody too well, but that don't sound right to me.'

Pete had straightened up. 'I did ask her.' *Still lyin' through me teeth. Surely to Christ he'll give up.*

'I meant it don't sound right she'd want anything to do with yer.' The trooper put his hand on his pistol.

Pete stepped back, hands in front of him. 'Orright, orright. Place is almost too far gone anyway, but when them girls do come back, it needs to be decent—at least for Miss Elsa.'

'I hear you been in the bakery, too.'

Pete's heart hammered. Shit, he was gonna do him for robbery or somethin'. 'Had to pay for Frank's funeral, Miz Putney gone an' all.'

'None of your damned business who pays for what. Empty your pockets.' His hand was still on his gun.

Pete let out a great sigh. He dug out a fiver and three one-pound coins.

'Ain't any of it yours, is it?' the sergeant asked.

'It'll pay for repairs. Look, they'll need fences fixed here, and the yards rebuilt. That well cleared—'

'Tell you what,' the constable said, and wandered further into the hut. 'Keep the coins, give me the fiver to take back.' He held out his hand for it. 'Maybe you need to go find them sisters and escort them home. Heard they were going to tell relatives about their pa's passing.'

Pete wondered what was being offered to him. Handlebar still had his hand out so he gave the note to him. It disappeared into a pocket.

'And better you go right now on that horse of yours,' the fella went on, looking around.

'What, to Penola?'

'Or wherever you have to go. Because if I see you back here without those women, or hear you haven't even left here, I'll put you in leg irons.'

Those flashing eyes and the grim mouth under that plank of a moustache surely meant he was all business.

Pete had sidled past him in the doorway. When he got outside there was another trooper, mounted and waiting. Pete blew out a silent breath. Even if he had thought of clobberin' Old Moustachio here, he wouldna got very far. Lucky he hadn't jobbed him one, after all.

Now, nearing Penola, the coins jingled in his pocket. There'd be an ale or two, maybe a rum in one of the coins, and then he'd think about his next move. He didn't much like the idea of going further than Penola but more so didn't like the idea of goin' back without the Goody women. That trooper might not be happy. Pete could always just keep goin', not bother coming back. But if he got Miss Elsa back to the farm, and Miz Putney—they'd both be grateful to him—he'd have a good chance of making something of himself.

He could almost smell a brew as the first dwelling of the town came into view. Riding on the thought of it, he headed for what he reckoned was the pub on the corner. Couldn't miss it—blokes standing out the front of a brick block of a place, pannikins and shot glasses in hand. One of them staggering over to lean against a hitching rail. There were a few kids hangin' around. Looked like they'd been out rabbitin'. One lad still had his haul over his shoulders. Might even be rabbit stew on the menu. That would suit him well.

Standing outside in the late afternoon, the air had turned chilly, but he'd had a rum, not a good one, but good enough, and its warmth swept through him. He had company, the men, and the rabbitin' kids—the tall lad was trying to sell the last of his catch— and one of the fellas told him that two women had travelled here a few days back.

'Publican sez they were ma and daughter. Coulda been sisters, but why say otherwise?' the fella said, and Pete shrugged. 'Not toffy lookin', these two, but the older one was in better nick than the other, her clothes an' all, like a townie. The younger one weren't no townie. Had a good grip of the reins. Handled the horse and cart orright.'

Coulda been them. Sounded like 'em. 'I'll ask the publican.'

'He won't tell yer. Only troopers wanna know that sort of information.'

'Right.' Pete backed away from that idea, didn't want to start anything to bring any more attention to himself.

'True enough,' another fella agreed, and blew out a plume of pipe smoke. 'Don't get too many folk through here who don't stay a while. You said they had people here?'

Pete hadn't got any names of relatives. He hadn't thought of doing that. 'They were comin' to pass along sad news. Goody was the family name in Robe and Miz Kitty, the old Goody lady, gone now, her people were from around here, but I dunno their name. The ladies were goin' on to Naracoorte from here, I been told.'

'An' why're you lookin' for them?'

No harm in saying. 'The missus, well, her husband dropped dead just a day or so after she'd gone. She's gotta be told. There's business of hers needs doing back in Robe.'

Hats tipped in reverence, nods all around. Tobacco smoke flumed, ale and rum slurped. Gobs of spit landed on the dirt road.

The lad with the rabbit carcasses over his shoulder spoke up. 'They wasn't on the road to Naracoorte. Them ladies was on the Casterton road when we saw 'em.'

Thirty-three

Nebo looked over at Rosie. 'She'd have found Zeke, for sure, by now.' He tossed the remains of his tea into the small campfire. The sun overhead wasn't as warm as it had been the day before, but intermittent cloud cover brought humidity. Sheens of perspiration had appeared on them both and he wiped a hand down his neck.

He stared at her, wondering if she'd regretted last night. He hoped not. But what did he know of ladies? She was real keen—it had been her idea. Shit, maybe he shouldn't have ... but what fella wouldn't have? He corrected himself. A fella who knew better. *Wait a minute.* Hadn't he said as much? That he knew better, and that he'd court her and— But then she got herself all breathless and urgent, and then somehow they were lying down beside each other and she was sidling closer to him, talkin' of not wasting any more time. Next thing, a few kisses, and she was taking his hand, lifting her skirt—

'She's very capable, is Elsa,' Rosie replied, and sipped from her cup.

'Those directions were good. She wouldna got lost.' He sat on a log close to where she sat.

Rosie nodded.

He rubbed his hands on his pants. Maybe he shouldna done it with her, long after dark last night. Long after he could hear Glen and Tillie's snores chorusing. After he could no longer hear Fred and Alice's murmurs. He'd heard nothing from Wally and Sal. They'd all moved their camps a little further away to let them cry in peace. Poor bastard, Wal; he didn't know what to do.

Nebo had been lying on his swag, hands behind his head, star gazing but not seeing stars, when Rosie had crept over to him, sayin' she needed to be close after the dead babe an' all, an' poor Sal.

When he'd woken just before dawn, she was back under her cart and had appeared to be asleep. 'More tea?' he asked her now.

She shook her head. 'No.'

He leaned towards her, keeping his voice low. 'Rosie, I meant what I said last night. I'm very much taken with you, and I don't want to think we made a mistake.'

'Was no mistake, Mr Jones,' she said and her face coloured red as if a bloom had opened on her cheeks.

That gladdened him. 'I'm happy you think that. I also think you can call me Nebo.'

There was silence between them for a few moments, then she spoke. 'It was no mistake because I wanted to know … I wanted to feel—' She stopped again, glanced at him and shifted her shoulders. 'Oh, I was being selfish, that's all, and because of what I wanted, I let Elsa go by herself.' Rosie checked where the others were, as if to be sure they wouldn't hear her. 'And then with Elsa gone, and the way you were looking at me,' she said, glancing at him again. 'I—wanted to see if things would be different, other than what I'd known before.'

She stopped, which was good. He was having trouble trying to take it all in. There were a lot of words.

She went on, 'To be with my husband, in the marital bed, was always a duty to be endured.' Her face got even redder.

He didn't think she'd been enduring duty last night.

When she'd first told him that she was married, Nebo hadn't been overly concerned. A smart man would've guessed she'd been married—she was of an age. She could have been a widow. He'd listened to her reasons for leaving this Frank fella—it had all come out in a jumbled rush, and his head hurt trying to keep up. It irked him that Frank had not appreciated a good wife. Nebo had been looking for a woman to make his wife, and if Rosie was to be that woman, he would take her as she was, married to another or not, and be good to her. He looked over to Glen and Tillie. She was laughing in his arms, happy, carefree, married to someone else, not Glen. It didn't matter to them. Why should it matter to him?

'So you are under no obligation to me.' She twisted her ring finger, but there was no ring on it, only a pale mark where one might have been.

'I'd like to be.' Sitting beside her on the sturdy bench seat that Fred and Alice had put together, he bumped her shoulder very slightly. 'We've just taken a shortcut in the courtship; moved to a more interesting stage.' He noted the beet-red flush was still in her cheeks.

Looking away, she said, 'You are a man without prospects, and I am now well and truly a fallen woman.'

He thought for a moment. He wanted to hear her sigh again, like she had last night. He wanted to hear her voice in his ear, urging him harder and deeper. 'Nobody but you and I need know any of our private business. Ever.'

'I would need to survive.'

'I'll look after you. Besides, I do have prospects. I can go see my brothers, work for them. They each have small farms.' He hadn't told her yet why he hadn't already done so. He hadn't said that he was a petty thief, a layabout, jealous of one brother and ignored by the other. Well, today was the day he would change his ways. He could do it. He hadn't held up the coach, he hadn't done that last job even though it had been the intention. His little band was breaking up, so he had the opportunity now to ... try to make good.

'People would talk if we lived together.'

Again, he took his time before he spoke. 'Nebo Jones has been gone from high society for years.'

A ghost of a smile was on that mouth of hers. 'Would your family accept me?'

He laid a hand over hers yet when she made no reaction, he took it away. 'I'm the only one who needs to accept you.'

'I can't have children,' she blurted.

He shrugged. 'Zeke has children. The way I feel right now, it doesn't matter to me that you can't have any.' How—why he felt so strongly, he didn't know. He'd had women before, women he'd taken when they offered, women he'd let go, or who'd let him go. None had affected him like this woman had, and it had been real fast.

She reached for his hand and her fingers squeezed his. 'It's very quick, this courtship,' she whispered.

'We were in a hurry,' he said, matching her whisper. The thought of her lush breast in his hand, her taut nipple in his mouth, and the warmth and wet between her legs ... The surprised little sigh that escaped her as he slipped in there to stroke and push, and touch and own.

'It was *never* like that for me before,' she said and ducked her head. 'Never.' She took a deep sigh. 'And I am so lewd to be discussing these things with a man, in the daylight, in the open air.'

'In that case, I'm impatient for the night.'

She shook her head, a worried laugh escaping. 'Will we get along, do you think? I've been a wife before, and I don't—'

'But you've not had a husband like me before.'

Rosie looked down at their hands. 'Elsa and I, we came looking for your brother, so that we could learn more about what happened to our George. And then we were to have our father's will read. Though now that I've left my husband, I don't know what that would mean for me. Or for Elsa.' She glanced at him.

Nebo shut up. Was she asking him to take on the sister as well? He moved on the seat, uncomfortable. 'I can't have—'

'She is all I've got to rely on,' Rosie went on.

Didn't seem to matter when you let her go yesterday. Nebo felt a prickle of shame. He didn't want Rosie to lose her sister, but nor did he want to look after the sister.

'Until we find what else George had with him.'

Nebo frowned at that. 'The locket, a few buttons.'

'Nothing else?' Rosie was very intent.

'Not that I saw. Zeke has everything I found.' Then he remembered a look that passed between the sisters yesterday. 'What else *is* there?'

'I'm trusting you, so you better tell me the truth. It was a tin of sovereigns. Thirty sovereigns, perhaps more.' Rosie stared at him.

Shit. Thirty sovereigns. 'There was no tin.'

'If we find that tin, it's half Elsa's and half mine. That way Elsa could live independently, to start, anyway. We could live without the farm, and I could live without—anything from my old life.'

'What farm?'

'The farm we had back near Robe. It would be in my father's will and Elsa has it with her. So as soon as we find the tin, we can hire a solicitor and find out who administers. If I'm not with my husband any longer, it won't matter, will it?'

He shook his head slowly. *Thirty sovereigns.* He let that swirl about in his head; he needed a plan. The petty thief was at work.

He looked at Rosie, couldn't read her. No, he couldn't let this layabout Nebo sneak back in.

He squeezed Rosie's hand again. 'It won't matter, don't you worry,' he said, although it didn't sound like his voice. 'We'll find a way around things.' He wanted to believe his words, he did, but unease settled in his gut, oily, something akin to fear. He didn't know what he'd just agreed to. Even to his own ears, it had sounded like it had come from someone else—from someone who was a grown-up.

Thirty-four

Zeke had heard the shot. His heart banged against his ribs as he left Mrs Hartman in his wake. *Sweet Christ, who were they shooting at? His kids? His brother?*

Elsa? Then he saw her drop on the verandah. *They've shot her, the bastards.* And where was his bloody rifle? In his room at the house with Jude. *Jesus, Jesus, Jesus.*

Poor Milo was galloping as fast as he could. Zeke was low over his neck, urging the horse with his heels. He turned and yelled to Mrs Hartman, 'Stay well back.' Shit, if he hadn't spent so much time waiting for her at her house while she dithered about …

He was closing in. He saw the troopers wheel about on their mounts and straighten up when they saw him. One of them dropped his rifle, threw his hands in the air. The other one was having trouble controlling his horse.

Milo skidded in alongside them, bumped the horse under the trooper whose arms were still over his head. In a rage, Zeke reached over and hauled him out of the saddle by the shirtfront, then slung him to the ground. Only a lad he was and scared to death by the look of him. He turned Milo about for the other.

'It weren't us, it weren't us,' the older trooper screeched. 'We didn't fire.' He threw his rifle to the dirt.

'*Liar.*' Zeke stepped onto Milo's back and lunged at the other man. He ripped him out of the saddle. The man's foot caught in the stirrup, twisted. He squealed, dangling upside down, as Zeke tumbled past. Scrambling back on his feet, Zeke bunched his hands in the man's coat. '*You fucking bastards*—'

'It weren't us, swear to God,' the man screamed, his face red. 'Me foot. Me *foot.*'

Zeke didn't let go until he checked the verandah and saw Gracie helping Elsa to her feet, a crutch of some sort tucked under her arm.

'We're all right, Pa,' Gracie yelled.

He wrenched the man's foot out of the stirrup and threw him off, left him in a writhing heap. He slapped the trooper's horse hard and it took no time stomping off. 'Stop your bloody squealing,' he shouted. 'What the *fuck* do you think you were doin'?' He spun around and descended on the boy.

The young fella scampered out of reach. 'We were lookin' for Nebo,' he said, his eyes large, and snot running over his lip. 'He done a hold-up. We knew Jude was banged up and we reckoned Nebo'd come 'ere, so we'd catch him 'ere.'

'You reckoned wrong, you stupid bastard.' Zeke spun back to the older man and pointed. 'If I find one splinter has harmed my family,' he said, teeth bared as he dropped to his haunches. His face was close to the other man's, his rage thrumming. 'I'll hunt you down, and Nebo Jones will be the least of your worries.' He stood, grabbed the trooper up and shoved him. 'So, get on your way. Get off my land.'

The trooper stumbled. He waved the younger one over and together they got him steady on his feet. 'I busted me ankle.'

'Not likely. Get lost, before I give you something else to whine about.' Zeke bounded up the verandah steps, anger leaching out of him and fear replacing it. He hauled Gracie into his arms, and she clung to him, her wiry arms around his neck. He rocked her, his heart thudding. He was suddenly wild and lost, light-headed.

'I'm all right, Pa,' she said into his shoulder. 'They did shoot once, after Uncle Jude shot his gun. But that last shot was Giff. He fired the rifle from inside.'

Mrs Hartman was helping Elsa to stand as she struggled up against the wall. Zeke's rage had been so blinding he hadn't seen the older woman gallop in behind him. Giff leapt out the door and ran full-bodied into him. Jonty followed, his little face bright red. He fell into the huddle and Zeke rocked all three, his arms tight around them.

Mrs Hartman steadied Elsa then she marched off the verandah. She bore down on the young trooper as he helped the other man limp towards his horse. 'When I see your mother, Tommy Broadbent, there'll be hell to pay. Shooting on women and children—what on earth possessed you, bailing up a young family and acting like a hooligan?'

'Miz Hartman, I swear I—'

'Don't you snivel at me.' She wagged a finger under his nose. 'Get back to that farm of yours and do some hard work for a change,' she snapped, her voice cracking. 'Don't be running around with the likes of this one.' She thumbed towards the man he was half carrying.

'Get me horse, boy,' the older trooper growled. 'Outta my way, missus.'

Mrs Hartman glared at him. 'You irresponsible great dolt, Ernest Kilby. You pathetic galumphing fool. Your senior officer will hear about this.' She spun on her heels and steamed towards the verandah. 'And you children, you're not to repeat those bad words of your father's.'

Zeke stifled a laugh in Gracie's hair. He watched the troopers snatch their rifles from the ground, clamber onto their mounts and ride off. He looked over and saw Jude's face in the window.

'Jesus, brother,' Jude said. 'What the hell have we got in these women here?'

His kids were untouched, unharmed. They were fine. Mrs Hartman was fine—in fact, in fine mettle. Zeke still had a smile, despite his fright. His estimation of Mrs Hartman had risen considerably. As for Giff, he'd frightened himself, so no need to go crook at him—though when the boy had picked up the rifle again, he'd snatched it from the lad's shaking grip. Zeke would put more time into teaching Giff how to better handle the Martini-Henry rifle and when to use it.

Mrs Hartman was attending to the other two children and Jude. She was soothing Jonty's wails but Gracie was her calm little self. Jude's protests were loudest of all, especially when she changed his dressing. His stitches had held together, but there was a small tear that had bled. She wasn't sounding overly patient when he whinged about it.

Miss Goody had shuffled, white-faced and wincing, along the wall of the hallway until he and Gracie got back to help her into the old parlour room. Despite spots of blood on her face and forearm where glass and splinters had flown at her, she seemed unhurt. When they angled her to sit on the cot, Gracie knelt and brushed debris off her sore foot and picked out a couple of tiny pieces of the shattered window. Nothing another bandage wouldn't fix after a wash with lye soap. She'd impressed him somewhat, but he had an issue about Gracie and he couldn't leave it unsaid.

'Miss Goody,' Zeke said. He was standing in the doorway of the room into which he'd always stuffed unwanted or unused bits and pieces: things he thought he might use one day and never had; things he thought his kids might enjoy. The cluttered space seemed different to him now, as if an extra presence had changed its purpose. He would clean it out. 'Thank you for all your help.' He took a breath. 'Though, I'd have much preferred my daughter hadn't been with you when you confronted an armed trooper.'

'Gracie was very brave out there,' Elsa said, still pale in the face. She rubbed her foot as she sat on the edge of the cot, then pulled her hem over it and tucked it back out of sight.

'She shouldn't have been there at all,' he said, hearing the censure in his tone.

There was a hesitation, a slight frown. 'No. She shouldn't have.' She glanced away. 'Thankfully, that idiot trooper wasn't stupid enough to shoot at a woman and a child.'

'Even so, he might have.' He watched her take in a silent, deep breath at his rebuke. Clearly, she'd done what she thought best at the time, but it had been reckless behaviour to allow a child out there in that situation.

'Quite right. I apologise. I never meant for your daughter to be in harm's way.' She gave him a tight smile that did not reach her eyes. She looked away and took another deep breath. 'In the morning, I'll be able to ride to my brother's grave by myself if you direct me, and then I'll depart your property afterwards. My brother's resting place, and finding the locket, were the sole reasons for my coming here—and to thank you, of course.'

Giff pushed into the room from behind his father. 'Miss Goody, I finished the other stick,' he said, a broad smile breaking his usually solemn features. He brandished the crutch. 'Uncle Jude said it's a fine job.'

Now her smile was genuine, and her eyes lit up as Giff thrust the stick at her. She struggled onto her feet to test both crutches. 'It is indeed a fine job. Thank you, Gifford.'

'Call me Giff,' he said expansively.

Elsa Goody didn't miss a beat. 'It will do me very well, Giff,' she said, and took a couple of awkward paces, dodging furniture. 'I'm grateful to you.'

His son beamed with pleasure, not something Zeke had seen for a long time. The boy nodded at her and ducked around his father out the door.

Elsa manoeuvred her way back to the cot. 'Perhaps someone would strap these to my horse tomorrow, so I might use them again after I leave. They'll be very handy.' She let them drop to the floor, side by side, and resumed her seat. Using both hands, she pushed back her long, thick wavy hair, which looked to be only partly secured. It hung more than halfway down her back in a heavy dense drop. 'I think I would like to take a nap, now, Mr Jones. I seem to be out of breath.'

Amazing. He had been dismissed. Swiftly she'd put the boot on the other foot. 'I'll ask Mrs Hartman to look in on you,' he said.

She glanced at him. 'No need,' she said politely.

'Nevertheless,' he answered, and not waiting for a protest, if any, reached over to pull the door shut behind him as he left. Her gaze, bright, intense and bold, stayed with him long into the afternoon and the night.

'I'll have to go with her, Jude,' Zeke said, his voice low. In his hand was a tin cup with a tot of rum in it. He gave his brother a sidelong glance as they sat on the verandah. 'Back to Nebo's camp. I can't let her go by herself. She was just lucky to make it to us the other night without any trouble.'

Jude nodded, eyes wide, mouth pursed. He lifted his own cup. 'Yeah, no, you can't let her go by herself.'

The children were abed after their bath, overseen by Mrs Hartman who had also returned Elsa's cleaned and dried chemise. After saying goodnight, then goodbye to Elsa and wishing her a safe journey, she had just gratefully taken her leave to collapse onto Gracie's bed once more.

Miss Goody had emerged for dinner but had also retired for the evening. She wanted to be up and gone by dawn, she'd said, so declared she needed an early night. But before she left for her room, and as his kids chattered away to her, telling her of their school, their chores, their animals, she'd looked at Zeke briefly. 'Do you have any story books, Mr Jones?'

He'd watched Jonty slip off his seat at the table to stand by her chair. The boy stared up at her before slipping his hand in hers.

'No, I don't,' he said.

'You must get one so you can read to your children before bed.'

She'd turned away, missed seeing his mouth agape, and was giving Jonty her attention. He'd climbed on her knee. Despite Zeke's lukewarm objection to that, she wrapped her arms around the boy and began to relate a tale of three bears and a little girl. Jonty, who didn't know what a bear was, kept interrupting and so the tale went on for a while. Her audience had been enraptured. Finishing the story amid demands for more, Elsa was readying to leave the table when Gracie offered to fix her hair for the night. 'Not tonight,' she'd told his daughter. 'But if you're awake very early I would certainly appreciate some help then.'

Gracie had smiled her delight. Zeke's heart gladdened at that, but his own delight had been diminished by the fact that Miss Goody would not make eye contact with him. Most likely she was still upset that he'd chipped her about having Gracie on the verandah when those fool troopers were aiming guns at her.

Zeke shook out of his thoughts and swirled the liquid in his cup before addressing Jude. 'Seems Nebo gave her exact directions. If we follow it in reverse, it should take us back to him and his camp. If he doesn't want to come here, at least I can warn him to keep out of sight.' He took a swallow of his rum. 'But I don't like the idea of leaving you with only the kids.' He looked across, straight-faced. 'And Mrs Hartman.'

'Very funny. She's a fine woman, and we can be friends. I shouldn't meddle with that.' Jude shot him a glance, then stared at his hands. 'Besides,' Jude said. 'You've seen her when she gets mad. A bloke wouldn't stand a chance.'

'A bloke might become a happy man again.'

Judah moved in his chair, as if easing a sore spot. The stitches in his side would be nipping at him. 'Happy,' Jude said, shaking his head. '*Happy* is just ripped away from ye. I have to wonder how and why I ever got there in the first place. Now they're all dead.' He glanced at Zeke. 'Not sure I want *happy* to happen again. It marks ye for doom.' He tapped a fist on the table and looked away.

Zeke saw the shake in Jude's conviction. 'Is that so? I reckon you do want happy again, I reckon you know what you're missing. And there's no better woman than that Mrs Hartman. She's set on you in any case, just you're too thick to see it.'

'I do see it, but I just got nothin'. Not even all of my own mind with this grief over my girls.' He rubbed his face. 'It never leaves ye.'

'It takes its place, Jude.'

Jude shifted and looked uncomfortable. Maybe after a challenge his thoughts didn't sit easy. 'I'm a broken-down fella who runs from his ghosts.'

'Maybe time to stop running.'

'Maybe. I've thought about it.' Jude tossed back his rum. 'And maybe for you, too. You listenin' to yourself?' He pointed a finger at Zeke. 'I know you got grief. But I've seen a light in your eye now that I haven't seen for a while. Reckon that Miss Goody has fired you up.' Zeke said nothing and Jude went on. 'If she takes your eye, Zeke, well, a man should grab the good while he can. You know how quick things can turn bad.' He threw his hands in the air. 'I can hear myself think. We're talkin' the same thing.'

Zeke let his thoughts run again. *Elsa Goody*. The way her face lit up when she talked to his kids. Or when she'd glanced his way, not realising he'd been looking at her. When that glance softened, before she remembered she was mad at him. *Too soon for her. Too soon to be* with *her*.

Jude pounced. 'Hah—I see it. Not to mention the flamin' red face she gets when you look at her. Lucky you two weren't sittin' together before, the place woulda combusted.'

'Bollocks,' Zeke sputtered, and cleared his throat. 'She wanted to kill me. I ticked her because she had Gracie out there on the verandah when those troopers were carrying on.'

Jude gave a laugh. 'Little brother, your daughter just marched on out there after Miss Goody directly told her not to.'

Shit. Should have known, Gracie could be pig-headed. *Shit*. Zeke coughed again. 'We were talking about you, just now. You have a think about Mrs Hartman some more. You know she tends your girls' resting places. It means something to her.'

Jude nodded. 'Figured it was her. Looks a right special place now, all those flowers growin'.'

'Don't pass her up.'

Jude cupped his pannikin. 'Might be right.'

'I reckon you've been thinking about her anyway, haven't you?'

'Might have.' Jude went quiet.

Zeke stared out into the darkened night. His mind wandered. The moon would be a full one, and its glow on the horizon bright. He swatted at insects. Wouldn't be long before they'd have to head inside or risk being eaten alive. At least all the lamps were out inside—they needn't attract any moths or other flying midges. Mosquitoes were another issue. The season was changing though: there might be some mercy in that.

Jude let out a long breath. 'What do you reckon about this Curtis Goody fella?'

'Whoever he is, he's gonna murder and maim until he finds something. You know he thinks the dead lad left something of value.'

Jude shook his head. 'But he didn't. We found nothin' at home. Nebo brought you the only things the boy had, didn't he?'

Zeke hesitated, nodded. 'But who knows how Nebo thinks, these days.'

'Yeah, Zeke, but Nebo, he's not a killer.'

'He's a thief.'

'Bah. He's just a nuisance. He's always been lost. He didn't shoot the boy, you know it and I know it.'

'Miss Elsa wants to visit the gravesite tomorrow.'

Jude downed the last of his rum. 'And a good thing you'll accompany her there, too.'

Thirty-five

By the time Elsa had made it to the cookhouse, a new dawn was streaking golden shafts of light over the horizon. She hoped she hadn't wakened the whole household as she'd swung herself along on the crutches down the short hallway. Outside, she got to the privy then headed in to stir up the coals for some tea. All very awkward, but at least she was mobile.

She wondered about trying to saddle up Salty and get on her way alone, but it was only a fleeting thought. Attempting that with her foot out of action would just be silly—it was struggle enough getting through her ablutions. After a hot and restless night, sleep had eventually come, although her thoughts, insistent and repetitive, vexed her. She didn't want an attraction to any man, not now, and especially not to a man who thought her reckless with his children. She'd kept going over and over the situation with the trooper, and the shock of finding Gracie behind her on the verandah.

She checked the water level in the kettle and then sat back to try and get her hair into some sort of order. Gracie hadn't appeared yet, and Elsa didn't want to have to wait if the girl was going to take her time. No sooner had she untangled the first ribbon of hair than the kitchen door was opened.

'Good morning.'

Ezekiel Jones stood in the doorway, shirt open a little and hap-hazardly tucked in at the waist, trousers buttoned, socks on his feet. His cheeks and chin had the darkened shadows of day-old bristles. His dark hair framed a serious face, and his eyebrows had a quizzical twist. But his eyes … His gaze made her heart race. Just like it had before sleep finally came last night. Thanks to him, a breathlessness was with her again. 'Morning,' she croaked, or thought she did, her voice whisked away.

Gracie darted inside, pushed around her father and ran behind Elsa's chair. 'I'll do it,' she cried, and plunged her hands into Elsa's hair. 'I brought the brush. It's in my pinny pocket. Good morning, Miss Goody,' she said and ducked her face around to give Elsa a toothy grin.

'Morning, Gracie,' Elsa managed. 'I have the kettle on for tea.' Then she said to Ezekiel, 'Then I'd like to be on my way.'

'Hmm.' He stepped inside the kitchen and headed for the stove, reaching up for the tea caddy on the mantel.

'Oh,' Gracie said, standing behind her and sounding annoyed, her hands tangling in Elsa's hair. 'It's fallen out of what I did yesterday. I'll have to start *all* over again.' She didn't sound that disappointed.

After a moment, Elsa felt the brush and Gracie began long downward strokes, tugging through the thick waves. 'Gracie, per-haps I could do it myself. I'm sure you'd have chores to do.'

'Not yet, Miss Goody. Have to have our tea first,' she answered, working steadily.

Elsa winced a little at Gracie's fervor. She glanced at Ezekiel. 'I'm ready to leave as soon as Gracie is done. Jonty told me that George is buried a little way up the hill so I should be able to find it. I'd only need help to pack the horse, and to mount.' She had to stop her voice shaking. She took a breath. 'I also need whatever else you found of my brother's.'

'Hmm.' He'd murmured again. He drew down three tin cups.

'Oh, Miss Goody, this *is* a mess,' Gracie said, matter-of-fact, still pulling through Elsa's hair with the big brush.

Looking up, Elsa caught Ezekiel's eye. He seemed amused by his daughter's claim, but content to have her continue. Elsa felt heat rise in her chest again.

Her restless sleep had done nothing for what was left of Gracie's previous attempt at a plait. Elsa should have re-wound her own hair for the night, but it was the last thing on her mind. Time and time again thoughts of Ezekiel Jones had hovered over all rational thought. Despite his growling about Gracie being with her on the verandah under the trooper's threat, the thrum of his presence glowed inside her, and those wicked thrills that made her squirm in secret delight had descended on her and hadn't let up.

She had rarely been taken by a good-looking face, or a knowing smile, but she recognised the feelings clearly enough—the same type when Henry Benson looked at her. Not that he had caused her this much pleasant discomfort—her response to Ezekiel Jones was more *the look* of the man, not being *looked at* by the man. This was anticipation of seeing him, of waiting for the hum and throb in her belly as she heard his voice, or for the sweet warmth to tingle between her legs as she watched him move. And how her heart had gladdened when he'd crushed his little girl to him yesterday, at how he kissed his boys before their bed. How, at one point, she swore his gaze had glinted when she'd spoken to him.

How she'd fled to bed before she started to stammer in conversation and began to flutter. *How girlish. How ridiculous. I am sensible Elsa. I am capable farm-girl Elsa. I am suffragist Elsa. I am not a debutante, not a schoolgirl.*

She had a job to do and that was to get whatever belongings of George's were here and get back to Rosie who was still with that other Jones brother in his poor camp. To find a solicitor. To take ownership of—or run from—the farm. She would think about a livelihood and her survival after she'd made it back to Robe, or elsewhere in South Australia, to vote. What would come after that, she didn't know, but she would not stay here a moment longer and be subject to her ... fancy whims about a man with a devilish, dark gleam in his eye.

She felt her face bloom now at the thought, and even though she was staring at his broad and straight back as he made tea, surely when he turned, he'd be able to read it for what it was. The sooner she was out of his way, the better, and that made her heart pound harder. She let a breath go. She hadn't realised she'd been holding it.

'Your tea, Miss Goody,' he said and slid a pannikin in front of her.

'Thank you.' Elsa, not able to look at him, just took up the cup and blew in it to cool down the brew.

Gracie was still resolutely tugging the brush.

He leaned back on the bench under the window. Elsa could only see his long solid legs, crossed at the ankles, the flap of his partly untucked shirt hanging over his trousers. The belt at his waist.

'I have tinned milk somewhere,' he said.

'Up by the candles, Pa,' Gracie said, dragging doggedly.

'I take it black, all the same,' Elsa said. 'We haven't had a cow for milking for some years. I'm quite used to taking my tea without milk.' She glanced at him.

'Hmm.' His gaze was on her, steady, unmoving.

Her heart thumped and she looked away, trying to concentrate on the fine-looking mantel over the squat iron cooker.

'Did you do the milking, Miss Goody?' Gracie rested a moment, letting the long drape of hair fall down Elsa's back.

'And the butter churning, and the shepherding—when we had sheep—and the skinning of the rabbits. Then I had to set the traps, too, when—' She stopped. She was running away with herself, her speech rapid and breathless. *Ridiculous.*

'So, a true farmer's daughter,' Ezekiel said.

'For the most part, *I* was the farmer,' she said, noticing he'd folded his arms and was studying her. She looked at her hands, the palms stained with the land, the backs of them weathered, her nails short, discoloured. She dropped them to her lap, out of sight. *For heaven's sake, why be conscious of that now?*

'Although you don't sound like a farmer, I believe you,' he said, his tone light.

'I was,' she said, annoyed that perhaps he was making fun of her. 'My father had been ill for some time, and George was really not that interested in the farm. He was always off exploring, he'd say. I'd always worked the land. Someone had to.' It would be too easy to rattle on, to have a lovely conversation when really, she needed to get going. She needed to drink some tea. She blew some more and ventured a couple of sips. Nearly cool enough.

'I believe it. I can see you are strong and natural in your disposition, as if used to hard physical work.'

Oh. Am I not ladylike in my appearance? Hackles rose. He was nothing if not forthright. She looked down at her dress, spot-cleaned, old and faded. Seeing it anew, she felt an unfamiliar dismay creep into her.

Gracie resumed a while, then sighed, pocketed the brush and tried to begin the plait. 'Oh dear,' she said. 'I've brushed and brushed so much, now it's too slippery for my hands,' she said. 'Pa, you'll have to do it like you do it for me.'

Startled, Elsa shook her head. 'Oh, that's not—'

'Gracie, why don't you go see if everyone else is up. I need to talk to Miss Goody for a while.'

'Pa does hair real good, Miss Goody,' Gracie said, smiling broadly. 'Here's the brush and the tie.' She put them on the table and took off for the house.

Elsa put her hands to her hair. 'Really, there's no need for you to do it, I can manage. Gracie just seemed to want to help so much, that I—'

'No trouble.' He pushed off the bench, his gaze on her. 'First, I now know that Gracie took it upon herself to stand by you on the verandah. I must offer you an apology.'

Under the intense scrutiny, Elsa felt the rush of colour again. No point hanging on to it. 'Accepted.'

'Good. I can get on with the plait.'

She protested again. 'It would be, um, unseemly for you—' She stopped short. *Good God, Elsa.* What is this ladylike rubbish—*unseemly*? This whole jaunt since leaving the farm was unseemly. *More tea, more tea.* She sipped again, swallowed, but it was too hot.

'Not in my household. I'm both father and mother to my children, so I've learned to do a few things that a woman would do, like my daughter's hair. Besides, there's no one to see me making a plait, so it's no bother to me,' he said. 'My brothers would think it a great lark.'

'Perhaps Mrs Hartman would do it for me?'

'The children are not to wake her. She's been through enough in the last couple of days.' He paused. 'As have we all.' She felt him take up the weight of her hair in his hands as he stood behind her. Shivers fled across her chest. 'Gracie and I learned to do hers, together,' he said. 'I'm sure I could be of some use here, as long as you don't mind simple and tidy.'

Elsa was transfixed. No man had touched her hair, ever. Those hands of his, the ones she'd stared at and wondered about, were in her hair. Strangely captivated by that, it made her a little light-headed. It was foreign. Exciting. Good. *Too good*. The warm tingle on her scalp, the glowing rush of sensation down both of her arms ... Her belly tightened.

As he separated three thick strands to make the plait, his fingers brushed her neck. Innocuous, a *nothing* touch, but her nipples squeezed and her secret place tightened. Every so often he tugged a little harder as he braided—how good that felt—and his fingers worked more magic. *Never, never, never. Never* had she believed there were sensations like this. The things he aroused in her ...

He stopped, and so did her breathing. She felt the plait being examined. 'Hmm. Now,' he said and resumed his handiwork, 'I'll be accompanying you to Nebo's camp.'

Her heart gave a jolt of a different sort. *What?* 'That's not necessary, either.' She half turned towards him.

'I think it is.' He took her head and gently turned her back. 'I'll either convince Nebo to come here and wait for this crook to be caught or convince Nebo to stay where he is until I let him know it's safe. Either way, I'll have to warn him, and even then, sometimes my brother doesn't know what's good for him.'

'I can warn him without—'

'And besides, it's not safe for you to be travelling by yourself with that fella out there.'

'Surely, in broad daylight there'll be no issue.' She took a good swallow of tea, pushed aside the memory of bushrangers bailing up a stagecoach in broad daylight.

Minor point.

He tugged a little. Turned the plait again. When he continued, his fingers grazed between her shoulder blades, warm and light. She felt it even through the fabric of her dress. He worked steadily, his knuckles skimming her back lightly as the plait grew. Acutely aware of him, she felt every minute scrape, every tiny stroke. Even imagined a linger of a touch when perhaps there was none. She squeezed her eyes shut. How was she going to sit still, or breathe, until he'd finished? When had this sensible farm girl, the woman she was, become such a dithery, twittery wreck?

'I'll be coming with you,' he said quietly. The fingers continued, plaiting and tugging. 'We'll ride for the camp after you've visited the gravesite. Your sister would be worried for you.'

The dithers and twitters continued. 'But—what about the safety of your children?'

'Jude is here, and Mrs Hartman.' Then he barked a laugh. 'Though I suspect she'd defend the place all on her own.' His fingers worked deftly. A touch of his hand tingled the hollow down her spine.

Why did it feel like it was just for her? Another shiver scooted along her arms and into her chest. *Oh, don't be so silly, Elsa.* Every twist of his hands working the plait was only confident ownership of a simple task, nothing more. But—even sure he would be feeling nothing like she was feeling—it was much more than simple. It was as if he'd stroked her, as if she was taking illicit pleasure in something she couldn't name. She hummed inside and held the secret of his touch close.

'And if your directions are as clear as you say,' he went on, 'I'll be back here by dark, and you'll be with your sister, preparing for home.'

Sharply brought out of her dreamy haze, she knew there was nothing to say to that. Anyway, his hands were nearing her lower back and showing no signs of stopping, and nor did she want him to. *Thank God he is oblivious to my nonsense. This can't be proper.* Her face burned all over again at that. First of all, a man fixing her hair, a man she barely knows. And—touching her, accidentally, of course, not by design, not the way Pete Southie had pawed her. But touching her, the feather-light scrapes and brushes of his fingertips and knuckles teasing their path down her back—

'Nearly finished.' His breath was on her neck as he bent forward. 'Hand me the tie, would you?'

Groping on the table for the piece of calico ribbon, she held it up to him as he handed her the end of the long plait. She watched as he tied it off with the strip of fabric, winding the long wide ribbon around the end of her hair. He knotted it and swung it behind her, letting it drop softly on her back. 'All done,' he said.

Her breath came back, but her heartbeat continued to gallop. 'Thank you.'

'Pleasure,' he said, and his gaze held hers for a moment.

Then he smiled, and his face transformed—

'Oh, I knew you'd have it finished, Pa,' Gracie said, a little disappointed as she burst back inside. She ran to Elsa and took the heavy plait in her hand. 'It's very fine, Miss Goody.' Admiring her father's handiwork, she said, 'One day I'll be able to do your hair just as good.'

One day? Elsa only said, 'Oh,' and took up her cup of tea. She put a hand on the plait, felt it for herself, but it left her—bereft. The hypnotic feeling of his hands on her hair had vanished, leaving nothing but a merciless need to have them in her hair again.

Ezekiel said, 'Gracie, tell the boys I want them to hitch Milo to Mrs Hartman's cart, saddle Salty, and tie him on side.'

Gracie stood for a moment, eyeing her patient father. Then she turned her attention to Elsa. 'You will come back again, won't you, Miss Goody, after you've found Uncle Nebo?'

'I'm sure she will in due course,' Ezekiel answered.

'Oh, that would be so grand.' Gracie's small strong hands squeezed Elsa's before she shot off again.

'I don't think I will be back,' Elsa said to him, a frown deepening. 'That wasn't fair to tell her that.'

He acknowledged that and shrugged a little. 'She's my daughter, I know her well. I'll explain to her when the time is right.' He peered into her near-empty cup and took it from her to the washbowl. 'She has enjoyed your being here.'

'All the more reason not to get ...' Elsa floundered for her words. *Get her hopes up? Whose hopes, Elsa Goody?*

'She understands that things change, that they come and go.' He hesitated, and gave her a rueful smile. 'Disappointment can come later.' Then he brightened a little. 'It's just nice for now, to see her happy and smiling.' He picked up her crutches and held them out. 'After you.'

Elsa found it easier to move today and, swinging along, was glad that she'd soon be on her way and nearing the end of this part of the journey. She wasn't looking any further forward, just wanted to be away from—him, and leaving behind her bewildering feelings for him and his family.

The day was cooler, though she could feel her face and neck dampen with the effort on the crutches. Spying the cart already harnessed, she cheered up and headed for it. They'd soon be underway.

Just as she got there, Jonty flew off the verandah and rushed into her, clutching her about the legs and burying his screwed-up face in her skirt. 'Don't go, don't *gooo*,' he wailed so loudly, the dogs started up their barking.

Staggering a little, she juggled the crutches, dropping one to hug the boy. She steadied and stood holding him as his snivels and sobs muffled into her. His sturdy little body was shaking with his distress.

'Stay with *meee*,' he howled, and his head came up as he pleaded tearfully with her. Then he buried it again, sobbing hard.

Her heart squeezed and her arm tightened about him. She looked across as Giff stood nearby, shock etched on his face, staring at his little brother. When he glanced at her, he looked worried, as if he needed to say something, as if he too didn't want her to go.

Gracie was standing alongside him, her eyes wide, her mouth open.

Ezekiel was rooted to the spot. 'Jonty.'

Elsa held the boy, rubbed his wiry back. Bent a little more, trying to soothe him. She murmured, 'Jonty, I have to go to my brother. You want me to do that, don't you?'

'Nooo. He went awa-ay, tooo.'

His head came up and the twisted little lips and the reddened eyes flooded with tears rocked her heart. She held on to him, wanting to cry with him. For him. For George.

Ezekiel stepped closer. 'Jonty.'

'I want a mama,' Jonty wept, and his grip tightened on her dress. 'Be my mama.'

Elsa shot a look at Ezekiel, mortified that the boy called on her for something she couldn't give, that he clung so desperately to her.

Ezekiel barely glanced at her. 'Jonty, come along, boy.'

Despite his father's encouragement, Jonty didn't let go until Ezekiel gently picked him up under the arms and took him from Elsa. He set him down, held him by one shoulder and squatted so he was eye to eye. Then he brushed the tears from Jonty's face with large, gentle hands. He cupped the boy's head, his gaze roving over him, as if he was drawing in the wonder of his little son. His other hand swept tenderly over the messy thatch of Jonty's hair, back and forth, until the boy was comforted.

Elsa swallowed the cry that came to her lips. That such open feeling was on display from a big, sun-browned man, whose eyes glistened as his callused hands held his bonny child, who listened attentively to the plaintive sobs—it nearly brought her undone. She had never seen such a thing, not from her father—for her, or for any of her siblings. She'd been right in her estimation of Ezekiel Jones. Here was a man who'd known deep sorrow himself, and the depthless grief of his family. Felt emotion keenly and expressed it, with dignity and courage. And that opened the tightly kept, aged hollow inside her and swept it away. As warmth and light flooded in, she held fast for fear that a cry would still escape.

Jonty's blubbers withdrew to hiccups, and he bit his quivering lip, his wet eyes blinking at his father.

'We must be brave, lad,' Ezekiel said quietly, his dark eyes creased as he smiled a little, his whiskered jaw sharply contrasted to the smooth cheeks of his son. 'Miss Elsa has to go.'

The boy's bottom lip came out again. 'I doan wanna be brave.'

'I know, but it's best to try.' Ezekiel cupped his boy's head again. 'Giff?' Giff shot forward and slipped his hand around Jonty's. 'Stay with Jonty now until we're gone then take him with you and let the dogs off for a while.' Giff nodded.

Jonty's bottom lip remained jutted forward. 'Bring her back,' he demanded, man to man.

Ezekiel stood and smoothed the boy's hair again. It seemed to Elsa, his jaw tight, his chin to his chest, that he couldn't answer.

She was grateful that Gracie had gone to gather her belongings. The girl held Elsa's other boot, and it dangled from her hand by the laces. 'I'll put this with your satchel, Miss Goody,' she'd said quietly over Jonty's gulping, and had marched past her brothers to the cart, dropping the boot over the side. Then she marched back to them and only lifted a hand to wave goodbye.

They left to the rousing chorus of three excited dogs. As they passed the back shed, Ezekiel roared at them to shut up, and except for one last yap, silence descended.

Elsa was grateful also to be sitting alongside Ezekiel in the driver's seat, and not mounted on Salty, trying to keep her sore foot in the stirrup. Or worse, stuck in the back of the cart alongside all Mrs Hartman's garden implements like some hefty sack of mulch.

Conversation was patchy. Elsa didn't broach Jonty's reaction. His children were not her affair, after all, but she couldn't help feeling for them; they'd all touched her heart.

'Are those working dogs?' she asked when the barks had stopped.

'Kelpies.'

'I haven't heard of that breed,' Elsa said.

'Been around a little while now, smartest dog there is. One of them, Bizzy, belongs to Jude.' Then he gave her a smile. 'Best farm workers.' Then looking dead ahead again, and clicking the reins, he said, 'Weather might hold.'

'Yes.' She glanced at the sky. Cloudy but not yet ready to rain.

It seemed a companionable silence for the most part after that. Only a short time later, he slowed the cart. She took a deep breath and adjusted her hat, pulling it a little lower over her face as the timber crosses appeared, signalling the gravesite. Her stomach lurched. A day of high emotion. Ezekiel hadn't said much more since leaving his house, and she wondered again how Jonty's cries might have affected him. Still, visiting this place would have a sombre effect on anyone.

Towering over the site was a massive gum tree, majestic, wide and strong, clearly one that had stood sentinel here for a long time. It would have seen drought, and fire—parts of its thick, broad trunk were blackened—howling wind and driving rain, for sure. It stood proud and alone on its grassy knoll, ravaged by the elements, and above the pale golden plains that flattened wide around it.

She'd watched it on the horizon. Now as they drew closer, she took deep and silent breaths else she feared the tears would well and plop on her cheeks, that her face would screw up, that her control would evaporate and she'd bawl her lungs out. For this would be the tree Ezekiel had written of.

He lies by a great eucalypt …

'I'll help you down, tend the other graves till you're ready to leave,' Ezekiel said and pulled up. He let Milo's reins dangle as he climbed out of the driver's seat and strode around to her side, where he reached into the back of the cart for her crutches. He leaned them on the cart and turned to her, holding out a hand.

To keep from falling into a weepy heap at the sight of the graves, to stop herself from breaking, she got on to the edge of the seat and stood carefully on her good foot. But she couldn't think for the life of her how to get down from the cart.

He reached up, big hands spread across her waist and lifted her down, as if it were long practised. She settled on one foot, her hands slipping from his shoulders to hang on to his arms. No thoughts rushed through her, but her belly filled with wild swoops at the warmth of him. When she steadied, he handed her the crutches and she put them in place.

'All set,' he said. He took a pace or two with her, a hand hovering at her elbow until she found her rhythm. Then he tipped his hat. 'I'll just be over there.' He pointed at the other two crosses.

She could not trust her voice to speak, only nodded her thanks. She looked at the wooden cross at the head of George's grave, vaguely aware of Ezekiel's footfalls as he walked away over leaf litter and twigs. A hum of blowflies passed her, a buzz of one close to her face. She tried to blow it away, reached up to swipe at it, unbalanced a little. Steadied.

The cross was simple. As she neared, she could see that someone—most probably Ezekiel—had etched her brother's name and his date of death on it. Barely a month gone. She'd seemed to have lost track of time. Suddenly, her throat scraped raw with her voice, as if the pain of grief was articulate, not put to words, yet not denied expression. The sound of it must have reached Ezekiel.

'You all right?' he called.

Still struggling to be quiet, she turned and nodded briefly, turned back and hung, stricken, over the crutches. Without them she would have sunk to the dirt and been unable to help herself upright again.

George. George.

The voice was hers. But her father's echoed over it. That brought more pain. Here, now, her throat tight, her chest demanding air, Elsa knew her grief opened the wound she'd tried to stitch closed far too early. She couldn't see George in her mind, she couldn't hear him, but she felt his presence. She stared down at the mound of dirt, at the cheeky sprouts of weeds dotting it, at the odd pebbles that were strewn across the patted-down earth, at the simple etching of his name in the wood ...

She sank to her knees then, the pain too much, the crutches falling from her grip.

Ezekiel was by her side, on his haunches, his voice soft. 'Let me.' He took her hand, held her, let her claw her way back to her feet. He tucked a crutch under her arm, retrieved the other for her, rested his hand over hers. 'He slipped away peacefully. There were no last words, no last-minute wishes.'

She felt the rasp of callused skin and the hard, warm fingers of his hand. Elsa gulped noisy breaths as much because of his words about George, as for the touch of his hand.

'There were no last memories coming from him, no nothing. He just slipped away.' Ezekiel had risen with her, steadied her. 'He did talk when Nebo first brought him home, about you and your sister. Mostly you, and the rest was delirium, I would say, although Gracie said he talked of your mother.' When she looked at him, Ezekiel nodded. 'He cried for her, as a boy in deep pain would. Giff might have heard a word or something, he's never said, but there was only one thing I heard that was clear. I'm not sure how coherent it was. He said "we'll save the farm", and then "it's in the dirt", but after that he wasn't really conscious again.'

Sniffing, wiping her nose on the back of her hand, Elsa said, 'He must have been feverish. The farm is nothing but dirt, barren now.' She sighed, and a little more composed, said, 'Please, continue to tend to your wife and your son's graves. I'm all right.'

His voice cracked. 'Who told you it's my son?'

'Jonty. He told me where I could find George, beside his mother and his brother. He said the graves were close.'

'Young Jonty amazes me,' Ezekiel said. He pinched his nostrils. 'Buried there is my last son. Born and then died not two days later. Healthy, it seemed, at first, and not a long or hard labour for my wife.' He shook his head, as if bewildered still.

'And your wife—what did she die of?'

'An aneurysm of the brain, they said. Not long after the baby.'

Emotion, that was not her right to have, surged inside her. Blinking hard, she shifted her weight, easing her good leg. She swung on the crutches to stand in front of the graves, the larger mound for his wife, whose cross bore her name, MAISIE JONES, her date of birth and date of death. She had only been twenty-eight.

The smaller cross was bare. 'What's your son's name?' she cried. 'His cross is not marked.' She took a breath, astonished to be so rude, so judging.

For a moment he seemed caught off guard. 'I had to bury him without—' He took a breath. 'Maisie couldn't bear to name him.'

Elsa watched as he stared at the little mound. Then he put the fingers of both hands to his forehead as if he had a terrible pain.

She knew that feeling, that taut band, the dry ache in the temples that thudded without ease. Grief.

'And did you name him?' she asked, surprised she'd even spoken the words.

He looked at her, his dark eyes bloodshot and bleary, as if he struggled to contain a deep reaction. He lifted his head a moment. 'He is Xavier. Maisie never knew that I named him. She just couldn't bear talking about it.'

'Will you write his name on his cross?' Elsa *couldn't bear* thinking the little grave would remain unmarked.

Raising his eyebrows, he looked at the grave, anew. 'I will,' he said.

In her mind's eye, Elsa could see Sal rocking her dead babe. She hoped she'd named the little girl. She hoped they'd buried her in a good place. *She hoped, she hoped*—she just wanted to get back to her sister. Hug her. Hug her tight.

There were so many things she didn't know. Rosie, who so desperately wanted a child, would have bought one from a baby farmer. Elsa herself, who had never thought of her own babies, only those of the animals she'd tended—was that a strange thing?—thought of Sal, whose dead infant had been held tight to her chest, not allowing anyone else to take the little body. And now, this man's wife—giving birth and having the baby die only days later—the suffering she would have endured.

'I don't think your wife would mind now that you name him,' Elsa said.

How dare she say such a thing? She could barely comprehend the anguish. All very well to watch a cow grieve, or to watch another woman grieve. But never knowing, never experiencing that loss herself ... how could she speak for another? And what of a man's grieving? Men, who think they shouldn't show emotion. Wally had seemed so stoic, even gruff, but was he only paralysed by grief, not just charged by society to never show it? It must have been gut-wrenching, destroying. She could not begin to—

'Not now, she wouldn't,' Ezekiel agreed. He rubbed his nose, sniffed loudly, pulled his hat lower over his eyes, and turned away from the graves. 'But back then? She minded. Maisie hadn't wanted him.'

Thirty-six

Sometime in the night, Nebo said, 'Are you not, with all intents and purposes, now my wife?'

Rosie rolled towards him, snug at his side and sighed. 'Mr Jones,' she started. She *still* called him that. 'I'm delighted with your attention and your sentiment and cannot be happier.' She pressed a kiss to his chest and flattened her hand on it, fingers tweaking the hair.

It echoed how Nebo felt, but he didn't have exactly those words. It felt good to hear it from her, all the same. He hadn't been sure she always looked as happy as she claimed, and she did go on a bit too much, too quick—there were a lot of words come out of her. Some he heard, some he just nodded as if he'd heard, as if he was listening.

He was staring up at the dark, starry sky, his arm tight around her shoulder, happy as a pig, when she said, 'But I won't allow my path to be hindered by the heady nights that have been incessant and prolonged.'

His chest expanded. *Incessant and prolonged*, that was him; he'd done that. What a bloke was he? Shit, he wanted to puff out his chest even more and strut around the camp. She craved it now, he could tell.

She tapped his chest, then allowed her fingers to drift under the blanket. 'So I'll keep my own counsel and nothing—*nothing*—will detour me from that.'

He frowned. *Whatever that meant.*

He'd had to take a moment here and there over the last couple of days and nights to sort all her words—she had a lot of words—and to catch what she might have meant, to keep up with her. He reckoned he'd got the gist of it, now. He smirked to himself. *Incessant. Prolonged.*

They couldn't marry, he knew that, but they'd live together, wouldn't they? That would make her his wife. It was a given. A contentment came over him. The stars looked brighter. The future looked brighter. He had a woman of his own.

She pushed away then and rolled onto her back and when he smoothed a hand over her luscious breasts, they seemed to float. He wanted to bury his face in them and slide inside her.

'Frank,' she said, and he imagined her lip was curling by the tone of her voice. 'Oh God, how his very name draws me down to the depths. But I must face facts. I don't want to be Mrs Putney, not for a moment longer, but I am.'

She had lain—gleefully and wantonly were her words earlier—with him, a man not her husband, and delight had opened for her, she'd said.

'The reality is, Mr Jones,' she said, her fingers reaching over to swirl lightly on his belly, 'unless I can prove cruelty beyond the law,' and she laughed then, 'and no one can actually see this particular cruelty, I am married to Frank until death.'

It didn't faze Nebo; he just didn't care. He had his hand on a full and firm breast, and when he tweaked the nipple, he heard her soft gasp. Then he put his hand on her bare thigh and slipped it higher to brush her damp pubic hair.

'You are most distracting,' she said, and rubbed against him, diverting him from her well-endowed chest. 'And it's no duty to undergo, whatsoever.' Her fingers crept around his hard cock.

He was just happiness itself with the fact that she couldn't seem to get enough of him. And he couldn't get enough of her—when he was in her, gliding back and forth and making her hum and quiver.

He couldn't wait … He needed her now. Gripping her sneaky hand, he tugged it away before she ruined him, lifted himself on top of her and slid between her open legs.

'You look right happy, Mrs Jones,' Nebo said to her. They were sitting at his campfire the next morning. He bumped Rosie's shoulder as he poked at the campfire coals with a stick. A chill lingered in the air. The seasons were changing, and summer was receding to autumn.

'Shouldn't call me that, Mr Jones,' Rosie chided, though she didn't seem unhappy about it: that little smile, that little lift in her eyes. She tugged his jacket around her.

'You just call yourself Mrs Jones,' he said. 'And that can be that.'

'When I am already Mrs Putney? I told you last night.'

'We'll just forget that Putney bit,' he answered. 'From here on in, no one else need know.' He waved a hand around the campsite. 'And no one here cares. You've left him, haven't you, my girl?'

She'd nodded and still went on about the same thing. He stopped listening; wished she'd stop going on about it. He had stated his needs, and they were simple. He was hers, she was his— the rest would be fun. No need to go on. *And on.*

He threw the stick into the fire, and interrupted her. 'If I had a decent tent, we would be there now, makin' you more *my* Mrs Jones.' He grabbed her hand, traced a finger down her palm and raised it to his lips. He felt a tremor pulse through her.

Rosie's voice wavered. 'It's not only delight you're after, is it, Mr Jones?'

'It's that, and more,' he said. 'You're my kind, Rosie. We're alike, you and me.'

She laid her head on his shoulder. 'What will we do? What will *you* do, no job, no prospects?'

He smoothed a hand over her hair and said, 'I have prospects, I said that. My brothers have small holdings, too small to make life easy. If they work the blocks together, make them worthwhile, I'll have work.'

Rosie pulled back. 'And you don't have a block?'

'I wouldn't live in the bush if I had a block. I was the lay-about son, so my parents put up a bit each for my brothers.' He shrugged. 'Pa had a little money stashed workin' the goldfields at Bendigo in the 'fifties, they bought some land, carved out a farm. They were careful, those two.' He snorted. 'I was to have worked the farm, but the rabbit plague of 'sixty-six ruined them before I was old enough to help. And Zeke was even younger than me, so it was hard times.' He flicked a few twigs into the fire. 'Jude was maybe eight. He could go work for someone, to bring in some money, but things were too far gone on our farm by then, so it got sold. We had to camp for a few years, but they'd hung onto a tiny stash of coin for that rainy day. Was the only way they could get ahead. So we lived on those rabbits. I never wanna see another pot of rabbit stew again in me life.'

He stayed silent a while. Rosie stopped talking, too. His life didn't seem so good, if he looked back. Mostly his doing, he knew. He *knew* it, clear as anything. The other two had picked themselves up, but not him. He'd gone wild. Seemed easier, believed he was owed something. It rankled, still.

He picked up a pebble and hurled it to the coals. Hard to look at yourself. Unruly, angry—no local girl had taken him as a serious contender for marriage. He had nothing, was a no-hoper without a crust to his name. The old farm had gone long prior, and his parents dead these last ten years. His brothers had made their own way, Jude had already been walking out with Anne in the early 'eighties. Maisie had chosen Zeke—the bastard—and not once had she looked back at Nebo, who'd been after her first. Didn't matter now. Maisie was dead. He should stop lookin' back.

'Stay with me, Rosie,' he said urgently. 'We'd be good together, you and me.'

She glanced at him. 'I could, I suppose.' She picked at her hands, like she was nervous or something. 'I mean, it's only been days,' she continued. 'I know we're grown-up people, but it's so forward, and unusual. Still—'

'We start from here, then.' He stopped her going on too much, smiled and held out his hand.

Rosie's slipped into his. 'Um, all right.'

His heart thundered, and a happy gallop of pulses shot through him. Nothing else mattered now. He was gonna make good. He'd go cap in hand, but serious, to his brothers and start a life on the land again. It wasn't like he was useless. He could do anything, he knew it.

Wally and Sal emerged from behind the canvas drop, the lifeless little bundle in Sal's arms. 'We're ready now,' Wally said, and gathered Sal close, an arm around her shoulders. 'We'll put this little one to rest.'

A thud landed in Nebo's chest. What was that, grief for his mate? Must be. He jumped to his feet. Rosie stood, her slim hand squeezing his as she pressed alongside him. When he glanced at her, he saw tears running down her cheeks.

Thirty-seven

Lily watched the cart, the extra horse tied behind, bob along the track until it took the bend and disappeared from her sight. Shading her eyes from the glare striking through the dense, rolling clouds, she hoped they'd get to wherever they were going without the heavens opening and drenching them. Oh well, at least Miss Goody would be all right with Ezekiel escorting her back to her sister.

She wondered whatever would become of the sister, left behind in Nebo's camp. Could be a scandal to that, but she knew there were other women there if the poor girl needed to be sheltered. Such a strange predicament for everyone—the dead boy, and his sisters searching for answers. And poor Jude, being stabbed like that.

Her heart warmed, then cooled almost as soon. He had rejected her … *Mrs Hartman, I thank you for your company, but I am a solitary man* … He faltered then, and she thought he'd perhaps been too embarrassed to go on. So she'd gone about other business in a hurry, couldn't even remember what she'd said. *Well, for heaven's sakes*—she hadn't proposed; it wasn't that bad. Still, she should be resigned and let it go. No point believing there'd be some magical turnaround from him. The man had made himself clear. The rejection was, after all, her own fault—wearing her heart on her

292

sleeve. What sensible woman ever did that? Her mood dropped even further. She sighed long and hard.

Whatever would her daughter think of it? 'Mama, you are just too old for that sort of thing,' she'd most likely say. Lily could just imagine Loretta tsk-tsking. If the mail had arrived in Melbourne on time today, Loretta would be doing just that as she read Lily's letter, as she read of her mother gushing (oh, the mortification now) over the possibility of Judah Jones in her life.

Still, it didn't matter that Loretta knew, or thought she knew. No one else was privy to how Lily felt, and Judah Jones had simply jumped to conclusions. She hadn't *declared* herself—God forbid. So, no harm done, except for a little bruising of her ego. She was of an age where her dignity came before all else. No one knew her private thoughts, and so her ego would survive this.

She sat on the end of Gracie's bed and looked around. The children's room was small, with hardly any furniture except the necessary, and no playthings whatsoever. Perhaps Gracie might like Loretta's old rocking horse. And surely there'd be something discarded by Edward and Oliver at her house that she could bring over for Gifford and Jonty.

Oh, to have family around again. Well, young family. The older her children got, the more distant they seemed. Perhaps that was her fault, and Stan's. Perhaps they'd given their children such an idea of independence and maturity that they hadn't wanted to revisit the past, the past that belonged outside of the busy city.

And really, she thought to herself a little exasperated, what on earth was she doing here, all by herself? Certainly, if the only man in the district who interested her was not interested, then what was the point?

Widows were hardly inundated with invitations for afternoon teas or lunches. Widows, except those who were in their dotage— and she was most certainly not—were given a wide berth, especially if they had no family. It had even been hinted, and out-right suggested when she came to think of it, that she should go to Melbourne and take up lodgings with her daughter. She shuddered and didn't study that too much. Loretta, at sixteen, had not been able to wait to governess in the city and Lily had barely seen her in the three years since. Her daughter's letters were more than a little stand-offish these days; hardly conducive to Lily suggesting a visit to the city.

She cast her glance around the little room again, straightened Giff's bed linens, and grabbed a small pair of discarded long-johns that had seen better days. Probably new when Giff wore them, passed down to Gracie before she wore dresses, and now to Jonty. *Oh no, was Jonty not wearing any unders today?* She folded them on his bed.

Perhaps she should go to Melbourne after all. Pack up her house and sell it, though talk was that she'd not get anything for it, such was the dismal state of the economy, especially house and land prices. And the way the banks were acting—disgraceful, all these foreclosures and bankruptcies.

So what point would there be to leave here and put herself in debt in Melbourne, where finding a decent house to suit her budget would be nigh on impossible, or worse, to burden her soon-to-be married daughter with her company? *One must be sensible.* Then again … *Oh, gracious me. I used to be so clear-headed.* She left the room, thoughts spinning, heart heavy.

Standing in the hall, she could hear a child crying somewhere outside, and she started towards it until she heard the soothing murmur of a man's voice following the sobs.

Jude was coming out of his brother's room. 'Mrs Hartman.' He shuffled into her path, a hand on the wall as he crept along.

Her steps faltered, her chest tightened. Seeing no signs of distress in him, she asked, 'Are you quite well, Mr Jones?'

'I am sore, but well as can be.' He had a few days' growth on his cheeks and chin, and salt 'n' peppery it was, too. She wondered—very fleetingly—what it might feel like to smooth her hand over it. She knew (of course she knew, from oh-so-long ago), what a man's bristly face felt like, but not Judah Jones's face. Her heart gave a little jump.

Goodness me. She had to stop this. *He'd made himself clear.* And the only reason she was still here in this house was that his brother Ezekiel had asked her to stay while he was gone—for her own safety as much as anyone's. And really, that was a very sensible reason for her to stay. Besides that, Jude was an invalid at the moment, and there were three young children to be cared for.

'Got me thinking, the boy cryin' out there,' he said and seemed to be choosing his words carefully as he edged towards the back of the house. He shoved the door open for her, beckoned her to go ahead of him. 'Let's have some tea.'

In the bright but cool early morning, the sunshine pale blue, she waited until he was level with her and then walked at his pace to the cookhouse. Their silence was awkward as far as she was concerned. Well, she had nothing of interest to impart.

Inside, she pulled out a chair and indicated he should sit. Removing a discarded hairbrush from the table, she thought to have Gracie come and put it away, which prompted her to ask, 'Where are the children?' She remembered the cry from before.

He sat carefully. 'They're saying goodbye to Miss Goody. They'll be in directly. If they're not going to school, they have to do chores before they get their damper and jam for the day.'

'Ezekiel is lucky he can still send them to school,' she commented, setting the half-filled kettle back on the stove. She checked the contents of the teapot and decided another brew could be eked from it.

'He won't be able to for much longer,' Jude said. 'Giff will have to work on the farm. Maybe on both our farms. Us brothers need to talk more.'

It gave Lily pause to think of her own place again, of how hard it was just to find spare money to pay someone to help her when she needed it. But if she sold … She dismissed the thought. *Don't think of it now.*

'You heard the boy cry, Mrs Hartman?' His voice was low, hoarse. His big hands smoothed the tabletop as if it had a wrinkled cloth on it, and he seemed to be studying his progress. 'It was the little lad, Jonty. I was watching.'

Lily glanced at him. *Oh my.* That wistful look on his face. Whatever is the poor man thinking? Perhaps missing his children, his girls, of course. Terrible thing. Terrible disease, diphtheria. She sighed inwardly. It wasn't her place to speak those thoughts. Many a time she'd been in trouble second-guessing what was on someone's mind. Who knew what he was really thinking?

'Upset for something, no doubt,' she replied evenly. She gathered the remains of yesterday's damper and brushed the crumbs and the crusts into a bowl for the chickens. Finding the flour bag, she poured a good measure into another bowl, added water and began to mix. Felt right; it was nice and easy in her hands. Something to do.

'Got me thinking.'

For goodness sake, man, you already said. The kettle whistled. Scraping sticky dough from her hands, she wrapped her pinny around the handle and poured the water into the pot. *Give it five minutes*, she decided. Back to the damper, and it was coming together nicely. 'I wonder if Ezekiel has any dried fruit?' she mused aloud.

Hands still doughy, she turned back to the mantel and as she did, she heard the chair scrape and Judah Jones was standing behind her. Without turning, she could feel the heat of him close to her back. She reached up for a tin on the shelf and his hand closed over hers.

'I came back, thinkin' the time was right to move forward. Got me thinkin' how much I miss a family life. Reckon I could be a help here with these children, 'stead of pushing them away.' He took the tin from her hand, set it on the table with a firm thump and picked a little dough from his hand. ''Stead of pushin' everyone away.'

And you were a solitary man only yesterday. But she didn't dare say that aloud—of course not. She turned, now so very close to Jude. She looked into those eyes that were always under a frown, always dark and enigmatic. Heat crept up her neck. It wasn't from the stove, and those burning flashes of heat other women talked of hadn't tormented her yet, and so it only left one thing.

'I said I was a solitary man. I am. I feel I have to be because my mind still takes me to dark days, every so often. The ghosts will never be gone, but they come less now than before.' He wasn't so much taller, and yet it felt as if he towered over her. 'I didn't finish sayin', yesterday before you ran off—'

I didn't run off. She gave him a look, sidled away from the stove and put her hands back into the dough. A light sweat broke out on her forehead and she patted it off with her forearm, hoping nothing would likely drip into the damper mix.

'—and I know I sounded like I was keepin' my distance, warnin' you off.'

One way of putting it, and you succeeded. Perhaps he was still too much attached to his dear and departed family. Well, she couldn't blame him for that, but it would certainly not do her any good to be hankering after a man who was unreachable. *Oh, make up your mind, Lily Hartman.*

She huffed out her determination and gazed at the bowl. She had a good dough, and another knead or two and she could put it in a pan. *Now. Where was a pan?*

'I just didn't have the right words.' Jude reached under a bench close by and a pan clattered to the table. 'When this is healed,' he said pointing to his side, 'I'll get back to my own place. Get it built up again.'

'Good for you,' she finally said as she kneaded. A blush rushed over her face to the roots of her hair. She'd felt like this for Jude for years. Still, he had put her straight yesterday. 'No need for you to explain—'

'Then maybe with that done, I'll have something to offer you,' he said, and stopped her hands working in the bowl. 'But for now, I'd like it if we stepped out together.' His eyes searched hers. He moved closer. 'Let me be proper about it and court you, Lily.' He pressed a hand over her wrist. 'If I may call you Lily?'

She stared. She took a deep breath and let it out. 'You've called me by my name before.' Still, her feathers were ruffled from yesterday. 'However, I've a mind to sell up and go to Melbourne, Mr Jones.' *Oh, and sounding petulant, now.* What on earth made her blurt that? She *had* thought of it, true, but really, so *very* fleetingly—

'Damn me,' he said softly. 'Not go, surely?' He shook his head a little, frowned as if worried all of a sudden. 'Why would you think of doin' that? Your farm, your friends are here. You know the place well.'

He looked surprised. *Did the man really have no idea? Oh, probably not.* 'My time would be better spent elsewhere, meeting new people. My children are all there, not likely to return. And you yourself know how hard it is to keep a farm.' She stopped short of saying what she most wanted to say: *especially as I'm a woman, and on my own.* That was most certainly not appropriate to say here and now, but it was true.

Still bemused, he looked at her. 'But people look out for you here.'

Do they? She supposed they did. And to date all *except* the one person she hoped would look out for her. And yet, now, here he is, hoping to court her. *Oh, my heart.* Could she dare think—

'Don't go, don't sell,' he said, and pressed her wrist again. 'We could work your place, too. With Giff, as well as us old boys, and maybe even Nebo, if he stops being the fool.' He looked as if something grand had just dawned on him.

Must be sensible. 'I need to get this in the cooker.' She reached past him, grabbed the dough and slapped it into the pan.

He turned and opened the oven with the tamp iron. He took the pan and shoved it inside. 'And you see? I'm good in the kitchen.'

'A very attractive attribute.'

'Thought that would impress.' He took one of her hands, rubbed off the excess dough. He brought it to his lips.

So very forward, Mr Jones. But the scratch of his beard stubble awoke her. She uncurled her fingers and let her hand rest on his cheek. Oh yes, those bristles were wonderful against her palm and the giddy tickle raced straight to her belly. She never thought she'd feel that again, that—wanting. That anticipation. However— 'I am not a woman with whom to trifle, Judah Jones.'

'I know it, and I would not.' His gaze never wavered. He waited.

A deep breath or two and then her other hand came up—all by itself—and cupped his face. A light sparked in his eyes and it so gladdened her heart. 'Because I've waited for you,' she said.

A strong arm slid around her, and despite her being acutely aware of her extra padding built up over the years—no longer the lithe girl—his easy warmth, his confidence was heartening.

He looked earnest, open. 'So don't be leavin' now that I'm here,' he said, and his eyes glinted. 'You'd never get to see the rest of my attributes.' He pressed his forehead on hers. 'I'm too old not to speak my mind about what I want, what I need, Lily, and it's you.'

Noises of the children playing in the yard—*perhaps not doing their chores*, the kettle puffing on the stove, the open pot of jam and the empty dough bowl on a hard-working family kitchen table … these were the sounds and signs of a life she missed, echoes of a life filled with company, and love. Her own children were distant now, disdainful—still, how she loved them. But here, a man was holding her close. She would be wanted again and useful. Productive, and with a life worth living to the full, surrounded by the thing she most treasured. Family.

But she'd waited too long not to guard her heart. She stared into those eyes, crinkled and bleary with years of life and love and loss. They were dear to her. She wanted her life again, not just the desperate filling of each day with simple routine to keep her alive. She wanted a new life, with him, but would he know what she needed to hear?

His hands pressed over hers again, large and warm, eyes searching hers. 'Grab the good while we can.' He took a breath. 'I'm letting my ghosts rest.'

Her breath caught. He had known. She touched her lips to his cheek, softly. *So very forward, yourself, Lily Hartman.* 'I think your ghosts would be happy to rest, Judah.'

'Aye, I think they would.'

Thirty-eight

Overhead, the sky had darkened. Roiling clouds, heavy and threatening, blocked out the sun. Every so often great fat drops had fallen, but a deluge hadn't come. Elsa tightened the tie on her hat as Ezekiel clicked the reins again, urging Milo faster.

'I have no brolly,' he said. 'And it looks like that could dump on us before we get much further. If it's a torrent, we'll have to go to the town. Going to Nebo's camp will be out of the question.'

'Why?'

'The ground doesn't drain well here. There's talk of digging great gutters by the roads, along the fields, but it hasn't happened yet. If it's rained hard over his way, chances are it's boggy. I won't risk Milo getting stuck.'

Many animals perished if carts and coaches got bogged and couldn't be pulled out. She'd certainly not endanger any animal, but she didn't want to go to the town. 'Could we turn around?'

'We could, but we're much closer to Casterton than the farm. We'll head there.'

She tried again. 'Surely we'd be fine on the track to the camp. It seemed quite sturdy.'

He glanced at her. 'It might be, but if it pours, and that's look-ing likely,' he said nodding towards the south-east and the wall of cloud, thick and grey, obscuring the horizon, 'we won't even get that far. Town it is.' He flicked the reins over Milo again and the horse stepped up once more, Salty picking up his pace too.

Ezekiel veered along to the right, onto a wider track, which Elsa assumed headed towards the township. She'd only seen faint twinkling lights when she'd ridden by it in the night not long ago, and now she had no real clue where she was.

She'd wanted to get to Rosie as quickly as possible, but she'd have to wait. The thing to do now was to secure the satchel so nothing inside it got wet, most importantly her father's will. She tucked it back further under the seat and checked that it would be well sheltered if it did rain. She hoped so.

A thought struck her. If they had to go to the township ... 'Would there be a solicitor there, by chance?'

'A visiting one at best.' Thunder cracked close by and Milo's ears twitched and flattened, and the cart lurched forward. 'Hang on tight,' Ezekiel said, and he let the horse have his head. 'Only a mile or so to go.'

The skies opened and the deluge hit them full force. Rain stung as it pelted and soaked their clothes through in only minutes. Milo tugged harder as the road began to puddle and muddy under him, but the sludge was slowing him down, sucking at the wheels. As the buildings of the town came into view, Elsa believed that they might just make it in one piece. She let her breath go and prayed for the satchel to remain dry—she didn't dare retrieve it now.

In front of them, pedestrians charged from the footpath across the slush and mire of the road to the opposite side, looking for shelter under verandahs. Not a lot around, Elsa discovered when she chanced a look through the sheeting rain. It was pouring in rivulets off a hill that rose like a great sentry at the eastern end of the street.

Ezekiel hauled Milo up at the Albion Hotel, a single-storey solid brick building that Elsa hoped had rooms. She also hoped that Ezekiel Jones could pay for rooms, for she had no money—Rosie had it.

'Wait while I check inside,' he shouted at her, the rain dripping down his face and running under his sodden shirt. He was off before she could answer.

Good God. Stuck on the cart for how long? She should grab the satchel out from its hiding place, but as her own clothes were wet through, weighty with water, that would not be a good idea. And she wouldn't be able to protect the contents from the bucketing rain.

He bolted back outside. 'Come on,' he shouted and held out his arms for her. He swept her off the cart, a confident, powerful swing that made her feel that she was as light as air.

'But—' She could only hold on, no time to grab anything. Rain cascaded over her head and she closed her mouth to stop sputtering water.

Then he clambered inside the hotel with her.

Shelter from the bombardment was swift relief. It was warm and dry, and close with the unmistakable ripe smell of hops. Loud male laughter roared through a doorway off to the side. So that would be the bar. Tobacco and firewood smoke mingled with the pungent sour aroma of sweaty bodies and floated in around her.

He set her down in the small foyer, checked that she rested easily against a wall and slapped his sodden clothes. 'Now for the things we need.' He turned for the door, dripping from his hat to his boots, and small puddles trailed him.

'Mr Jones, please, get my satchel,' she called after him.

He pulled open the door, and the roar of the downpour was staggering. Long moments later, utterly soaked, he returned with a rifle, the crutches and the satchel.

A sigh of relief when she saw it tucked under his arm. She sagged back against the wall and smiled at him. 'Thank you.' She put it under the seat nearby, which stood by a raggedy-looking aspidistra. Sopping, she wasn't game to sit on the nicely upholstered chair for fear she'd ruin it.

Ezekiel snatched off his hat, wrung it over the plant, and dropped it on the floor. 'They have rooms and have given me a credit note.' He looked grim. 'This weather looks set in. There's no guarantee the roads will be safe for the cart even in a day or so, even if it stops raining.'

'Should we have turned back for the farm after all?'

He snorted. 'We wouldn't have made it. We'd be stuck out in this, in the open somewhere.' He pushed wet hair off his face and swiped water from his arms and chest. Great plops settled on the timber floor. 'I'll try to find cover for the cart and horses.' He leaned down and grabbed his hat. 'We'll be right.'

Elsa wasn't so sure. She'd been days away from her sister, no idea when she'd see her next. Her only clothes were saturated. She had a broken bone in her foot, had no money … and she was in a hotel with Ezekiel Jones.

Bursting from the bar room in a tumble, a big redheaded man with a sizeable middle that hung out of his shirt was clutching another man around his neck. They chortled, drunk as lords. Cackling about some joke, the redhead straightened up and wobbled his pink and ginger-furred belly in both hands. Then he caught sight of Ezekiel.

Elsa caught her breath and shrank. She knew exactly who these men were. She tugged her hat rim around her ears.

'Hey, Jones,' Redhead said, and shoved into the other man, who staggered back against the wall.

Ezekiel was still swiping rainwater from his clothes. He looked up. 'Billy Watson, they let you back in here again?'

Elsa smoothed her own clothes and tried not to attract attention. But she was on one foot, and crutches rested nearby. Surely that awful man would recognise her, or his friend might—the one who'd dragged her out from behind Peppin's hind legs. She lowered her head.

Redhead wobbled closer. 'Funny bugger, Zekey. Nobody keeps me out of a pub,' he said. He threw a smirk at his mate and stared back at Ezekiel. 'Hey, heard your brother bailed up a coach like some flamin' bushranger.'

'Did you now?'

'Yeah, had some wild women with him. Decoys, they was. Their cart was across the road an' all. Coach had to stop for 'em, is how they got held up. Clever, that Nebo, gettin' women to do his work for him.'

Elsa squeezed her eyes shut and kept her hands on her dress. She hardly dared breathe. Glancing, she saw Ezekiel had stilled a moment. He'd cocked his head, as if considering what Watson had said.

'That so? Never heard of either of my brothers bailing up any coaches.' He flicked a narrow glance in Elsa's direction.

'C'mon, Nebo done one years ago.'

Ezekiel shook his head. 'Don't think so.' His mouth flattened. His hands flexed.

'Yeah, well.' Then Watson thumbed towards the bar. 'I was just talkin' to a bloke about Nebo in there. Told 'im where he might be, hidin' out in that camp of his at five-mile. Got me good coin for it, too. He's real interested in you Jones boys. I might just go right back to 'im and earn me some more, now I seen you here.' He nodded, smirked again, his guts wobbling as he tried to stand upright.

Ezekiel's face looked set as if carved in stone.

Watson didn't notice. He nodded again, imparting more news. 'He's the fella been huntin' Jude for killin' his son. He reckons Nebo might have somethin' what don't belong to 'im. As usual.'

Elsa sucked in a breath and froze. *Could Nebo have had something of George's after all? Oh God. Rosie.*

Ezekiel's gaze nailed the drunk. Then he snaked out an arm and grabbed Watson by the collar. 'It isn't my brothers he has to worry about,' he said between his teeth.

'*Jesus*, Zeke, yer killin' me.' Bug-eyed, Watson gurgled. 'Boffa, get that bloke—'

A man exploded out of the bar. Stocky, with a grimace glinting gold, he head-butted Boffa in the doorway, sending him out cold and sliding down the wall. The man spun hard, barrelled full-bodied into Watson, knocking Ezekiel flat on his back. The man flew out the door, into the driving rain.

'That was 'im, that was the fella,' Watson shouted from the floor.

Ezekiel shoved Watson off and scrambled to his feet. He bolted outside into the deluge.

Watson fumbled around trying to stand up, and once back on his feet, spotted Elsa. He squinted at her. 'Hey,' he said, and staggered towards her. 'You, girlie. I know you.'

She shied away, she could smell his breath, and the rest of him. Worse than a fly-blown sheep.

Boffa, awake, was holding his head. His nose was bleeding into his mouth as he crawled towards the door. 'Let's go, Billy,' he said, his teeth red.

'Look who it is, Boffa.'

'Billy, come on, Zeke's on his way back.' Boffa spit blood as he dragged himself up the door jamb.

'It's one of Nebo's doxies.' Watson leered at her as if he'd won a prize. He glanced at the crutches and then down at her feet. 'It was you at the cart.'

In spite of good sense, she screwed up her face and shouted, 'You'd only know that if you were there.' And Watson understood her, she could see it on his face, even drunk as he was.

He lurched and knocked her hat off. 'Well, maybe my mate the coach driver can tell the troopers that I caught me his lady bushranger, all by accident—'

Ezekiel crashed inside, lunged at Watson and grabbed him by the waistcoat, swinging the bulky redhead towards the door. Watson stumbled and dropped to the floor with a grunt. Ezekiel put a foot to his backside and rolled him outside and into the mud as if he was a sack of beans. He wheeled around to the man holding his own head, trying to stand. 'You next, Boffa,' he growled, dripping with muddy water and breathing hard.

Holding his nose as blood slid over his fingers, Boffa mumbled, 'Not me, Zeke, I'm goin'. No trouble outta me.' On bowed legs he wobbled past Ezekiel and staggered outside.

Elsa propped herself against the wall with both hands to keep from falling. What a relief—

'Tell me you didn't help Nebo bail up a coach.' Ezekiel's eyes were fiery-red. He stormed towards her. 'Tell me you haven't bloody lied the whole time.'

She stormed right back, just under his chin. 'I haven't lied about a damned thing.' She swatted at drips running from her hair to her chin. 'Don't you yell at me,' she cried. 'I just heard that your brother might have something of George's after all, and my sister is out there with him,' she finished, a finger in the air, done with *polite*, done with waiting.

A man stuck his head out the bar door and shouted, 'Hey, Zeke, I just got rid of two drunks making a noise. You got rooms, take it up there.'

Raucous laughter followed from the bar, and a sudden hot bloom burst in Elsa's cheeks. She glared at Ezekiel and watched as the fight flickered to nothing in his eyes before he turned away.

He bent, picked up her crutches, and thrust them at her. He snatched the satchel from under the chair, then cradled the rifle.

'This way,' he said, and didn't wait for her as he stalked past the bar door.

The laughter had drowned under the pounding rain on the roof. Behind Ezekiel, Elsa swung carefully along a short corridor, mindful of puddles forming on the floor as rain found its way inside in steady streams from above.

When she caught up, Ezekiel was jiggling a key in a door and it swung open. He looked inside, then stood by so she could get past him.

She'd expected only one single bed, but there was one big bed and a smaller one beside it. She flared. 'I'm not—'

'I'll take that room, there,' he said, gruffly cutting her off. He swung open the door opposite, and three single beds were close together in the middle of the room. 'I'll bring a bowl and a pitcher of water. There's a chamber pot under the first bed.' He pointed at it, then nodded down the hallway. 'A privy is out that way.' He tossed the satchel onto one of the beds in her room. 'I'll see if I can get us some food.' He stopped and looked at her. 'Maybe some dry clothes from somewhere, and shelter for the horses and cart.' He turned to go.

'Wait.' Elsa's face still flamed and her heart had begun to pound, but not because of their spat. The real enormity had dawned on her as she recalled Lily's description. *'They're capped in gold ...'* As he turned back, she said, 'That man with the gold teeth—'

'He's the one I took to your brother's grave, the one who says he's Curtis Goody, the man we reckon killed George. The one who stabbed Jude.' He looked at his hands and back at her again. 'And now Watson has told him where Nebo is likely to be. He'd disappeared by the time I got outside.'

She took in the slump of his shoulders, the resigned look on his face. 'If he's gone to where Nebo is, Rosie is there. My sister—'

'What the hell is he after?' Ezekiel cut in. 'What the hell does he think George had that was worth killing him for, that was worth trying to kill Jude? George had something, he must have.' His eyes were bleak, searching hers. Water dripped from his hair and slid down the bristly dark cheeks, dropping to his neck and shirt. Beads trickled onto the expanse of his chest, mingled with the hair there, and disappeared.

Rain roared down overhead. Now her fury had evaporated, Elsa was chilled to the bone, standing in drenched clothes. Her one boot was heavy and squelchy with water, and the bandage on her sore foot was soaked. Her toes felt numb, on both feet.

'It's a tin,' she said hoarsely. 'A tin with at least thirty sovereigns in it.' She lifted a hand to wipe over her lips. Her fingers were biting cold. She licked the droplets off them, her mouth was so dry. Water still dripped from her hat and she snatched it off, letting it dangle by its tie around her neck.

'*Thirty*—' He stared at her for some moments then looked at a leak starting in her ceiling. 'I'll find a bowl and a bucket, clean water for drinking.' He handed her a key. 'Let only me back in.' He didn't wait for her to answer, just turned on his heels and pounded back towards the bar.

The barman filled a pitcher of water and told Zeke where to get towels. He agreed to find a dry dress for Zeke's lady friend. Then he sent a boy out into the weather to stable Zeke's cart and horses.

'Not one of the tart's dresses, either, Bernie,' Zeke told him, flicking a glance at a couple of women entertaining the patrons. Though any sort of dress would suit Elsa. She was the most effortlessly beautiful woman he had ever seen. Strong, and natural in her disposition—he'd told her that—no airs and graces, just a normal down-to-earth woman. Elsa out of any sort of dress would suit him, too.

What?

The barman laughed. 'Might be they're the only ones that are dry today, mate. Hope the river don't flood, else there'll be nothin' dry for months. 'Ninety-three was bad enough, you remember?' he said and looked at the old water stains running on the wall beside him. 'Heaviest drop in three years, today.' He nodded towards one of the women. 'I'll have Emily bring something along directly. She'll be finished soon, and I don't reckon she'll be in a hurry to leave in this lot.' He put a shot of rum in a cup and slid it across the bar.

Zeke grabbed it and took a swallow. When he remembered how Elsa had looked after he accused her of lying, he had cause to shift uncomfortably on his seat. Those big green eyes and her spitfire temper … She'd been dripping wet, angry, and glaring at him.

Get your mind out of your pants, man.

Right, right. Thirty sovereigns in a tin. No wonder the bastard had killed for it and had tried to kill Jude. He was sure Jude didn't have it and never had. Who'd been with the boy, other than Nebo, before he found him and brought him in—

Nebo. Zeke thought hard, shook his head. Nebo wouldn't still be in the district if he'd found thirty sovereigns. He'd have gone, quick as snatching up a rum. Zeke went over the last conversation he'd had with him—there was no indication that his brother had had a stroke of that sort of luck.

Zeke stared into the pannikin. All there'd been with the boy was the locket and those few buttons.

No bloody thirty sovereigns in sight.

Thirty-nine

Jaysus, glad I made it.

Pete Southie shook off his oilskin and stepped into the main bar at the Glenelg Inn in Casterton. Others had crowded inside before him and the air was thick, all tobacco smoke. Blokes were yellin' across the crowded room, ale was spilled, rum slopped. *Busy place.* The bar counter was packed with men except for a corner on the other side. Only one fella sat there, nursing a glass filled to the brim. He didn't look happy.

It was the only place to stand and Pete angled his way over. He kept his coat close to him and his hand in his pants pocket, feeling the warm coins there. He got to the vacant space, called over the din to the barman for a rum. He slapped a coin into the man's hand and took his change.

The fella alongside was surly. Barely even looked up. No matter. He didn't need conversation. Not yet, anyway. Soon as he'd had a drink, found something to eat, he'd check around for those Goody girls, see if they'd headed here like the rabbito-kid said. Well, he would if the bloody rain let up. *Was only luck me horse didn't slide off the road and do a fetlock comin' into town.* As it was, he had to tie up his poor nag out the back with others. There was little shelter around.

If Miz Putney was here, he'd tell her about Frank. Come right out and say it, he reckoned. *Miz Putney, Frank is dead.* He'd tried out other ways, kept himself occupied with it gettin' over here, but he kept coming back to simple, and to the point. *Frank is dead.*

Old town back home weren't the same with the bakery shut. Miz Putney would take it over, for sure, when she got back, and have young Elsa help her out. Pete could run the farm, get a few trees in, get a vegetable garden going. The ladies like a good garden. Get a crop in maybe, this year if he was lucky. If he was smart. Some sorta crop, anyhow. He'd figure it out learning from a few of the others. He'd never been a croppie before. Would be better to run sheep. Maybe dairy cows. Yeah. He could see himself doing a fine job. Having a fine time. If he got it right.

He'd get Miss Elsa on side, he could see she was itchin' for him, playing that hard-to-get game. She'd see his way of thinking. And he'd have none of her independent-lady thinking. He'd wear the pants. 'Course, that other thing she done was just a mistake—messing up his tea that last day. Poor little lady woulda been all sad, and her mind woulda been turned upside down. Damned near poisoned a man, whatever she give him 'stead of sugar. Can't have a woman all blithered in the head like that, allowed to vote like she wanted to do. No wonder everyone was agin it. Gov'ment's gone damn stupid—dunno what it's doin' givin' women the vote. He shook his head.

He took a long gulp of rum. Looked at the fella next to him and nodded. The man eyed him, nodded back, and took a long swallow of whatever was in his glass. Whisky, maybe. Lucky bastard. No one dirt-poor could get whisky. Must be a rich local.

Pete still had a bit of money left, could buy another drink for himself. He signalled the barman, then he'd strike up a conversation, see what he could get out of the bloke standing all quiet-like beside him.

Could be an interestin' conversation with a rich fella—never talked to a bloke with gold in his teeth before.

Forty

Elsa didn't know how long she'd been asleep. She hadn't believed it was possible to doze off with the rain still hammering above. But she had, and now the rain had stopped. The leak was still running and the chamber pot under it was catching most of the drips.

Trying to rouse herself, she heard a knock at her door. She sat up, pushed off the covers and swung her feet to the floor. She'd stripped down to nothing earlier, pulled her hair out of the tie, and used a sheet from the other bed to dry herself off. Then had slipped under the covers of the big bed to warm up.

Her clothes hung over the other bed's rail, and small puddles had formed under the hems. Her dress was still heavy with water, her chemise was just a little more than damp. Still nowhere near dry enough to wear. Her ruined stockings were almost dry, but they would hardly help and she wondered what to wear to answer the door.

'Elsa, are you in there?' Ezekiel's voice was urgent through the door.

'I'm coming, I just have to— I won't be a moment.' Wrapping the thin bedsheet around her and tucking it secure, she draped a light, short blanket over her shoulders. Something smelled a bit mouldy, but it was bearable. Then she tried her weight on her sore foot—it wasn't too bad—and hobbled to the door, unlocking it and pulling it open.

It looked like shock on his face as he stared at her.

'What is it?' she cried, now fully alert. She was perfectly decent, she knew, but her hair was all over the place—would that have shocked him? Surely not.

'Nothing.' He gathered himself, shook his head. 'I found this for you.' He held up a light gown in an amber-coloured fabric. 'I left the water pitcher here before, and a bucket,' he said and pointed at the foot of the door. 'I knocked, but couldn't get you to answer.' Still he stared. Then, 'Here, I'll bring it all in.'

She hopped aside and he brushed past, laying the dress on the bed. He was only in his shirt and his trousers. His feet were bare. Looked like he'd tried to dry off, too. He went back to the door and picked up the pitcher and bowl, set it on the dresser. He emptied water from the chamber pot into the large bucket. 'Towels are somewhere. I think there's a bathroom down the hall a bit.' He looked as if unsure of what to do, then bemused, turned to go.

'When will we leave here?' she asked, one hand clutching the sheet around her, the other holding the blanket closed over her chest.

'Tomorrow, if the rain stays away. The river hasn't come up, it might not, but if it does, we'll be here for a while.' He headed for the door again, seemed to be in a hurry. 'The cook will have a couple of bowls of mutton stew and potatoes for us. Will that do?'

Her mouth watered immediately. 'Yes. I'll dress and come down—'

'No. Too many men in the bar, and they've spilled into the dining room. It's crowded.' He waited, and only once met her gaze.

'Then I'll eat here,' she said, and her mouth flattened. She was to be locked in a room while he went off and had a fine old time in the bar.

Still he hesitated, but then said, 'I'll be back directly, with the food.' And he marched out.

Sighing, she shut the door and shuffled to the bed, eyeing the dress he'd left for her. Wouldn't make sense to put it on now that she was going to be in the room all night. She might as well stay as she was, even sleep without unders to give all her clothes a chance to dry more. The smalls that were still in the satchel were damp—the will had been dry, thankfully—and there was nothing worse than that stale water smell on clothes, the smell of things not dried properly but worn, nevertheless. She'd stay in the blanket and sheet, dry and warm.

She sat on the bed and tried to wrangle her hair. The blanket slipped from her shoulders and the sheet drooped. She adjusted them and tried again with her hair. Drying, it was becoming voluminous, and not for the first time she thought about lopping it off. George had done her a favour all those years ago. She bit her lip. If she cut it off, would Ezekiel ever put his hands in it again? It would grow, of course. Heat crept through her chest as she remembered him plaiting her hair, the gentle tugs on her scalp as he worked, his warm fingers brushing her back. Would there ever be a chance he'd do that again?

He did it for his child because she had no mother to do it; he did her own hair because Gracie insisted on it.

Would he do it for a wife?

Such an intimate act it seemed to Elsa, personal, innocent yet charged with something she couldn't name, didn't know how to name.

Wife? She gave a little huff and tried to quell the glow inside.

No lopping off my hair.

'Elsa?' His voice was muffled at the door.

Startled, she adjusted the sheet and, clutching the blanket, opened the door. A tantalising waft met her. She looked down. 'Oh, that smells wonderful.' In his hands were two bowls of steaming, aromatic stew with a dumpling atop each. She couldn't take them otherwise she'd lose her clothes. She pointed at the dresser with an elbow. 'But I couldn't eat all that,' she said.

'I thought to eat here with you, for company,' he said, carefully placing the bowls. He took two spoons out of a pocket. 'That is, I'll eat here if you've no objection. We'll leave the door open.' He looked as if he was waiting for her to tell him what to do.

The mutton stew called her, and her stomach groaned a little in response. 'That's a fine arrangement.'

'Good.' He seemed pleased with that and stood there.

'I must change in order to eat in company.'

'Certainly.' He seemed pleased with that, too, and with a deep breath headed for the door. 'I'll wait across the hall.' Seemed he couldn't get out fast enough and he shut the door with a loud click.

First, she swiped a finger through some gravy and took a quick bite of dumpling. Then Elsa shed the blanket and sheet and pulled on the dress. She didn't need to fumble with too many buttons— it was a little big in the bodice, soft, well worn, but it would do. It smelled of lavender and was only a bit musty, but she was grateful to whomever had supplied it.

She dipped her finger in the gravy again. Perhaps she could eat both bowls after all, it smelled so delicious.

Pulling open the door, she could see directly into his room. He sat on the end of a bed, waiting, his dark head bowed, his hands laced between his knees. 'Come in,' she called. As he stood and walked towards her, she thought suddenly that perhaps she'd never seen anything better in all her life. Until he smiled. Then she was absolutely sure she'd never seen anything better. Her belly swooped as she met his glance. *What would it feel like to see that face every day for the rest of my life?* She cast her eyes down and blinked. *How can I be thinking that? Pa just gone, George gone. There's something the matter with me. Oh, for goodness sake, the world is all topsy-turvy—Pa would want a good man for me. George would laugh out loud.* She could almost hear him.

Standing aside, she left the door ajar as he strode past her to pick up a bowl and spoon. He waited until she'd hobbled to a bed and sat before handing them to her.

'I'm so hungry, I could eat my poor horse, and yours,' he said. Taking his bowl, he sat on the edge of the bed opposite and spooned a large scoop into his mouth.

Elsa glanced at the open doorway. Noises from the bar threaded their way along the hall, but it wasn't too bad. She tucked in, mutton stew bursting onto her tastebuds.

'I want you to know,' he said between mouthfuls, 'Nebo would never hurt your sister. Never.'

She lifted a shoulder. 'I know nothing about you, or your brothers. Mr Judah was very quiet, for good reason of course, and Mr Nebo is—different. You seem a decent man.' She felt heat creep again. It was the look on his face when he'd glanced up. 'You all seem decent men.'

He chewed, watching her. 'I know nothing of you or your sister.' He spooned another mouthful. 'Or your family. George was in no state to befriend anyone.'

She ate more before answering. No point being hungry. 'There were five of us. With George gone, and our older brothers long gone, there's only my sister and me. Rosie left her husband recently.' Elsa looked away, then decided it was not for her to be worried what he thought of that. 'She's unsure she should be ashamed of herself or happy for herself. She wants to be happy. I was a farmer, as I told you. I intend to go back, but perhaps I mightn't be able to go back to the farm. Rosie's husband stands to inherit, or at least administer. We won't know until the will is formally read, but we do know Frank is not in favour of independent women. And I certainly doubt he'd look kindly on a woman who's left him, or look kindly on her sister.'

'Hmm.' Ezekiel waved his spoon. 'I hear there are many independent women in South Australia, and all women there are about to cast a vote for the first time. Second in the whole world only to New Zealand women. You see? I read, too.'

She let the remark pass her by. 'And I'm to be one of them. The ballot is set for the twenty-fifth of April and I will be there in Robe for election day, no matter what.'

'Even if you don't find that tin of sovereigns?'

Was he teasing her? Her chin came up. 'I'll drive myself to get back there, with or without the tin.'

'Is that right, by yourself? What of your sister?' He wrangled meat from between his teeth with a fingernail.

Elsa let a little breath huff out. 'I think she might not want to— return.' She sat her bowl on her lap and stared into it.

'Ah. A runaway. So, both lady bushrangers, then.'

'By accident,' she cried, looking at him. 'A ridiculous incident. Our cart was ahead, and the coach came roaring up behind us. There was no space on the road to overtake us or time to stop, and then that big fat redhead jumped out on the road on his horse. I'd been thrown onto the brace poles, and my horse had just stomped on my foot.' She thrust out the bruised foot, and when Ezekiel glanced down, she quickly withdrew it. 'Boffa, the other man, grabbed me and threw me off the road, luckily, else I could've been killed. It was only luck that no one was killed.'

Everyone knew stories of horrific coach accidents. Men, women, children and horses killed outright, or maimed terribly, only to die agonising deaths by the side of the road.

'Then they bailed up the coach,' she went on. 'And that Watson man yelled that he was Nebo Jones, and that Rosie and I were his accomplices. The driver had said he'd remember me, and that redhead idiot thought it was a huge joke and had fun with it. Then they took off.'

'And Nebo was where?'

'Not far away.' She ate some more then set the bowl aside.

'Hmm.' That seemed to be Ezekiel's thinking sound. 'That'd be Nebo,' he said, a wry twist on his mouth. He reached over, took her plate and spoon, and set them on the dresser. He poured two cups of water from the pitcher, handed her one and sat down again.

'Why do you three have such unusual names?' she asked.

Ezekiel gave a laugh. 'Not mine or Jude's so much. But Nebo's is certainly unusual. My mother, Mary Brown, married my father John Jones. Seems she didn't want plain names for her boys. They're all old biblical names. Years ago, I could have told you chapter and verse where to find them. Not now.' He took a long draught of water. 'Tell me about your farm.'

His gaze was so intense, it was as if he'd asked her something else completely. Flustered, she took a moment. 'Uh, a small holding my father secured before the land grabbers came in. Back then, I think in the 'sixties, land agents and the big pastoralists would make sure to run the price of land up at the auctions. Smaller farmers lost out.'

'Sounds the same everywhere. Even still,' he said.

Elsa nodded. 'My father always said things never changed much. Just to bid, they had to put down a twenty per cent deposit, the balance due within a month. Anyone with more money, a pastoralist for instance, could bid over the price and win at the auction. Pa was lucky early on, and grateful he'd had at least that chance so he never bid again for another piece. He couldn't afford to.'

She lifted a shoulder. 'But it's all we have. And while it's owned outright, it's not earning anything now. I'm not allowed to secure a loan in order to build it up even if I did inherit.'

'And your brother-in-law?'

She glanced at the satchel, emptied of its contents, and at the will that lay propped beside it, drying out. 'He mightn't want it at all now, especially if Rosie doesn't return.'

'Why wouldn't she return? It'd be hard finding her way alone in the world. Almost impossible if she wishes to live reasonably well. She'll have to change her mind.'

Elsa rankled. 'She knows how hard it'd be. We all do. She won't change her mind, won't suffer going back to him.' Warming again under that dark-eyed, intense stare, Elsa couldn't help but remember the looks that passed between Rosie and Nebo. Remembering what Rosie had said to her about Nebo, she said, 'I think my sister believes she's found someone else. She is very firm in her convictions. Always has been.'

His eyebrows rose. 'And who might the lucky man be? I doubt he'd be in your home town, would he?'

Of course not. The scandal of it. Elsa frowned. 'Your brother.' She couldn't look at him, but she heard his little laugh of surprise. Yes, she could understand that reaction. She remembered that Rosie had inferred dislike for what goes on between a man and a woman in private, and then she'd seemed to make a complete about-face on that same subject. *Surprise? Oh yes.*

'Nebo?' he said, astounded. 'That amazes me. How? Had they met before, somehow, somewhere?'

Elsa did look at him then. He was waiting for an answer, surprise still on his face. 'They met only after the hold-up.'

'A few days ago?'

Elsa reddened. He need not be so sceptical. It was about as long as it had taken her to become enthralled by him, Ezekiel Jones.

Clearly, not the done thing, this speedy developing of emotion.
And *clearly* Ezekiel didn't feel the same about her. His reaction
just now showed he couldn't believe it. Her heart thundered for
a different reason; thank heavens she hadn't let her feelings show.
'Nevertheless, she's quite taken with him.'

'And—did my brother appear to, uh, feel the same?' She nodded. 'Well,' he said, and laced his hands on his knees, not far
from her as she sat on the bed. 'That would impact on your life,
wouldn't it?'

'Of course but things are so unknown, aren't they? I'm trying
not to think too far ahead.'

'Except for insisting on returning to your father's farm to front
your brother-in-law, and to vote.'

She heard the note of criticism but ignored it. 'Voting is only
five weeks or so away, not a lot of time to endure whatever the
consequences of Frank's decision.'

'It's a long time if you have nowhere to live,' he said sharply.

'There'd be a bit of time after the will is read, won't there?
I only need a little time to gather myself. I wouldn't be put out
straight away, would I?' He only lifted a shoulder to show his
doubt. She flustered. 'I'm sure a direction will emerge,' she said,
hoping she sounded strong. But her current plan was pathetic and
without substance. It was hardly a plan—it was just all she had.
She'd have to find somewhere to live, find work to provide a living. She wasn't sure she'd even be allowed to keep Peppin, or the
cart. Her chest felt tight. She most certainly had to come up with
something. 'For me, right now, there is nothing more important
than that vote,' she said firmly. 'What happens with the farm is
out of my control. It's secondary.'

'How can that be if it's at least a roof over your head?' He
sounded incredulous now. 'Think about that.'

'I have thought about it,' she cried, and that was the truth of it. 'Even if Frank were to maintain the farm, even if he did allow me to live there, I couldn't stay knowing Rosie was elsewhere.'

'So going back is hardly an option, really.' His mouth set.

Elsa took a moment. 'I have to go back. I can't leave Robe, or stay away, with nothing.' She knew that much for sure. 'I'll find a place, and work. People know me there. I'll be all right.'

He studied his hands, back and front, in considered silence. He was very fine to look at. The dark and wavy hair, a lock falling forward. Such a handsome face with its strong jaw and searching eyes, that slight frown, the tilt of his head ... *If only. If only.* If only they'd known each other well enough to meet again, to explore the feeling she knew was between them. How to say she wanted the opportunity to see him again without making some awkward mistake?

The noise from the bar receded as rain began to fall. Then a huge downpour dropped out of the sky and crashed onto the roof. Just as suddenly, it stopped. Collective male voices groaned and then laughter began again.

'Maybe you'll find that tin,' Ezekiel said, still concentrating on his hands.

She snapped out of impossible dreams. 'I have no illusions about it. After what you've told me, I doubt George even had it with him.' Her thoughts went to the man in the hotel with the gold in his teeth. 'I hope that terrible man believes it, too. I never want to see him again.'

He was quiet for some moments then cleared his throat. 'Miss Goody, whatever happens,' he began, 'until you're on your way back to Robe, I'll ensure to the best of my ability that you come to no harm.' He took a breath. 'For now, you might need your foot re-bandaged. I'll ask the publican to send a woman to help.' He got to his feet.

Elsa stared at him as he stood. 'No,' she said, more sharply than she'd intended, and struggled to get to her feet. His hand shot out and gripped her elbow as she steadied. 'My foot is much better. Perhaps not quite ready for full weight on it, or riding, but it is better, hardly painful at all.' She took a step to show him but she faltered. It felt sore.

He hesitated before he let her go. 'I should've insisted you take more time to heal at my place.' He gave her a lopsided smile. 'God knows, my kids would've loved you to stay longer.'

Words rushed out. 'If I can, I'd like to visit again—when all this is over.' Reaching for his hand as it slid from her elbow, she was intent only on words that would not be stopped, words that were coming from her heart. 'I'm very much taken by your children. And their father.' *Oh Lord.* She'd said it.

His warm gaze, which had been on her hand in his, lifted to her face.

Oh my dear heavens, could he see what's written there, plain as day?

And by the looks of him ... *Good God, Elsa. You've just said something so, so wrong.*

Forty-one

Zeke stared down at those serious and luminous green eyes. Stared at her wild hair, its joyous spirals of dark honey-coloured waves waiting to tumble in his hands once again. It framed her face, a face he was desperate to hold against his. His heart leapt, and he itched to grab her up and press his mouth against her throat.

And she looked very much as if she wanted it, too. His cock had stirred; *Christ*, he needed to be careful. He dropped her hand as if it were molten.

She blinked. 'I beg your pardon. I've said the wrong thing.'

He let out his breath. 'Not at all, Miss Goody. I'd enjoy it if you would return to us. To visit,' he qualified, to be proper. 'I know the children would enjoy it, too.' He tried a smile, and that didn't work. *Jesus. What to do here?* He'd been thinking about how he could stop her leaving altogether, and failing that, how to see her again if she left; where she might go if Robe was no longer for her. Now she was offering—

'Please call me Elsa,' she said, and her chest rose and fell.

He watched a little beat at the base of her throat. He wanted to touch it, put his finger on it.

'I'm flattered.' *Lame, you idiot. Lame.* The way she just stood there … She had to stop looking at him like that. He knew she was waiting for him. He looked to the door. Open door, he was safe. Fool—*she* was safe. He wanted to toss her on the bed, slide his hand over a velvety firm little breast, and after, down those strong, lean legs he knew were hidden by her dress. More than that, he knew it deep inside that he wanted to care for her, love her, have her by his side. He'd known it from the first moment he laid eyes on her. *How can that be? Too soon, too soon.*

'Flattered?' A fierce blush coloured her face. 'Oh, I see. It was forward, I'm sorry. I'm well known to be forthright. My father always told me that. I had to be that way, you see, growing up with boisterous older brothers, and then because of all the no-hopers that arrived at the door. I had to be very clear and plain-spoken. My father began to see it was probably a necessity after all.' She was talking too fast, rattling, and her hand appeared to be waving her words away. 'Don't be alarmed, it's my nature. I meant only to—'

'I'm not alarmed by your nature.' He stood rigid. 'It's too quick, this feeling between us. It's too strong to make light of it or make decisions that might one day be regretted. We don't know each other.' He stepped back, he had to; she was delivering herself, and he wasn't ready. Not like this, not without thought for the future. He wouldn't just take her and—let her leave. 'I don't want you to make a mistake.'

'Me?' She looked bewildered, surprised. 'I'm sure of my feelings.' Her gaze was warm and welcoming, her small smile tentative.

She was an open book, no guile, but he sensed hesitation. 'The feelings are strong, it's true, but being quick, they might be without depth. It takes time to be sure.' *Dammit—wrong way to say it.*

The smile faltered. 'My feelings are not without depth.'

'I meant, I won't take advantage and jeopardise our friendship.'

'You wouldn't be *taking* advantage. I have my own mind,' she said, her tone clipped, the smile now empty, taut. 'But thank you for your considerations. Please close the door on your way out.'

'Elsa,' he began.

'Just let me know when I need to be ready tomorrow.'

He'd dug his own hole. He set his mouth. 'If it hasn't rained through the night, we'll leave at dawn.'

'Good.' She nodded. 'Good night.'

He held onto his temper. Dismissed, he strode out the door and yanked it shut behind him.

Forty-two

Elsa wasn't stupid. No matter how much she wanted to pull open the door and clump down the hall on these ridiculous crutches, leave this awful pub, find Salty, and disappear, she knew she wouldn't.

She would not put herself in danger—or the horse—just because she was exploding with embarrassment and—and more embarrassment. Waves and waves of it. She'd let the man know that she'd jump all over him like some wanton baggage.

She was trying to plait her unruly hair. (The bloody stuff would *not* be contained. No matter how she tried, her hands were shaking too much.) Now her arms were tired. *For goodness sake.* Frustrated, she jerked a handful high on her head until it hurt.

But *was* she stupid? She barely knew what she'd have done with him if he had given in. *Given in? Oh, don't fool yourself, Elsa Goody. The man had been staunch.*

She'd ruined it. Forthright, oh yes. *A forthright idiot.*

Her insides had been all warm and whooshy. And it certainly hadn't felt like it would've been a duty to be endured—*thank you for nothing, Rosie.* All she wanted was to feel those arms around her, feel his face slide down her neck and—would those bristles scratch? What else would she feel? What else *could* she feel? She'd never been there before.

He had been a gentleman. And it was true: they didn't know each other.

But they did. She knew him well enough. She knew him in her heart, had known him so well since she'd read his letter that had carried the awful news about George. She'd been drawn to Ezekiel, and he hadn't disappointed. He was a kind man. A family man. His children were loved. His brothers were loved. *She* would be loved. She knew it. Did she dare think it? Did she dare think that they might become close, much closer, and that she would become his wife?

It takes time to be sure. She *was* sure. But he was being honourable, *so* honourable, and she had embarrassed herself. *You fool, Elsa. Fool.* What to do? How to keep face in the morning? And the night would be long—it was barely dusk now—with only her self-pitying whimpers to keep her company.

She started to pace but only limped along. Her foot wasn't too bad, perhaps she should strap it again. The bone would have hardly healed at all, not least enough to stay strong—*if* she were to be rash, *if* she were to go galloping off on a horse like she'd just sworn to herself that *she would not.*

But she was about to do *something.* She could feel it. It drove her. She needed to impress upon him that she was a serious person, and not taken lightly by whims of nature that were frivolous or glib. Her feelings already had depth.

He'd be unsuspecting, the poor man. He'd answer the door and she'd just rush in and he wouldn't be able to resist and she would have no care in the world.

And he hadn't said no to her. Not exactly.

Would he think it rash? Do I care? I should have a care. I'm not married to him, he has no obligation to me …

He hadn't said yes, either. Had he only been polite, trying to discourage her? She held her head. *So confusing. I am sensible Elsa ... usually.* She slumped. Oh, that delicate, teasing, intense craving down deep inside wouldn't let go. The ache was physical, that feeling of *needing* something. Needing him.

She spun awkwardly, limped full of determination to the door and wrenched it open. She crossed the hall to stand at his door. *I know my feelings.*

She hadn't the chance to knock before he pulled it open. His hat was on his head, the rifle was in his hand, and boots were on his feet. *Oh no. He's going somewhere.* Breath shot out of her. 'I was just about to knock.' She swiped wayward tendrils from her face. *Should have tied it. Should've at least looked sensible, and not like some mad street woman.* She put both hands on her head.

'I can see that.' He smiled a crooked smile. 'Do you need your hair tied?' There was an unusual gleam in his eye.

'No.' Short and to the point. 'I came to say that I know my own self and my own depth of feeling, I don't make light—'

'I'm sorry. I never meant it to sound like that.' His mouth was set, his gaze on her.

Oh.

He took a step closer. 'I made a mistake earlier,' he said softly. 'I misspoke what I meant.' He reached out to slide a lock of hair from her face.

'You didn't listen properly.' Her face was flaming. Elsa had passed her own point of no return. 'Nor are you now.'

He tilted his head. 'I did listen, I am listening, but if we take this step, we need to address going forward beyond it.'

Oh. 'Yes. To mutual terms, perhaps.' *For goodness sake, Elsa, you have to have terms before you demand them.* Nevertheless, she took a step closer.

'Mutual terms,' he said, and gave a breath of laugh. 'And consent, open and honest. I want you,' he said, and slipped a hand behind her neck, tugging on her hair and drawing her close. 'Is this presumptuous?'

'No.' Her heart lifted. Her lips felt lush and her belly was whooshy again. But the rifle? She pointed at it. 'Were you going out?'

'Only across the hall to knock on your door. It might as well be by my side. There are dangerous people about.'

A deep breath. *Consent.* 'I want you to be with me tonight.'

'Sure?'

She nodded. He nudged her back to her room, a hand on her hip. When he closed the door and turned the key, he set down the gun, threw off his hat and toed off his boots. He took her face in his hands.

So close she could feel his mouth and yet it hadn't touched her. He smelled of soap, at some time he'd washed ... She gripped his wrists and hung on and he swayed with her as if they were dancing. He dipped and his nose touched hers briefly, but his mouth did not. He held her still, away from him, his gaze roving until it settled on her mouth.

'I meant consent, as well, to be my wife.'

She breathed short and sharp. 'So soon?' She hardly expected that. 'Are *you* sure?' She almost backed away. 'You said it was too quick. You said—'

'I'm sure,' he insisted, and angled her face to see her mouth, to trace a finger over her lips. 'I want you, I want a wife. You, as my wife,' he said, his eyes on hers. 'And if we do this, here tonight, marriage will protect you. I'll protect you, as your husband.'

A baby. He meant if she was to have a baby because of tonight. Something deep inside tingled and sparks flew through her belly, into her breasts. But still if she was to become a wife ... 'I must vote.'

Eyes wide, he said, 'You can think of the vote, now?'

She laughed a little at herself. 'I must.' She took a breath as his arm slid around her waist, drawing her closer. 'It's so important to me to be a part of it. To have a say as a person.'

'And you will, whenever you need to, that's my promise to you, here and now.' He held her fast. 'Will you marry me?' His lips brushed hers, but still he held back.

She needed his mouth on hers again, but then it was pressed to her throat and oh yes—the bristles scratched and zinged, and delicious need fluttered when his chin scraped her neck. She shouldn't be thinking but thoughts were twirling. 'What about your family?'

'You don't think they'd be happy? Marry me,' he whispered, voice rough, his mouth on her ear. The tip of his tongue slid to her nape.

'I will, whenever we're ready.'

He paused and murmured on her neck.

Elsa couldn't make out the words. Instantly worried, she cried, 'What? *What?*' and pulled away.

'I said, thank Christ for that. We have mutual terms.'

They slow-shuffled to the big bed, her hands splayed over strong, densely muscled forearms. The bed base pressed behind her knees. He dropped his hands low on her hips, and the sweet pressure of his thighs against her was driving her mad. This was pleasure—*to be endured, yes, yes, happily and greedily*—

Hands on her backside, he pulled her closer. The hard line of him sat rigid between her legs, through the light fabric of the dress, and a wave of longing irresistibly bloomed inside, left her without breath.

He touched the buttons at the back of her neck and stopped. 'May I help you?'

She nodded. *Though I'll hardly need it.*

He sucked in a breath, gripped her dress at her hips. As she swung her arms high over her head, the dress came off and he dropped it on the floor. Brushing her fallen hair from her face, he stood a moment, staring at her. He rested a finger between her breasts then lazily traced each nipple. *Oh my. How to endure a heaven such as this?* He took the weight of each breast in his hands and bent to suck, and nip, and lick.

Mad swirls of delightful torment streaked their way to her centre, little pulses which sent her ragged. 'I cannot stand up any longer,' she breathed, hands on his shoulders, fingers digging in.

He tugged off his shirt, undid his belt, dropped his pants, and stepped out of them.

She gazed from the broad patch of dark hair across his chest—she just had to put a hand on the solid expanse and down, down to the surprise spring of his penis, warm and smooth as her hand closed around it.

Arms scooped her up and laid her down and he slid alongside her on the bed. He kissed her, his mouth long and slow over hers, languid, inviting, teasing. His hand flattened on her belly, near her secret place that tingled with want and warmth. Fingers swirled in the hair there, played with it, brushing softly, rhythmically, lower until he found her cleft. He stroked long and sleek until she writhed, lifting her hips for him. His fingers slipped inside, his thumb, wet and warm, glided silkily over the tiny nub until her low breathless cry of wonder escaped and exquisite rolling waves of pleasure rocked over and over her. Pressed against his hand, at each peak she cried into his chest, and when she could stand it no longer, she stopped him.

'No more,' she breathed. 'You. I need you.'

He lifted her over him and drove deep. She moved with his rhythm, under his control, then he tensed, and the muscles in his arms bunched as he held her. She clung on. His gaze fierce, he let himself go, spent hard with a thrust and a lingering shudder as her hips met his. Then, with gradually measured breaths, he gathered her down to him.

Wrapped in his big arms, she thought that it was all a wonder, a superb, heady wonder. 'Is it always like this?' she asked into his neck, pressing her mouth here and there.

'Oh, that'd be a beautiful thing,' he answered, his voice a murmur. 'But if so, I might not survive to old age.'

Forty-three

Elsa woke long before him and rested her head on his warm chest. She listened for sounds of the outside world above the strong, steady beat of his heart.

Daylight was only a hint above the curtain over the window. She should rouse herself and dress; she could hear that others had risen from their beds and were going about their business at the start of the day. Although eager to get going, she couldn't fight the urge to slide her hand down the trail of hair that would lead to—

'As much as I wish it, my love, we shouldn't linger. We must make tracks.' He held her hand fast before it reached him. 'I fear I have created a monster.'

'You have,' she said. 'But a monster who's also keen to get going.' The night's many delights had tantalised into the small hours. She should have been satisfied … Resisting another touch, and sighing, she sat up and stretched.

At that, he groaned and rolled over, swung his feet to the floor. 'I'll bring the horses and cart to the front,' he said, and dressed swiftly. He pulled on his boots and donned his hat, bent and planted a hard kiss on her mouth, then gently tugged her thick plait that had survived the night. He'd fashioned it late, and after bathing, they'd slept. 'No more than ten minutes,' he said. And he was gone, rifle in his grip.

She used the chamber pot, washed again in cold water, shrugged into the dress, and pulled on her one boot. She strapped her sore foot, quickly, inexpertly, but better than no strapping at all. With the satchel slung over her shoulder, she picked up the crutches and followed him.

Clumping down the hall, she was glad she'd become used to Giff's sturdy sticks but hoped that soon she wouldn't need them. As she neared the bar door, she realised her chin felt a little tender, and wondered if it had been pinked-up by the bristles of his beard. Head down, sure her face was aglow, she smiled a secret smile and made her way outside.

Forty-four

'That's her,' Pete Southie told the other two, his voice a rough whisper as he peered over the rump of his horse. Elsa Goody had emerged from the Albion Hotel. He was glad to find her. He wanted to go right there—she was on crutches, for God's sake—but he'd been told to keep out of sight. For her own benefit, the man with the gold teeth had added.

Jesus, lucky he'd befriended the surly stranger in the bar the night before. Seemed he'd heard about Elsa and Miz Putney, and that they'd been taken by bushrangers.

Watson, who stood beside him now, had told him that they were dangerous blokes, a band of brothers who roamed the place, causing trouble. The fat redhead stank of last night's grog; musta had a skinful. He looked as if he'd been dragged backwards over a bullock track.

'Yeah, that's her, Mr Curtis.' Watson turned to the man, who nodded.

That's what started the ball rollin' last night—the name of the fella with the gold teeth. After a rum or two, Pete had mentioned that he had to find the Goody sisters from Robe. Heard they'd come this way lookin' for their brother's grave. The man had looked real interested and introduced himself. Dropped the grumpy attitude quick smart. Funny that Elsa's pa was named Curtis, too, Pete had remarked. Mr Curtis had laughed a bit at that, and said he'd be happy to help find the women.

Pete watched the cart pull round the corner, a spare horse tied at the back, and park at the hotel's front door. The fella driving didn't look familiar, but when he jumped down and helped Miss Elsa onto the coach, Pete felt a punch slam into his guts. The man had swooped her up, and laughing, had sat her on the seat of the cart, the crutches she'd used dropping to the ground. She'd put her hand on his cheek.

Jesus, Miss Elsa. What's that all about?

The crutches were thrown in the back, a bag removed from around Miss Elsa's shoulders and shoved under the seat, and then the man climbed aboard and gee-upped the horse. He musta been in a hurry, they'd taken off quick enough.

Mr Curtis grunted. 'Where they goin'?' he asked as the cart headed out.

'Need to follow them a ways,' Watson said, his stink-breath flying over Pete's shoulder. 'They could head south, goin' to Mt Gambier, or they could take the turn-off going west to Penola. Nebo's camp is off the Mount road. There's a track goes in at about the five-mile mark. Tracks all over the place in there but I reckon I can find which one.'

Curtis nodded. 'Stay here, Mr Southie. We'll bring our horses and then follow at a reasonable distance.'

'You done this before, Mr Curtis?' Pete asked him. 'You a law man?'

'Can't say too much, Mr Southie. I just know how to find what I'm lookin' for.'

Forty-five

Wally and Sal were leaving. Wally lifted a hand to wave before heading for the scrub. As they trudged on, a sack each on their backs, their figures morphed into the landscape and were soon out of sight.

Glen was standing beside Nebo. 'Sad business.'

'Aye.' Nebo was standing with Rosie, watching them leave. He didn't know what he felt. Sad, maybe. Strange. Too many things were changing quickly.

Glen and Tillie would wait for Salty to come back, and then they'd be the last to leave besides him and Rosie. Fred and Alice had said their goodbyes just as the sun had risen.

Nebo had no clue where to go, or even if they needed to leave. They couldn't yet, anyway, Rosie had told him. Not until Elsa returned. She'd got a bit shrill about that when he tried to put another case forward. He'd managed to calm her down, especially when he said they'd wait, no matter what.

He couldn't get near her after that, she'd been all agitated. But she'd be right later on. They had a good thing between them, and tonight he'd make her feel even better again.

The rain had held off last night, hadn't dumped a drop on the camp although they'd all been worried about it. They'd packed their horses then, their tools and implements tied tight to each saddle, ready for an early morning start. They all just looked like plenty of others who were trooping around the countryside, seeking work, shelter, their next meal. Rabbits were aplenty, but a good mutton stew or a beef roast was always welcome.

At least Fred and Alice would always find work. They could turn their hands to anything.

Glen and Tillie. Well, Tillie wasn't good for much, or not that Nebo had seen. Musta been good at something, for Glen was happy enough to keep her. He said she was a good stick, nothin' surer. Nebo shrugged. Who the bloody hell was he to say?

He'd miss them all. They were his mates, and they'd been through a lot over the years. Some bad things, some not so bad, but there'd been plenty of mischief. Back in the day they were the boys who didn't care about anything much, except for having fun. As he'd watched Wal trudge away, and Fred ride off with his horses packed, Nebo saw them in a different light. Still mates, but with the sharp edges worn off. Or worn down. They were gettin' on in age. And who was he foolin'? He was no boy anymore, either. He set the thought aside.

Tillie called over, hands on her hips. 'Reckon your sister will be back with my Salty sometime soon, missy?'

Rosie sighed aloud. 'I hope so.'

She glanced at Nebo and looked away, not as happy as the other night, but she'd have been worried about her sister. His chest expanded. He had himself a good woman, finally. Now he had to keep her.

Forty-six

A flat, dull grey mass of cloud sat overhead covering the whole sky as far as Elsa could see. She stared up, but the sun was well hidden. It didn't feel like there'd be more rain, and thankfully so. The track leading out of town was heavy and Milo was doing his best.

She was relying on her memory to retrace Tillie's directions and Ezekiel seemed to know exactly where they were. Over a crossroad, and when the track dropped to barely a path, she wondered how on earth she'd managed that night to stay in the right direction. She was lost in daylight.

When the rough track eased here and there, Ezekiel would reach across and take her hand. He'd squeezed it while he talked, and she'd squeeze back.

She learned he'd planned to buy dairy cows, maybe cattle, because the market had dropped out of wheat. 'If I can use Jude's place as well, we'll both be better off.'

It was the same where she came from, but her father had no one, and no money, to expand. 'Bigger holding,' she agreed. She was used to cows around but knew nothing of a dairy. She thought of her father's farm. It would belong to Frank now, or near enough belong to Frank. There was nothing left there for her in South

Australia, except the right to vote—while her address was still officially in that colony, she would do that.

If moving—that's what marrying Ezekiel meant—then she had to hope that the vote for women would soon be passed here in Victoria. Surely after Federation in a few years, every civilised colony would adopt a suffrage for women. It made sense that if laws were passed governing all, then all were to have a say in the governing.

Ezekiel had commented on the matter when she raised it. 'It would seem an obvious choice to make. But there are some hard and stoic heads out there wrangling the reins on our laws.'

'I read that some parliamentarian argued that men would have their home comforts destroyed if we get the vote and want to be a part of governing the country.'

Ezekiel looked at her. 'Who would wear the pants at home if you entered parliament?' he asked, teasing her.

'The one who best fits them,' she retorted, then blurted a laugh with him.

Not long after, he said, 'I think this is the track. I vaguely remember coming somewhere close by as kids. Nebo would know this area well.' Salty, tied alongside, stepped up his pace. 'Seems I'm not the only one who thinks so.'

A lazy drift of wood smoke on the breeze seemed to confirm it. Elsa felt her stomach swirl, as much for anticipating seeing her sister again, as worried for Rosie's situation. Then, chiding herself, Elsa realised that she was in the same situation. Still, her nerves were on edge.

Milo had slowed, picking his way carefully along the narrow track. Ezekiel let him lead. Once or twice the horse threw his head, the whites of his eyes showing as he looked around. Salty answered him, a confident nicker, but Milo wasn't placated.

Ezekiel turned to look behind them and saw nothing to worry him. But the horse had always been trustworthy, so he pulled the rifle from its holster and sat it across his lap. 'Mrs Hartman's bullet box is under the seat. If she's packed rounds, load this up for me.'

Startled, Elsa groped under her feet and pulled a box forward. Cradling the rifle, she cracked it and checked the bullet casing to see that it was dry, then loaded a bullet into the chamber. Once done, she looked over her shoulder, but couldn't find fault in the disappearing track and the scrub behind her.

Now her stomach was indeed fluttery. The wood smoke was stronger, and she fancied she heard voices on the wind. Salty was impatient, Milo was not happy, but still Ezekiel drove on, calm and quiet. The cart bobbed and jumped, and Elsa banged against his shoulder from time to time, not minding at all. She cared not to look a moment further into the future than where she was, and at least for the time being, she was happy with that.

They heard a gleeful female voice first: 'Salty.' The horse replied with a little dance as a woman appeared from nowhere out of the bushes, her reddy-gold hair piled haphazardly on her head.

'That's Tillie,' Elsa said quietly. 'Mr Barton's wife.'

'Hmm,' was all she got from Ezekiel.

'Glad to see you back, missy, and just in time,' Tillie said to Elsa, and flashed Ezekiel a big grin. 'And you have to be Nebo's kin, no mistakin' that,' she said to him and went straight to untie her horse. Leaping into the saddle, she drew alongside Elsa. 'You missed Wal and Sal, they've gone. They buried the little 'un over yonder.' She lifted her chin in the direction beyond the campfire. 'They left just after Fred and Alice. And now that Salty's back, me and Glen will be off. New South Wales, doncha know.' She nudged Salty and he trotted ahead of the cart.

'A lot of information,' Ezekiel commented, his brow raised at Elsa.

'I helped Sal when we first got here, but her baby was stillborn.'

He nodded, silent, a frown deepening.

Milo, still not happy, surged forward, following the other horse. Ezekiel steered him but let him have his head. Elsa's nerves still fluttered. 'Why do you think he's so worried?' she asked.

Then Rosie was running, holding her skirt as her feet dodged hollows in the soft earth. 'Elsa,' she cried as she reached the cart. She darted a look at Ezekiel.

'Rosie, this is Mr Ezekiel Jones, the gentleman who wrote the letter about George,' Elsa said. 'Ezekiel, my sister, Rosie Putney.'

'Mr Jones,' Rosie said, breathless as she jogged alongside the cart, her eyes on her sister. 'Thank you for your letter.' Rosie skittered along holding Elsa's hand until Ezekiel pulled up at the campfire. Then she clambered aboard and took her sister into a tight hug.

Tillie had immediately begun to load Salty with the remainder of their possessions. Her bags were tight, tidy and she slid a small, slim rifle into a holster on the saddle. Glen's horse was already packed, so he stood to greet Ezekiel as he climbed off the cart.

Nebo called from the campfire but didn't stand. 'Welcome to my kingdom, little brother.'

'I see it's a fine place,' Ezekiel replied. He reached into the back of the cart to grab Elsa's crutches. He nodded over to Glen, who was packing his rifle. 'Mate,' he said, without warmth.

Ezekiel came to Elsa's side of the cart and reached to lift her down. Rosie stared as he fitted Elsa with the crutches. Satisfied with her safety, he brushed his fingers along her cheek and turned for his brother at the fire. Rosie was wide-eyed at her.

Nebo gave Ezekiel a light punch on the shoulder. 'Ezie,' he said, with affection. 'Come sit a while. Got somethin' to tell you.'

There was no mistaking the other horse Elsa heard. Peppin, tied up next to his cart, which had a new draught pole and brace on it, had been whinnying. She clambered across and stroked his face. 'I've missed you, too, beautiful boy.' She looked over her shoulder at Rosie. 'I see they took good care of him.'

Rosie was beside her. 'Was only a few days, at most. But did I see what I thought I saw between you and that man?'

'What did you see?' Elsa continued to stroke Peppin.

Glen yelled out as he mounted his horse. 'We'll be off, good friend,' he said to Nebo. 'No girly kisses and hugs for me, and I'll knock you dead if you touch me missus.' Tillie had ridden up alongside as Nebo stood beside Glen's horse. He held out a hand and Glen gripped it hard. 'Off on another adventure, old mate,' Glen said and wheeled his horse and headed for the scrub.

Tillie waved and followed him, a gleeful smile as Salty leapt to catch up.

Rosie had waved but turned her attention back to Elsa. She studied her a moment. 'You have a pink chin, Miss Elsa.'

'I thought as much.'

'And a sly smile on your face.'

'Not sly. Happy.'

Rosie flicked a glance at the brothers sitting by the campfire, talking, hands waving, a laugh or two between them. They both looked over and back again, though Ezekiel's glance lingered. 'Perhaps you were not strict, Elsa,' she said, her voice low and her brow arched.

'Perhaps I was not,' Elsa replied in a whisper. 'Don't look at me like that, Rosie. I was as strict as you, I'll wager.' Her sister's mouth popped open. Elsa looked around. 'Do you have any food here?' And turning on her crutches to inspect the camp, she saw a man on horseback crash into the clearing.

'Miz Putney, Miss Elsa,' Pete Southie shouted. 'Don't be 'fraid. It's me, Pete. I've been trying to find ye.'

Forty-seven

Zeke heard him before he burst into view. A lone man on horse-back, yelling at Elsa and Rosie. He leapt to his feet and Nebo took the campfire in a bound and sprinted for his rifle.

Zeke glanced at the cart, Milo still harnessed. His own rifle was there. He went for it, and although seeing no threat from a man who addressed the women by name, he lost no haste.

Nebo had his aimed, but the man hadn't noticed.

'Mr Southie,' Rosie cried. 'What on earth are you doing here?'

Zeke saw Elsa flinch, move a little, distancing herself. He eyed the man as he dismounted then grabbed up the loaded rifle. He waved his brother down, but Nebo ignored him.

'Miz Putney.' Pete snatched off his hat. 'I have some terrible news for ye.'

Rosie was frowning. 'About Frank?'

'Aye. Dead, the day after you left. His heart business.' He shook his head. 'Just up and died on the floor of the bakery. They found him while they was lookin' in the window waitin' for him to open—'

An explosive crack rocked the quiet of the clearing and Pete Southie dropped like a stone, the side of his head blown clean away.

Shrieking, Rosie fell in a heap. Elsa tumbled over, crutches falling with her.

Nebo swung the rifle towards the scrub, but another shot burst. Blown off his feet, his chest a bloom of colour, he landed in slow motion on his back, silent. The rifle dropped close by.

Zeke was almost paralysed. *I got one bullet.*

'Don't try it, Zeke, I've loaded again,' someone shouted off to the side. Billy Watson appeared out of the bushes, on foot, his own rifle aimed. 'I got you good as dead, mate,' he yelled.

Zeke glanced over at Nebo. *Get up, brother. Sit up, dammit. Yell. Let me hear you.*

Rosie, still screaming, pulled away from Elsa, trying to get to Nebo. Breaking free, she scrambled on all fours to him.

A rider emerged from the scrub, a rifle resting over his saddle. The man pushed his hat back a little as if in a greeting. 'Afternoon, Mr Jones.' And the grin he flashed gleamed with gold.

Zeke stared.

'Recommend you drop the rifle and move away.' The gold gleamed again. 'All I'm after is the boy's tin. And as I believe these good ladies are his sisters, I'm reckoning it's here somewhere.' He waved his gun at Zeke, who put his rifle on the ground and stepped back from it.

Rosie, beside Nebo, was clutching at his shredded waistcoat, blood slicking her hands as it bubbled out of him.

Watson, still with his gun aimed, sidled over to her. 'Get over to yer sister, slut.'

Rosie screeched, threw herself up at Watson, beating his chest and arms with flailing fists. He *thwacked* her hard on her shoulder with the butt. Down she went, but not out. Angry keens poured out, and Elsa scrambled to her.

The man with the gold teeth had his rifle up, aimed at Elsa. 'She's dead if you move,' he said to Zeke.

Zeke's rifle was too far from his reach. 'You don't know who's got that tin. You won't kill any more of us till you find out.'

'Oh, but I will,' he said, aimed over towards the women, and fired.

Rosie and Elsa screamed.

Behind them, Billy Watson dropped to the ground with a thud. His legs kicked and then were still. The top of his head had a hole in it.

'And when I get it, I'm not sharin' the tin with nobody.' The man on the horse reloaded, a slick move, loud, well practised. He aimed the rifle again at Elsa.

Zeke kept his eyes on Elsa. He shook his head at her but she untangled herself from her moaning sister and crawled to Nebo.

'Had a big mouth, that brother of yours, Miss Elsa.' The man walked his horse around Zeke, pushing him further away from the rifle. 'Oh yeah, I know which is which of you two. Georgie-boy gave me good descriptions, he was proud of ye both. Is why he told me about your pa's tin. How he was gonna get your farm out of a hole, make yez all rich. He just didn't tell me exactly where the tin was. Not even when I tried to tickle it outta him with a round or two. He already talked of the tin bein' at the graves, so I wandered along and checked around both sites.' He pointed the rifle at Zeke. 'Nothin' at the graves on your brother's place, Mr Jones, and nothin' at yours. So no point leavin' him alive to finger me to the troopers.' He snorted a laugh. 'But your brother found him before I could finish him off.' He nodded across at Nebo.

Zeke couldn't look at his brother. He clenched his fists, and his voice broke. 'And Jude? Why'd you go there? Why stab him?'

'Poor timin' on my account. I knew the boy had camped there, but I thought the place was abandoned. I hadn't made up any bullets so when I saw a fella was already there, it took me by surprise. Couldna use me gun.' He shook his head. 'He alive or dead?'

Zeke didn't answer.

The man made a noise with his tongue, like he was geeing up his horse. 'Ah. Must be alive. Seems I'm not real good with a knife. You shoulda said he were dead, that way I wouldna have to go back and finish him off.' He cocked his head. 'Or do in those nice kids of yours.'

Zeke's heart boomed, his sight wavered. His pulse thundered so hard he rocked. *I can't move. If I go for him, I'm dead, and so are my kids. He'll kill Elsa, and her sister. If I— If I ...*

Elsa had edged to Nebo's side, and clambered on her knees to sit by his head. She leaned close to his mouth, put her fingers to his throat. When she looked at Zeke, ashen-faced, she held his gaze, then placed her hand softly over Nebo's eyes and closed them.

Zeke's heart broke. A roar ripped out of him as he lunged for the man on the horse.

Another shot cracked but Zeke felt nothing.

Forty-eight

Elsa sat hunched over Nebo's body. She dared not look any-where but at her hand covering his eyes. Couldn't bear to see what she might see. Her own breath ragged, she heard Rosie sob-bing breathily, but the raw scraping in her sister's throat had been silenced after the last gunshot. From Ezekiel, she heard nothing after his agonised bellow.

Was she next? Or Rosie?

Eerie, terrifying silence from the gunman.

She couldn't turn her head. Did not want to see Ezekiel, his life gone, her heart gone with him.

Dear God. Footsteps. Boots.

A slim hand landed on Elsa's shoulder and squeezed. 'You can breathe, missy.' It was Tillie. 'Take a look. Your man's alive and well.'

Elsa stared. *Ezekiel*. He was unharmed, staring at his brother's prone body. She heaved in a breath past the lump in her throat. Reaching up, she grabbed Tillie's hand, trying to get off her knees.

'I can still shoot straight,' Elsa heard Glen Barton say. She looked up and he was scratching his head. 'Thought I mighta got soft.' Then he wiped his eyes, bowed his head and fell to kneel by Nebo, his shoulders shaking as he bent over the body. 'I was too late for ye, me old mate,' he said. 'I'm sorry for it.'

'We seen Watson creeping around and had decided to circle back,' Tillie said, her hand under Elsa's arm. 'Bastard woulda been up to no good. But murder? Never thought it of 'im.'

Elsa lurched to her feet. Saw the man who called himself Curtis slumped, dead, over his saddle, blood pouring from a large hole in his neck. Then his body leaned over and fell off the saddle, one foot stuck in the stirrup. The horse skittered nervously as imposter Curtis's head bounced on the dirt.

George had resisted this man, paid with his life, all for a tin of coins, all for a worthless piece of dirt. Ezekiel reached her, caught her as she stumbled trying to step away from the sight.

Rosie hadn't wanted Pete Southie loaded in the back of their cart, but Elsa insisted. 'He has to go home, Rosie.' Elsa had her eye on Ezekiel. He stood over his brother's body.

Rosie paced. 'But that means he'll be in the back of our cart for three days and nights. I won't allow it. What if we break down— we'll have to bury him where we stop. We can't do that. The ground is like granite.'

Elsa rubbed her eyes with her knuckles. That was true enough. 'Yes, but—'

'He's got no family at home, Elsa,' Rosie cried, still pressing her point. 'I know that from Frank. We should bury him here.'

'Not with those other two,' Elsa said, and pointed at a mound made of tree branches on the edge of the clearing. 'He might've been a stupid, leery galoot but he was just caught up in it, not a part of it. Didn't deserve to be murdered.' Her shakes had stopped, finally, and her head was clearing.

Rosie stamped her foot. 'I insist his body stays here. Otherwise, it's all too much.' It sounded like the beginning of a wail, and her face had screwed up, her eyes fierce.

Glen had stepped in. 'Tell you what. After dark tonight, follow Tillie and me, take his body in your cart to the old cemetery in Casterton and leave him at the gate. The good folk there will look after him in the morning. He'll get buried, all proper-like. How's that?'

Ezekiel's eyes were red-rimmed, his face gaunt. He stood by Elsa's side. 'That's a good idea. Then you and Rosie can come on to my place before you decide—'

'Rosie needs to get home, Ezekiel,' Elsa said softly, and looked at her agitated sister. 'Best to leave quickly.' She almost couldn't believe what she was saying, knowing what it would mean to her. To him. The weight of it filled her chest. 'I have to go with her,' she said, hoping the tremble in her voice wasn't noticed.

Ezekiel, bleak, started. 'I know, but Elsa, I can't let—'

'Please don't. If I wait it'll hurt too much,' Elsa whispered, gripping his arm. She turned to the others. 'If someone is willing to do it for us now, we need to get supplies for three days. Rosie has money to pay. Then we follow Glen tonight like he said and leave Pete at the cemetery.' She took in a breath and glanced at her sister. 'We'll head straight back to Penola from there.'

'In the dead of night?' Ezekiel wasn't happy.

'And you and Judah can bury your brother.' Her chin wobbled. Ezekiel had said earlier that he'd take Nebo in Mrs Hartman's cart and bury him at home on the hill.

Rosie threw her hands in the air. 'At last,' she grumbled, 'someone making sense.' She looked away, and Elsa knew that her sister felt she'd won a small victory.

'I'll go get your supplies,' Tillie said then pointed to where the two dead men lay. 'No one will find that lump over there in a hundred years but let's not waste time, just in case.' She memorised a list from Elsa, took Rosie's money and on Salty, headed into town.

'Let's get Nebo into your cart, Zeke, before we deal with that.' Glen tilted his head at the other two bodies.

In the cart, they covered Nebo with his swag and Ezekiel sat with him. Tiredly, he wiped a forearm over his face then palmed his eyes. Glen took up Mrs Hartman's shovel and the pick and headed towards the other two bodies. Ezekiel followed, reached for Elsa's outstretched hand as he passed her, pressed it to his lips and let her go.

Wielding the pick, Glen swung hard. Ezekiel shovelled out the loosened soil until the hole was deep enough. They rolled both bodies in and returned the dirt, pounding it down. Evil had been buried, and the earth would deal with it. In silence, Ezekiel headed back to the cart where Nebo lay, and hung his head.

'Rosie,' Elsa said quietly so no one else could hear. 'You need to pay your respects.'

Cutting her sister a look, her mouth pressed in a thin line, Rosie trudged to the cart and climbed in. Hesitating, she patted Ezekiel's arm and sat by his dead brother.

They waited for Tillie. Blowflies buzzed, leaves rustled, and the pure fragrance of a flowering shrub drifted here and there on a cool breeze. Time passed. Elsa was sitting by the campfire, the crutches close by, lost in thought when Ezekiel came to sit with her.

He took her hand. 'Write to me, Elsa, after you get Rosie home. I'll come and get you.'

'I'll write,' she said, and squeezed his hand. She had to think some more, had to sort all this out in her head. In her heart. She looked across at Rosie. 'I—need to be with her now. She'll have a great deal to do when we get back, a lot to cope with.'

'So will you,' he said, frowning.

Elsa knew he could hear what she was saying. 'But her more so. If it's known she left Frank, if Pete told anyone, there'll be hell to pay for her back there.' She pressed her head to his. 'I am so very sorry about Nebo.'

Ezekiel folded his hand over hers and took a deep breath. 'At the last, he'd found some happiness, he finally had hope, wanted to marry. We'll hold onto that.'

Elsa remembered the look on Nebo's face when he'd first laid eyes on her sister. Now Rosie would have to start a new life as a widow in Robe; not the new life she'd expected. Elsa looked down at her hands linked with Ezekiel's. *Finally had hope*. Her own hopes were slipping away.

Tillie returned with supplies and dumped them into a corner of Elsa's cart. Glen smothered the campfire with dirt and poured the last of the billy water onto it. Then he headed for where Rosie still sat with Nebo in Mrs Hartman's cart. 'Time you and your sister was off in your own cart, Miss Rosie,' he said kindly.

She nodded, and after a moment waved him away, climbing out unaided. Straight-backed she headed for her cart. Elsa stood and limped over, Ezekiel carrying the crutches. He slipped them into the back alongside Pete Southie's shrouded figure.

Glen, on his horse, and leaning down to Ezekiel, said, 'We'll not meet again, Zeke,' and held out his hand. Ezekiel took it in both of his but couldn't speak. Glen called over to Tillie. 'Let's go.' He nodded at Elsa. 'Ladies, get on board and gee-up that horse of yours.'

Ezekiel reached for Elsa's hand, pressed it to his cheek. 'Don't forget,' he said, his eyes searching hers. He reached around and gently tugged her hair. He kissed her cheek, hugged her, and after helping her on board, draped the reins in her hands.

'I won't.' She thought she'd feel a rock in her chest, or the emptiness in her heart, but she felt only numb. She was leaving him behind.

'Elsa, my love, I don't want to have to tell Jonty that I failed him.'

She gave a sob, a laugh. She had nothing to say that would change things. She didn't know about anything anymore, only that leaving him so overwhelmed her that words would not come.

At her silence, he pushed away and trudged to his cart, climbing into the driver's seat. He lifted his hand in a wave and gave her a long, last look before he flicked the reins. Milo trotted away, taking Ezekiel, and Nebo.

Elsa glanced at her sister who stared without tears into the distance. Dry-eyed herself, her throat aching, she thought how hollow her life would be without Ezekiel Jones in it. She couldn't face that yet, wouldn't weep. She'd never get home otherwise. There were things she had to do. Rosie. Frank. The farm. The bakery. Her last brother was gone. Her pa was gone. There were things … She felt the shriek rise in her throat, but she couldn't scream. *Wouldn't.*

She gee-upped Peppin and he trotted after Mrs Hartman's cart. Following Glen and Tillie to the Casterton cemetery at the turn-off, she knew Ezekiel had gone on, straight ahead. Her heart wrenched. Tears came.

They left Pete Southie's body by the gates. As Glen and Tillie waved them off, Elsa turned the cart for Penola. Now leaving Ezekiel was real.

Forty-nine

Elsa had given up trying to draw Rosie out. The first night had only been about finding a safe place to camp. Glen had directed her to the Penola road and had given her clear instructions about how far she could travel before stopping. 'It narrows in some places,' he said, 'and in the dark you might veer off the main road by mistake.'

Peppin had to be unharnessed for the night. Rosie refused to touch anything in the back of the cart that had touched Pete Southie. Ridiculous, Elsa thought. A few snappish words were exchanged before they bunkered down, huddled together on the thin mattress. They only used one blanket against the cool night air.

In the morning, drawing well away from Casterton, Rosie was still quiet—answering only when spoken to, not offering conversation. She'd taken over the reins from time to time, but never for long. She was too distracted. By the third morning, their arrival back in Robe due sometime later that day, Rosie was becoming increasingly agitated.

Home felt close, but Elsa couldn't be sure. They hadn't dilly-dallied driving back, so as the sun began to lower, she hoped she'd recognise some landmarks soon. Every so often, she imagined she could smell salt air on the breeze but wondered how much of that was wishful thinking. Elsa reached across and squeezed her sister's hands. 'I'm sure everything will be all right, Rosie,' she said, then flicked the reins. Peppin picked up a little pace.

Rosie was hanging on to her seat, her hat tied tight, her face creased in a frown. Rigid, she looked as if she was hanging on to more than just the rail of the cart, almost as if letting go meant that she'd fall apart. Elsa feared all would come crashing down on Rosie if she didn't let go of *something*.

Elsa understood. So far, her own life felt as if it had already fallen apart. Everything had been so ordered before they received Ezekiel's letter about George, before Pa died, before they'd left to seek out their dead brother's belongings. How was she ever going to be able to go to Ezekiel Jones now? It was beyond her.

'I'll keep the door slammed shut on the damned bakery,' Rosie had burst earlier.

Elsa thought about that. 'But perhaps if you re-open it instead, you'd have an income.' She hoped it might allow her to return to Casterton but as another tirade erupted then it didn't seem likely.

Rosie needed her, she'd said, with or without the bakery. She made it plain and even if she hadn't said so, it was clear Rosie would not fare well on her own. Her throat tight again, Elsa tried to push thoughts of Ezekiel away, just as she'd done time and again, unsuccessfully, since leaving him.

'First thing I'm going to do,' Rosie said suddenly, 'is go and see Mr Milton about Pa's will.' But she hadn't spoken of Frank at all.

Elsa had to ask. 'Did Frank make a will?'

'Would I know if he had?' Rosie snapped.

'You were his wife. He should have said.'

'Well, hopefully Mr Milton will have a copy of it if he did.'

Salt was on the breeze again. 'Can you smell the sea, Rosie?'

Her sister squinted into the afternoon light and twitched her nose. 'I think I do.'

'Not far now then.'

'I want to go to the farm,' Rosie said, staring ahead.

Elsa inclined her head. 'All right. We have enough food for tonight if we're frugal.' Tillie had done well on the small budget Rosie had given her.

'Then we'll go to the town tomorrow morning, although I can barely bring myself to face it.' Rosie looked away, her chin puckering, her mouth tightly closed.

'It might not be as bad as you think.' Elsa bumped her shoulder but got no response.

Peppin knew where he was. He picked up speed, his ears flat, and threw his head back and forth. Elsa let him speed up. She, too, was keen to get off this road.

They'd arrived at the hut to see the place almost devoid of any possessions—someone had been along and helped themselves to what little there was. Dismayed, feeling the weight of futility and the injustice of it, they spent a restless night's sleep on the floor on their old mattresses that they'd carried in from the cart.

Despite being deflated, crotchety, and tired beyond measure, Elsa couldn't muster the rage at the loss of their meagre pieces of furniture.

The next day, they harnessed poor Peppin once more and drove into town. Mr Milton welcomed them back, agreed to see Rosie that same afternoon, and no, to his knowledge Frank had not left a will, certainly not left one with him. Perhaps there were papers at the bakery, he'd said. Which meant they'd have to go there, despite Rosie's aversion.

Opening the back door of the bakery, stale air rushed out. There was a pong of something dead just inside, probably a rat.

Neither felt like striding through the store. Instead, they crept about—Rosie, as if being inside was not her right, and Elsa, because she wasn't sure what she'd step in. Rodents had been having a lovely time amongst the goods in the heat, and thanks to Frank having laid poison, there was more than one dead rat strewn on the floor.

Rosie huffed and steadied herself on the shop counter. First thing she did was yank open the cash drawer, and merely raised her brows. 'Not only home has been ransacked,' she said, looking up at Elsa.

'Wish they'd taken these old buns as well. Not even the rats wanted them,' Elsa replied. She'd found a box and emptied the trays of mouldy and chewed pastries and cakes into it. 'Good for someone's pigs.'

'Oh, Elsa.' Rosie bit her lip and sagged against the bench.

'Let's get to his papers. Is there a safe box or something?'

In the back room, Frank had kept a large leather bag under his desk. Rosie hauled it out and together the sisters trawled through it. There were his bank books, his investment papers—Rosie hadn't known of any investments—and there, shining a light on their day, was an envelope marked 'Last Will and Testament of Francis Putney'. Rosie sighed and began to open it.

'Don't do that. You know what Mr Milton said.'

'Pa's will, yes, because there's more than one but I'm not so sure about Frank's will—'

'Your appointment is at two, Rosie. Leave it till then,' Elsa urged.

'That's more than three hours away,' her sister cried.

Elsa took a deep breath despite the stink in the store and squared her shoulders. 'Time enough to visit the cemetery then.'

Rosie squeezed her eyes shut, slapped the sealed envelope on her palm, and nodded.

That afternoon, they sat in Mr Milton's 'office', an old table in Mrs Milton's parlour room. It was jammed against a wall, and a pigeon-hole shelf had been hammered above it. It did feel strange to sit crammed against one another in the front room watching the retired solicitor peer at the wills.

'Quite right,' he said, after reading. 'All in order. This one of Frank's is straightforward. In the event of his death, you are to administer his business, Rosie, and take over the ownership of the bakery property. Any debts are to be paid from his bank account and the residual paid to you. You are entitled to keep the account open and operate it yourself, and the bank looks favourably on you keeping his investment shares.' He studied the names and figures. 'Small as they are. However, he has left no stipend, my dear, and the shares don't look worth overly much.' He checked Rosie's response over the rim of his spectacles. Taking her silence to mean she didn't understand, he said, 'That means you must work for your living, or marry again. I presume you could re-open the bakery.'

Rosie remained stony-faced.

He studied Rosie. 'My dear, Pete Southie was known for his tall stories. Whatever he said about the situation between you and Frank, rumours are all they are.' Today, instead of bugs, he had remnants of his lunch in his beard. Crumbs periodically worked their way out of the healthy white bush on his face and fell onto his lap.

Rosie took a deep breath, tapped her clasped hands on her chin and nodded.

Elsa filled the silence. 'And our father's will, Mr Milton?'

He set Frank's will aside. Found his letter opener again—in front of him—and sliced open the envelope he'd had stored in his files. 'Now, this one says all goods and chattels and the farm to go to his only surviving son, George Curtis Goody, dated, oh let me see …' He glared at the date on both wills. '… Two years before this one.' He shook the unopened one at them, the one they'd carried to Casterton and back.

Rosie huffed, her impatience evident. Well, not evident to Mr Milton.

Elsa nodded at him. 'Please go ahead.'

He opened it with a flourish, read down the page and began at the top again. 'It's been crudely written, but it has a witness. Tell me, is this his handwriting?' He waved it at Rosie first, who looked at Elsa.

Elsa checked. 'Yes, it is.' Rosie would scarcely have known if it was her father's handwriting. 'And who is his witness?' She had tried to catch the name.

Mr Milton glared at the page. 'Peter Southie.'

Rosie groaned and so did Elsa.

The old lawyer looked from one to the other. 'Heard Pete trooped off after you. I suppose he caught up with you before you went on to Naracoorte.'

'Yes,' Elsa said, nodding. 'He did. We saw him near Penola and—'

'And he informed me of my husband's passing,' Rosie said, shooting a glare at her sister. 'He won't be coming back this way.'

'Not surprised,' Mr Milton said. 'Some men get the drifts, late in life, especially if they don't have anything to stay for. Work is tight, all of that. Probably a good thing. Wasn't a great addition to society around here, was he?' He missed Rosie's squinty glare. 'Now, you two ladies. You should have your own wills prepared. Let's get that underway for you.'

'Our father's new will, Mr Milton?' Elsa pressed.

'Ah. Mind like a sieve.' Mr Milton skimmed the paper and looked over his spectacles at both women. 'He has written that the farm and goods and chattels should go to his last remaining child or children, to be owned jointly if that is the case.' He sat back and stroked crumbs from his beard. 'Most unusual not naming names. But clearly, you both have ownership.'

Rosie sighed and flattened her hands on her lap. Elsa felt like a pond into which a large stone had been dropped. The implications of her father's will kept coming at her in ripples, wave after wave, rolling over her thudding heart and opening possibilities she never really believed would come her way.

An hour later they left Mr Milton's, their own simple wills done, and were driving back to the farm.

'Pa must have had an idea that George might not survive us,' Elsa said, as the revelation kept breaking over her.

'That would appear so. And Pete Southie, Pa's witness, already knew one of us would inherit.'

'I didn't think he could read. He never said.'

'No wonder he was keen on you, Elsa.'

'Thanks very much.'

For the first time, Rosie cracked a laugh.

At the farm, Elsa dug out a pair of George's cast-off trousers and one of his old shirts, shook them out, and changed into them. She pulled on a pair of boots. Rosie only raised her brows.

'I'd been wearing these for work, and there's work to be done, Rosie. Weeds to be pulled, the well to be cleared. If we're to stay here at the hut, then we need the vegetables harvested, what's left of them, and to replant for a new crop. The house needs repairs, the fences need—' She stopped at the look of despair on her sister's face.

'Do you even want the farm, Elsa, really now?'

'I can't manage it all by myself, but together—' She floundered again. 'Do you even want the bakery, Rosie?'

Both stared at the other. Shoulders drooped.

'Perhaps one business could help support the other,' Rosie said. 'I need the bakery, I know it. You help me there, for wages.

And—we could lease the farm to someone, couldn't we? We have no animals, no stock to worry about.'

Elsa nodded, resigned. She'd already thought as much. The door that had briefly opened to her here on the farm, after her father's will, was closing. And the glimpse of a new life in Casterton further away than ever. Rosie, the runaway woman, needed her here in Robe. Elsa, who'd been the stoic stay-on-the-farm woman, had found life elsewhere but wouldn't go. Couldn't go and leave her sister.

She looked around the hut, at its gaps and its cobwebs, its floor with broken boards, and with dirt and dust clinging to every surface. She thought of Ezekiel's home of timber, of smart tongue-and-groove, of a big verandah, of lively children. Of his smile. Of his arms around her. Of promise. She thought of what she'd found, the very thing she'd never known she was missing.

Elsa breathed in long and quietly, and slowly let it out. She was letting go of something so new, so untried—why did it hurt so badly, so deeply? She'd been swiftly cut with a blade, and healing from it would be long and hard.

She would write to him but only once she'd found the right thing to say. She didn't have the right words just yet.

Fifty

Voting day has dawned at last. The 25th of April, 1896, will go down in history! Elsa sprang out of bed. The weather, rainy and cold all week, had turned fine, and so far this morning the sky was blue and cloudless.

Oh, *nothing* would take Elsa's mood down today. *Well, something will if I let it.* But just for once, today, she must try and not think of him while she went about her business. She'd written once, and he'd replied. She must get his letter out again, safe and sound by her bed, and re-read it for the—*oh, there I go again, thinking of him.* She couldn't help it. Thoughts of Ezekiel Jones had not left her, not ever, not for a minute. Although she fell into bed so wearied and went straight into a deep sleep, she was sure that she even dreamed of him.

Elsa had got up early this morning, and made sure Rosie was comfortable. Her sister had been ill for the last couple of days and Elsa had gone to the bakery at all hours ensuring there would be goods to sell. (She was tired as tired could be, but today she would vote for the first time—what was sleep compared to that?) She'd said to Rosie that as a baker, she made a very good farm girl, still tending the repairs and chores at the hut. Exhaustion was her latest routine.

She set out her new dress. New-ish. It was a hand-me-down from Mrs Bourke who lived in the street back from the bakery. Elsa had made a careful job of taking in the seams and it was in reasonable repair now. It was her going-to-vote dress. A nice blue, a calming colour, and one that matched the muted colour of the ocean today.

'Rosie.' She called across the room to her sister who'd cocooned herself in the bed. 'We have to vote today. You haven't forgotten. Come along.'

Rosie mumbled something.

'Yes, you must,' Elsa replied. 'Come on, the sooner it's done, the sooner you can get back to bed.'

The moan was muffled. 'I think I'm dying.'

Elsa tut-tutted. 'I think not. I'm going to harness Peppin, then get changed. Hurry up.'

Elsa parked their cart close by the District Council offices.

One of the men waiting to vote held up his timepiece. 'Ye're late on such an auspicious day, I'da thought, Miss Elsa—it's nine forty-five. But y'are the first lady to vote, I'll give ye that. Well done.'

She waved gleefully. She was about to be the first woman to vote here. How *grand*. But she didn't need congratulations on her legal franchise. 'I'm glad to finally have my basic right to vote, Mr Simmons, so any time I can do that is a very civilised time.' She waited impatiently for her sister who looked anything but enthused. 'Come on, come on, come on, Rosie,' Elsa urged. 'I have to be the first.'

Grumbling and pale, Rosie said, 'I'm only glad it's Saturday and we don't have to open the bakery. You'll have to tell me what to do, so hurry up and let's get this over with.'

Elsa marched into the council office with great purpose in her stride. She nodded her thanks to the gentlemen who lined the walkway, allowing her to go ahead of them. *How wonderful—they're all extremely polite on this historic day of all days.* Did that mean they truly understood the importance of the day that had dawned? She clapped her hands under her chin, as if holding onto her enthusiasm.

One man said, 'I heard ye ladies would most likely vote for the good-looker, Miss Goody.'

Clearly that man has not understood the importance. Elsa turned and spotted him. 'A good thing then that you're not running for election, Mr Williams. You'd be vastly disappointed by the results in the polls.' And that wiped the smirk off his face and brought knee-slapping guffaws from his mates.

'Elsa,' Rosie admonished from behind her, but there was a smile in her tone.

'You look right smart in that dress, Miss Goody,' someone else called.

'Ignore them, Elsa,' Rosie said. 'Now, Mr Gell, do tell us what we do here?'

Mr Gell, the returning officer, handed her over to an assistant. Elsa felt her hackles rise. Rosie had addressed him and he saw fit to pass her off to a man whose spectacles slid down his nose as he stared kindly at them, and spoke as if he were addressing imbeciles. Handing them voting papers, he took his time explaining exactly what was required while male voters waited patiently in line behind. 'Number the candidates one to four as you prefer. No words, no identifying marks as to your person. All sections, including the education question on the referendum paper, must be filled out correctly—a cross in only one box against either yes or no on that paper, else your vote will be invalid.'

'Thank you, sir, for your kind explanation, although I do see that it is plainly written as such on the papers,' Elsa said, her eyes alight.

He ducked his head towards her and smiled. 'Ah, but we don't want our first vote to be an invalid one, now do we, miss?'

'We most certainly do not want that,' she answered sweetly, instead of stomping on his foot. Elsa tugged Rosie with her, heading for the curtained recesses to cast their vote. Between her teeth she said, 'After all this time, Rosie, we absolutely don't want that, do we?'

'Now you'll have to tell me who to vote *for*,' Rosie said, still snippy.

'Vote as you think best, and keep it secret.'

Once the vote cards were handed back to the box at Mr Gell's table, Elsa beamed for the first time since returning from Casterton.

'I am so happy today, Rosie, that I—that you and I—have cast our first vote to have a say in who governs us.'

'Still so naïve, Elsa.' Rosie pushed her way outside, heading as quick as she could for their cart. She flew around the other side once she got there.

Startled, worried, and hurrying to reach her, Elsa saw her sister double over and retch.

It had been a slow journey home—they'd had to stop a number of times along the way. Once back at the farm Elsa had put Rosie to bed again. Now she sat with Ezekiel's letter on her lap, open but not re-read this time, and tried to absorb what Rosie had told her.

There was no doubt in her sister's mind that she carried Nebo Jones's baby.

Elsa had blinked at her. 'Not Frank's?'

'For goodness sake, Elsa,' Rosie had said, cross and tired at the same time. 'Definitely not Frank's.'

'But you'd said that—a duty to be endured.'

Rosie had sighed. 'It was different with Nebo. Very different. I wanted to find out— I found that it was a thing to be enjoyed, after all.' Then she pitched forward over the bowl. Elsa had rubbed her back, wiped her face with a wet cloth. 'And only you and I know that my life with Frank was anything but what it seemed,' Rosie said pointedly, sliding a glance at her before spitting out the last of the bile. 'You're to tell no one of Nebo.'

Elsa had taken a moment to work out what she meant. 'You mean to say you'd let people think that the baby is Frank's?'

'What else to do?' Rosie cracked at her, bleary eyes red-rimmed and streaming. 'I am a forty-something-year-old woman, who laid with a man not my husband, and before I was widowed. Of course I must say it's Frank's.' But she held onto her middle and her features softened. 'But I never dreamed I could have a baby. I never dreamed I could.'

Astounded on all fronts, Elsa had sputtered, 'But you loved Nebo, you must have, to have been with him and—'

'Not love, Elsa. It was far too soon for love. It was a need, or something. A longing. Oh, I think he could've loved me. For me, he was—a delightful, irresistible rogue, but ...' She faltered, seemed to search for the right words. 'He had no house, no land, no work. I would've been living in a camp—'

'Many people do.'

'—with no prospects and that is not for me. I knew even before you returned from Ezekiel's that I'd been hasty being with him. So very hasty. And now,' she'd said and lifted her shoulders. 'This.'

'But it is a baby for you, Rosie,' Elsa said in wonder.

'Yes. A baby. If only I can keep it.'

A thought pounced on Elsa. Horrified, she said, 'You wouldn't think to sell it to one of those despicable baby farmers, would you?'

Rosie had rolled her eyes. 'Elsa, I simply meant that at my age, I might miscarry.'

But it had stayed, and its little life beat strongly inside her sister. Perhaps Rosie's body had not been at fault at all over the years. Perhaps it had been Frank's body. But everyone knew that the woman was always at fault, either for being barren, or for having female offspring, or for having a baby at all, especially out of wedlock. Always *her* fault. She was congratulated if a boy was born. Where was the science? Certainly not in any newspapers she'd read.

Elsa was thankful that her own monthly course had arrived, right on time. Far too soon for love, Rosie had said. And even though it had only been a few days for Elsa too, she was sure of her feelings. They hadn't changed. Was it far too soon for love? That may well be, but she knew her mind. And heart. She would follow where it took her. It felt too good to dismiss. But how to keep it?

They both resided in the rooms over the bakery, and it was just about dawn. Hours before, Elsa had already been downstairs firing up the ovens and had rolled the dough ready for proving. Thinking to encourage Rosie to have something for breakfast, she took a cup of cooled, sweetened tea for her and a dry slice of bread. Yeasty, warm wafts had followed her back upstairs and flour covered her just about head to toe.

The first of Rosie's morning heaves reached her ears. *Gracious, how long will this last?* If all went well, it would be mid-December or thereabouts before the baby was born. Elsa looked over at the dining table where Ezekiel's letter lay open, waiting for her to pen a reply. She'd made a decision and would put it to paper. It seemed unavoidable—so why was she still hesitating?

At Rosie's side, she sat the teacup and the plate of bread on the bedside table then drew open the curtain. Weak daylight streamed in. Helping her sister to sit, she bunched the pillows behind her.

'Oh, I can't even look at the bread,' Rosie said, her lip curling.

'Then sip some tea.' Elsa held up the cup. 'There's something I want to talk about before I fall asleep on my feet.'

Rosie glanced at her, her frown dark. 'Oh, is that right? I am the one throwing up my stomach all day and night, yet you are asleep on your feet. Poor you.'

Elsa let it go. It wouldn't make any difference reminding Rosie that working for twenty hours of the day was taking its toll. Instead, she took a deep breath. 'Yes, poor me. And so I've come up with a solution to our predicament.'

Rosie waved a hand dismissively. 'What predicament? It's only a short time until the baby is born, and you're quite right, I'll be able to work after. So I don't see things need to change now. You'll just have to find the energy until then to—'

'Stop.' Elsa held up a hand. 'That's not what I meant. I'll write to Mr Jones and tell him of our situation.' Even firm in her convictions, she felt the burning flush spread across her face and rush down her neck.

Rosie's mouth dropped open. 'You will not.'

'I will.'

'But it's a *scandal*, Elsa, about me—'

'And about Nebo. We will tell his family.'

Rosie looked aghast. 'We won't. I can't have you telling anyone. You know that.'

'I, for one,' Elsa said, 'will not be telling anyone *here* about the father of your baby, therefore no scandal.' She sat up straight, the cup of tea in her hand hovering close to Rosie. 'It's sensible. It's right and proper that—'

'No, it's illegitimate,' Rosie shrieked, throwing her hands up before she snatched the bowl and coughed over it. 'I forbid you,' she barked between spits.

'Forbid me? I don't think so.' Elsa whisked away the cup of tea before her sister knocked it from her. 'We must also put the bakery up for sale to see if it attracts a buyer.'

'Elsa, no. You must work the bakery, you must.' Rosie groped for her hand. 'We can't sell it. How will we survive without it?'

'Be reasonable. I can't work the bakery and the farm. It's too much for me and we can't afford a worker for either place.'

'Sell the damn farm. It's useless.'

Elsa's shoulders fell. 'There's not much point to trying to sell the farm.'

'Abandon it, then. God knows, it looks derelict.'

That hurt, but it was close to the truth. Rosie gulped again, screwed up her face and clutched the bowl. Elsa handed her the damp cloth and watched her sister drag it over her face and neck. 'I'm not a baker, Rosie. I'm a farmer, or, if you'd rather not call me that, I'm a woman who knows how to work a farm. I can't abandon it.'

'And I'm not a farm person,' Rosie shrilled. 'I can't live out there on that lump of dirt without even a decent roof over my head.' She thrust the cloth back at Elsa, fear and anger etched on her face.

Drawing in another deep breath, Elsa said, 'Then I'll be writing to Ezekiel, and I will post the letter today.'

Rosie stared at her and began to gulp. The bowl hovered under her chin but nothing happened. Her eyes widened and her breathing was shallow, but it wasn't anything to do with pain or with the baby. Rosie was thinking. 'I can't stop you writing,' she said.

'You can't,' Elsa replied. 'I have to do what's right. For all of us.'

'I will not take charity.' Rosie was tremulous. 'You must stay with me and we will work this out, together. You must, Elsa. No one here must know about Nebo's child. Their family would be disgusted with me. Nebo is dead, they might think— Promise me you will not write to him,' she cried.

Elsa's heart pounded. Suddenly she wanted to be sick, too. The future was so unknown. But if she didn't explain to Ezekiel, didn't give him a reason for her absence then she hadn't tried everything she could—for herself, not only for Rosie and the baby. For Ezekiel, too. She wouldn't be dishonest with him. She couldn't be.

Rosie seemed to be weighing up her options. Her mouth pursed and her voice cracked. 'You don't have to write to him about it today, do you? Just give me a little more time to become calm, to think more clearly. I'm—not my best right now.'

Elsa thought it over. Anything could happen in the next few weeks, she knew. Early life in the womb could be quite precarious, Rosie had said. 'All right. I won't tell him yet.' She had a sinking feeling.

Rosie reached across and squeezed Elsa's hands. 'I'll feel better soon, I know it.'

'I hope so.' An overwhelming fatigue struck, and Elsa tried to disengage her hands.

Rosie's grip tightened. 'But no matter what, Elsa, you won't leave me alone, will you, even though I know your heart is elsewhere?'

Gracious me, Rosie, acknowledging I have feelings. Elsa sighed inwardly as the ache grew. She removed her hands from her sister's and rubbed her eyes. 'I won't leave you, Rosie. I wouldn't do that.'

All evening, thoughts of how life here at Robe might look were only interrupted by mopping Rosie on the half-hour. Her sister had grown increasingly waspish. 'Yesterday, the dough for the bread hadn't proved long enough. What a waste. Where is the icing for the sweet buns? You've used the wrong jam. And just look at them—they're not exactly works of art, are they? They'll have to be thrown out.'

'Which is totally unnecessary.' Although when Elsa looked again at her handiwork, the buns did look more like cowpats.

Her sister huffed. 'You'll have to lease out the farm, Elsa, or get rid of it altogether. No more indecision about it. Put all your energy into making the bakery work. How will we survive if—' *Retch.* 'You will take over everything here at the bakery. I know it's a big job: the early mornings, the baking itself, the deliveries. Manning the shop counter. But you'll have to do it.' *Retch.* 'Who knows when this daily sickness will stop? Until it does, I can't be expected to work—'

'Here's another damp towel, Rosie.' And on and on it went.

Later, Elsa collapsed into her bed. Her life was never meant to be in the bakery, a life Rosie had built with Frank. Perhaps instead of leasing the farm, they could sell the bakery. Sell to whom? No one in the district would have any money—the banks weren't lending.

Please, please, please let me find a solution.

Her mind went around and around, and at each turn, her heart thumped as Ezekiel popped into her head. If Rosie had a disturbed night that evening, Elsa hadn't heard her. She'd dropped into a deep, exhausted slumber.

Next evening, Rosie had retreated to her room early. Hopefully she'd not be attacked again by the wretched vomits.

Elsa sat at the tiny dining table with Ezekiel's letter under her hand. Shaking off the weight of exhaustion, she looked down at the beloved handwriting and read it again.

'*My Lovely,*

'*The nights grow cooler, the dawn comes later. My children groan about the crisp air they must endure getting to school. Perhaps not for much longer. It appears I must soon take Gifford from the classroom and put him to work on our farms.'*

Elsa thought about Giff, the serious boy who'd delighted in her using the crutches he'd fashioned. She wiggled her foot. Barely a twinge in it now and she tried not to favour it at all.

'Gracie is doing so well, it seems a shame to remove her to the kitchen.' Elsa frowned at that. Surely not that bright little girl? There would be a better future for Gracie if she stayed at school. She would write and tell Ezekiel so.

'And Jonty is, well, Jonty. My delightful little lad.'

'One wouldn't think winter is coming, but rather spring if Jude were anything to go by. I have never seen a happier man than when he is in the company of Mrs Hartman, and even when he is not, there is certainly a <u>spring</u> in his step.' He'd underlined the word. *'And as for Mrs Hartman, she cannot seem to stop cooking. I presume that to be a good thing, and I, for one, do all I can to encourage it.'*

Each reading of his letter made her want to start another to him. She'd worried that she wouldn't have anything to say. She certainly had no hope to offer that she'd visit—*ever again*—and her heart nearly gave out at that thought. She wanted to tell him so much, but knew it best to chatter about the farm, the bakery— she'd told him Rosie had re-opened it. Now that the vote had been made, she would send him clippings of the *Naracoorte Herald* reports of polling day. She was sure it would make headlines, and not only here but right across all the colonies.

He went on. *'Despite my sore loss of you, I've been keeping busy. In part, telling my children of their uncle's passing. No easy task. A sorrowful time, and I would keep the full circumstances from them. It grieves me further that few will ask after my brother, but if they do, we'll only say that he's gone to God. Our doctor's hand on the death certificate will suffice. The other business at Nebo's campsite remains forever unspoken.'*

Elsa paused then but could not think of any reason why it needed to be otherwise.

'Nebo rests next to my infant son and both now have their names over their graves. Xavier Jones's resting place looks very fine, especially as Mrs Hartman is also tending my family's plot as well as Jude's.'

Mrs Hartman. Kind woman. Elsa had felt very good about her. Surely Judah Jones would find happiness with her. Even the little time Elsa had spent there, it appeared they might have been well matched.

She read on. 'My children enjoy helping her and she has such a good way with them. We all look after George's grave for you until you return.'

Her heart gave a thud again. George's grave. She bit her lip. Until you return.

But it was his next few words that had surprised her when she'd first read them. It shouldn't have—she knew Ezekiel was kind and generous. She let that thought linger before revisiting his words.

'Mr Southie also has a marker with his name on it over his grave in the town cemetery.'

Ezekiel Jones was a kind man; he was her kind man. (She'd have to think harder about how she could return to him.) She thought of what he'd done for George, and George's resting place, beneath that majestic gum tree. She smiled to herself that George would be able to see far and wide from his vantage point as befitted his roaming nature.

George. Whatever he'd done with the sovereigns, he hadn't told a soul. Not even that terrible man who'd beaten him up and shot him trying to get the information. What could George have done with that tin? The thought popped into her mind every so often, surprising her, as if nudging her to see something, or remember something. She'd left Casterton believing with every part of her being that the tin was gone, and with it, all its contents.

She looked down to the last few lines of Ezekiel's letter. *'And so, my love—you are that to me—I will close and have the children post this on their way to Mrs Hartman's today.*

'Yours most faithfully, Ezekiel.'

My love, he'd written.

Last night she'd woken with a start, remembering Ezekiel had told her something, something about what George had said. On the edge of her memory, it had refused to be coaxed forward. And just this morning she remembered something of what that horrible man had said.

Rosie called out again and Elsa tramped to her room. Her sister's head pitched over the bowl, the retch loud as Elsa wrung out a cloth and wiped her face.

Gracious me. Rosie and a baby, a bakery, and a farm. Only Elsa to provide the hard, physical work. How was she going to survive all that?

Fifty-one

Lily stood up and stretched. Thank goodness it was a cool day again. At least the rain had loosened the soil enough to pull the weeds, without her pulling a muscle.

Her *Anaïs Ségalas* rose cuttings looked very healthy indeed. Soon dear Nebo would have mauve blooms at the head of his grave, just like the others had. She was sure that now, he wouldn't mind having a pretty display when the flowers came out, even though he had been a very tough man—like all the Jones men. She gazed at the handsome timber cross Ezekiel had turned for Nebo's grave. Even tough men could show great emotion for those they loved.

She dusted off her hands. The children were packing the cart with the tools now that they'd finished tending their mother and their little brother's resting places. She glanced at the tenderly crafted sign Ezekiel had made for Xavier—another beautiful name for a Jones boy. He'd promised that they'd both have proper headstones as soon as it could be afforded.

Jude was here today. He looked across and winked at her, lifting her basket of fruit pies from the cart. The children let out whoops of delight. Since arriving, they'd been looking forward to the sweet treats.

Oh, family. Family.

'Your bellies are full,' Jude said, nodding towards Giff and Gracie sitting on the cart, legs dangling, and Jonty splayed in the dirt. 'Off you go to your father.' With an extra pie each, and gleeful, the children started out for home. Jude watched them go then turned to Lily. 'I'll take you home before the afternoon chill comes in.'

Pulling the cart under Jude's reins, Cricket pranced down the gentle slope and away from the silent old gum tree. Lily reached over the back for a blanket and threw it across their knees. She sat close to him.

'A letter arrived from Loretta yesterday,' she said. 'She's coming home for a visit, she says. I wonder if our letters crossed in the mail, somehow. Seems she had little to say in reply to my last one.' She tucked her hands under the blanket and Jude slipped a hand into hers. Lily thought of the clipped letter her daughter had written. *'We will talk about things, Mother.'* Not Mama anymore. 'I have a feeling she'll be wanting to have a few words regarding my friendship with you.'

He nudged her with his shoulder and squeezed her hand. 'Well, we'll have to give her something to have a few words about, and it won't be just our friendship. When we get to your place, I have a paper for you to look at.'

Lily turned to him, delighted. 'You have it with you?'

'Aye.'

'Come on, out with it,' she cried. 'I'm not waiting the whole drive home without seeing it.'

Cricket danced at her lively voice. The serene plains drifted by, and white-grey cumulus clouds crowded the sky.

'Judah Jones,' she warned.

He tilted his head, side to side, as if thinking what he should do. 'Inside my waistcoat. I don't want to let go of your hand.'

She rummaged around and pulled out a folded paper, printed back and front. When she read it, she looked at him, amazed.

He gave her a sidelong glance. 'No sense waitin' and courtin' when we know what we want. We're old enough and can't get into no trouble about it.' He shrugged. ''Cept maybe from your kids.'

She waved the paper at him, beaming. 'If it wouldn't upset Cricket, I'd kiss you on the spot.'

'He's got his back turned. He'll never know.'

'Eyes on the road,' she said and kissed him hard on the cheek.

'If that's all there is now, I'm lookin' forward to gettin' to your house,' he said, gazing into the distance.

'So am I,' she replied, the marriage licence clutched in her hand.

In the days after Nebo's funeral, they'd drawn closer, laughed more, shared more. Jude had needed Ezekiel and the children, and they'd needed him, as she did. It was after one of those days, in the early evening a week or so ago when Jude had driven her home, that she'd made up her mind.

'I have an apple pastry that needs a man's appetite. Would you join me, Judah?'

He'd whipped off his hat, kicked off his boots and followed her inside.

Well, after watching him demolish the pastry, she'd certainly made a good job of seduction, if she did say so herself. When she took his plate away and topped up his glass with an elegant madeira—she'd need to find herself another bottle—she took his face in her hands and kissed him. And when he stood up, happily dazed, she took his hand and walked him to her room.

How splendid he was without his shirt on. Her gaze had drifted to the thick wad of bandage at his side, nearly ready to be removed, and she reminded herself to be careful of that. But it was the broad flat chest, with its sprinkling of silver and dark hair, that most took her attention. He worked tough, this man, and he'd been tough on himself. The years on him showed proudly and they warmed her heart. She loved him for it, loved the scars here and there, a crude stitch mark, the bent forearm where a break had not healed properly. She ran her hand down to his belly, a little plump, attesting that perhaps he'd started to enjoy life. She loved that, too, and smoothed her palm over it.

She'd turned for him to unbutton her dress, and she stepped out of it, letting it sigh to the floor. Her shoes shaken away, she waited for his pants to drop. He'd lifted her chemise over her head and loosened the strings on her knickers.

'I'm not youthful anymore,' she said standing still under his gaze, a game tilt of her chin.

He took the soft weight of her breasts in his palms. 'You're ageless, my dear girl.' He broke away, looked at her, down, up, stepped in close to crush her back to him. 'You're beautiful, Lily,' he said, into her neck.

In his arms, she shivered. 'I'm also a little bit cold. Let's just get in that bed and warm up.'

Oh yes, I'm so good at this seduction business. And warm up we did.

Under the covers, pressed against one another, legs wrapped around legs they'd rocked delightedly, laughing, kissing, loving, with an abandon she was sure young people believed only they owned. Jude was strong and giving, and she enjoyed the easy familiarity, the tacit understanding that this was right, and good, and all theirs.

How she loved this man. How she wanted more. And in the morning, just as he was to head back to his place to fix fences, he had said he didn't want to wait to marry.

Now she gazed happily at Judah. He glanced briefly at her, grinning widely as she waved the paper overhead, before he snapped the reins for more speed. The document she held in her hand meant they could be married as soon as they found a pastor agreeable.

They took the turn-off into Lily's driveway and Cricket sped up on the home stretch. As the cart rattled and shook over the wheel ruts, she hooked her arm around Jude's and pressed closer. It was a grand feeling, this feeling of belonging, of being loved for herself again. This knowing that she could start her life all over with a man she trusted without reserve. A man she knew would be by her side for as long as was forever for them.

She'd closed her eyes, had her head on his shoulder a short while as her thoughts drifted when she felt him stiffen. Lily looked at him as he stared ahead and turned to stare at what had caught his attention.

They weren't far from her house, and she could clearly see that two young women stood on the verandah, one of whom she knew. 'Loretta. That's my daughter, Jude. Oh, how delightful.' But the vision of her daughter gave her a start. There must be something wrong for her to visit unannounced. *Perhaps it was about Edward, or Oliver …*

'All growed up. Hat, gloves, fine-looking dress. Pacing up and down too. Looks like your daughter might be worried about something, Lily.'

His voice was soft, and his words worried her a moment. She clutched his forearm. 'My thoughts, too. I'm so pleased to see her, but this is such a surprise.' She straightened in the seat as the cart drew closer and waved.

Loretta's response was merely a half-hearted, quick lift of her hand. Her companion, standing alongside, seemed poised and prim, her dress similar to Loretta's. Perhaps a friend who'd accompanied her home.

Tucking the precious piece of paper into her apron pocket, Lily didn't wait for Jude to assist her from the cart; she climbed down while he braked. She was well used to getting on and off by herself all these years. Anxious to grab her daughter and hold her in her arms before hearing of whatever terrible news Loretta might have, she clutched her skirt in both hands and ran towards the verandah.

Loretta met her at the bottom of the steps. 'Mother,' she cried, and then, 'Mama,' and threw herself into Lily's outstretched arms.

Lily's heart bloomed as she enveloped her daughter in a fierce hug. 'Good gracious, Loretta. I'm so happy to see you. What brings you home so suddenly?' As she took Loretta's shoulders and stared into the so-familiar hazel-eyed gaze, she remembered the other young woman who'd come down the steps. 'And who is your friend?'

'Mother, this is Miss Cassandra Drake, Bertie's sister.'

Well, that sorted his name. Lily made a mental note of it.

The young woman greeted her solemnly. 'Good afternoon, Mrs Hartman.' Ebony eyes, blue-black hair, and about Loretta's age, she'd nodded politely. 'My brother also sends his regards, as do our mother and father.'

'How do you do?' Lily responded and when Miss Drake's gaze went beyond her, Lily held out her arm towards Jude. 'Loretta, you remember Mr Jones. And Miss Drake, this is Mr Judah Jones who lives on a neighbouring property.'

The young women spoke as one. 'Good afternoon, Mr Jones.'

The warmth of the previous happy greeting had dissipated in a puff of air.

'What is it, Loretta, one of the boys?' Lily's hand slid to her daughter's. She squeezed it. 'What's the matter? Why are you here out of the blue without letting me know?'

'I wrote I was coming today.'

Lily did not believe that. Unease crept through her as Loretta glanced at Judah.

'Miss Loretta, I'm happy to see you again. It's been a very long time.' He introduced himself to her friend. 'Miss Drake, I am pleased to meet you. But now that I have delivered Lily back here, I'll make my way home, leaving you ladies to your afternoon.' He said to Lily, 'If there is anything you need me for, you're to come and get me.'

She smiled at him, a hand briefly on his arm. 'You needn't go now, Jude.'

He looked at her, his eyes crinkling at the corners, his voice kind. 'I think I do. Perhaps Miss Loretta needs to talk to you in private.'

'Wait,' she breathed to him. Facing Loretta, she asked, her voice steady but her heart rocking, 'Are your brothers well?'

'Yes, Mother.'

Relieved but bewildered, she gave a little laugh. 'Then it can't be bad news.'

Jude's callused fingers touched her cheek, ever so gently. 'You ladies have a lot to catch up on.' He took her hands to his chest, pulling her close. 'We have a date to make, my love,' he whispered.

She knew then why Loretta had come, and knew that Jude was aware too. 'We do, and we will. Do not doubt me,' she whispered in return, then on her toes kissed his cheek, allowing the two girls to see. She said to him loudly enough, 'I'll see you tomorrow, Jude.'

Lily's mood lifted. His kindness, his perception that she and her daughter would need time alone was not lost on her. As she watched Jude doff his hat and walk away, she now wished he'd tied his horse to the cart so that he'd have a ride home. Still, it wasn't a long walk for him and—

'Mother. It appears I was right to come.'

Turning towards her daughter, noting the tight indignation in Loretta's voice, Lily smiled. 'I'm parched for a cup of tea. Come on, girls.' She headed up the steps, arms wide, herding them along with her. 'You must tell me all about your travel and how long you intend to stay.' The little tremor under her rib cage didn't surprise her. One way or another Lily would have a battle on her hands, either with her daughter or with herself.

Settling in Lily's small parlour, tea in the pot and the first cup poured, the girls told her that they worked at big houses next door to each other.

'Cassandra's employer has closed the house for a week to visit a sick relative and has given her leave,' Loretta said, sitting very straight in her chair. 'Without wages, and having to find somewhere else to lodge while they were away, we decided that we could possibly take this break together.'

How strange; hired help often had shared quarters within a big house. What was a young woman to do without a roof over her head? Some people were more than thoughtless. Poor girl.

Cassandra nodded, a small smile lighting a youthful face. Loretta's own fresh smooth features were only beginning to take on some maturity. Barely women, Lily thought of both girls. Just on the edge of it, with their whole lives ahead of them.

Loretta went on, her shoulders back. 'I told my employer that I thought you were not well and that I needed to travel home quickly to ensure myself of your wellbeing. They were very kind, giving me the time. They needn't have.'

Lily realised that Loretta had deliberately misinformed her employer, for her own end, of course. She gave a short laugh. 'As you can see, dear girl, I'm quite well.'

'And because Cassandra was free to come as my companion, we thought of it as a holiday,' Loretta went on. 'We only have one week to travel to and fro, so the visit is short. We misjudged how long it takes to come here from Melbourne, so we must start our return tomorrow to be back in time.'

Loretta was after something; she wouldn't have misjudged a thing. Disappointing. 'Tomorrow? Oh, that's hardly any time at all,' Lily cried lightly. 'Certainly better than nothing, though,' Lily said when Loretta frowned. *Definitely after something.* She poured each another cup and glanced at Cassandra, who shifted in her seat, then dabbed at her mouth with the serviette. No one had touched the little silver tray with freshly baked jam drops on it.

Loretta glanced at her companion, who stood, cup and saucer in hand and excused herself. 'I'll take some fresh air on the verandah, if you don't mind, Mrs Hartman, and take my tea with me.' She almost bobbed as she passed Lily's chair. A rehearsed departure.

Lily carefully set down her cup. 'If you're to leave tomorrow, my dear,' she said to her daughter, 'you must speak your concerns quickly, for if nothing else, I know you're up to something.'

Loretta blushed, no doubt at the tone in Lily's voice as well as the implication. She too put down her cup and folded her hands in her lap. 'Mother, seeing Mr Jones here confirms my suspicions about what it is you thought you'd so carefully tried to disguise in your letters.'

'Is that so? And what is that?' Lily maintained a small smile.

'That you intend to marry again.'

My girl is so snippy these days. 'It's true, I do,' Lily said, 'and it's come around more quickly than even I had thought.' At the shock on her daughter's face, she continued, calm and trying to sound reassuring. 'Loretta, my dear, whatever you might think, I do have a life left to live. Your father has been gone for some time,' she emphasised.

Loretta pressed her lips together, then, 'I—we, Oliver, Edward and I don't wish that you marry again,' she burst. 'It's as if you've forgotten our father.'

Lily gave a worried sigh. 'That's not true.' She reached across the table between them to take Loretta's hand, but her daughter pulled back.

'We think that this Mr Jones is out to get your ...'

'My what?'

Suddenly unsure of herself, Loretta took a deep breath. 'You're pushing aside our father's memory for him,' she said sharply.

Lily knew that was not all her daughter had intended to say, but she'd heard the plea in Loretta's voice. 'You—all you children— and I will never lose the memory of your father. Not ever,' she said softly.

'Your marrying again diminishes that, dishonours it,' Loretta cried and tears, borne out of the vehemence now in her voice, popped into her cheeks. 'You'll lose this place to Mr Jones. It will belong to him and his family.'

That astonished her. Her children seemed worried about their inheritance. She'd not seen that in any of them before—none of them could hardly bear to come home to the farm, and now they were worried they'd lose it. Speechless, she stared at her daughter.

'You won't be here for us,' she wept. 'We won't have you to share our memories of our father—'

'I'll always be here for you.' Lily held herself back in the face of her daughter's distress.

Loretta sniffed. 'I'm to tell you, from all of us, that we forbid you to marry.'

'I beg your pardon?' Surely Lily had misheard.

Loretta didn't look at her, instead grabbed her cup and took a slurp. 'One day, one of the boys will have the farm—Oliver stands to inherit but he's not sure he wants it, and Edward, well, is Edward. He'd sell it as much as anything. I'll be married. I'll need you. And where will you be? With him,' she seethed, pointing outside. 'I don't want my father's memory pushed aside. I don't want another man to take the place of my father in your affections.' The outburst had run its course. Red-faced, Loretta set down her cup again and tried to pour a refill. A shake in her hand prevented her filling her cup, so she gave up. She said, 'You'll betray our father. Us.' But still she hadn't looked at her mother.

Lily sat in silence. Her children were jealous of her, of material possessions—inheritance had entered the tirade—but were also jealous enough to try to keep all others from her door. Had it not crossed their minds that she deserved another chance at happiness with a man of her choice in her life?

She sighed. When Stan died, Loretta had been only thirteen. Old enough by law to be married off, although, God forbid, that hadn't happened. *Barbaric consent law.* Of her three children, Loretta had been closest to her doting pa. The shock of his dying had left her scarred, the young teen's grieving fused in, and she couldn't accept it.

Lily reached over again and took her daughter's hands. Reluctantly, Loretta allowed it. She waited a beat until she was sure her daughter would let her speak. 'No one will take your father's place.'

Quick as a wink, Loretta asked, 'You won't remarry?'

Lily frowned at her. 'You will give me the respect to hear me properly, to listen.' Her daughter dropped her chin but didn't move away. 'No one will push our memories aside.'

Loretta scowled. 'If you marry, we'll have to share everything with another family,' she said.

Lily gave her a look. 'That would be lovely if ever the three of you came home once in a while.'

Loretta's mouth fell open. 'I work, and the boys are studying. We can't just drop everything and—' She stopped, seemed to have heard herself.

Lily nodded. 'Indeed. I know you have your lives to lead, and I'm happy for it.' She patted Loretta's hands. 'You've indicated perhaps you and Bertie might soon be tying the knot. So far, I haven't heard any more news on that front.'

'Nothing to tell,' she said, too sharply. Loretta's blush burned. 'Besides, that's different.'

'It's just as important for you to live your life as it is for me to live mine.'

'We won't come to the wedding,' Loretta burst, her lip curling. 'We don't give our blessing. We will hate him, despise him.'

Lily took in a sharp breath. 'How beneath you, Loretta.' She could cope with the immaturity but hadn't noticed earlier that her daughter had developed a sneer, a haughty twist on her mouth that made her look petty, nasty. It distorted her beautiful features, and the desperation in her shrill voice tore at her, broke her heart. 'Look at you, believing you have a right to speak so churlishly.'

Loretta sobbed. 'Why would you do it to us?' She pulled a handkerchief from her dress pocket and dabbed her eyes.

Lily's hand went to her own pocket and felt the paper there, felt it crinkle under her fingers. 'Loretta, I'm not doing anything to you. You are not babies. I don't need a man, I want one. Judah Jones. And if I marry, it is for me.'

Loretta looked up again, hopeful.

Lily held up a hand. 'I will marry, but it's not to slight you.' She sat up straight. 'As for your suggestion that our property will be absorbed into Judah's, I should remind you children, and you especially being a young woman, to revisit the *Married Women's Property Act*, of which I am reasonably well acquainted.'

'What?'

'You might also inform your brothers—who don't actually sound deserving of the farm—and your beau for that matter, that whatever a woman brings to the marriage, she is within her rights to keep as hers.' Loretta's mouth dropped open again. 'It is a plain fact,' Lily confirmed. 'Tell your brothers that their inheritance of this land is intact but that if I choose to leave part thereof to you, I will do so. In fact, now I've mentioned it, I'll consult with our lawyer, Mr Milton, on that very thing, as soon as possible.' It didn't seem as if Loretta could close her mouth, so Lily went on. 'Now, I'll tell you another thing plainly. I love you children, and I love that you're making your way in the world as responsible adults. But this woman,' Lily tapped her chest, 'your mother, has found no better man living than Judah Jones, and I will marry him. What you decide to think of that is up to you.' If she'd had any guilt about marrying, it had been completely banished. She sat back, taking her cup, and sipped cooled tea. 'It must have escaped your notice that I am also a person in my own right, not just your mother, not just working this place by myself all these years for your benefit only,' at which Loretta bit her lip and looked away, 'and certainly not just as a widow who has nothing left to live for.'

Wiping her eyes, closing her mouth, Loretta glanced around her, as if trying to find something else to say. When she finally did, it was with a whimper. 'But I have to go back tomorrow. You have to agree—'

'Then there's very little time to be together this visit,' Lily cut in, exasperated. 'My last word on the matter is that you're all welcome here at home whenever it suits you to visit, but you'll be courteous to Judah if you can't be anything else.'

Loretta stood up. Her chin had puckered. 'If I can't change your mind, Cassandra and I will walk into town to take lodgings for the night.'

Lily's heart dropped again, thudding against her ribs. 'You know you don't have to do that,' she said, keeping the panic from rising. 'There's room here for both of you.'

'I can't bear what you're going to do.' Loretta's face crumpled. 'You're choosing him over us, over our father.' She turned and fled the room.

Lily followed, torn. *No, no, no.* She wasn't being disloyal to her children, or to Stan. During his illness, they'd never discussed her remarrying, but surely as he loved her, he'd have wanted her to be happy? She wouldn't be disloyal to herself, either. Her children, adults now, could not dictate how she'd live her life. She'd given everything for them in the past, but she would not give this.

When had her daughter become so terrified of losing her? Perhaps she'd been too young to send to the city to work, though God alone knows how hard it was to prevent her. When her older brothers had received their uncle's bequest, there was no stopping her going as well. Even at sixteen she'd been determined, and had threatened to run away.

In the hallway, Lily watched her daughter pick up her friend's hat and gloves from the tallboy and tuck them under her arm. 'My dear girl.'

Loretta pulled on her own pair and donned her hat. 'I'll still write, Mother,' she said and pressed her wet cheek quickly against Lily's before she marched to the front door and onto the verandah.

Cassandra took her hat and gloves. 'Good day, Mrs Hartman,' she said. 'I was pleased to meet you.' Her glance was brief as she took the steps off the verandah and began to walk.

Loretta followed but stopped on the bottom step, twisting her handkerchief. Lily, leaning on a post, was weary with a new grief she couldn't name. *One last try.* 'If you marry your beau and make a life with him like I did with your father, think about what it might be like to lose that love and companionship and end up alone, yet knowing you have so much more to give.'

Loretta set her mouth, then head down, strode past Cassandra, who skipped along to keep up with her.

Lily rubbed her eyes. Was it enough, or would she never see her daughter, or her sons, again? Surely, she would. Surely, it would be all right.

Loretta stopped and turned. She called out, her voice teary. 'I hope it's a happy wedding day, Mama.' Then she ran back, leaping the steps two at a time and hugged Lily fiercely.

Lily wrapped her up and rocked a little, her daughter's tears on her neck. Loretta let her go, rushed down the steps again and ran to catch her friend. Sagging against the verandah post, waving as Loretta turned one last time, she smiled away the quiet despair. *It would be all right. It would.*

Fifty-two

Zeke met the kids at the gate. Giff shook his head sadly. 'No letter, Pa,' he said. He'd check the mail in town every day after school before coming home. Gracie looked at her father with sympathy. Jonty had no clue, he was already nearly asleep bareback on Milo.

Zeke reached up and took him off the horse, settled him on his shoulder.

No letter. There'd only been one from Elsa in the seven weeks since she'd left, written maybe two weeks after they'd have got back to Robe, and although he knew he needed patience, he didn't feel he had enough of it.

Dearest Ezekiel—his heart had soared—*we arrived home safe and sore, and glad to be home.*

Should that have worried him? He'd read the last words of that line over and over. She'd written of the farm and that it had been pilfered in their absence, of the bakery that was in a neglected state, but how Rosie had soon re-opened it. He wasn't sure how he felt about that. Elsa was also working at the bakery, so it seemed she had gainful employment. She might not want to leave that.

She continued, telling him of her excitement of the election day coming in the weeks ahead.

'… *the candidates, Mr Ash, Mr Handyside, Mr Smeaton and Mr Barker. Forgive me not saying for which party, or for whom I will cast my vote.*'

And to add to the complexity of it, the women would also be among voters who would answer a referendum, a first for the country. Her tenacity, her determination to vote made him feel proud for her. No wonder—it was a fierce part of who she was. How could he possibly have tried to deny her, even with the knowledge that he might well lose her to her home colony.

'… *I am well, dear Ezekiel, and my thoughts are constantly with you and your children.*' He took a deep breath at that. '*For now, all I have are these written words, but know that they are sent with deep affection.*'

His heart was still soaring when he headed inside with Jonty. He put the boy down to sleep for a while.

Jude was winding vinegar-soaked bandages around one of his hands. He held it up. 'Fencing. I hadn't realised how soft I'd got until pulling wire through posts,' he said, and took a look at Zeke. 'No new letter, I take it?'

Zeke shook his head. 'Mrs Hartman not coming today?'

'Her daughter was at her house when we got back from the graves. I think Lily's anxious about that.' He held out his hand and Zeke tied off a bandage. 'She believes her kids are not impressed by her remarrying.'

'And?'

'I didn't stay, I'll let them sort it out. I have confidence in my wife-to-be.' Jude inspected the bandage.

'So she's still remarrying?' Zeke asked, wide-eyed.

'Aye, she is. Without a doubt. I know it, and don't sound daft. We have it planned for next week.'

'Jude, family can be persuasive.'

His brother nodded. It was clear Jude had thought of the possibility that Lily might be talked out of their decision. 'They can. As I said, I have confidence.'

If nothing else, he was stoic.

'Ah, well then, a wedding.' Zeke reached into a cupboard and brought out a rum pot and two snifters. 'We'll enjoy that.' He poured.

Jude lifted his in salute. 'Nebo would have enjoyed it too.'

'He would have.' Zeke leaned over his glass. *Nebo.* He felt a pain in his heart. *My brother.*

'He was a good lad, deep down, our brother,' Jude said. 'Silly bugger.'

'Sad bugger,' Zeke said.

'Aye. I miss him.'

'We all do.'

In silence, they sat until the kids had finished their chores.

The next day at the gate, Gracie and Giff were running alongside a slow trotting Milo, and Jonty, high on the horse, was gleefully waving an envelope in his hand. 'Pa, Pa, it's from Ma Goody,' he cried.

Gracie yelled at him. '*Miss* Goody.'

Zeke closed his eyes a moment. *That boy.*

None of them could wait. They jogged to the house. Chores waited, tea waited and the four of them huddled around the table while Zeke read the letter. Then he had to read it again, before deciding which of the parts of the letter to read aloud.

'... *so I hope everyone is well. We are well here, and think often of you all* ...'

Jonty was very pleased. 'She thinkin' of me.'

'Of all of us,' Gracie said, leaning over her father's shoulder, and he edged the letter away from her eyes.

'... *not many animals on the farm. The fences are in need of mending* ...'

'I could mend her fences,' Giff said, and looked expectantly at his father.

'... and so I still work at the bakery. Speaking of my sister, Rosie is not as good as Gracie at managing my hair ...'

Gracie preened. 'She means I was good at it, Pa.'

Zeke smiled at her, remembering Elsa's hair in his own hands.

The letter went on, but the children were satisfied with their mentions and their interest waned quickly. Zeke folded the letter and tucked it in his pocket. He would study the rest of it at his leisure, when he could pore over her pages—the many pages—detailing her life.

From then on, her letters arrived every few days, causing much excitement and chatter after school. Again, he would read the children the mention Elsa made of each of them, then he'd put the letter into his pocket and wait until he could savour reading and re-reading for an hour or so in the quiet of the evening.

Some letters were only a page. He wondered if she'd been tired when her hand penned those missives. And when he set down to reply, he made sure to ask. He tried to reply to each separate letter and didn't succeed but always made sure he answered all her questions in a long letter back to her.

Over the weeks he noticed that hers began to slow. Maybe she had truly overworked herself. He wondered if mail might have been going astray, but that didn't seem likely. Gifford had also noticed the lack of regular mail from Miss Goody. The boy would shake his head ruefully when he'd come home after school.

Then at last, Giff had been successful on his mission. The last one received mentioned the results after the election. Elsa had written about the local polls, and about how they returned a resounding 'no' to the first of the three questions of the referendum: should any changes be made to the free and secular education for state schools? She listed the other questions, but he was impatient to read more personal news.

Satisfied that she was well, and happy, in reply he'd quickly written a short letter to tell her of his own visit to the polling booth, returning home to more work. He'd wondered if he'd hear news of a visit from her soon. He didn't ask. She knew how he felt. But he did tell her of Jonty's growing impatience, of Gracie's careful tending of her mother, Maisie's brush, readying for Elsa's return. He promised Elsa a new brush—maybe Gracie needed to have her mother's brush all to herself. He wrote of Judah and Lily marrying.

It was now nearly the end of May, three weeks after that last letter and as autumn drew to a close, winter advanced more boldly by the hour. The letters from Elsa had stopped. Zeke wrote, and wrote again, and waited.

On a cold day at the end of June, the afternoon sun bright in a pale sky, Giff greeted him with a wave and a big toothy grin. Gracie, laughing and singing, skipped alongside Milo and Jonty, rugged up on the faithful horse, flapped two letters, and cried, 'We got two, and this one's from her. It's from Ma.'

Zeke rubbed his face and pocketed the other letter; he didn't recognise the writing on it and put it out of his mind. He slipped Elsa's letter inside his shirt. After so long, would it be bad news? He'd have to read it all through first before imparting anything to his kids.

As they all clamoured around the table in the cosy kitchen room, the oven chugging out happy warmth, he took a ragged breath, reading quickly. Zeke couldn't believe his eyes. He couldn't believe what she'd written.

'Come on, Pa. What does she say?' Gracie asked, peering over his shoulder. 'Pa.'

He snapped out of his shock. 'She says that she's well, that her sister is well.' Newspaper cuttings drifted to the floor. Giff picked them up, squinted to read them. 'And that she sends everyone her best wishes and hopes you've all been very good.'

'We have,' Giff and Gracie said.

'When she comin' home?' Jonty.

Zeke was greedy for time alone. 'And now it's time for chores,' he said to his kids, distracted. 'Jonty, eggs. Gracie, fruit. Giff, the dogs, and give them a run.' He grumbled at their groaning protests. 'Go on, hurry it up.' When the kids had gone, he sat and stared at the letter.

While Jude continued working to fix his place, he'd gone to live at Lily's now that they were husband and wife. Zeke was on his own with Elsa's news. *'And so, Ezekiel, my love, forgive me for my tardiness, but I don't know how to use the right words for this ...'*

He read and re-read as a pulse beat strongly in his neck.

'I must look out for my sister ...' and *'... don't want my words to be misconstrued as "unseemly" when I speak of what was between us—do you remember when I used that word before? It seems so long ago ...'*

He thought of her wild head of hair, and Gracie struggling to contain it. Of how he'd taken over from his daughter and been completely entranced, his hands working the plait—nothing *unseemly* about it. Thought of her grit, her honesty, her need to be independent in her thinking. Her love of family, and of the land.

'I cannot see another solution. It appears the only way.'

How could it be so?

'If there were another way for me, for Rosie, I wouldn't be writing any such thing.'

He'd had hope, but now ... He hadn't realised how badly it would hurt, until now, not to have her. Never to have her with him. His heart thudded, his temples hurt. He held his head in his hands and breathed.

'You must put me out of your mind, and trust that this is the best thing to do.

'With my love and deepest affection, Elsa.'

Fifty-three

Close to tears again, Elsa tried hard not to think of what Ezekiel might've felt when her last letter landed in his hands. There'd been no answer from him but what else should she expect—she'd broken her own heart, so what must her letter have done to him?

Rosie had reached out and gripped her hand in both of hers. At first Elsa thought her sister had been about to show some heart. 'It's for the best, Elsa,' she'd said. 'For me,' she added matter-of-fact. 'No one must know the baby's real father, not only of the disgrace for me, but also for the child if it were to be known.' Rosie wanted Elsa to look at her, had tried to move into her line of sight, but Elsa pulled her hand away. *Always about Rosie.* 'And you do know we couldn't survive without you, don't you?' Elsa only nodded. Still more nervous, Rosie had asked, 'You won't leave, will you?'

Trying to muster a smile, glancing at Rosie over her shoulder, Elsa had said brightly, 'Of course not.'

The mornings had been the hardest of all, getting up in the wee small hours and toiling in the bakery with nothing but the roar of the heating ovens to break the silence in her head and heart. In those hours, thoughts of life at Casterton with Ezekiel

and the children crowded in over the top of the dough proving for bread, over the dried fruit plumping for the buns, over
the spreading of jam in thick swathes ... (One thing had happily
occurred—her buns no longer looked like cowpats.) Then she'd
go upstairs and try to stay awake to get Rosie up and about, with
tea, and something to entice her to eat.

Her sister had lately begun to feel better for she woke ready to
chatter, ready to give orders and finally ready to do a little work.
That was a good thing, because Elsa's steps had begun to slow,
and life appeared only burdensome. When the day was done, Elsa
would climb to her room above the bakery and sink into the
mattress, exhausted. What hope had ever looked like for a future
with Ezekiel was well extinguished, and her sorrow couldn't be
relieved under the heavy curtain of fatigue. Her last thoughts
before sleep were that she really had to lift her spirits. She wasn't
a maudlin person.

One day not long ago, Rosie had been in the bakery surveying the baskets of fragrant breads and the pastries in their display
cabinets. 'You have developed a knack for this, Elsa, but oh dear,
I do wish you'd look after yourself better. Whatever will the customers think?'

Elsa smoothed wayward locks back to her haphazardly put
together bun. 'In that case, perhaps if you're feeling well enough,
you'd look after the shop while I have a sleep for an hour or so.'

'Yes, all right, but do it after lunchtime. I have to go down the
street myself this morning.' She looked very healthy and stood
there protectively cupping her belly. She'd taken to doing that
when she thought no one was looking. It was a good thing for her
to be happy about her coming baby.

Rosie had returned and Elsa had taken a nap. Her sister had
let her sleep for an hour in the afternoon each couple of days
since then.

Today was the day they'd leave the farm behind; no more talk of working the land. Elsa had only been able to visit the farm from time to time anyway since arriving back, and now the land had been leased to a farmer from the next section. Elsa took it in her stride; she'd continue to live with Rosie in the small residence over the bakery.

She'd woken to Rosie holding her hand.

'Is everything all right?' Elsa struggled to sit, groggy with sleep.

'I realised I've never said thank you for all you do, Elsa.'

Peering at her sister, Elsa wondered if she was feeling unwell. She swung her stockinged feet to the floor and reached for her work boots. She'd head for the farm with Peppin and the cart for one last time. 'I'm sure you have, Rosie.'

'You must know that I never meant to hurt you, even though my situation might have caused that.'

Was her sister becoming soft? *Well, that wouldn't hurt.*

Rosie had gripped her hand again. 'I've been a selfish and shrill woman all my life. Oh, I've certainly heard myself lately, don't worry, but I realise how happy this baby makes me. I am aware, though, that my happiness is at the expense of yours, and for that I'm sorry. And I'm sorry you—haven't yet heard from Mr Jones.' She'd looked very worried still, even furtive, but that was Rosie.

Elsa gently shook her off; it was too hard to dwell on that. Before she lost the ability to summon her voice, she said, 'I must get to the farm. I'll be back by tea. I hope the store isn't too busy for you until then.'

After deciding to lease the farm—they could only get a pittance and Elsa had already signed the lease papers—the bakery was all they had to keep them going for now. But once again, Rosie had changed her mind and was all for getting rid of that, too. Elsa couldn't keep up, she just plodded along.

Out at the farm, clutching one of Rosie's shawls about her shoulders, Elsa looked around the dusty yards of their property. Rain had come and gone. It was another cloudless day, and now the cool drift of early spring swirled on the sea breeze.

Standing in the paddocks of home, she inhaled a deep breath of fresh air. Elsa would miss the farm, despite how much extra work it added. It would be hard to leave the place of her childhood, and where her parents and her brothers lay. Leased or not, no matter what, she'd still come here to visit the graves.

The graves. She shook off a strange sensation, as if in her mind she'd heard an echo and couldn't make it out. Just her nerves jangling—all this planning, changing the plans, the fatigue, the waiting. That was the worst. What would Ezekiel's reaction have been, if he had answered? She was anxious for mail, waiting for his letter to arrive, telling her that he understood and forgave her. Telling her anything. If he chose to write.

Elsa turned, heartsore, and walked inside the family's old house, hugging the shawl against the crisp air. She picked up the milking stool, rested it against the wall of the hut and sat down. The kettle was still on the cooker, but the oven was cold. The hutch was empty, clean, and the one remaining pot hung from a nail in the wall nearby. Leaning back, she looked around, idly wondered who on earth would have left one lone pot and stolen most everything else. Some people were just too desperate, and still no end of the depression in sight. Besides, as Rosie had said long ago, the place must have looked abandoned to those who had come here. She could well imagine that.

Drifting, closing her eyes, she let the events of the last long weeks whirl around. She pushed aside the memories of the danger, and the murders. Too horrible to relive. She wanted only to think of Ezekiel, of his children. Of Jonty, the little boy who wanted a mama, of when he told her he knew where George's grave was. Of what Ezekiel had told her George mumbled when—

She opened her eyes. *The graves.* A wraith-like touch feathered along her arm.

Ezekiel's voice. *'He said something like "we'll save the farm ... It's in the dirt."'*

That horrible man's voice. *'He talked of the tin bein' at the graves ... Nothin' at the graves on your brother's place, Mr Jones, and nothin' at yours.'*

The graves. *Oh, George—the graves here!*

Elsa shot off the stool and crashed outside, throwing off the shawl. Her feet pounded on the cold, hard dirt. Ignoring the recently healed bone in her foot, she ran, stumbling and tripping across the yard to where her parents were buried, to where the earth was still soft over her father.

And there—something she'd seen oh-so-long ago but had barely noticed—was the loosened dirt by her mother's marker. She dropped to her knees and cried an apology to her mother. Tearing at the foot of the marker, she tossed aside the dirt and pebbles and twigs and ants and ... was now scraping, *scratching* and digging with her hands, fingers gouging the deeper, damp soil. Tears were falling as she swept open a small hole and—*oh my Lord*—it's here, the tin.

She pushed grazed fingertips down and lifted it out, hearing the unmistakable clink and slide of coins. Falling on her backside, the grave marker lying flat beside her, she stared at the narrow, weighty tin. Rectangular, only an inch or so deep, its lid was clapped on, no hinges. She tilted it this way and that, tried to pry it open. Etched crudely on the lid were the letters 'R', 'G' and 'E'.

Dear George. He'd hidden the tin here for the three of them.

Fifty-four

Poor Peppin had probably never galloped as hard pulling the cart back to town. Elsa was laughing as she flicked his reins. In the back, she'd barely tied down the milking stool or the lone pot and they slid and jangled in the cart. She didn't care.

She'd found the tin, and George had left it right in front of her all this time. No matter how hard life had looked, it would ease considerably now if they were careful—if there were indeed thirty sovereigns inside the tin. *A fortune.*

Oh, she couldn't wait to tell Rosie.

In town, she braked the cart next to another horse in front of the bakery, and with the tin tucked under her arm, she ran to the door and rushed inside.

Rosie was finishing with Mrs Collins, and handing her change of a pound coin. Fit to bursting and barely being able to wait, Elsa hopped from one foot to the other. Dust from the drive floated from her, and her hair had become unruly again—she puffed it out of her face, swiped it with her free hand, and rubbed her scraped and dirt-filled fingernails on her dress. She didn't care. The tin tucked under her arm—oh joy—was such a bright light after the awful events of the last months. And then Rosie did an unusual thing. As soon as Mrs Collins left, she walked to the front door and shut it, turning out the CLOSED sign.

'Finally,' Elsa burst. 'Oh, Rosie, look, It's George's tin.'

Rosie, coming back to her at the counter, lit up. She reached to grab it. 'Oh, that's so wonderful. It'll come in very—'

'It was at Ma's grave all this time.' Elsa brushed Rosie's hands aside. She slapped the tin onto the counter, grabbed the towel tucked into Rosie's pinny and wiped dust from the lid. 'It all just seemed to come to me when—'

'Elsa.'

'—I was sitting out at the farm and … What's the matter?' She realised Rosie's tone was strange. 'You're not excited? But it's the best thing that could've happened—'

'Elsa.' Ezekiel stepped out from the back of the shop. Her breath caught. He came around the counter to her. 'Hello, my love,' he said, reaching for her.

'You're here,' she breathed, and slid into his arms, touched his cheeks to make sure he was real. Her heart was light, her head woolly. 'Oh, finding the tin is nowhere near … This is the best thing that could *ever* have happened.' She stared unblinking into his handsome, smiling face, his darkly glinting eyes searching hers. 'Ezekiel.'

He took her hands, brought them to his chest. 'I was summonsed,' he said, tilting his head towards Rosie.

Elsa, wide-eyed, looked from him to her sister.

Rosie folded her arms, looked a little flushed. 'Well,' she said, in a huff. 'I'd been selfish for too long, Elsa, and despite the—' she took a breath, '—indelicacy, I could no longer allow the, um, whole burden of it, and the bakery, and with me being with—all … to fall on your shoulders.'

Elsa blinked in surprise and then suspicion of her sister's motivation descended. A frown threatened.

Ezekiel bent to Elsa. He smelled of horse, and leather, and the dust on his shirt was grainy under her fingers. 'How could I not come for you, and for your sister, when I learned of Nebo's child?' He smiled and swung Elsa with him to speak to her sister. 'I knew my brother well, Rosie. He's sorely missed and the child you carry is part of him, so part of our family.' At Rosie's prim nod, her colour high, he said to Elsa, 'And I was so affected after your last letter that I forgot a second one had arrived at the same time.'

Rosie cleared her throat. 'I wrote to Mr Jones and mailed it the same day your last letter. Told him myself of the, er, my predicament.'

Elsa stared at Rosie, increasingly stern. *Rosie's 'predicament'.* 'How hard that must have been for you to tell Ezekiel, Rosie.' Ezekiel's arms shifted, tightened around her but she went on, 'To take such a risk.'

Rosie, her eyes downcast, waved a hand. 'Oh, was only, er, uncomfortable while I was writing.' She went on in a hurry. 'I told Mr Jones you wouldn't come to him because you wouldn't leave me, that was the whole reason.' She glanced at Ezekiel. 'And I believed by telling a gentleman, such as Mr Jones, of—family news, that my reputation would've been protected.'

Rosie's *effrontery*. Astounded, Elsa could hardly believe her ears. Rosie had ensured the security of her own future and that of her child. Why, she'd begun to do that from the moment she knew she was with child: having Elsa leave the farm, having her slave in the bakery, half dead on her feet, mopping up after her …

But it had brought Ezekiel.

Rosie, rushing on, ducked back behind the counter, clearly believing it to be a safe distance. 'So in the light of that, because *of course* I knew you wanted to be with Mr Jones, I also asked that I might be allowed to accompany you both to Casterton.' At Elsa's amazed glare, she said hurriedly, 'To make a new life for myself there.' She paused, looking from one to the other. 'If my presence would not disturb his family.'

Ezekiel shook Elsa a little as if to distract her. 'A child arriving is not disturbing. It's disturbing that there've been too many in my family already departed. We welcome Rosie and Nebo's child, Elsa.' He pulled her closer. His eyes were merry, and a smile twitched. 'Nebo told me that he wanted Rosie as his wife. I thought then how well suited they were to each other.' The wry smile remained.

Poor Nebo.

Rosie smarted, had the grace to look uneasy.

Ezekiel kissed Elsa's forehead. 'I would've come to you anyway, to hear with my own ears that you didn't want to be with me. I refused to believe it from your letter. Then Rosie's letter confirmed it, gave me the best excuse to come,' he said.

Ezekiel's grip on her hadn't lessened. He was a good man; she'd known it from the very first. *I would've come to you anyway.* Elsa's glare softened towards her sister.

Rosie saw it, and triumphant, broke the silence—back to her bossy self. 'Now, if you'll both kindly take yourselves into the parlour,' she said, 'I must re-open the store. We are expecting prospective purchasers for the bakery.'

'What?'

'I wouldn't move colonies and be as poor as a church mouse, too. For goodness sake, Elsa,' Rosie tut-tutted. 'And take that grubby little box of coins with you. It's made a mess.' She walked to the front of the store, opened the door and effusively greeted a man and woman there.

Elsa clutched the tin and tugged Ezekiel into the small well-lit parlour warmed by the bakery ovens in the next room. Daylight cheerfully swathed the room in a pale, yellow haze. Dropping the container with a clatter, she spun in his arms and held his face in her hands. 'I still cannot believe you're here, Ezekiel, in front of my eyes.'

He whirled her around and hugged her. 'That's from Giff and Gracie and Jonty. They're with Jude and Lily, desperate for your return.' Then he kissed her hard. 'And that's from me.'

She stopped him, anxious. 'Ezekiel, Rosie planned all this, orchestrated that you come here. I would never trick—'

'I know that, and good, I'm glad she did. Here I am.' He brushed wisps of hair from her face, planted another kiss on her brow. 'Besides, I really am happy to know that Nebo's child is coming.'

Still annoyed at Rosie, she whispered, 'Do you believe the child is Nebo's?'

'Do you believe it?' At her nod, he said, 'That's all I need.' Ezekiel leaned close to her. 'I could see at the campsite that my brother and your sister were two peas of the same pod, my love, and I knew Nebo well. They're both childlike in their selfishness. They're transparent, needy, jealous.'

'She didn't love him.'

'Ah, but we loved him and so we'll care for her as Nebo's widow. The babe will be a happy, well-loved Jones child. You leave dealing with Rosie to me.'

She touched Ezekiel's face tenderly then took his hand. 'I'm so sorry I disappointed you with my letter.' She pressed her lips to his fingers. Her eyes squeezed shut. She was right to love this man.

'Disappointment is not what I'd call it. It was a good thing Jonty reminded me of the other letter; I might not have recovered so fast. Not the first time the lad has pointed me in the right direction.' He gave a short laugh. 'Now I can personally deliver my reply,' he said and took a wrinkled, folded page out of his pocket. 'It's very short. "My dearest Elsa, you must come home to us as quickly as you can. Jonty is very impatient for your company."'

Raising his gaze from the letter, his dark eyes were now regarding her intently. 'Not only Jonty,' he said and kissed her head, burying his face a moment in her hair. 'Hmm. Dust from the paddock.'

'I rushed in from the farm with the tin.' She bent and picked it up.

'The infamous tin.'

Huddled, they sat together at the little table and pried it open to count the sovereigns. 'Only twenty-nine,' Elsa said. 'George must have found a way to spend one.' She let her thoughts run to her mop-haired brother. *Well, good for him.* Then she cheered up. 'Come on, read the rest of your letter, you haven't finished,' she said.

He dropped his hand over hers. 'It says, "On second thoughts, I'll come and get you, just to be sure you don't gallop off on other adventures, my lady bushranger. You are loved and missed, and my life is not complete without you."' He tucked a long wavy lock of hair behind her ear. 'To tell the truth, I didn't even write that. I plain decided to get on my horse and ride.' He smoothed her frown. 'Come home to me. To us.'

'I will.' With her head against his, Elsa thought of her family's farm. She'd leased the place, but it was still her address in South Australia. She leaned back to look at him. 'I'll have to come back here to vote though, in the future. Victoria doesn't allow it yet.'

'Of course. We'd make it a holiday by the sea each time.'

She leaned back to look at him. 'I'll work on your farm,' she said.

'You'll work beside me. You're a farmer.'

'I am.' She thought of Giff and Gracie, and the little lad, Jonty. 'And I'll be a mother to your children.'

'And to ours who'll follow.'

Her fingertips idled over the stubble on his cheek. 'I'll have a good life with you. We'll have a good life.'

'We will, my love. I have no doubt.'

Her thoughts strayed to family, and children laughing, hens bustling and kelpies barking. Soon on their farm, there'd be dairy cows, or cattle roaming on those golden plains of Casterton. She smiled. 'No doubt whatsoever.'

Author's Note

As usual, any mistakes or omissions are mine.

Rosie and Frank's bakery in Robe is fictional.

At the time of writing the name of the first woman to vote in the 1896 election in Robe is not known. According to a journalist's article, she did cast her vote at 9.45am. The State Library of South Australia informed me that electoral roll records from the area for that particular election have not been found. We do hope they still exist, and if they ever come to light, I hope Elsa Goody has done the lady justice.

The story behind the thirty sovereigns was true in part in my own family history going back to the early days of the Depression on the land in Victoria. My great-grandfather discovered the stash after he took up a land division. When no one came forward for them, he was very careful how he spent the find. A dirt-poor farmer would've had a hard time trying to change a sovereign back in those days, much less thirty of them.

Acknowledgements

Thanks to my readers, I remain deep in the batcave and in nine-teenth-century Australia—long may it continue. Once again thanks to Susan Parslow who casts her eagle eye over my first draft—she always knows when I've fallen asleep at the wheel. To Fiona Gilbert who abandons husband Tony to travel with me on our book tours, and who keeps up the flow of essential road trip items, especially for happy hour. To Leon and the team at Leon Bignell MP's office Aldinga and Kingscote, SA—my day job keeps me connected to the outside world. To the fabulous history in Liz Harfull's *Almost an Island: The Story of Robe*, to the many jour-nals and articles found via my go-to Trove, to the State Library of South Australia. The amazing townships of Robe and Penola in South Australia. The Penola Coonawarra Visitor Information Centre was a gem and a mine of information, as was the wonder-ful Casterton Visitor Information and Kelpie Centre in Victoria. As always thanks to the booksellers everywhere, especially on the home front, Kangaroo Island: Kingscote Newsagency, Kingscote Gift Shop, Big Quince Print for being so supportive, and to the library in Kingscote and in Penneshaw. My island home had a hell of a finish to 2019 which led into more devastation and desperate heartache of January 2020; the road to recovery will be a long one. Big thanks to the fab team at HarperCollins Harlequin Mira— my publisher Jo Mackay, editor Chrysoula Aiello, and Annabel Adair, Brand Manager Sarana Behan and the creative magic of Darren Holt who brought an evocative *Elsa Goody, Bushranger* to life on the cover. To my friend, Barbara Goody Ward, for lending her surname for Elsa. And finally, to my writing partner (part kelpie himself), Hamish the Wonder-dog without whom life in the batcave would be very different.

Turn over for a sneak peek ...

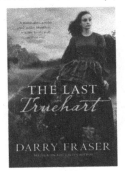

THE LAST
Truehart

by

DARRY FRASER

Out Now

mira

One

1865
Alice and Leo

Deep inside beyond the heart is a place where truth can't be denied.

Alice knew it as she hunched over the heavy weight in her chest, her hand on her belly as if protecting the life within. Hollow, her breath short, she swivelled to stare left and then right along the busy wharf, over the top hats, the caps and the bonnets. There were many onlookers here at the Victorian port where the *Shenandoah* had been berthed for so many eventful weeks. Some were in finery, some in rags, some so wrapped up in their own affections—they all streamed by with their inane chatter and their ridiculous fawning over the dark and gleaming American ship. The awe was too much for Alice and certainly misplaced.

This afternoon she was to have been married to a man who had gleaming chestnut hair, a sunny smile and a twinkle in his eye, and yet now she stood alone watching and waiting. *No, no— he said he'd come back. He will come back. He will.*

But Alice knew the truth. That he wouldn't. That he'd gone.

At first, grappling reality, she slapped her hands over her ears to shut out the noise so she—sensible Alice Truehart—could gather her galloping thoughts. Not a sign of him. Not on the ship, not on the wharf, not in any of the row boats that pitched and swayed on the busy waves in the American clipper's wake.

Leo had gone.

The Confederates' SS *Shenandoah* (which had no place in her home port, for goodness sake) glided out from its sturdy mooring into Hobson's Bay, sailing on greater Port Phillip Bay, past the rotting prison hulks and onto the heads, proud and majestic on her journey. A fierce huntress carrying her greedy hunters, she steamed away, sleek and sly, from the Victorian colony's bustling shores.

Something on the water caught Alice's eye. A bird? White, calm and bobbing on the low laps, enjoying the sunshine, it was odd, out of place. It sat on the gentle, sooty foam and the speckled froth of the ship's long wake. But it wasn't a gull. It was a white cabbage tree hat, Leo's hat, its raven's feather still tucked tightly in place.

Her heart clenched, her body shook. He'd gone. He was on that ship.

She shouldn't have told him about the baby coming—she knew it, she'd seen something in his eyes—even so, how could he *do* it? How *could* he?

'I don't like it one bit, Leo Smith. Not one bit.' She'd shaken her head at her fiancé. It was not long after first light, and she'd stood back on the wharf and stared up. Moored at the Williamstown dock was an American ship of war. Astounding; *the effrontery of its Captain Waddell*. 'Why did we come here to visit again, and especially this early?' She squinted against the morning glare. 'These Yankees shouldn't even have their ships in our docks. We're a neutral colony.'

'Keep your voice down, Alice.' Leo had darted a look over his shoulder, as if checking to see if anyone heard her. 'They're not Yankees. They're Confederates on this ship, they're from the South.' He pulled his cabbage tree hat low over his forehead, tucking the raven's feather deeper into the band. He swiped at his dark curly hair as it spilled over his collar.

'Ahoy, mate,' someone had yelled in a terrible, flat accent. Laughter erupted. 'You got yeself a purty little golden-haired beauty. Looks mighty fine in her gown. We don't see that blue colour on our ladies' dresses much anymore.' Three sailors chuckled, leaned over the rail high above and doffed grey caps. 'Mornin', ma'am.'

'Huh,' Alice bridled but dropped her voice when she saw a couple more heads look over the side at her. 'They're called Belligerents, Leo. It means they're slavers. Going on board that thing is against the law in the colonies.' He was awestruck by the ship and nothing she said would change that. It made her nervous.

'What do you know?' Leo scoffed. 'The law didn't bother when thousands of folk came to gawk and gander inside her the other day. And I wanted another look without all the crowds.' His gaze roved over the hull. 'She's a wonder, a real beauty. Iron-rigged, beautiful teak planks. Seventeen knots under full sail, they say. What adventures would there be, eh?'

He always did have his head in the clouds, always off dreaming. She could never be sure it was *only* dreaming—now he seemed to be making something romantic out of this horrible ship.

It was hot; there'd been no breeze across the water—the great ship had blocked it. And if there had been, it would have carried the stench of sewage—from the ship as well as from land—and the briny, ripe odour of fish guts as the ship dropped its garbage.

Alice had frowned. 'She's sat here in all her snooty glory for nigh on three weeks being repaired. Everyone decent has got their innards in a knot over it yet you sound quite taken with this *boat* that acts as a privateer.' She'd noted with some satisfaction that Leo winced a little at her words. 'You *did* read that scathing article in *The Age* the day after she arrived?'

Leo's eyes lit up. 'I bet she's as fast as they say. I know she'll sail today.'

Alice had stopped in her tracks. 'How do you know that?'

'When we came to look, when she first arrived—'

'And you had to spend a shilling for that harbour trip out with a boatman.' So annoying. They were meant to be saving, not spending.

'Yes, yes, but after that, when we both went on board. You were with the other ladies, and I heard a few of the sailors say that men from here had enlisted already'—if only there wasn't that gleam in his eyes—'but had to hide below, said it was on the quiet.' He looked up at the gun turrets, his gaze fervent.

'I know,' she'd whispered furiously. 'Because the governor wanted the police to arrest them. Enlisting locals is *against the law*.'

'The cap'n said it'd be an act of war if all them police and such went traipsing around on his ship. So, it didn't happen but the poor fella was ordered to leave the harbour, wasn't he?'

'Poor fella indeed. The captain's braggartly threat of war was called out,' she said, astounded at just how starstruck Leo had become.

'The Yankee consul fella didn't like it either that a Dixie ship was taking repairs here,' Leo went on, not seeming to have heard her. 'So we were gonna lose her anyway.'

Leo sounded so unhappy about it. Jiggling the tiny bag of coins that dangled from her wrist, she adjusted her bonnet and tidied wisps of hair back to her neat bun. The palms of her hands had been damp with perspiration.

The ship's timbers had creaked amiably, the vessel rocking gently in the water by the pier—no sly threat at all—why, just a benign presence in Victoria's calm waters. She was smug, reeked of self-importance as if in this colonial port she deemed herself of higher worth than her hosts. *Indeed, some of her officers undoubtedly thought they were above the rest of us. Silly Dilly Ashworth had got herself in a right fix with one of those so-called gentlemen.* Alice had squared her shoulders, uncomfortable at her swift judgement. She shouldn't cast aspersions on Silly Dilly. Alice found herself 'in a right fix' but after telling Leo, at least he agreed and they were to be married this afternoon. Elopement, it was, although they weren't running away. Both were well old enough to marry without consent, and neither had felt it necessary to post any banns. She'd patted her pocket, feeling the blank marriage licence deep within, happy that she'd kept nudging Leo's acceptance of the nuptials.

Leo had shifted his stare and waved at a man high up, who leaned over the side and whistled appreciatively. 'Hey there, Leo.'

Startled by the familiarity, Alice rounded on her fiancé. He shrugged first and then grinned at her in that devilish way, making the deep twist in his left brow more pronounced. It was scarred thanks to a chunk of timber that had speared it after flying off his axe. Then he'd tapped his nose. 'And now, me darlin' *golden-haired beauty*,' he said, teasing her, 'with the doleful brown eyes a man can never forget, I'm just goin' on board for another look.'

I should have known then.

'Don't think yourself a Confederate pirate, Leo. No one's allowed—'

'Don't nag, Alice. I'll be right back. Then we'll go down to the registry, become mister and missus to give our comin' baby a good name, just like you decided.' He'd smacked a kiss on her cheek and more laughter had erupted from above. 'What a great day.'

Alice's belly had fluttered with nerves, as well as with the little heartbeat she knew was pulsing strongly within her. She grabbed hold of Leo's arm and squeezed it. 'Better not go. They could be hostile after all, despite our weak-kneed attempts to be gracious to them. They say the captain is a very strong-minded man. Don't— don't go, Leo.' She heard it in her voice, the pleading.

He pried her hand from his arm, impatient as he frowned, glancing this way and that. Was he worried someone would see?

'Yeah, but none of them government bods have taken him on yet,' he said, 'they're too busy keepin' their noses out of it. And look around. Half the older folk here prob'ly came out in chains on the convict ships. No love lost for England.'

'Oh, not that old whining again, Leo,' she said, exasperated. 'Your pa and ma did just fine on the goldfields after they were transported. I didn't hear them complaining too much after arriving here.'

'But we don't all love Queen and country. Bad enough her picture's lookin' at me all bleedin' day at the bank.' Then he waffled on, something about Dixie boys are more our types, and Cap'n Waddell was a champion for playing the governor right well. Alice had enough of this hero worship; it was all just noise she wanted to block out. Then he cleared his throat, his eyes furtive. 'Every man on the street knows it.'

'Leo, that's fanciful,' Alice chided, and tried to reason with him again. 'Did you miss that it's said Waddell is a pirate? That the newspapers say this ship's a man-o'-war. Look at those big guns over there. If someone really did upset him, he could blow a hole in Melbourne from here.'

'I *am* looking at those big guns.' He'd peered at the gun turret. 'I can't wait to get a closer look before they sail. Word has it that the cap'n is goin' to take her into the open sea and go to war on Union ships in the Pacific.' Leo angled upwards at sailors who were staring back at him. One man impatiently beckoned him on board. 'He's goin' to cripple their merchant whaling fleet.'

'You don't even know where the Pacific is, Leo,' she hissed. 'Besides, with your two left feet, you'd fall down the ladder and drown in the bilge water before they set sail.' Not that she had any idea about bilge water.

He'd ignored her, muttering something about sailing the seas, and gazed along the length of the ship.

Alice had clutched both his arms, not caring who thought what of her. 'Don't you dare consider—'

'Just wishful thinking, my sensible Alice.' His damaged right hand clamped on hers and flicked it away. His two remaining fingers and thumb were painfully strong despite the hand missing its ring finger and little finger at the knuckles—the result of another clumsy accident with a rabbit trap when he was a child.

Then his next words had chilled her.

'But I'm goin' on board now to have another look. They'll be sailing by eight so it's now or never.' His bravado thinned for a moment. 'Don't wait, though. I'll come get you from your place.'

'No, Leo.'

He'd pulled away and moved through the early morning throng that hovered around where the gangway had already been withdrawn. Waving at someone high above, he lifted his hat to reveal his shiny, dark head of hair. Then he'd disappeared towards the bow and in the crowd. She lost sight of him.

I should have known then. I should have known.

As if to mock her, a groan from the ship had rolled around her ears. She stepped back, watching where she was going, then faced the ship and looked up once more, one hand on her hat, the other on her belly. She stared at the three massive masts, the sails furled tight on each one. The Confederate flag flew, its white background stark against the red square in one corner, and the huge blue X in the middle of it dotted with white stars.

As if you'd know anything about sailing a ship such as this, Leo Smith.

Despite Leo telling her to go home, Alice had waited for him. She'd waited and waited. Paced alongside the length of the ship— nearly eighty yards long, it was said—and back again. And waited some more. But when the sun rose higher overhead, and no one looking remotely like Leo Smith had been back on the dock, pushing his way through the crowd, deep inside she'd known. When she'd heard the chug of steam engines rumble and throb, heard the slap and flap of huge swathes of sailcloth unfurling and billowing up the masts, she'd known.

At the shouts of the men on board, and the thump of running feet on the deck, Alice stepped back further. She stared up, calling out, but her voice had been lost. She couldn't catch anyone's attention on board, and passers-by in the crowd jostled her, giving her strange looks. Tears had come and gone. Anger surged and died. She could not afford to be frantic. She'd tried to still the wild beating of her heart; she was sure she felt the scampering, worried little trill that followed it.

The tugboat and accompanying yachts bobbed in the bay as the *Shenandoah* had slid out of the canal on this warm and moody February morning. Straggling well-wishers still on the wharf waved at the sailors who yelled and laughed and hooted.

Now, the glossy raider finally slipped out of her sight, futility swamped her. Bewildered, numb, she stood rigid as shadows lengthened on the wharf.

He's really gone. She finally, utterly believed it. Resigned, unable to do anything about it, sensible Alice Truehart put her hand in her pocket, closed her fingers around the paper there. No more tears; she knew what she had to do.

It was time to put her *what-if-this-happens* plan into action.

It wasn't a difficult task and Alice had a fine penmanship. She was back in her room at her parents' modest home in Williamstown, sitting at her writing table, her ink pot and nib pen ready.

Daughter of a local doctor, Henry Truehart and his wife, her mother Ellen, Alice had had a good education as far as it went. She could read and write well, and her father had often said that she'd learned to think for herself.

So it was with great care, a cool head and hand, and with precision that Alice wrote on the official certificate: *Feb 18th 1865, Williamstown, Leo Thomas Smith, bachelor, Williamstown* and *Alice Jane Truehart, spinster, Williamstown*. She took a steadying breath and continued. I, *Wm B Cooper* (she thought) being a *Wesleyan Minister* (she hoped) do hereby certify that I have this day at *Williamstown* celebrated the Marriage between *Leo Thomas Smith* and *Alice Jane Truehart* after Notice and Declaration duly made and published, as by law required (and with written consent of *The Guardians of the Bride*) dated this *Eighteenth* day of *February* 1865. Signature of Minister, Registrar-General, or other Officer *William B Cooper* (she couldn't really remember his name—they rarely went to church—and scribbled something barely legible). There was a small column preceding the first date and place but unsure if it needed anything written there, she left it blank. Checking the rest of the paper, she realised she didn't have to sign anything, nor did Leo. Satisfied, she thought it excellent work.

Damn you, Leo Smith. It was bad for a lady to use an expletive, but no one could hear her.

Damn me. I should've known he couldn't keep his word. I should never have let him talk me into laying with him. Serve myself right.

She sat back, careful not to let new traitor-tears drip off her chin and on to the paper. Straightening her shoulders, she sniffed, wiped a hand over her face and squinted at her handiwork. Once the ink dried, it would be a perfect foil if anyone dared question her marital status. Alice was reasonably sure no one she'd ever meet would even ask to see such a thing.

Taking a deep steadying breath, she rested her elbow on the little desk and pressed a fist to her mouth. She stared at the small valise opened on her bed, and the pathetic trifling pile of folded smalls, day dresses and chemises in it. A pair of boots and a pair of house shoes were at the foot of the bed waiting to be packed into a drawstring bag and put on top of her clothes before she'd fasten the case closed. Her coat, hat and gloves were on the chair, ready. She'd been about to be married.

Her parents, attending a concert in Melbourne, had travelled early and wouldn't be back until tomorrow. The plan had been to leave them her already written note of her elopement. She'd hardly been able to contain her excitement—or the trepidation. She was twenty-two, well over twelve years old, the legal age for a girl to be married with her father's consent. Barbaric to be married at that age—she agreed with her mother. Marriageable age for a man was fourteen, but Leo at twenty-five was evidently still not mature enough for it. He'd needed to be mature enough for it; she'd missed her monthly courses twice now, and he had known it.

Damn you, Leo.

Both sets of parents had fully expected Alice and Leo to marry. But in her present condition and with Leo now nowhere in sight, she had to present herself as a married person. So she'd become an abandoned married woman.

All very well to fool a stranger, but she wouldn't be able to fool her parents right away. She bit her lip, decided to leave as planned and go to Geelong—where she and Leo were to spend their so-called honeymoon. Her family holidays were always there.

Before she was born, her parents had often visited Geelong, and they'd loved it, had made friends there over the years. They swore they'd move there where her father would open a practice, one day. The Trueharts were well respected in Williamstown—her father, born here, was a fine physician—but their hearts lay in Geelong.

Leo had said he couldn't afford a honeymoon on his own wage at the bank. Alice, about to be married, had given up her job in the local tearoom, so they'd have had to live on one wage. Alice knew Leo was uneasy about it but entertained the idea that he'd grow into his responsibility. She'd been almost sure he would. Well, she hoped he would. *Fool.*

She idly wondered if his parents knew he'd intended to 'travel' at some point, and not marry her after all. *Oh, surely not.* Alice didn't like his parents—his mother was mean, his father sly—but perhaps instead of being so hasty, she should go to visit them. Was Leo hiding from her and cowering at his parents' place? If so, she would confront him there.

She huffed. There would be no point in doing that. No, she wouldn't go squalling on their doorstep, crying foul, to then become the pity of the town. And if he wasn't there, if he truly had gone on that boat as she suspected he had, how could she tell his parents …? *Oh, damn* me *for being a coward.*

Then there were her few friends to confront. Oh heavens, they'd be scandalised. Or titillated and there'd be laughs all round. Perhaps they'd scorn her. She was never really sure what to expect with them.

No, she *had* to be 'married'.

'Oh, damn you, Leo Smith,' she muttered darkly. 'Damn you.'

Her stomach fluttered again and she swooped her arm over her belly. This little child coming—would he or she be in her image? Golden hair and brown eyes, a calm person, a reader of long books, a serious child, responsible. Perhaps a little taller than she was, but not if the child was a girl. A boy might become taller than she was, be more Leo's height, and take after him with his dark looks … *Damn you, Leo!*

She picked up the licence paper, waved it in the air to make sure it was fully dry. Then pressed it on the blotter—a double-check that it wouldn't smudge—and slipped it into the envelope she'd had ready. As she held it, she knew that it was now her most prized possession; that and the photograph they'd taken weeks ago. She tucked the licence into the suitcase, sliding it alongside the stiff card of the photo.

She propped the other envelope she'd prepared onto her pillow. Its contents she knew by heart. *Dearest Mama and Pa, Leo and I married today and have gone away to live. I will write when we are settled. You are not to worry, you know that we are well grown up and can look after ourselves. I do promise I will write. Your loving daughter, Alice.*

Standing still a moment she glared at the suitcase. What on earth did she think she'd do in Geelong, with child, alone? Without a husband or a family? She caught the swirling thoughts and concentrated.

This was not the way to do things now.

Her parents loved her and wanted the best for her. They'd understand. They'd understand how—and why—she'd wanted to protect herself. They were not like other parents who would cast aside their wayward daughters or lock them up in misery, forever untouchable. Not her mama and pa. But it did make her a little nervy again, having to tell them, to confess the truth—well, perhaps not all of it—but she would be brave and be almost honest. She'd *almost* been married after all.

She reached into the case and removed the envelope containing the licence then put it on top of her bureau. The accompanying daguerreotype she slid into a drawer, with the image down. She would face it another day.

Her heart thudded as she thought about the date she'd put on the licence—today's date—and wondered if she should change it, backdate it for the sake of her parents. But an attempt to alter it now would look fumbled, and wrong. *No.* She'd done the best she could do with that, and she hoped she'd never have to use it in the distant future. It would be the only lie she'd tell: that she was Mrs Leo Smith, albeit abandoned.

Taking the letter from her pillow she tore it into shreds and threw the remains into the fireplace. Then, from the valise, she lifted out the folded clothes and set them back into the drawers, and her dresses she hung in her small wardrobe.

Much better idea.

Alice checked her hair in the bureau's mirror. Still tidy, still gleaming dark golden in its demure bun despite the warm, insistent breeze that had followed her as she'd scurried home. She settled her hat, tied it under her chin. She jiggled the little bag—their eloping money—and slipped it once again onto her wrist, and took another deep breath. Giving her face one last swipe to dry any residual tears, she walked down the short hallway to the front door, left her home and headed for the police station.

There was a missing person to report. She was, after all, still sensible Alice Truehart.

Two

1898

Ellen's reedy voice whispered in the wind, '_You'd make your mother proud, Stella. She was a strong girl, like you._' Stella Truehart-Smith stood at her mother's grave, the damp umbrella open by her side. Six years ago, Alice had been buried in the Geelong cemetery; she'd lost her short, fierce battle with cancer of the womb.

Glancing at the larger gravesite next to her mother's, the plot in which Grandmama Ellen and Grandpa Doctor Henry Truehart (her Pa Henny) were both now interred, her chest was taut and her throat seemed to close a moment. Her most treasured people were here, side by side.

Reluctantly, with the barest nod to custom, Stella's gaze swept to the furthest corner where Lowry Hayward lay. (He couldn't besmirch any of them from there.) He'd been her husband for a short awful time after a whirlwind courtship and now lay in an unmarked grave; unmarked because of a lack of finances, she'd insisted. Truth was, now he was dead, she hadn't wanted to mark his grave at all. He could stay in an unmarked grave forever.

She'd learned, from the constables during their many visits after he'd disappeared, that at some point in his short but vigorous thieving career in Geelong he'd upset the wrong man; it was said that he'd had a run-in with a dangerous 'push', a street gang. The leader of which, a violent thug named Rawlins, had wanted two men dead: Lowry, and a friend of his—whose name she'd forgotten if she ever knew it.

Lowry had courted her so determinedly and swept her into marriage with great charm. They were heady, rushed days filled with a promise she thought had bypassed her. Even though she considered herself a smart, clear-thinking woman, she'd soon let down any guard she had and became dazed by his romantic onslaught. All she'd been worried about then was that he'd die from an appendix attack, the agony of which had plagued him from time to time.

Once the ring was on her finger, it hadn't taken long for his true colours to spew out. Abuse and painful blows had landed on her, strange women with painted faces reeking of cheap perfume would hammer on her door. Shock accompanied her horror that thugs were coming after him, calling at all hours with shouts and threats. And then somehow, he'd gone and got himself gruesomely murdered. Pity his reputation hadn't been killed off as well.

'I won't continue to bear his name one day longer,' she'd told her grandmother as they sat in the parlour. Ellen's good Meissen tea service was in use—a rare occurrence—to mark the solemnity of the occasion. 'Hayward just spells trouble. Even mention of it brings on the nightmares. I will hyphenate your name and my maiden name.' Stella took up her handkerchief and blew her nose. (It seemed even relief, not only grief, brought on tears.)

Ellen had liked the idea. 'Smith is such a common name, it seems that every second person is a Smith.' She'd winked. 'Now, Truehart is a name to be proud of. You always wanted to be a Truehart,' she'd then said with feeling. In the past she'd uttered it softly; Alice would've frowned darkly if ever she heard Ellen or Pa Henny say it.

Funny what you remember.

Stella had said, 'I'll be known as Mrs Truehart-Smith from now on.'

'You could be just Truehart now,' Ellen suggested. 'I can't see why not since your mother's gone. You can do what you want, forget about the gossipers.'

Stella had faltered. Smith had been her mother's married name. Her mother, Alice, and her parents had moved to Geelong from Williamstown before Stella was born, so Pa Henny could open another medical practice.

Better not drop 'Smith' altogether, after all; she'd been born to it, albeit *such a common name.* She'd declared that gossip would not deter her one—

'Mrs Hayward?'

Stella spun from her mother's gravestone, instantly wary. There was a man, but thankfully he didn't look like the tall person she thought she'd seen lurking near her house the other day. She calmed herself, blinked hard to clear the threatening tears, and shook the dripping umbrella before closing it. He stood straight. He'd taken his hat off, and his dark hair, barely damp after the recent downpour, featured a streak of white from the widow's peak at his forehead. The man's eyes were intense and alight with interest.

Her heart leapt. She hoped that in her surprise her eyes hadn't lit up nor that she'd inadvertently offered a smile. But there was something about him, something in that instant that charged her pulse—

How could that be? She didn't know him, had never met him. Sense flooded in, and with it came a fierce blush, the likes of which had cursed her all her life.

He'd addressed her by her married name—he knew her or thought he did. She hadn't used that name for some time. All the same, why would anyone be here at the cemetery on a day such as this, asking after her? The thought started a shake.

'Mrs Hayward,' he repeated. 'I'm sorry to have startled you.'

His candid stare unsettled her still. Taking a moment more to steady herself, she inclined her head at the stranger. 'It's not a name by which I call myself these days. Who might you be?' she clipped. A sliver of fear scuttled down her spine. Might he be one of Lowry's shady acquaintances come after some perceived gain from her? The police had warned of it.

He indicated the headstones. 'I don't wish to intrude if you're still paying your respects. I would make an appointment—'

'Conversations with my mother and my grandparents can be made at any time, Mr ...?'

'I am Bendigo Barrett, ma'am.' He bowed slightly.

When he offered no more, she shook her umbrella, careful that no drops of rain splashed either of them. 'Bendigo?'

'Exactly named for the town in which I was born,' he pre-empted, clearly used to the query his name prompted. 'Such was the imagination of my parents. I'm only glad I wasn't born later, I might have been called Sandhurst.' He smiled a little.

Stella knew the town name changed to Sandhurst, and following a plebiscite recently had reverted to Bendigo. She smiled politely in return but wasn't yet prepared to share humour with the stranger. 'I haven't made your acquaintance before, have I? I would remember such a name.' *And your face.*

'No, Mrs Hayward—I beg your pardon. How do you prefer to be addressed?'

'I now call myself Mrs Truehart-Smith.'

He shook water from his hat and put it on his head. 'Ah. You have taken your family names,' he said and nodded towards the graves.

How did he know they were family names? She stared at him.

A light patter of rain began again. Mr Barrett stood to one side as she shook the umbrella. 'Perhaps we could move to the rotunda; it affords some cover from the weather,' he said.

'I see no reason to do any such thing.' *This is all disconcerting.* 'You've made no prior appointment with me, and I have no idea why you've sought me out at the cemetery, of all places. If you'll excuse me, I'll be on my way.' With a lift of the brolly, she stalked past him, clutching her skirt in one hand and dodging the puddles as she headed for her buggy.

'You have no driver?' he called after her.

'I have no need of a driver. I drive myself. And my horse is perfectly capable of taking instruction.' Did she just hear him stifle a laugh?

'So you'll not hear me out?' he called out again.

'If you know anyone in the district I might know, please have them introduce us. They might drop their card in my post box requesting afternoon tea at Mack's Hotel on Corio.'

She heard him step along the path behind her, the gravel crunching under his boots as rain began to plop heavy drops and then fall in a rush from the dense clouds. At that, she turned, fully aware she hadn't been mannerly, and thinking that perhaps she should at least offer the shelter of her umbrella. She beckoned him and he caught up, ducking underneath with her and removing his hat to shake it. 'You have a buggy nearby?' she asked.

'No.'

As they neared her small two-seater, she said hesitantly, 'I could take you to your lodgings. This weather looks to be set in.'

'I appreciate the gesture but it's not necessary.'

He just stood there, drenched from earlier, and staring at her with a small smile as if he couldn't be happier being sodden. *Perhaps he's one of these poor afflicted people who just go about grinning at strangers all day long.* She placed her foot onto the buggy's step and hauled herself up. Settled in the seat, she thrust the umbrella at him. 'Do take this, then.'

He accepted it with a gracious nod, and opened it over his head. 'My thanks.'

Gathering up the reins and feeling strange, quite peculiar in fact—her heart pounding, her hands shaking—wanting to flee, she said loudly over the pelting rain, 'Good day, Mr Barrett.'

'Mrs Truehart-Smith, did your mother leave you any papers, any family business?' His hazel gaze was earnest now. Gone was the smile and a slight frown puckered an otherwise smooth forehead.

Stopped cold by the question, Stella glared. 'What sort of papers?'

He raised his voice over the downpour. 'Anything about your father?'

'I know nothing about my father,' she snapped. She thrust off the buggy's brake. Flustered, aware she hadn't answered his question, she said, 'Excuse me.' She cracked the reins and her horse startled forward.

He stepped back. 'I have information about him.'

Her horse was leading away. Impatient, she pulled him up. 'What information could you possibly have? This is most'—she waved skywards—'inconvenient.' The heavens had well and truly opened.

He dipped his head as heavy rain smacked the umbrella. 'It is inconvenient. But as you suggest, I'll have a card delivered to your post box and will await summons to Mack's Hotel.' Bendigo

Barrett doffed his hat. 'Good day.' Then he turned on his heels and squelched off in the opposite direction.

Well might he squelch, she decided and flicked the reins again. *Await summons.* The cheek. He was mocking her and it gave her pause. She frowned as she drove. Who of her friends would know such a man? And what information could a stranger possibly have about her father, a man about whom she knew little? He'd absconded to parts unknown, disappeared on the day he married her mother.

Stella never knew any more than that—as far as she was aware, Alice hadn't received a word from him in thirty-three years. He was most probably dead, anyway. She hardly thought any longer about what type of man he'd been. No point—he'd *absconded*. She could wonder all she liked, there'd be no answers. But Pa Henny had said that he'd liked 'the lad'. He said that Stella had Leo's looks—the same chestnut brown hair, the dark eyes and an olive complexion—due to some marauding Spaniard no doubt, Henny had winked—and a big, ready smile matching Leo's happy personality. When she was happy, Henny conceded. Stella had liked his description of Leo, but when she'd ask Henny for more information, he'd just shaken his head. 'We'll never know more, my little Truehart.'

You were my champion, Pa Henny. How I miss you. Stella's chest expanded as the memories came flooding in: his soothing voice close to her ear after she'd had a fall, or his solemn face as he listened to her relate a bad day at school or following a nasty comment in the street. 'Bear up now, Stella,' he'd whisper. 'You're our last Truehart.' She would stand taller under his encouragement, her bottom lip still thrust out, tears unshed. She'd loved hearing she was a Truehart but knew never to say anything about that in front of her mother. Alice had said over and over that she herself had married a Smith, and therefore her daughter Stella was a Smith.

I know whose name I'd rather have.

Grandmama Ellen would put a finger to her lips whenever Alice was in earshot of the conversation. What little more there was to learn about Stella's father had come from Ellen: a woman with a delight for the humour in life, and a sense of *que sera, sera.* Over the years, *what will be, will be* had been the old lady's answer to Stella's many questions.

Stella's mother Alice would simply scoff at the merest mention of the man who was her absent husband. She'd fob Stella off with a wave of her hand, her face grim and say, 'Not worth bothering about, dear child.'

The rain continued to pelt. Stella drove on, careful not to flick the reins incessantly. Inflicting her frustration on Clod, her horse, would not do; a buggy accident and an injured horse would mess things up completely—she had no extra funds to cope with a disaster. Not to mention the heartache that losing the faithful old horse would cause. Since Ellen had passed away two months ago, the house and the horse and cart had come to Stella but with only a little cash. Most of the family's hard-earned savings had all gone to Alice's medical care, such as it was, and what with the banks on a downturn, and Lowry, her husband—

Oh, for heaven's sake. I have an income, slight as it is. I have the house, and it's paid for. I just need to be careful.

Stella had often wondered if she should look for a cheaper house, in a cheaper area, sell up so she could realise some cash. As always, though, she came back to the fact that her friends lived here, and that as a widow now without extended family, she was on her own—more in need of friends than ever.

The other side of that, of course, was as a widow, she'd begun to feel as if her two married female friends were wary of her. Stella hadn't been invited to tea by either of the women lately. Despite herself, she gave a little laugh. Real friends would have known her better. Truly, their husbands were among the least attractive men she knew. Their habits, their condescension ... she was unimpressed. Perhaps the women weren't friends, after all.

Constance and Isabella Leonard, however, were definitely her good friends. She was at ease with them, trusted them, enjoyed their light-hearted, teasing banter. In their company she rarely needed to be reticent or mindful; she could be herself, unguarded and have some fun. They knew of her sleeplessness, and of the nightmares that had begun to plague her and ruin what little sleep she managed.

She'd met the sisters in their father's pawnbroking shop when she'd visited one day. They'd agreed, even as strangers, that a piece she'd chosen, a simple brooch for her grandmother, was a wise and delightful choice. Over time, their beaming open smiles and happy hearts had chipped away her icy diffidence born of Alice's reserve and latterly Lowry's ill-treatment. Their kindness was unconditional; they'd even offered to go to the morgue with Stella to be there for her when she identified her husband's body. She'd spared them that horror.

They were a little younger; had a spark of life about them, open warmth and were not dulled by the drudgery of housewifely duties and all its ties. They were modern women, like she was. Her mother at least had taught her to think for herself.

Stella's only lapse of judgement, in hindsight, anyway, was Lowry Hayward. And what a lapse that was. He'd taken her for a fool—and she had been, she'd admit it. She'd allowed him to sweet-talk his way past her prickly exterior and win her over. At first after they married, it seemed that life would be all right. He'd treated her well, in the marital bed too at that time (she shuddered now), never lifted his voice but then it all changed. Something to do with jewellery. They fought about it and he began to stay out of an evening, would tell her he took loose women one after the other, and she'd heard rumours of his stealing. She then had to suffer his profanities, 'you dull, cold bitch', and worse, while he'd scream at her to hand over this *jewellery* she was supposed to have had. The worst of it was the beating. It was easy to keep quiet about it for there were never marks on her face. In any case, to whom would she complain? She was married, so she just got on with things as best she could. Ellen had known, though. Ellen always knew; she appeared at Stella's house each time she was most needed, a pot of arnica cream emerging from her bag to help soothe the deep bruises. Other bruises couldn't be soothed; after she'd thought Lowry dead, the nightmares had begun. Why on earth would that be? It was as if something inside her had been damaged and was screaming for attention, trying to tell her something. But what? She never remembered what the horrors were once she'd woken, only that her heart pounded, and terror filled her. How could she fix what was broken if she didn't know what it was?

Clod faltered. Rain was coming down so hard it looked like an impenetrable grey wall immediately ahead. She directed the poor horse to the side of the road. Braking, and tucking herself to the back of the buggy under its cover, she wished that she hadn't—in a fit of unaccustomed generosity—given her umbrella to the enigmatic Mr Barrett. It might have protected her boots from getting wet.

Bendigo Barrett. He'd introduced himself in a well-modulated calm voice and with a smile. She'd been instantly entranced at the sight of that angled, shaded jaw, the dramatic white streak in his hair, and the candid dark-eyed gaze. His large hands, stained perhaps by ink or the earth, had gripped his sodden hat. Caution now slowed her gleefully idiotic racing pulse and she remembered what he'd said ... *information about him.* Her father.

Silently bewailing her saturated skirt, she remembered that Ellen had a box of papers and such. She'd kept 'things' she believed to be of importance to the family. Stella knew that Grandmama Ellen had long ago put Alice's 'things' into that tin box. At the time of her mother's death, Stella had not been too curious, or keen, to fossick her way through any of it. She hadn't thought to look at the box again until Ellen had passed. Even then, Stella could still not face what else might have been in there. Three of her most valuable treasures—her mother and her two grandparents—would be represented in some way, and she couldn't bring herself to look. Too painful handling mementoes or letters. Or was she simply delaying the inevitable? The grief would be overwhelming. Time and again she wondered how to release it, and not have to endure the strangling weight of it locked inside. Time and again, she shied away from letting it go. She hadn't gone near the box.

Perhaps now it was time.

The rain eased, and with it the grey wall parted like flimsy curtains revealing the way ahead. First, home and stable Clod. Inside the house, secure the back door. Take the poker at the oven for a weapon and check each room. Inspect the windows for damage. Only then, convinced of her security, could she be satisfied.

Then she'd change out of her wet clothes. Boil the kettle. She would seek out Grandmama Ellen's Box of Things. She'd face whatever was in there, step into the grief, and go forward.

BESTSELLING AUSTRALIAN AUTHOR

DARRY FRASER

Discover thrilling Australian historical adventure romance ...

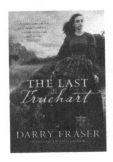
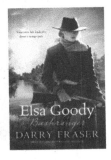
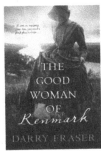
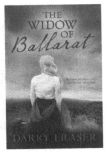
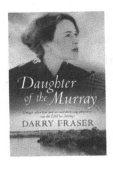

talk about it

Let's talk about books.

Join the conversation:

 facebook.com/romanceanz

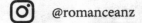 @romanceanz

romance.com.au

If you love reading and want to know about our
authors and titles, then let's talk about it.